D0449514

# The Adventure of the Missing Detective

EDITED BY

Ed Gorman

AND Martin H. Greenberg

CARROLL & GRAF PUBLISHERS
NEW YORK

THE ADVENTURE OF THE MISSING DETECTIVE
*And 19 of the Year's Finest Crime and Mystery Stories*

Carroll & Graf Publishers
An Imprint of Avalon Publishing Group Inc.
245 West 17th Street
11th Floor
New York, NY 10011

Copyright © 2005 Ed Gorman and Tekno Books

All rights reserved. No part of this book may be reproduced in whole or in part without written permission from the publisher, except by reviewers who may quote brief excerpts in connection with a review in a newspaper, magazine, or electronic publication; nor may any part of this book be reproduced, stored in a retrieval system, or transmitted in any form or by any means electronic, mechanical, photocopying, recording, or other, without written permission from the publisher.

Library of Congress Cataloging-in-Publication Data is available.

ISBN-10: 0-7867-1643-6
ISBN-13: 978-0-78671-643-2

9 8 7 6 5 4 3 2 1

Book design by Maria E. Torres
Printed in the United States of America
Distributed by Publishers Group West

# Contents

# The Year in Mystery and Crime Fiction: 2004

Jon L. Breen

**It's tempting to call 2004** the Year of *The Da Vinci Code.* Though actually first published in 2003, Dan Brown's monster bestseller had an iron grip on the popular fiction reading public throughout the year. In what may be an unprecedented publishing event, a 2004 illustrated edition took its own place on the lists in competition with the original version. Early 2005 even saw a book-length parody, *The Asti-Spumante Code* (Time Warner UK/Trafalgar) by Toby Clements. Though you shouldn't look for elegant prose or deep characterization, there's no denying *The Da Vinci Code,* which resembles by turns an old movie serial, a dime novel, an Ellery Queen dying message puzzle, and an anti-Catholic jeremiad, makes for compelling reading.

However, in a nod to quality over commercial success, I'll call 2004 the Year of the Paperback Original instead. You may ask, why this year more than any other? Paperback originals have been around a long time, and in today's market they could include any kind of mystery. Indeed with the increasing inroads of trade paperbacks, the distinction between hard and soft covers may become less and less significant.

But to readers of a certain age, mostly but not entirely male, the phrase Paperback Original has a more distinctive and specific meaning: the tough, fast-paced crime novels of the 1950s and '60s, typified by the Gold Medal line. They were brief and hard-hitting, sexy and violent, usually urban in setting and noirish in flavor, often with an illusion of greater reality than more genteel mystery fiction. While most of the authors of these novels were men, at least one of the best of them, Vin Packer, was a woman writing under an androgynous pseudonym.

The year 2004 brought a new appreciation to this paperback tradition, both in reprints and new books. Among the notable revivals were James McKimmey's 1962 *Squeeze Play* (PointBlank), introduced by Jason Starr; Paul S. Meskil's 1954 *Sin Pit* (Gryphon), introduced by Gary Lovisi; and James Reasoner's almost legendary late example from 1980, *Texas Wind* (PointBlank), introduced by Ed Gorman. Stark House offered a pairing of two Douglas Sanderson novels, *Pure Sweet Hell* (1957) and *Catch a Fallen Starlet* (1960). Two publishers revived Packer's work, Cleis Press with the non-criminous Lesbian novel *Spring Fire* (1952) and Stark House with a pairing of *Something in the Shadows* (1961) and *Intimate Victims* (1962). Both editions had new matter by Packer (a.k.a. Marijane Meaker), and the Stark House volume reprinted my article on her work from *Murder Off the Rack*.

A new paperback publishing imprint, Hard Case, was established to capture both the look, with evocative period-style cover illustrations, and the spirit of the classic originals. They included some reprints, notably Lawrence Block's *Grifter's Game*, a minor classic originally published in 1961 as *Mona*, and *Two for the Money*, a pairing of Max Allan Collins's first two published novels, *Bait Money* and *Blood Money* (both first published in 1973 and revised in 1981). But equally notably, Hard Case offered some very good new books in the tradition, including Max Phillips's *Fade to Blonde*, Domenic Stansberry's *The Confession*, and Richard Aleas's *Little Girl Lost* (published earlier in the year as a Five Star hardcover). That the latter two were both honored by the Edgar judges, Stansberry the winner in the paperback category and Aleas (anagramical pseudonym of Charles Ardai) a nominee in the first novel category, should bode well for the new imprint's future.

The rise of the paperback original in the 1950s was fueled by the bestselling success in paperback reprint of a writer whose books usually appeared first in hardcover: Mickey Spillane. Prominent mystery publisher, bookseller, and all-around expert Otto Penzler, writing on the AmericanHeritage.com Web site for their Overrated/Underrated feature, called Spillane underrated and attributed his dismissal by critics and academics to left-wing political bias. Meanwhile, Penzler chose the Ellery Queen team as his overrated writer, in a squib seemingly based only on their early S. S. Van Dine-influenced output. If he had made this claim in the 1950s or '60s, when Queen (the Frederic Dannay half) was the most influential editor in the mystery world and Spillane was rejected by the critical establishment and only loved by his millions of readers, I still wouldn't have agreed with Penzler but he might have had a case. Certainly Spillane's alleged denial of membership by the Mystery Writers of America was an unconscionable black eye on that organization. But today the situation is reversed. Though the Queen name still fronts the most prestigious magazine in the field, the Queen novels are mostly out of print and criminally underappreciated, while Spillane, clearly more significant as a commercial than an artistic phenomenon, has in his elevation to Grand Master by that same MWA arguably become overrated.

What else happened in 2004? Michael Connelly served an unprecedented second term as MWA president in 2004 and turned down an Edgar nomination for best novel on grounds of conflict of interest. . . . Rinehart Potts closed up shop after more than twenty years on one of the longest-running fanzines devoted to a single author, *The Linington Lineup*, which began as a celebration of Elizabeth Linington (a.k.a. Dell Shannon and Leslie Egan) and later came to cover a greater variety of mystery-related and wider-world topics. . . . Deaths in the mystery community included Jane S. Bakerman, a prolific mystery critic and scholar; William F. Deeck, one of the best known, most industrious, and most widely respected of fans; Joseph Hansen, one of the key American writers to emerge in the 1960s or '70s; Hugh B. Cave, one of the last surviving '30s pulp writers, who was still productive into his nineties; and Willo Davis Roberts, a leading practitioner of young adult mystery fiction. For other passings in the field, see Edward D. Hoch's yearbook.

## Best Novels of the Year 2004

The following fifteen were the most impressive crime novels I read and reviewed in 2004. Once again it shows my historical bias, with no fewer than eight taking place in times other than the immediate present, but as any reference librarian will tell you, bias is not necessarily a dirty word. The standard disclaimer applies: I don't pretend to cover the whole field—no single reviewer does—but try to find fifteen better.

Boris Akunin, *Murder on the Leviathan*, translated from the Russian by Andrew Bromfield (Random). Russian diplomat Erast Fandorin investigates murder on the 1878 maiden voyage of a luxury steamship. Classical detection at its games-playing best.

Lee Child, *The Enemy* (Delacorte). If you wonder why Child and his series hero Jack Reacher have built such an admiring following, look no further than this wide-ranging Military Police procedural.

Max Allan Collins, *The London Blitz Murders* (Berkley). Agatha Christie and Bernard Spilsbury join forces to solve the Blackout Ripper murders in 1942 London. Another triumph from a master of fact-based mystery fiction.

Mat Coward, *Over and Under* (Five Star). In their third case, bipolar London cop Don Peckham and his understanding partner Frank Mitchell reaffirm their status as one of the best new police teams on the mystery scene.

Loren D. Estleman, *Retro* (Forge). In any selection of the half dozen greatest private eyes in the Chandler tradition, Detroit's Amos Walker would have to make the cut.

Hal Glatzer, *A Fugue in Hell's Kitchen* (Perseverance). The combination of fine puzzle-spinning, great period ambience (late ’30s, early ’40s), and knowledgeable musical background make the Katy Green series (of which this is the second) one of the mystery field’s underappreciated treasures.

Oakley Hall, *Ambrose Bierce and the Trey of Pearls* (Viking). In a year many famous writers of the past played fictional detective, Bierce’s performance was a standout.

Milton Hirsch, *The Shadow of Justice* (ABA Criminal Justice Section). The American Bar Association picked a winner for their first publication of a novel. This is one of the best fictional depictions of the trial process I’ve ever read (and I’ve read quite a few).

Annette Meyers, *Repentances* (Five Star). Repressed memory and the desperate efforts of American Jews to get their relatives out of 1930s Europe are features of an extraordinarily effective mystery saga.

T. Jefferson Parker, *California Girl* (Morrow). Ranging over several decades in Orange County, California, the Edgar winner for best novel is both a tantalizing whodunit and an involving family saga, somewhat in the vein of John Gregory Dunne’s *True Confessions* and some of Thomas H. Cook’s work.

Rebecca Pawel, *Law of Return* (Soho). The second novel about Carlos Tejada Alonso y Léon, Guardia officer in Franco’s Spain, is a match for its Edgar-winning predecessor.

Steven Saylor, *The Judgment of Caesar* (St. Martin’s Minotaur). Cleopatra figures in the latest novel about Gordianus the Finder, best of the fictional Roman sleuths.

Martin Cruz Smith, *Wolves Eat Dogs* (Simon & Schuster). Moscow cop Arkady Renko’s murder investigation at the site of the Chernobyl nuclear disaster is a haunting addition to a classic series.

Joseph Telushkin and Allen Estrin, *Heaven's Witness* (Toby). One of the year's most absorbing mysteries combines a serial killer whodunit with an exploration of the issues of reincarnation.

Gary Zebrun, *Someone You Know* (Alyson). This novel of a closeted gay journalist must be among the most nail-bitingly suspenseful of the year.

## Sub-Genres

Private eyes. My reading in this category was somewhat limited in 2004, apart from Estleman among my top fifteen, but Walter Mosley's latest Easy Rawlins novel, *Little Scarlet* (Little, Brown), was a standout, illuminating the African-American experience in 1960s post-Watts riots L.A. Also in commendable form were Robert B. Parker's Spenser in *Bad Business* (Putnam) and Ed Gorman's Sam McCain in *Breaking Up is Hard to Do* (Carroll & Graf). Parnell Hall's Cora Felton, cozy as she may appear at first glance, is also a tough private eye, and she certainly talks and acts like one in *And a Puzzle to Die On* (Bantam), until she starts playing Perry Mason in a hilariously Gardneresque courtroom climax. Michael Connelly's Harry Bosch was still working private in *The Narrows* (Little, Brown) but by evidence of that book he'd be well-advised to rejoin the LAPD. (As shown in the far better early-2005 novel, *The Closers*, he did.)

Amateur sleuths. Making welcome returns to action were Lawrence Block's bookdealer/burglar (should I have put him in the crook section?) Bernie Rhodenbarr in *The*

*Burglar on the Prowl* (Morrow); Aaron Elkins's Skeleton Detective Gideon Oliver in *Cold Blood* (Berkley); the husband-and-wife team of Reb and Melissa Pennyworth in Michael Bowen's farcical *Unforced Error* (Poisoned Pen); Bill Crider's English teacher Carl Burns in *Dead Soldiers* (Five Star); Father John O'Malley and Vicki Holden in Margaret Coel's *Wife of Moon* (Berkley); Laura Childs's tea expert Theodosia Browning in *The Jasmine Moon Murder* (Berkley); and PGA golfer Jack Austin in John R. Corrigan's *Snap Hook* (Hardscrabble Crime/University Press of New England). New and welcome additions to the ranks were Sandy Balzo's coffee merchant Maggy Thorsen in *Uncommon Grounds* (Five Star) and Martin Edwards's historian Daniel Kind in *The Coffin Trail* (Poisoned Pen).

Police. Stuart M. Kaminsky's *The Last Dark Place* (Forge), about Chicago cop Abe Lieberman, was another gem from one of the very best contemporary procedural series. Among other series cops in good form were Ed McBain's 87th Precinct bunch in *The Frumious Bandersnatch* (Simon & Schuster); Boston's Jane Rizzoli (now very pregnant a la the *Fargo* police chief) in Tess Gerritsen's *Body Double* (Ballantine); and L.A.'s Kate Delafield in Katherine V. Forrest's *Hancock Park* (Berkley).

Lawyers. Sam Cogley, ace defender from the *Star Trek* universe, plays twenty-third-century Perry Mason in *The Case of the Colonist's Corpse* (Pocket) by Bob Ingersoll and Tony Isabella. John Grisham's *The Last Juror* (Doubleday) belongs among the perennial bestseller's better books. In Robert Reuland's *Semiautomatic* (Random), Brooklyn Assistant District Attorney Andrew Giobberti faces a legal ethical dilemma in a trial book with a strong whiff of reality. Other series advocates in effective action included William Bernhardt's Ben Kincaid in *Hate Crime* (Ballantine); Perri O'Shaughnessy's Nina Reilly in *Unlucky in Law* (Delacorte); Jay Brandon's Chris Sinclair in *Grudge Match* (Forge); and John Mortimer's immortal barrister in *Rumpole and the Penge Bungalow Murder* (Viking).

Crooks. Max Allan Collins produced a sequel to his excellent (and memorably filmed) *Road to Perdition* in *Road to Purgatory* (Morrow). John Dortmunder and his cohorts attempt classic car theft with the usual comic results in Donald E. Westlake's *The Road to Ruin* (Mysterious).

Historicals. Past literary figures taking on fictitious detecting chores had an especially busy year. Aside from Christie and Bierce (see the list of fifteen), they included Geoffrey Chaucer in Philippa Morgan's *Chaucer and the House of Fame* (Carroll & Graf); William Shakespeare in Leonard Tourney's *Time's Fool* (Forge); Edgar Allan Poe in Harold Schechter's *The Mask of the Red Death* (Ballantine); and Beatrix Potter in Susan Wittig Albert's *The Tale of Hill Top Farm* (Berkley). Among non-literary series characters in good form were Anne Perry's nineteenth-century team of William Monk and Hester Latterly in *The Shifting Tide* (Ballantine), Gillian Linscott's suffragette Nell Bray in *Blood on the Wood* (St. Martin's Minotaur), Peter Tremayne's seventh-century Irish Sister Fidelma in *The Haunted Abbot* (St. Martin's Minotaur), Michael Jecks's fourteenth-century Sir Baldwin Furnshill and Simon Puttock in *The Tolls of Death* (Headline/Trafalgar Square), Lindsey Davis's ancient Roman Marcus Didius Falco in *Scandal Takes a Holiday* (Mysterious), and David Dickinson's early-twentieth-century Lord Francis Powerscourt in *Death of an Old Master*

(Carroll & Graf). A better than average Sherlockian pastiche was Lora Roberts's *The Affair of the Incognito Tenant* (Perseverance). Two novels entertained history/mystery buffs while straining reader credulity with their use of the old Shakespearean cross-gender disguise ploy: Laurie R. King's *The Game* (Bantam), about Sherlock Holmes and his wife Mary Russell, and Claudia Gross's fifteenth-century academic *Scholarium* (Toby), translated from the German by Helen Atkins. Finally, a non-series historical concerned a meeting of Marilyn Monroe and Nikita Krushchev: Barbara and Max Allan Collins's *Bombshell* (Five Star).

Satirical thrillers. Larry Beinhart's *The Librarian* (Nation Books), released shortly before the Presidential election, had political fish to fry. Lee Goldberg's hard-to-classify but not-to-be-missed *The Walk* (Five Star), set in the aftermath of a major Los Angeles earthquake, pokes fun at the TV industry in the midst of disaster.

## Short Stories

It was another banner year for single-author collections. Literally this time. Crippen & Landru's Lost Classic series added a volume by the undeservedly obscure John Dickson Carr acolyte Joseph Commings, *Banner Deadlines: The Impossible Files of Senator Brooks U. Banner.* Other additions to this distinguished publishing project included T. S. Stribling's *Dr. Poggioli: Criminologist*; and Erle Stanley Gardner's *The Danger Zone and Other Stories*, the latter launching a new series of collections from an author whose backlog of unreprinted fiction seems inexhaustible. Outstanding C&G volumes from contemporaries included Margaret Maron's *Suitable for Hanging*; and Kathy Lynn

Emerson's *Murder and Other Confusions*, short stories from the Elizabethan series about Susanna, Lady Appleton.

From other non-Manhattan publishers came a notable volume of mostly humorous crime stories, Joan Hess's *The Deadly Ackee and Other Stories of Crime and Catastrophe* (Five Star); previously uncollected stories by E. Phillips Oppenheim, *Secrets & Sovereigns* (Stark House); a collection about L.A. private eye Ivan Monk by Gary Phillips, *Monkology* (Dennis McMillan); and James Sallis's partly criminous, partly science fictional, all downbeat *A City Equal to My Desire* (PointBlank).

Most significant collection from a New York publisher was probably *The Easiest Thing in the World: The Uncollected Fiction of George V. Higgins* (Carroll & Graf), but there were others. Some of the shorter cases of Peter Tremayne's Sister Fidelma were gathered in *Whispers of the Dead* (St. Martin's Minotaur). Jeffery Deaver's *Twisted* (Simon & Schuster) gave lessons in how to fool the reader. Francis M. Nevins edited a new collection of Cornell Woolrich stories, *Night and Fear* (Carroll & Graf/Penzler), commemorating the suspense master's 2003 centenary.

The two remaining annual best-of-the-year anthologies from American publishers, *The Best American Mystery Stories 2004* (Houghton Mifflin), edited by Nelson DeMille with series editor Otto Penzler, and the present volume's predecessor, *The World's Finest Mystery and Crime Stories, Fifth Annual Collection* (Forge), edited by Ed Gorman and Martin H. Greenberg, agreed on the merits of only two stories published in 2003: Jeff Abbott's Edgar-nominated "Bet on Red" and Dick Lochte's "Low Tide." G. Miki Hayden's Edgar winner, "The Maids," and the other three nominees by Shelley Costa,

David Edgerley Gates, and Kristine Kathryn Rusch, appeared only in Gorman/Greenberg, who also had the Anthony Award winner, Rhys Bowen's "Doppelganger." Joyce Carol Oates appeared in both anthologies but with different stories, "Doll: A Romance of the Mississippi" in DeMille/Penzer and "The Hunter" in Gorman/Greenberg. What does it all mean? Only that there was plenty of good short fiction to choose from.

Other reprint anthologies of note included *The Mammoth Book of Roaring Twenties Whodunnits* (Carroll & Graf), edited by Mike Ashley; and the Jewish themed *Murder is No Mitzvah* (St. Martin's Minotaur), edited by Abigail Browning. Wildside offered a facsimile reprint of the entire August 1935 issue of *Spicy Mystery Stories*, appropriately anchored by pulp wildman Robert Leslie Bellem.

The most notable original anthology of the year was probably *Shades of Black: Crime and Mystery Stories by African-American Writers* (Berkley), edited by Eleanor Taylor Bland. The same publisher brought out several others: the Mystery Writers of America's *Show Business is Murder*, edited by Stuart M. Kaminsky; *Death Dines In*, edited by Claudia Bishop and Dean James; and *Death by Dickens*, edited by Anne Perry. Two of the most prolific current anthologists stayed busy: Robert J. Randisi edited *Murder and All That Jazz* (Signet), while Michael Bracken edited a pair, *Small Crimes* and *Fedora III: Even More Private Eyes, Even More Tough Guys* (both Betancourt). Dana Stabenow edited the wilderness-themed *Wild Crimes* (Signet). One of the most specialized anthologies of the year was the Kentucky Derby-themed *Derby Rotten Scoundrels* (Silver Dagger), edited for Sisters in Crime's Ohio Valley chapter by Jeffery Marks.

As usual, see Ed Hoch's yearbook for the full list.

## Reference Books and Secondary Sources

The reference source of the year was Leslie S. Klinger's Edgar winner, *The New Annotated Sherlock Holmes* (Norton), superseding W. S. Baring-Gould's annotated edition of several decades ago. Two biographies concerned world literary figures with strong connections to the crime fiction field, Norman Sherry's *The Life of Graham Greene, Volume Three: 1955–1991* and Edwin Williamson's *Borges: A Life* (both Viking). It was an especially good year for admirers of old radio crime drama, with Jack French's *Private Eyelashes: Radio's Lady Detectives* (Bear Manor) and Martin Grams, Jr.'s *Gang Busters: The Crime Fighters of American Broadcasting* (OTR). Also notable were Ray B. Browne's *Murder on the Reservation: American Indian Crime Fiction* (University of Wisconsin Popular Press); Rita Elizabeth Rippetoe's *Booze and the Private Eye: Alcohol in the Hard-Boiled Novel* (McFarland); *Latin American Mystery Writers: An A to Z Guide* (Greenwood), edited by Darrell B. Lockhart; Gary Lovisi's *The Pulp Crime Digests* (Gryphon); Laurence Roth's *Inspecting Jews: American Jewish Detective Stories* (Rutgers University Press); Max Allan Collins and George Hagenauer's *Men's Adventure Magazines in Postwar America* (Taschen); and the second edition of Richard J. Bleiler's *Reference and Research Guide to Mystery and Detection* (Libraries Unlimited).

Again, Ed Hoch will give you the full story.

## A Sense of History

In 2004, mystery fiction continued to honor its rich past. Apart from the paperback original reprints and historic short story collections noted elsewhere, there were a wealth of notable revivals. Hard Case brought back the team of Donald Lam and Bertha Cool in the 1952 novel *Top of the Heap*, by Erle Stanley Gardner writing as A. A. Fair. Rue Morgue's always exciting program included vintage titles by Stuart Palmer, Kelley Roos, Constance and Gwenyth Little, Margaret Scherf, and others. A particularly notable Rue Morgue revival was Lucy Cores, whose two novels about exercise trainer Toni Ney, *Painted for the Kill* (1943) and *Corpse de Ballet* (1944) struck me as far better than most of the current cozy crop. Walker brought out hardcover reprints of the first two John LeCarré novels, *Call for the Dead* (1962) and *A Murder of Quality* (1963), with introductions by the author and new forewords by P. D. James and Otto Penzler, respectively. Penzler's series of Edgar winner reprints for Forge added Brian Garfield's *Hopscotch* (1975) and Adam Hall's *The Quiller Memorandum* (1965). Stark House continued its Elizabeth Sanxay Holding revival with a double volume of *The Death Wish* (1934) and *Net of Cobwebs* (1945). Two suspense classics, Evelyn Piper's *Bunny Lake is Missing* (1957) and Dorothy B. Hughes's *The Blackbirder* (1943) joined the Feminist Press's Women Write Pulp series. (Neither fits my definition of pulp, but who cares?)

Academy Chicago resumed its revival of Leo Bruce's Carolus Deene with the first American edition of *Death in the Middle Watch* (1974). Wildside continued its rediscovery of Arsene Lupin's creator, Maurice Leblanc, with *The Golden Triangle* (1917), while Ramble House still has some previously unpublished late works by the one-of-a-kind Harry Stephen Keeler, most recently *The Riddle of the Wooden Parakeet*, a two-volume opus completed in the early 1960s, with an introduction by Francis M. Nevins.

## At the Movies

It was an unusual year for crime films. The best of the lot concerned an offense that is now not usually considered a crime: Mike Leigh's *Vera Drake*, about a sympathetically observed abortionist, brilliantly played by Imelda Staunton, going through the criminal justice process in early-'50s Britain. Another best-actress Oscar nominee, Catalina Sandino Moreno, appeared in Joshua Marston's *Maria Full of Grace*, a disturbing, graphic, and all-too-believable look at heroin-smuggling from Columbia to the United States.

The best *mystery* film I saw in 2004 was not a whodunit, whydunit, or howdunit but an example of the most pervasive current trend in big-screen mysteries, mostly those from independent filmmakers: a whatsgoingonhere. *The Machinist*, directed by Brad Anderson from Scott Kosar's script, gradually reveals how an insomniac machine-shop employee, played by an alarmingly reduced Christian Bale, reached his precarious mental state. Adding to the sense of disorientation, this is officially a Spanish film (original title *El Maquinista*), though acted in English.

In a time of excessive remakes and sequels, two well-remembered films of the past had new versions. While nearly everyone agreed Jonathan Demme's updated remake of *The Manchurian Candidate*, with screenplay by Daniel Pyne and Dean Georgaris based on George Axelrod's screenplay from Richard Condon's novel, was not as good as the 1962 version, most still found it a creditable job. Less well received was a film I found better than reputed, albeit still not quite up to the original: *The Ladykillers*, which Joel and Ethan Coen refashioned from a 1955 Alec Guiness vehicle to a 2004 Tom Hanks vehicle, adapting William Rose's original screenplay.

Pieter Jan Brugge's *The Clearing*, scripted by Justin Haythe from Brugge's story, was an unconventional kidnap drama, more character based than suspense based. *Cellular*, directed by David R. Ellis from Chris Morgan's script of Larry Cohen's story, struck me as an effective pure suspense outing if you can live with a few improbabilities. (I neither have nor want a cell phone, so some of them were probably lost on me.) A typically fine performance by Ben Kingsley marked *Suspect Zero*, directed by E. Elias Merhige from a script by Zak Penn and Billy Ray, in which a serial killer is targeting other serial killers. David Koepp's *Secret Window*, from Stephen King's story, was a pretty good paranormal thriller that enjoyed a symbiotic publicity relationship with *Ellery Queen's Mystery Magazine*. *Man on Fire*, directed by Tony Scott from Brian Helgeland's adaptation of A. J. Quinnell's novel, was a terrific revenge thriller.

Two of the four Edgar nominees were foreign films: the Italian childhood kidnap story *I'm Not Scared* (*Io non ho paura*), directed by Gabriel Salvatores from the screenplay by Niccolò Ammaniti and Francesca Marciano based on Ammaniti's novel; and the winner, the French *A Very Long Engagement* (*Un long dimanche de fiançailles*), adapted from Sébastien Japrisot's novel by director Jean-Pierre Jeunet and Guillaume Laurant. (Much as we love French films, my wife and I passed on that one, having OD'd on the trailer and incessant radio ads.) Representing the home team in the Edgar contest were *Collateral*, directed by Michael Mann from Stuart Beattie's script, which cast Tom Cruise in the unconventional role of a hired killer;

and *The Bourne Supremacy*, directed by Paul Greengrass from Troy Gilroy's adaptation of Robert Ludlum's novel, a well-made addition to a new international intrigue and action franchise.

## Award Winners

Awards tied to publishers' contests, those limited to a geographical region smaller than a country, those awarded for works in languages other than English (with the exception of Crime Writers of Canada's nod to their French members), and those confined to works from a particular periodical have been omitted.

### Awarded in 2005 for Material Published in 2004

**EDGAR ALLAN POE AWARDS**

(MYSTERY WRITERS OF AMERICA)

BEST NOVEL:

T. Jefferson Parker, *California Girl* (Morrow)

BEST FIRST NOVEL BY AN AMERICAN AUTHOR:

Don Lee, *Country of Origin* (Norton)

BEST ORIGINAL PAPERBACK:

Domenic Stansberry, *The Confession* (Hard Case Crime)

BEST FACT CRIME BOOK:

Leonard Levitt, *Conviction: Solving the Moxley Murder* (Regan)

BEST CRITICAL/BIOGRAPHICAL WORK:
Leslie S. Klinger, ed., *The New Annotated Sherlock Holmes: The Complete Short Stories* (Norton)

BEST SHORT STORY:
Laurie Lynn Drummond,
"Something About a Scar"
(*Anything You Say Can and Will Be Used Against You*, HarperCollins)

BEST YOUNG ADULT MYSTERY:
Dorothy and Thomas Hoobler,
*In Darkness, Death* (Philomel)

BEST JUVENILE MYSTERY:
Blue Balliett, *Chasing Vermeer* (Scholastic)

BEST PLAY:
Neal Bell, *Splatter Pattern; or, How I Got Away With It* (Playwrights Horizons)

BEST EPISODE IN A TELEVISION SERIES:
Elizabeth Benjamin (teleplay and story) and René Balcer (story),
"Want" (*Law & Order: Criminal Intent*)

BEST TELEVISION FEATURE OR MINISERIES TELEPLAY:
Paul Abbott,
*State of Play* (BBC America)

BEST MOTION PICTURE SCREENPLAY:
Pierre Jeunet,

*A Very Long Engagement*,
based on the novel by Sébastien Japrisot (2003 Productions)

GRAND MASTER:
Marcia Muller

ROBERT L. FISH AWARD (BEST FIRST STORY):
Thomas Morrissy,
"Can't Catch Me" (*Brooklyn Noir*, Akashic)

ELLERY QUEEN AWARD:
Carolyn Marino

RAVEN:
Cape Cod Radio Mystery Theatre (Steve Oney, founder);
DorothyL listserv (Diane Kovacs and Kara Robinson, founders);
Murder by the Book, Houston, Texas (Martha Farrington, owner)

MARY HIGGINS CLARK AWARD:
Rochelle Krich, *Grave Endings* (Ballantine)

SPECIAL EDGAR:
David Chase; Tom Fontana

## AGATHA AWARDS

(MALICE DOMESTIC MYSTERY CONVENTION)

BEST NOVEL:
Jacqueline Winspear,
*Birds of a Feather* (Soho)

BEST FIRST NOVEL:

Harley Jane Kozak,

*Dating Dead Men* (Doubleday)

BEST SHORT STORY:

Elaine Veits,

"Wedding Knife" (*ChesapeakeCrimes*, Quiet Storm)

BEST NONFICTION:

Jack French,

*Private Eye-Lashes:*

*Radio's Lady Detectives* (Bear Manor Media)

BEST CHILDREN'S/YOUNG ADULT:

Blue Balliett, *Chasing Vermeer* (Scholastic)

LIFETIME ACHIEVEMENT AWARD:

H.R.F. Keating

POIROT AWARD:

Angela Lansbury

## Awarded in 2004 for Material Published in 2003

### EDGAR ALLAN POE AWARDS

(MYSTERY WRITERS OF AMERICA)

BEST NOVEL:

Ian Rankin,

*Resurrection Men* (Little, Brown)

**BEST FIRST NOVEL BY AN AMERICAN AUTHOR:**

Rebecca Pawel, *Death of a Nationalist* (Soho)

**BEST ORIGINAL PAPERBACK:**

Sylvia Maultash Warsh,
*Find Me Again* (Dundurn Group)

**BEST FACT CRIME BOOK:**

Erik Larson, *The Devil in the White City* (Crown)

**BEST CRITICAL/BIOGRAPHICAL WORK:**

Andrew Wilson, *Beautiful Shadow: A Life of Patricia Highsmith* (Bloomsbury)

**BEST SHORT STORY:**

G. Miki Hayden, "The Maids"
(*Blood on Their Hands*, Berkley)

**BEST YOUNG ADULT MYSTERY:**

Graham McNamee, *Acceleration* (Wendy Lamb)

**BEST JUVENILE MYSTERY:**

Phyllis Reynolds Naylor,
*Bernie Magruder & the Bats in the Belfry*, (Atheneum)

**BEST EPISODE IN A TELEVISION SERIES:**

Peter Blake and David E. Kelley, "Goodbye" (*The Practice*, ABC)

**BEST MOTION PICTURE SCREENPLAY:**

Steve Knight, *Dirty Pretty Things*
(BBC, Celador Productions, Jonescompany)

**GRAND MASTER:**

Joseph Wambaugh

**ROBERT L. FISH AWARD (BEST FIRST STORY):**

Sandy Balzo, "The Grass is Always Greener" (*Ellery Queen's Mystery Magazine*, March)

**RAVEN:**

Ray and Pat Browne Library for Popular Culture Studies at Bowling Green State University;
*Vanity Fair* magazine (Graydon Carter, editor)

**MARY HIGGINS CLARK AWARD:**

M. K. Preston, *Song of the Bones* (Intrigue)

**SPECIAL EDGAR:**

Home Box Office

## AGATHA AWARDS

**(MALICE DOMESTIC MYSTERY CONVENTION)**

**BEST NOVEL:**

Carolyn Hart, *Letter From Home* (Berkley)

**BEST FIRST NOVEL:**

Jacqueline Winspear, *Maisie Dobbs* (Soho)

**BEST SHORT STORY:**

Elizabeth Foxwell, "No Man's Land" (*Blood on Their Hands*, Berkley)

BEST NONFICTION:

Elizabeth Peters and Kristen Whitbread, eds.,
*Amelia Peabody's Egypt:*
*A Compendium* designed by Dennis Forbes (Morrow)

BEST CHILDREN'S/YOUNG ADULT:

Kathleen Karr, *The 7th Knot* (Marshall Cavendish)

LIFETIME ACHIEVEMENT AWARD:

Marian Babson

POIROT AWARD:

Ruth Cavin and Thomas Dunne

## ANTHONY AWARDS

(BOUCHERCON WORLD MYSTERY CONVENTION)

BEST NOVEL:

Laura Lippman, *Every Secret Thing* (Morrow)

BEST FIRST NOVEL:

P. J. Tracy, *Monkeewrench* (Putnam)

BEST PAPERBACK ORIGINAL:

Robin Burcell, *Deadly Legacy* (Avon)

BEST SHORT STORY:

Rhys Bowen,
"Doppelganger" (*Blood on Their Hands*, Berkley)

BEST CRITICAL/BIOGRAPHICAL:
Gary Warren Niebuhr,
*Make Mine a Mystery* (Libraries Unlimited)

BEST YOUNG ADULT MYSTERY:
J. K. Rowling, *Harry Potter and the Order of the Phoenix* (Bloomsbury)

BEST HISTORICAL MYSTERY:
Rhys Bowen, *For the Love of Mike* (St. Martin's Minotaur)

BEST FAN PUBLICATION:
*Mystery Scene*, edited by Kate Stine

LIFETIME ACHIEVEMENT:
Bernard Cornwell

## SHAMUS AWARDS
(PRIVATE EYE WRITERS OF AMERICA)

BEST NOVEL:
Ken Bruen, *The Guards*
(St. Martin's Minotaur)

BEST FIRST NOVEL:
Peter Spiegelman, *Black Maps* (Knopf)

BEST ORIGINAL PAPERBACK NOVEL:
Andy Straka, *Cold Quarry* (Signet)

BEST SHORT STORY:

Loren D. Estleman, "Lady on Ice"
(*A Hot and Sultry Night for Crime*, Berkley)

THE EYE (LIFE ACHIEVEMENT):

Donald E. Westlake

## DAGGER AWARDS

(CRIME WRITERS' ASSOCIATION, GREAT BRITAIN)

GOLD DAGGER:

Sara Paretsky, *Blacklist* (Hamish Hamilton)

SILVER DAGGER:

John Harvey, *Flesh and Blood* (Heinemann)

JOHN CREASEY AWARD (BEST FIRST NOVEL):

Mark Mills, *Amagansett* (Forth Estate)

BEST SHORT STORY:

Jeffery Deaver, "The Weekender"
(*Twisted*, Hodder & Stoughton;
first published in *Alfred Hitchcock's Mystery Magazine*,
December 1996)

BEST NONFICTION (TIE):

John Dickie, *Cosa Nostra:
A History of the Sicillian Mafia* (Hodder & Stoughton);
and Sarah Wise, *The Italian Boy:
Murder and Grave Robbery in 1830s London* (Jonathan Cape)

**DIAMOND DAGGER:**

Lawrence Block

**ELLIS PETERS HISTORICAL DAGGER:**

Barbara Cleverly, *The Damascened Blade* (Constable & Robinson)

**IAN FLEMING STEEL DAGGER:**

Jeffery Deaver, *Garden of Beasts* (Hodder & Stoughton)

**DAGGER IN THE LIBRARY (VOTED BY LIBRARIANS FOR A BODY OF WORK):**

Alexander McCall Smith

**PEOPLE'S CHOICE AWARD:**

Reginald Hill, *Good Morning, Midnight* (HarperCollins)

**DEBUT DAGGER (FOR UNPUBLISHED WRITERS):**

Ellen Grubb, *The Doll-maker*

**LEO HARRIS AWARD:**

Joan Lock, for the best contribution to the CWA monthly bulletin, *Red Herrings*

## MACAVITY AWARDS

**(MYSTERY READERS INTERNATIONAL)**

**BEST NOVEL:**

Peter Lovesey, *The House Sitter* (Soho)

BEST FIRST NOVEL:

Jacqueline Winspear, *Maisie Dobbs* (Soho)

BEST CRITICAL/BIOGRAPHICAL WORK:

Gary Warren Niebuhr,
*Make Mine A Mystery* (Libraries Unlimited)

BEST SHORT STORY:

Sandy Balzo,
"The Grass Is Always Greener"
(*Ellery Queen's Mystery Magazine*, March)

## ARTHUR ELLIS AWARDS

(CRIME WRITERS OF CANADA)

BEST NOVEL:

Giles Blunt, *The Delicate Storm*
(Random House Canada)

BEST FIRST NOVEL:

Jan Rehner, *Just Murder* (Sumach)

BEST NONFICTION:

Julian Sher and William Marsden,
*The Road to Hell: How the Biker Gangs Are Conquering Canada*
(Knopf Canada)

BEST JUVENILE NOVEL:

Graham McNamee,
*Acceleration* (Wendy Lamb)

BEST SHORT STORY:

Gregory Ward, "Dead Wood"
(*Hard Boiled Love*, Insomniac)

BEST CRIME WRITING IN FRENCH:

Jean Lemieux, *On finit toujours par payer* (La Courte Echelle)

DERRICK MURDOCH AWARD FOR LIFETIME ACHIEVEMENT:

Cheryl Freedman

## NED KELLY AWARDS

(CRIME WRITERS' ASSOCIATION OF AUSTRALIA)

BEST NOVEL:

Jon Cleary, *Degrees of Connection* (HarperCollins)

BEST FIRST NOVEL:

(tie) Jane Goodall, *The Walker* (Hodder);
Wayne Grogan, *Junkie Pilgrim* (Brandl & Schlesinger)

BEST TRUE CRIME:

Peter Rees, *Killing Juanita* (Allen & Unwin)

LIFETIME ACHIEVEMENT:

Bob Bottom

## BARRY AWARDS

(*DEADLY PLEASURES* MAGAZINE)

BEST NOVEL:

Laura Lippman, *Every Secret Thing* (Morrow)

BEST FIRST NOVEL:

P. J. Tracy, *Monkeewrench* (Putnam)

BEST BRITISH NOVEL:

Val McDermid, *The Distant Echo* (HarperCollins)

BEST PAPERBACK ORIGINAL:

Jason Starr, *Tough Luck* (Vintage)

BEST SHORT STORY:

Robert Barnard, "Rogues' Gallery"
(*Ellery Queen's Mystery Magazine*, March)

DON SANDSTROM MEMORIAL AWARD FOR
LIFETIME ACHIEVEMENT IN MYSTERY FANDOM:

Ted Fitzgerald

## NERO WOLFE AWARD

(WOLFE PACK)

Walter Mosley, *Fear Itself* (Little, Brown)

## DILYS AWARD

(INDEPENDENT MYSTERY BOOKSELLERS ASSOCIATION)

Jasper Fforde, *Lost in a Good Book* (Viking)

## HAMMETT PRI

(INTERNATIONAL CRIME WRITERS)

Carol Goodman, *The Seduction of Water* (Ballantine)

# A 2004 Yearbook of Crime and Mystery

Edward D. Hoch

**COLLECTIONS AND SINGLE STORIES**

**Anderson, Lars.** *Domino Lady: The Complete Collection.* Somerset, NJ: Vanguard Productions. Six stories from 1936 pulps, with a new story and introduction by the cover artist Steranko.

**Atkinson, Lisa.** *Yule Be Sorry.* New York: The Mysterious Bookshop. A single new short story in a Christmas chapbook from a Manhattan bookstore.

**Berkeley, Anthony.** *The Avenging Chance: and Other Mysteries from Roger Sheringham's Casebook.* Norfolk, VA: Crippen & Landru. Eight stories including a previously uncollected novelette, plus the author's own brief parody of his character and a checklist of all Sheringham novels and tales. Edited by Tony Medawar and Arthur Robinson.

**Blanchard, Al.** *The Stalker and Other Tales of Love and Murder.* Hamilton, MI: Koenisha. Twenty-five stories.

**Bonnett, Hal Murray.** *Crusher O'Shea.* Sidecar Preservation Society. A pamphlet containing two stories from 1930s pulp magazines.

**Capote, Truman.** *The Complete Stories of Truman Capote.* New York: Random House. Twenty stories, a few criminous.

**Coel, Margaret.** *Bad Heart.* Mission Viejo, CA: A.S.A.P. Publishing. A single short story, the seventh in the Arapaho Ten Commandments series. Introduction by T. Jefferson Parker.

**Commings, Joseph.** *Banner Deadlines: The Impossible Files of Senator Brooks U. Banner.* Norfolk, VA: Crippen & Landru. Fourteen "impossible crime" stories, one co-written with Edward D. Hoch and one previously unpublished. Edited by Robert Adey, with a memoir by Hoch.

**Connolly, John.** *Nocturnes.* London: Hodder & Stoughton. Twelve fantasies, one featuring the author's private eye Charlie Parker.

**Constiner, Marle.** *The Compleat Adventures of the Dean.* Shelburne, Ont., Canada: Battered Silicon Dispatch Box. Stories of a fortune-teller detective, from *Dime Detective,* 1940–45. Edited by Robert E. Weinberg.

**Davis, Frederick C.** *The Compleat Adventures of the Moon Man, From Ten Detective Aces, The Silver Spectre—Volume*

*Two*. Shelburne, Ont., Canada: Battered Silicon Dispatch Box. Commentary by Gary Roberts and Gary Hoppenstand, compiled and edited by Robert Weinberg. *Lost Treasures from the Pulps* #6.

**DeBra, Lemuel.** *The Tribe of the Tiger.* Bloomington, IL: Black Dog Books. A single secret service story from *Blue Book,* February 1940.

**Doctorow, E. L.** *Sweet Land Stories.* New York: Random House. Five novelettes, mainly criminous.

**Doyle, Arthur Conan.** *The Captain of the 'Pole-Star': Weird and Imaginative Fiction.* Ashcroft, BC, Canada: Ash-Tree Press. Thirty-seven stories, some criminous, including "The Speckled Band." Edited by Christopher & Barbara Roden, preface by Michael Dirda.

———. *The New Annotated Sherlock Holmes: The Short Stories.* New York: Norton. A two-volume illustrated edition of the fifty-six stories, with historical and cultural details by editor Leslie S. Klinger. Introduction by John LeCarré.

**Drummond, Laurie Lynn.** *Anything You Say Can and Will Be Used Against You.* New York: HarperCollins. Ten short stories about women cops.

**Dunsany, Lord.** *In the Land of Time and Other Fantasy Tales* New York: Penguin Books. Forty-two stories, mainly fantasy but including the author's classic mystery "The Two Bottles of Relish." Edited by S. T. Joshi.

**Ellroy, James.** *Destination: Morgue! L.A. Tales.* New York: Vintage. Four new stories mainly about LAPD detective Rick Jenson, plus eight nonfiction pieces from *GQ.*

**Emerson, Kathy Lynn.** *Murders and Other Confusions.* Norfolk, VA: Crippen & Landru. Eleven historical mysteries, five new, about a woman herbalist in Elizabethan England.

**Estleman, Loren D.** *Sweet Women Lie.* New York: ibooks. A novel reprint with a short story added.

**Fleming, Ian.** *Octopussy and The Living Daylights.* New York: Penguin. An expanded version of this collection of three James Bond stories, with the addition of an eight-page tale, "007 in New York."

**Gardner, Erle Stanley.** *The Danger Zone and Other Stories.* Norfolk, VA: Crippen & Landru. Eleven pulp reprints, 1931–52, in the first of a series reviving Gardner's lesser sleuths. Edited by Bill Pronzini.

———. *Early Birds.* Norfolk, VA: Crippen & Landru. A fourteen-page pamphlet reprinting a story from *Detective Fiction Weekly,* 3/25/33, distributed to attendees at Malice Domestic XVI.

**Gores, Joe.** *No Crib for His Bed: A DKA Files Story.* Norfolk, VA: Crippen & Landru. A single new story in a holiday chapbook.

**Higgins, George V.** *The Easiest Thing in the World: Uncollected Fiction of George V. Higgins.* New York: Carroll & Graf. Fifteen stories by the late suspense writer, some previously unpublished, only a few criminous. Edited by Matthew J. Bruccoli.

**Howard, Robert E.** *Graveyard Rats and Others.* Holicong, PA: Wildside. All of Howard's detective fiction, some previously unpublished.

**Kantner, Rob.** *Trouble Is What I Do.* Holicong, PA: Point-Blank/Wildside. A collection of the author's Ben Perkins stories.

**Kellerman, Jonathan & Faye Kellerman.** *Double Homicide.* New York: Warner. Two collaborative novellas set in Santa Fe and Boston.

**Krieg, Joyce.** *Who Stole the Agatha Teapot?* A single detective story printed by the author and distributed at Malice Domestic 2004.

**Lansdale, Joe R.** *Mad Dog Summer and Other Stories.* Burton, MI: Subterranean Press. A mixed collection of eight stories, some fantasy, one new. The title novella was expanded into the Edgar-winning novel *The Bottoms.*

**Maron, Margaret.** *Suitable for Hanging: Selected Stories.* Norfolk, VA: Crippen & Landru. Twenty stories, 1970–2004, two new, some about Judge Deborah Knott.

**McCulley, Johnston.** *The Spider Strain and Other Tales from the Pulps.* Holicong, PA: Wildside. Pulp crime stories.

**McInerny, Ralph.** *Slattery: A Soft-Boiled Detective.* Waterville, Maine: Five Star. Four new novelettes.

**Mertz, Stephen.** *Fade to Tomorrow and Other Stories.* Waterville, Maine: Five Star. A novel and two stories about the music industry.

**Mill, Robert R.** *Murder on the Island and Other Stories of "Tiny" David of the Black Horse Troop.* Bloomington, IL: Black Dog Books. Four stories from *Blue Book,* 1933–35.

**Millar, Margaret.** *The Couple Next Door: Collected Short Mysteries.* Norfolk, VA: Crippen & Landru. Six stories and novelettes, 1942–87, in the Lost Classics series. Edited by Tom Nolan.

**Oates, Joyce Carol.** *I Am No One You Know.* New York: Ecco/HarperCollins. Nineteen stories, several criminous, two from *EQMM,* two reprinted in *Best American Mystery Stories.*

**Oppenheim, E. Philips.** *Secrets & Sovereigns.* Eurika, CA: Stark House. Early stories of intrigue. Edited by Daniel Paul Morrison.

**Phillips, Gary.** *Monkology.* Tucson, AZ: Dennis McMillan. Thirteen stories about a black L.A. private eye.

**Pronzini, Bill & Barry N. Malzberg.** *On Account of Darkness and Other Stories.* Waterford. Maine: Five Star.

Twenty-five science fiction and fantasy stories, some criminous, one from *AHMM.*

**Rathbone, Julian.** *The Indispensable Julian Rathbone.* London: Do-Not Press. A brief autobiography, stories, poems, essays, a 1985 novel *Lying in State* and a bibliography by the British crime writer. Introduction by Mike Phillips.

**Rawson, Clayton, writing as Stuart Towne.** *The Magical Mysteries of Don Diavalo.* Shelburne, Ont., Canada: Battered Silicon Dispatch Box. Four novellas from *Red Star Mystery Magazine,* 1940, plus five additional pulp stories, 1940–44, three featuring "Mr. Mystery." Introductions and commentaries by Douglas Greene, Hugh Rawson, Robert Weinberg, and Garyn Roberts.

**Robinson, Peter.** *Not Safe After Dark.* London: Macmillan. An enlarged edition of the thirteen-story 1998 collection, with the addition of six stories and a new Inspector Banks novella.

**Sallis, James.** *A City Equal to My Desire.* Holicong, PA: Pointblank/Wildside. Short crime stories.

**Schoenfeld, Howard.** *True and Almost True Stories.* Brooklyn: Gryphon. A mixed collection of fiction and nonfiction, including science fiction and crime tales. Introduction by Michael Kurland.

**Spillane, Mickey.** *Byline: Mickey Spillane.* Norfolk, VA: Crippen & Landru. Short story versions of two Mike Hammer novels plus a previously unpublished Hammer story, a playlet, three comic book reproductions of Hammer's predecessors and fourteen nonfiction pieces. Edited by Max Allan Collins and Lynn F. Myers, Jr.

**Stribling, T. S.** *Dr. Poggioli: Criminologist.* Norfolk, VA: Crippen & Landru. Nine uncollected stories, 1929–35, in the Lost Classics series. Edited by Arthur Vidro.

**Sturgeon, Theodore.** *And Now the News . . . Volume IX: The Complete Stories of Theodore Sturgeon.* Berkeley, CA: North Atlantic Books. This volume of fifteen stories, 1955–57, by the noted science-fiction writer includes three from mystery magazines, two from *The Saint.*

**Suter, J. Paul.** *The Memoirs of Horatio Humberton, The Necrologist Detective.* Shelbourne, Ont., Canada: Battered Silicon Dispatch Box. Stories of a mortician-detective, from *Dime Detective,* 1933–37. Edited by Robert E. Weinberg.

**Thomson, June.** *The Secret Notebooks of Sherlock Holmes* London: Allison & Busby. Seven new pastiches.

**Tinti, Hannah.** *Animal Crackers.* New York: Dial Press. Eleven strange stories about animals, a few criminous, one reprinted in *Best American Mystery Stories 2003.*

**Torrey, Roger.** *The Frankie and Johnnie Murders.* Bloomington, IL: Black Dog Books. A pamphlet containing two stories from *Private Detective,* 1939–42.

**Tremayne, Peter.** *Whispers of the Dead: Fifteen Sister Fidelma Mysteries*. New York: St. Martin's. More stories about a seventh-century Irish nun, three new, one from *EQMM*.

**Westlake, Donald E.** *Thieves' Dozen: The Dortmunder Stories*. New York: Mysterious Press. Eleven stories, 1981–2004, about a hapless thief, seven from *Playboy*, one new.

**ANTHOLOGIES**

**Alexander, Skye, Kate Flora & Susan Oleksiw,** eds. *Undertow: Crime Stories by New England Writers*. Prides Crossing, MA: Level Best Books. Eleven new stories, some fantasy.

**Ashley, Mike,** ed. *The Mammoth Book of Roaring Twenties Whodunnits*. New York: Carroll & Graf. Twenty-three stories, seventeen new.

**Bishop, Claudia & Dean James,** eds. *Death Dines In*. New York: Berkley. Sixteen new stories about food and drink, with recipes.

**Bland, Eleanor Taylor,** ed. *Shades of Black: Crime and Mystery Stories by African-American Writers*. New York: Berkley. Twenty-three original stories.

**Bracken, Michael,** ed. *Fedora III: Even More Private Eyes and Tough Guys*. Holicong, PA: Betancort & Co. Seventeen new stories.

———, ed. *Small Crimes.* Holicong, PA: Betancourt & Co. Fifteen new stories about small crimes with big consequences.

**Browning, Abigail,** ed. *Murder Is No Mitzvah: Short Mysteries About Jewish Occasions.* New York: Thomas Dunne/St. Martin's. Twelve stories, mainly from *EQMM.*

**DeMille, Nelson,** ed. *The Best American Mystery Stories 2004.* Boston: Houghton Mifflin. Twenty stories. Series editor: Otto Penzler.

**Dennis, Pat,** ed. *Who Died in Here? 25 Stories of Crimes & Bathrooms.* Richfield, MN: Penury Press. New stories by midwestern writers.

**Edghill, Rosemary,** ed. *Murder by Magic: Twenty Tales of Crime and the Supernatural.* New York: Warner Aspect. All new stories.

**Gorman, Ed & Martin H. Greenberg,** eds. *The World's Finest Mystery and Crime Stories, Fourth Annual Collection.* New York: Forge. Forty-two stories, with five reports on the year in mysteries. (2003)

———, eds. *The World's Finest Mystery and Crime Stories, Fifth Annual Collection.* New York: Forge. Thirty-two stories, with six reports on the year in mysteries.

**Hutchings, Janet,** ed. *Ellery Queen Presents Great Mystery Novellas.* Waterville, Maine: Five Star. Five novellas from *EQMM,* 1996–2001.

**Jakubowski, Maxim,** ed. *The Best British Mysteries 2005.* London: Allison & Busby. Second in an annual series.

**Kaminsky, Stuart,** ed. *Show Business Is Murder.* New York: Berkley. Twenty new stories in the latest anthology from Mystery Writers of America.

**Kurland, Michael,** ed. *Sherlock Holmes: The Hidden Years.* New York: St. Martin's. All new stories.

**Marks, Jeffery,** ed. *Criminal Appetites.* Johnson City, TN: Silver Dagger. Fourteen tales of culinary crime, with recipes.

———, ed. *Derby Rotten Scoundrels.* Johnson City, TN: Silver Dagger. Stories with a Kentucky Derby theme by members of the Ohio River Valley Chapter of Sisters in Crime.

**Massey, Brandon,** ed. *Dark Dreams: a Collection of Horror and Suspense by Black Writers.* Elmont, NY: Dafina Books. Twenty new stories.

**McLoughlin, Tim,** ed. *Brooklyn Noir.* Brooklyn: Akashic Books. Twenty previously unpublished stories set in various parts of Brooklyn.

**Penzler, Otto,** ed. *Dangerous Women,* New York: Mysterious Press. Seventeen new stories.

**Perry, Anne,** ed. *Death by Dickens.* New York: Berkley. Eleven new stories inspired by the fiction of Charles Dickens.

**Radcliffe, Martin,** ed. *The Masters of Mystery.* London: Do-Not Press. Twenty-seven stories of crime and mystery, 1842–1918, mainly by British authors.

**Schooley, Kerry J. & Peter Sellers,** eds. *Revenge: A Noir Anthology About Getting Even.* Toronto: Insomniac Press. Twelve stories, three new.

**Slaughter, Karin,** ed. *Like a Charm.* London: Century. New mysteries with stories built around a charm bracelet.

**Stabenow, Dana,** ed. *Powers of Detection: Stories of Mystery and Fantasy.* New York: Ace. Twelve new stories by mystery and fantasy authors.

———, ed. *Wild Crimes: Stories of Mystery in the Wild.* New York: Signet. Eleven new stories.

**Stevens, Serita,** ed. *Blondes in Trouble & Other Tangled Tales.* Denver: Intrigue Press. Eighteen new stories with blond protagonists.

**Turner, Gary & Marty Halpern,** eds. *The Silver Gryphon.* Urbana, IL: Golden Gryphon Press. Twenty new stories, mainly fantasy, a few criminous.

**Webb, Betty; Terence Faherty, Nancy Baker Jacobs, Jonathan Harrington.** *Desperate Journeys.* Toronto: Worldwide Library. Four new novelettes of murder in motion.

## NONFICTION

**Albert, Walter.** *Detective and Mystery Fiction: An International Bibliography of Secondary Sources.* Oakland, CA: Locus Press. Third edition, revised and enlarged. Available on CD-ROM.

**Ashley, Mike & Robert A. W. Lowndes.** *The Gernsback Days: A study of the evolution of modern science fiction from 1911 to 1936.* Holicong, PA: Wildside Press. A detailed description and bibliography of Hugo Gernsback's pulp magazines, including *Scientific Detective Monthly* and *Amazing Detective Tales.*

**Barnes, Alan.** *Sherlock Holmes on Screen: The Complete Film and TV History.* Richmond, VT: Reynolds & Hearn/Trafalgar Square. An updated second edition.

**Bleiler, Richard J.** *Reference and Research Guide to Mystery and Detective Fiction.* Westport, CT: Libraries Unlimited. Second edition, much enlarged, of a 1999 guide to book and online reference sources.

**Borges, Jorge Luis.** *Jorge Luis Borges Autobiography-Autobiografía.* Barcelona: Grupo Planeta. Borges's original English manuscript with a Spanish translation.

**Capote, Truman.** *Too Brief a Treat: The Letters of Truman Capote.* New York: Random House. Letters from the author of *In Cold Blood.*

**Decharne, Max.** *Hardboiled Hollywood: The Origins of the*

*Great Crime Films.* London: No Exit. A study of eleven well-known crime films.

**Derie, Kate,** ed. *The Deadly Directory 2004.* Tucson, AZ: Deadly Serious Press. The ninth edition of an annual guide, with over 700 listings of booksellers, associations, events, periodicals, reviewers, and publishers.

**Emerson, Kathy Lynn.** *A Cautionary Herbal, being a compendium of plants harmful to the health.* Norfolk, VA: Crippen & Landru. A sixteen-page pamphlet describing some of the poisonous plants found in Emerson's mysteries, distributed with the limited hardcover edition of the author's short stories.

**Estleman, Loren D.** *Writing the Popular Novel: A Comprehensive Guide to Crafting Fiction That Sells.* Cincinnati: Writer's Digest. Advice from the well-known mystery writer.

**French, Jack.** *Private Eyelashes: Radio's Lady Detectives.* Boalsdburg, PA: Bear Manor Media. A survey of female radio sleuths starting in 1932.

**Frey, James N.** *How to Write a Damn Good Mystery: A Practical Step-by-Step Guide from Inspiration to Finished Manuscript.* New York: St. Martin's Press. A guide for beginning writers.

**Gannon, Michael B.** *Blood, Bedlam, Bullets and Badguys: A Reader's Guide to Adventure/Suspense Fiction.* Westport, CT: Libraries Unlimited. Over 3,100 titles listed, about 2,000 annotated.

**GEORGE, ELIZABETH.** *Write Away: One Novelist's Approach to Fiction and the Writing Life.* New York: HarperCollins. Views on the craft of writing from a best-selling mystery novelist.

**HITZ, FREDERICK P.** *The Great Game: The Myth and Reality of Espionage.* New York: Knopf. Comparing great works of spy fiction with actual espionage operations.

**HOLLAND, STEVE.** *The Trials of Hank Janson.* Moulton, England: Telos. A biography of Stephen D. Francis, author of a series of British paperbacks about hardboiled pulp hero Hank Janson.

**JANCE, J. A.** *After the Fire.* Tucson: University of Arizona Libraries. Poetry and bits of autobiography by the mystery writer.

**JORDAN, JON.** *Interrogations: Author Interviews.* Milwaukee: Mystery One Books. Interviews with twenty-five mystery writers. Introduction by Deborah Morgan.

**KESTNER, JOSEPH A.** *Sherlock's Sisters: The British Female Detective 1864–1913.* Aldershot, Hampshire, UK: Ashgate Publishing. A study of thirteen books featuring women sleuths.

**KNIGHT, STEPHEN.** *Crime Fiction 1800–2000, Detection, Death, Diversity.* New York: Palgrave. The changing patterns of crime fiction over two centuries.

**LOBDELL, JARED,** ed. *The Detective Fiction Reviews of Charles Williams 1930–1935.* Jefferson, NC: McFarland &

Co. A study of the mystery reviews of the English novelist and theologian, not to be confused with the American author of the same name.

**Lockhart, Darrell B.,** ed. *Latin American Mystery Writers: An A to Z Guide.* Westport, CT: Greenwood. Signed biographical/critical essays on fifty-four Latin writers, mainly from Argentina and Mexico.

**Lovisi, Gary.** *The Pulp Crime Digests: A History, Checklist & Value Guide to Traditional Mystery and Crime Exploitation Digest Magazines of the 1950s and 1960s.* Brooklyn: Gryphon. Introduction by Harlan Ellison and comments by several other writers of the period. Afterword by Peter Enfantino.

**Lownie, Andrew.** *John Buchan: The Presbyterian Cavalier.* Boston: David R. Godine. A biography of the author of *The Thirty-Nine Steps* and other thrillers.

**McCarty, John.** *Bullets Over Hollywood: The American Gangster Picture from the Silents to "The Sopranos."* New York: DaCapo Press. A detailed study.

**McCrum, Robert.** *Wodehouse: A Life.* New York: Norton. A biography of the famed British humorist, many of whose novels and stories contain criminous elements.

**Meyers, Jeffery.** *Somerset Maugham: A Life.* New York: Knopf. A biography of the British novelist and author of *Ashenden*, the earliest example of realism in spy fiction.

**MIZEJEWSKI, LINDA.** *Hardboiled & High Heeled: The Woman Detective in Popular Culture,* New York: Routledge. Female investigators in crime fiction, TV and film.

**OLSON, BRIAN & BONNIE OLSON.** *Tailing Philip Marlowe.* St. Paul, MN: Burlwrite LLC. Three tours of Los Angeles based on the work of Raymond Chandler.

**PANEK, LEROY LAD.** *The American Police Novel: A History.* Jefferson, NC: McFarland & Co. An illustrated history from Julian Hawthorne to the present.

**PARINI, JAY.** *One Matchless Time: A Life of William Faulkner.* New York: HarperCollins. A new biography of Faulkner, who occasionally turned to crime and detective fiction, as in his Gavin Stevens stories.

**PENZLER, OTTO & THOMAS H. COOK,** eds. *Best American Crime Writing: 2004.* New York: Vintage. Twenty true crime essays, a few by noted mystery writers such as Scott Turow and James Ellroy. Introduction by Joseph Wambaugh.

**PERRY, DENNIS R.** *Hitchcock and Poe: The Legacy of Delight and Terror.* Blue Ridge Summit, PA: Scarecrow Press. A study of the relationship between Poe's tales and Hitchcock's films.

**PRIESTMAN, MARTIN,** ed. *The Cambridge Companion to Crime Fiction.* Cambridge: Cambridge University Press. Fourteen essays on the genre's history.

**Rippetoe, Rita Elizabeth.** *Booze and the Private Eye: Alcohol in the Hard-Boiled Novel.* Jefferson, NC: McFarland. Individual chapters on Hammett, Chandler, Spillane, Parker, Block, and female private eyes.

**Roth, Laurence.** *Inspecting Jews: American Jewish Detective Stories.* Piscataway, NJ: Rutgers University Press. A history and guide to the principal authors.

**Scowcroft, Philip L.** *Railways in British Crime Fiction.* South Benfleet, England: CADS. A fifty-page booklet surveying over 200 novels and short stories.

**Sherry, Norman.** *The Life of Graham Greene: Volume III: 1955–1991.* New York: Viking. The concluding volume of Greene's definitive biography.

**Strauss, Marc Raymond.** *Alfred Hitchcock's Silent Films.* Jefferson, NC: McFarland. Descriptions and interpretations.

**Tapply, William G.** *The Elements of Mystery Fiction: Writing the Modern Whodunit.* Scottsdale, AZ: Poisoned Pen Press. A revised and expanded edition of a 1995 volume, now including advice by experts on editing, publishing and bookselling.

**Thomas, Milt.** *Cave of a Thousand Tales: The Life and Times of Pulp Author Hugh B. Cave.* Sauk City, WI: Arkham House. A biography of the mystery and fantasy writer.

**Vickers, Kenneth** *W. T. S. Stribling, a Life of the Tennessee Novelist.* Chattanooga: U. of Tennessee. A biography of the

Pulitzer prize winner and author of the Professor Poggioli short stories, starting with *Clues of the Caribbees.*

**Wagstaff, Vanessa & Stephen Poole.** *Agatha Christie: A Reader's Companion.* London: Aurum Press. Plot summaries, jacket photos, and memorabilia.

**Warburton, Eileen.** *John Fowles: A Life in Two Worlds.* New York: Viking. A biography of the British novelist and author of *The Collector.*

**White, Terry.** *Justice Denoted: The Legal Thriller in American, British and Continental Courtroom Literature.* Westport, CT: Praeger. Over 1,800 entries covering books, films and plays.

**Williamson, Edwin.** *Borges: A Life.* New York: Viking. A biography of the Argentinean author of *Ficciones* and other stories, many criminous.

## OBITUARIES

**Joan Aiken** (1924–2004). Prolific British author of more than one hundred books including some thirty-eight novels and short story collections in the suspense genre, 1965–2003, as well as numerous fantasy and juvenile titles. MWA Edgar winner for best juvenile, *Nightfall* (1971).

**Lawrence P. Bachmann** (1912–2004). Author of seven suspense novels, 1943–72, starting with *Death in the Doll's House,* a collaboration with the late Hannah Lees.

**Andrea Badenoch** (1951–2004). British author of four novels starting with *Mortal* (1998).

**Jane S. Bakerman** (?–2004). Edited *And Then There Were Nine . . . More Women of Mystery,* and contributed fanzine essays and interviews.

**Leo G. Bayer** (1908–2004). Co-author, with his late wife, of four mysteries under the pseudonym of "Oliver Weld Bayer," starting with *Paper Chase* (1943).

**T. J. Binyon** (1936–2004). Author of two suspense novels and a nonfiction book, *Murder Will Out: The Detective in Fiction* (1989).

**Al Blanchard** (1945?–2004). President of MWA's New England chapter, author of five mystery novels starting with *Murder at Walden Pond* (2001), and a story collection, *The Stalker and Other Tales of Love and Murder* (2004).

**Martin Booth** (1944–2004). British author whose many books included two suspense novels, 1980–87, and an Edgar nominee, *The Doctor and the Detective: A Biography of Sir Arthur Conan Doyle* (U.S. edition, 2000).

**Mary Branham** (1929–2004). Author of at least three novels about sleuth Sydney Reardon, starting with *Little Green Man in Ireland* (1997).

**Vincent Brome** (1910–2004). Author of two intrigue novels, 1972–76, starting with *The Ambassador and the Spy.*

**Gordon Brook-Shepherd** (1918–2004). British author of a single suspense novel, *The Eferding Diaries* (1967).

**Larry Brown** (1951–2004). Southern writer whose books include a single crime novel, *Father and Son* (1996).

**Jack Cady** (1932–2004). Science fiction writer who authored two mystery novels in 1994 as well as a collaborative 1993 mystery under the name "Pat Franklin."

**Finn Carling** (1925–2004). Author of a single suspense novel, *Commission* (1993), unpublished in America.

**Hugh B. Cave** (1910–2004). Long-time pulp writer, author of nearly 1,200 stories in numerous magazines, under his own name and as "Justin Case." Also published nearly fifty novels and collections, notably *Long Live the Dead* (2000) and *Come Into My Parlor* (2002), collecting respectively his stories from *Black Mask* and *Detective Fiction Weekly*.

**Elizabeth Chater** (1910–2004). Professor of English and author of 23 romance novels, who also published some science fiction stories and a single mystery novel *A Course in Murder* (1969) under the name of "Lee Chaytor."

**Jerome Chodorov** (1911–2004), Screenwriter and playwright who collaborated on the 1935 Perry Mason film *The Case of the Lucky Legs* and on a 1982 play *A Talent for Murder.*

**Anna Clarke** (1919–2004). Author of some twenty-six mystery novels, 1968–96, starting with *The Darkened Room.*

**Judith Cook** (1933–2004). British author of nine mystery novels, five about Elizabethan physician Dr. Simon Forman, beginning with *Death of a Lady's Maid* (1997).

**Whitfield Cook** (1909–2003), Author of a single crime novel, *Taxi to Dubrovnik* (1981) and a story in *EQMM,* 6/46, who also co-authored the screenplays for Hitchcock's *Stage Fright* and *Strangers on a Train.*

**William P. Cooke** (1934–2003). Mathematics professor who authored a statistics textbook and two paperback novels, *The Nemesis Conjecture* (1980) and *Orion's Shroud* (1981).

**Alfred Coppel** (1921–2004). Science fiction author whose work included three suspense-intrigue novels as by "A. C. Marin," 1968–71, plus eight more under his own name, 1974–94. He also published fiction as by "Sol Galaxan," "Robert Chan Gilman," and "Derfla Leppoc."

**Barbara Davey** (c.1948–2004). Canadian editor and publisher of *The Mystery Review,* a fanzine published from fall 1992 until fall 2003.

**Bradford M. Day** (1916–2004). Science fiction publisher and bibliographer whose work included *Sax Rohmer: A Bibliography* (1963) and *Bibliography of Adventure* (1964).

**Babs H. Deal** (1929–2004). Author of four suspense novels, 1966–75, notably the Edgar-nominated *Fancy's Knell* (1966).

**William F. Deeck** (1936–2004). Fan guest of honor at Bouchercon and Malice Domestic who compiled indexes for *The Armchair Detective, CADS,* and other fan publications.

**Michael (Aiken) Elder** (1931–2004). Scottish actor and science fiction writer who authored two mystery novels starting with *The Phantom in the Wings* (1957).

**Carole Epstein** (1945–2004). Canadian author of three mystery novels starting with *Perilous Friends* (1996).

**Morton Cooper Feinberg** (1925–2004). Author, as Morton Cooper, of at least eleven crime and suspense novels, 1953–77, among other works.

**Janet Frame** (1924–2004). Mainstream New Zealand author who published a single suspense novel, *The Adaptable Man* (1965).

**Lucy Freeman** (1916–2004). Former *New York Times* reporter and author of seventy-eight books including the bestseller *Fight Against Fears* and three mysteries, 1971–75, featuring psychiatrist William Ames. Longtime Board member of MWA.

**Jose Giovanni** (1923–2004). Corsican novelist and screen-writer whose work included a single crime novel, *The Break* (1960).

**Richard Lancelyn Green** (1953–2004). British Sher-lockian who published several nonfiction books and co-authored *A Bibliography of A. Conan Doyle* (1983), winner of a special Edgar Award.

**Arthur Hailey** (1920–2004). Best-selling author whose work included two crime novels, *The Evening News* (1990) and *Detective* (1997), as well as two collaborative suspense novels with John Castle.

**Joseph Hansen** (1923–2004). Author of nearly forty books including twelve novels about homosexual investigator Dave Branstetter and five short story collections. He published eight novels as "James Colton" and two as "Rose Brock."

**Mollie Hardwick** (1915–2003). British author of seven mystery novels about Doran Fairweather, plus four Sherlockian books written with her husband Michael and three collections of short stories adapted from a British television series.

**Nathan C. Heard** (1936–2004). Ex-convict author of three crime novels, notably *Howard Street* (1968).

**William Herrick** (1915–2004). Author of two suspense novels, *Love and Terror* (1981) and *Bradovich* (1990).

**Karla Hocker** (1946–2004). Author of Regency romances including two historical mysteries about governess sleuth Sophia Bancroft, 1991–92.

**Jack Holland** (1947–2004). Belfast-born author whose work included a single crime novel, *The Prisoner's Wife* (1981).

**Ken Jackson** (c.1926–2000). Author of four suspense novels starting with *The Cutting Edge* (1970).

**Barbara Jefferis** (1917–2004). Australian author of five mystery novels, 1953–63, beginning with *Undercurrent.*

**M. M. Kaye** (1908–2004). British mainstream author, born in India, whose work included some fifteen mystery and suspense novels, notably *Death in Kenya* (1958), *Death in Zanzibar* (1959) and the bestseller *The Far Pavilions* (1978). Two of her novels were first published as by "Mollie Hamilton" and "Mollie Kaye."

**William Kelley** (1929–2003). Author of three crime novels, notably a novelization of the movie *Witness* (1985). Kelley won both the Oscar and the Edgar for his co-written screenplay of the film.

**Jean Alexander Kemeny** (1930–2003). Author of a single intrigue novel, *Strands of War* (1984).

**John M. Kimbro** (1929–2004). Author of some fifty romantic suspense novels as "Katheryn Kimbrough," with others published under the pseudonyms "Ann Ashton," "Charlotte Bramwell" and "Jean Kimbro."

**Beatrice La Force** (1908–2002), Author of a single romantic suspense novel, *The Sound of Hasty Footsteps* (1963).

**James R. Langham** (1912–1999). Author of two mystery novels, 1940–41, the first of which, *Sing a Song of Homicide,* was filmed as *A Night in New Orleans.*

**Jerome Lawrence** (1915–2004). Well-known playwright who co-authored a single suspense drama, *A Call on Kuprin* (1962).

**Lange Lewis** (1915–2003). Best-known pseudonym of Jane Lewis Brandt, author of five mystery novels, 1942–52, notably *The Birthday Murder* (1945). She also published one suspense novel as by "Jane Beynon."

**Adrian Lopez** (c. 1906–2004). Magazine publisher who contributed articles to *Black Mask* and *Dime Detective,* as well as short fiction to *Greater Gangster Stories,* 1/34 and 3/34.

**Nicholas Luard** (1937–2004). Author of six intrigue novels under his own name, 1967–96, starting with *The Warm and Golden War,* plus three as by "James McVean," 1977–81.

**Robert David MacDonald** (1929–2004). Scottish playwright who authored a 1988 play based upon James Hadley Chase's *No Orchids for Miss Blandish.*

**Milt Machlin** (1924–2004). Editor of *Argosy* magazine and co-author of four novels with Robin Moore, notably a novelization of *French Connection II* (1975).

**Yvonne MacManus** (1931–2002). Author of two suspense novels starting with *With Fate Conspire* (1974).

**Lee Magner** (1947–2002). Ellen Lee Magner Tatara,

whose work included a single novel of romantic suspense, *Dangerous* (1996).

**William Manchester** (1922–2004). Noted historian, author of *The Death of a President*, who published three suspense novels in the 1950s starting with *The City of Anger* (1953).

**Ted Mark** (1928–2004). Pseudonym of Ted Gottfried, author of erotic spy thrillers and one suspense novel, *A Stroke of Genius* (1982).

**Clayton Matthews** (1918–2004). Author of more than twenty suspense novels, 1960–95, some in collaboration with his wife Patricia Matthews and some under their joint pseudonym of “Patty Brisco.” Ten of his short stories were collected in *Hager’s Castle* (1969).

**Brian McNaughton** (1935–2004). Horror writer whose work included two mysteries, *The Poacher* (1978) and *Guilty Until Proven Guilty* (1979).

**Robert Merle** (1908–2004). French author whose novels included *The Day of the Dolphin* (1969) and *The Idol* (1989).

**Rex Miller** (Spangberg) (1939–2004). Author of eight crime novels, 1988–95, notably *Chaingang* (1992).

**Joan Morgan** (1905–2004). British silent film actress who became a playwright and novelist, authoring a suspense play and a single mystery novel, *The Hanging Wood* (1950).

**Jane Muskie** (1927–2004). Widow of Senator Edmund Muskie, who collaborated on a single suspense novel, *One Woman Lost* (1986).

**John North** (1942–2004). British/Canadian author, editor and mystery reviewer, active in the Crime Writers of Canada, who published short stories in the *Cold Blood* anthology series and co-edited *Cold Blood V* (1994) and *Best of Cold Blood* (1997).

**Jeff Nuttall** (1933–2003). British author of two suspense novels, 1975–78, unpublished in America.

**John M. Reilly** (c.1933–2004). Professor of English who edited the Edgar-winning *Twentieth Century Crime and Mystery Writers* (1980) and authored *Tony Hillerman: A Critical Companion* (1996). He was also one of the editors of *The Oxford Companion to Crime and Mystery Writing* (1999).

**William Relling Jr.** (1954–2004). Novelist and short story writer who authored three mystery novels, 1995–2003, the first two about private eye Jack Donne.

**Willo Davis Roberts** (1928–2004). Prolific author of one hundred suspense novels, romances, and young adult mysteries, three of which were Edgar winners, starting with *Megan's Island* (1989).

**Philip Rock** (1927–2004). Author of five crime novels, notably his novelization of the film *Dirty Harry* (1971).

**Bernice Rubens** (1928–2004). Author of five suspense novels, 1980–99, starting with *Sunday Best.*

**Pierre Salinger** (1925–2004). Former presidential press secretary and U.S. senator who authored three intrigue novels beginning with *On the Instructions of My Government* (1971). The final two were written in collaboration with Leonard Gross.

**Cathleen Schurr** (1916–2003). Author of a single suspense novel, *Dark Encounter* (1955).

**Hubert Selby Jr.** (1928–2004). Mainstream author whose work included a single crime novel, *Requiem for a Dream* (1979).

**Milton Shulman** (1913–2004). Author of a single crime novel, *Kill 3* (1967).

**George Harmon Smith** (1920–2004). Juvenile author who published at least one adult thriller, *The Age of the New Barbarians* (2001).

**Susan Sontag** (1933–2004). Mainstream novelist and essayist who authored a single crime novel, *Death Kit* (1967).

**Elsie W. Strother** (1912–2003). Author of eight romantic mysteries, 1975–87, beginning with *Rendezvous at Live Oaks.*

**Winona Sullivan** (1942–2004). Author of four novels about Sister Cecile, 1991–2000, starting with *Sudden Death at the Norfolk Café.*

**Beatrice Taylor** (?–2004).Treasurer of Britain's Crime Writers Association, 1975–87, who published a single suspense novel, *Journey Into Danger* (1973).

**Robert E. Thompson** (c. 1924–2004). Co-author of the published screenplay for *They Shoot Horses, Don't They?* (1969).

**Peter Ustinov** (1921–2004). Famed British actor who authored two crime novels and a pair of novelets, starting with *Krumnagel* (1971).

**Janet Gregory Vermandel** (1922–2002). Author of six suspense novels, 1968–74, starting with *So Long at the Fair.*

**Donald S. Vogel** (1917–2004). Author of four mystery novels, 1991–95, all featuring Joe Jensen and Heather.

**Walter Wager** (1924–2004). Author of some fifteen mystery and intrigue novels, notably *58 Minutes* (1987), filmed as *Die Hard 2.* He also published ten thrillers as by "John Tiger" and one as by "Walter Hermann." Past executive vice president of MWA.

**Amelia Walden** (1909–2002). Author of twelve novels about sleuth Lisa Clark, 1964–75, intended for younger readers.

**Gerald Walker** (1928–2004). Author of a single crime novel, *Cruising* (1970), filmed in 1980.

**Anna Mary Wells** (1906–2003). Author of five detective novels, 1942–56, starting with *A Talent for Murder.*

**Basil Wells** (1912–2004), SF and fantasy writer who authored four stories under the pseudonym of "Gene Ellerman," One of these, "Crusader" (*Fantasy Book* #5, 1949), is criminous.

**John Harvey Wheeler Jr.** (1918–2004). Co-author with Eugene Burdick of the 1962 nuclear thriller *Fail-Safe.*

**Dana Wilson** (1922–2004). Author of a single suspense novel, *Make With the Brains, Pierre* (1946). With her late husband Albert Broccoli she controlled the rights to the James Bond film franchise.

**Muriel "Mickey" Ziffren** (c.1917–2004). Author of *A Political Affair* (1979), a novel with criminous elements.

# The Mystery in Great Britain

Maxim Jakubowski

**It was, all in all,** a good year for British crime and mystery fiction with an invigorating brace of good titles by the more established authors and a reasonable crop of new names making it into print. However, one of the worrying aspects that could bear bitter fruit in times to come was the increasing difficulty many middle of the road authors were having in getting their books published, with midlist talent being dropped left, right, and center by the mainstream publishing houses, and not all of the writers in question finding new hospitality within the ranks of the smaller independents like Allison & Busby, Severn House, and others.

To add insult to injury the most prestigious of the Crime Writers' Association awards this year went to big-name American authors! The Gold Dagger was given to

Sara Paretsky for *Blacklist,* with the consolation Silver Dagger being taken by John Harvey for *Flesh and Blood.* Also shortlisted were Mo Hayder for *Tokyo,* Val McDermid's *The Torment of Others,* New Zealand author James Nichol for *Midnight Cab* and Laura Wilson's *The Lover.* The Ian Fleming Silver Dagger for best thriller of the year (although the judge's definition of a thriller yet again was open to much interpretation) was swooped by Jeffery Deaver for his wartime suspenser *The Garden of Beasts,* while Mo Hayder was again left at the altar together with Dan Fesperman, Joseph Finder, Stephen Leather, Adrian McKinty, and Daniel Silva. The indefatigable Deaver also took the Short Story Dagger, for which Mat Coward, Val McDermid, Mark Billingham, and Don Winslow were also competing. To continue in an American vein, the John Creasey Dagger for best first novel went to Mark Mills for *Amagansett,* a wonderful debut novel set in the United States, by an author who is coincidentally the son in law of leading British editor Jane Wood (although she was not his publisher . . . ). Other Creasey nominees were Denis Hamilton, Catherine Shaw and Stav Sherez. The remaining CWA Awards (in their final year of sponsorship by Book Club Associates) were Barbara Cleverly who won the Ellis Peters Historical Dagger for *The Damascened Blade,* ahead of Marjorie Eccles, Matthew Pearl, Tom Franklin, Steven Saylor, and Laura Wilson; Alexander McCall Smith, the Dagger in the Library; and Reginald Hill whose *Good Morning, Midnight* was awarded the People's Choice prize.

Organized by *Sherlock Magazine* (who went through a change of ownership this year but survive as one of our few specialist magazines alongside *Crime Time* and *Cads*), the Sherlock Awards went to Val McDermid and *A Distant Echo* for best crime book, Paul Johnston and *The Last Red Death* for best detective, Christopher Brookmyre and *Be My Enemy* for best comic novel and added a life achievement kudo to P. D. James.

It was also a year in which we lost relatively few friends, with just Joan Aiken and veteran pulp and horror writer Hugh B. Cave departing this mortal coil.

Another pleasing development was the continuing success and acceptance of crime books in translation by the book buying public, thanks to sterling efforts from publishers like Harvill, Serpent's Tail, Canongate, Arcadia, Weidenfeld & Nicolson, and Bitter Lemon Press. This was confirmed when the Richard and Judy TV show chose Carlos Ruiz Zafon's wonderful *Shadow of the Wind* as their weekly selection and provided an Oprah-like boost to the book, propelling it straight into the bestseller lists. On the retail front, the customary marketing wars continued with chains dominating the market, with the power to make or break books, thanks to heavy discounting and special offers abetted by publishers, while non-lead titles were sadly often left to languish on the shelves. Crime In Store returned from the dead yet again with new premises near the British Museum (and have since disappeared once more, most likely for good this time), while Murder One after thirteen years on the famous Charing Cross Road had a notice of eviction due to their block being redeveloped in a controversial scheme which made newspaper and TV News headlines (they have since moved across the road, thus providing their customers no excuse to no longer finding them . . .).

On the social front, the three annual festivals are all

alive and well. The National Film Theatre's Crime Scene took place in July, blending film and literature, while Harrogate had a successful second year and the St. Hilda's Conference, albeit smaller and more exclusive, continued.

So, what about the books? They still flood the groaning bookshelves and the following round-up is, as ever, just the tip of the iceberg.

Big titles of the year included Rennie Airth, *The Blood Dimmed Tide;* Kate Atkinson, *Case Histories;* Robert Barnard, *The Graveyard Position;* Mark Billingham, *The Burning Girl;* Simon Brett, *The Hanging in the Hotel;* Ken Bruen, *The Dramatist;* Lee Child, *The Enemy;* Martina Cole, *The Graft;* Lindsey Davis, *Scandal Takes a Holiday;* Ruth Dudley Edwards, *Carnage in the Committee;* Ben Elton, *Past Mortem;* Jasper Fforde, *Something Rotten;* Nicci French, *The Secret Smile;* Frances Fyfield, *Looking Down;* Jonathan Gash, *The Year of the Woman;* Robert Goddard, *Play to the End;* Caroline Graham, *The Ghost in the Machine;* John Harvey, *Flesh and Blood;* Mo Hayder, *Tokyo;* Reginald Hill, *Good Morning, Midnight;* Anthony Horowitz, *The Killing Joke;* Val McDermid, *The Torment of Others;* Michael Marshall, *The Lonely Dead;* Denise Mina, *Field of Blood;* Magdalen Nabb, *Property of Blood;* David Peace, *GB84;* Anne Perry, *The Shifting Tide, Shoulder the Sky,* and *Christmas Visitors;* Ian Rankin, *Fleshmarket Close;* Ruth Rendell, *Thirteen Steps Down;* Peter Robinson, *Playing with Fire;* Alexander McCall Smith, *The Sunday Philosophy Club* and *in the Company of Cheerful Ladies;* Boris Starling, Vodka; Mark Timlin, *Answers from the Grave;* Minette Walters, *The Tinder Box;*

Laura Wilson, *The Lover;* Robert Wilson, *The Silent and the Damned.*

Also noteworthy and notable, although maybe not always as visible were Paul Adam, *Sleeper;* Jane Adams, *Heatwave;* Vivian Armstrong, *Murder Between Friends;* Jeffrey Ashford, *Evidentially Guilty;* Marian Babson, *Retreat from Murder;* John Baker, *White Skin Man;* Adam Baron, *It Was You;* Colin Bateman, *Driving Big Dave;* Jo Bannister, *Depths of Solitude;* Simon Beaufort, *Coiner's Quarrel;* Ingrid Black, *Dark Eye;* Veronica Black, *Vow of Evil;* Hilary Bonner, *Reason to Die;* Stephen Booth, *One Last Breath;* Caroline Carver, *Black Tide;* Glenn Chandler, *Dead Sight;* Alys Clare, *Whiter than Lily;* Judith Cook, *Keeper's Gold;* Natasha Cooper, *Keep Me Alive;* Clare Curzon, *Last to Leave;* Judith Cutler, *Scar Tissue* and *Drawing the Line;* Jonathan Davies, *The Piano Factory;* Sarah Diamond, *The Spider's House;* Joolz Denby, *Billie Morgan;* Eileen Dewhurst, *Naked Witness;* David Dickinson, *Death of an Old Master;* Paul Doherty, *The Magician's Death, Assassins of Isis,* and *Song of the Gladiator;* Maureen Duffy, *Dead Trouble;* Robert Edric, *Siren Song;* Marjorie Eccles, *The Shape of Sand;* Martin Edwards, *Coffin Trail;* Ron Ellis, *City of Vultures;* Geraldine Evans, *Bad Blood* and *Dying for You;* Liz Evans, *Sick as a Parrot;* Jason Foss, *Blood and Sandals;* Christopher Fowler, *The Water Room;* Anthea Fraser, *Jigsaw;* Janet Gleeson, *Thief Taker;* Philip Gooden, *Mask of Night;* Carol Goodman, *The Drowning Tree;* Paula Gosling, *Tears of the Dragon;* Anne Granger, *That Way Murder Lies;* Alex Gray, *Small Weeping;* Christine Green, *Deadly Choice* and *Deadly Night;* Susanna Gregory, *Hand of Justice;* J. M. Gregson, *Wages of Sin* and *Just Desserts;* Peter Guttridge, *Cast Adrift;* Georgie Hale, *Hear No Evil;* Patricia Hall, *False Witness* and *Masks of Darkness;* Gerald Hammond, *Saving Grace, The Outpost, Dead Letters,* and *The Hitch;* Tom Harper, *Mosaic of Shadows;* Cynthia Harrod-Eagles, *Dear Departed;* Veronica Heley, *Murder in the Garden;* Mandasue Heller, *Tainted Lives;* Mick Herron, *The Last Voice You Hear;* David Hewson, *The Villa of Mysteries;* Susan Hill, *The Various Haunts of Men;* Joanna Hines, *Angels of the Flood;* Joyce Holms, *Hidden Depths;* Hazel Holt, *Silent Killer;* C. C. Humphreys, *Jack Absolute;* Graham Hurley, *Cut to Black;* Graham Ison, *Hardcastle's Spy, Hardcastle's Armistice,* and *Whiplash;* Lee Jackson, *Metropolitan Murders;* Bill James, *Easy Streets;* Quintin Jardine, *Unnatural Justice, Stay of Execution,* and *Alarm Call;* Michael Jecks, *Tolls of Death* and *Chapel of Bones;* Paul Johnston, *The Golden Silence;* Alison Joseph, *Darkening Sky;* H. R. F. Keating, *The Detective at Death's Door;* Jim Kelly, *Fire Baby;* Susan Kelly, *Death of a Ghost;* Simon Kernick, *The Crime Trade;* Alanna Knight, *Ghost Walk* and *Unholy Trinity;* Deryn Lake, *Death in the Setting Sun;* Frank Lean, *Raised in Silence;* Stephen Leather, *Hard Landing;* Roy Lewis, *Headhunter;* Joan Lock, *Dead End;* Gaye Longworth, *The Unquiet Dead;* Keith McCarthy, *The Silent Sleep of the Dying;* Jill McGown, *Unlucky for Some;* Edwards Marston, *The Railway Detective;* Andrew Martin, *The Blackpool Highflyer;* Priscilla Masters, *River Deep;* Peter May, *Chinese Whispers;* Glenn Meade, *Web of Deceit;* Fidelis Morgan, *Fortune's Slave;* Fiona Mountain, *Bloodline;* Margaret Murphy, *Dispossessed;* Amy Myers, *The Wickenham Murders;* Barbara Nadel, *Petrified;* Reggie Nadelson, *Disturbed Earth;*

Hilary Norman, *Guilt;* Maureen O'Brien, *Fear* and *Every Step You Take;* Ed O'Connor, *Primal Cut;* Pat O'Keeffe, *Blowtorch;* Nick Oldham, *Dead Heat* and *Big City Jack;* Stuart Pawson, *Over the Edge;* Michael Pearce, *Dead Man in Trieste;* Anne Purser, *Theft on Thursday;* Sarah Rayne, *Dark Dividing;* Elizabeth Redfern, *Auriel Rising;* Will Rhode, *White Ghosts;* John Rickards, *A Touch of Ghosts;* Phil Rickman, *Prayer of the Night Shepherd;* David Roberts, *The More Deceived;* Rosemary Rowe, *Ghosts of Glevum;* Betty Rowlands, *Sweet Venom* and *Deadly Obsession;* Nicholas Royle, *Antwerp;* Denise Ryan, *Blood Knot;* Robert Ryan, *Night Crossing;* C. J. Sansom, *Dark Fire;* Simon Scarrow, *Eagle's Prey;* Kate Sedley, *The Midsummer Rose;* Chris Simms, *Pecking Order;* Carol Smith, *Hidden Agenda;* Sally Spedding, *Night with No Stars;* Sally Spencer, *Witch Maker, The Butcher Beyond,* and *Blackstone and The Golden Egg;* Cath Staincliffe, *Blue Murder;* Veronica Stallwood, *Oxford Remains;* Andrew Taylor, *Call the Dying;* Marilyn Tod, *Widow's Pique;* Rebecca Tope, *A Cotswold Killing;* Peter Tremayne, *The Leper's Bell;* M. J. Trow, *Maxwell's Grave;* Peter Turnbull, *Dance Master, Hopes and Fears,* and *Reality Checkpoint;* Martyn Waites, *The White Room;* Louise Welsh, *Tamburlaine Must Die;* Stella Whitelaw, *Jest and Die* and *Veil of Death;* John Williams, *Temperance Town;* Derek Wilson, *The Nature of Rare Things;* David Wishart, *The Parthian Shot.*

Debut mystery writers who took their bow this year included Liz Allen, *Last to Know;* Anthony Eglin, *The Blue Rose;* Robert Collins, *Soul Corporation;* Vena Cork, *Thorn;* Tom Franklin, *Hell at the Breach;* Mark Gattis, *The Vesuvius Club;* Neil Griffiths, *Betrayal in Naples;* Boris

Johnson, *72 Virgins;* Simon Levack, *Demon of the Air;* Ken McCoy, *Mad Carew;* Anthony McGowan, *Stag Hunt;* Pat McIntosh, *Harper's Quine;* Adrian McKinty, *Dead I May Well Be;* Adrian Magson, *No Peace for the Wicked;* Mark Mills, *Amagansett;* Toby Moore, *Sleeping with the Fishes;* Sheila Quigley, *Run for Home;* Michael Robotham, *The Suspect;* Tony Saint, *Blag;* Catherine Shaw, *The Three Body Problem;* Stav Sherez, *The Devil's Playground;* Paul Southern, *The Craze;* Megan Stark, *Game of Proof;* Sue Walker, *The Reunion;* Herald Williams, *Dr. Mortimer and the Carved Head Mystery.*

In the real of thrillers, spy, and adventure stories, an area still much in demand in Britain, we had the choice of Ted Allbeury, *Hostage;* Geoffrey Archer, *Dark Angel;* Campbell Armstrong, *White Rage;* Tom Bradby, *God of Chaos;* Paul Carlkson, *Ambush;* Michael Dobbs, *Churchill's Hour;* Clive Egleton, *Never Surrender;* Ken Follett, *Whiteout;* Clare Francis, *Homeland;* Brian Freemantle, *Death by Dividend;* John Fullerton, *Give Me Death;* John Gardner, *Angels Dining at the Ritz;* Jack Higgins, *Dark Justice;* John LeCarré, *Absolute Friends;* Ken McClure, *Gulf of Conspiracy;* John McLaren, *Blind Eye;* Andy McNab, *Deep Black;* Stella Rimington, *At Risk;* Chris Ryan, *The Increment;* Julian Jay Savarin, *Hot Day in May* and *Hunter's Rain;* Gerald Seymour, *Unknown Soldier;* Terence Strong, *Cold Murder;* Guy Walters, *The Occupation.*

There was a paucity of anthologies and author collections however, with even the traditional CWA annual compilation skipping a year. But, nonetheless, we had the opportunity to read my own *Best British Mysteries 2005;* Mike Ashley, *The Mammoth Book of Roaring '20s Whodunits;*

Martin Radcliffe, *Masters of Mystery;* Shelley Silas, *Twelve Days;* John Connolly, *Nocturnes;* Peter Robinson, *Not Safe After Dark;* Peter Tremayne, *Whispers of the Dead.*

And, as the song from *My Fair Lady* goes (in an alternate world, that is . . . ) I could have typed all night and still not come to the end of the 2004 British crime and mystery (over)production. The Brits still appear to have an appetite for crime books and an undeniable desire to get into print (Robert Hale, a small publisher who concentrates mainly on sales to the library sector increased their mystery output by a factor of 8, including fifteen debut novels in this year alone, although few made a genuine impact and are as a result not listed above; likewise a new imprint Creme de la Crime has also launched a half dozen new British authors, although here again quality is lacking . . .).

So, read on. Life is short enough as it is when you have so many books to catch up on!

# The Newest Four-Letter Word in Mystery

Sarah Weinman

**It is a truth universally** acknowledged among denizens of the World Wide Web that the word "blog" may be one of the ugliest in the English language. But the term—short for weblog—stuck, and as the number of them grows by leaps and bounds, the word's not about to go away anytime soon. It's getting so ubiquitous that the entire lyric of Cole Porter's "Let's Do It" might well apply to blogging:

> Birds do it
> Bees, do it
> Even educated fleas do it!

All kidding aside, weblogs are perhaps the fastest-growing and most popular new Internet application, a tool that's not only allowed ordinary citizens to share their thoughts with the world, but also highlighted the brightest and fiercest minds in politics, entertainment, media, science, and literature. They've been written about so much in major papers that some, like the *New York Times*, have special beat reporters and separate sections devoted to them. Even celebrities are getting in on the blogging game, viewing them as a way to promote themselves in an unfiltered manner. And, as I'll get into at length here, blogs are changing the way writers communicate directly with other writers and other readers.

So what exactly is a blog, anyway?

In its purest form, a blog is a frequent, chronological publication of personal thoughts and links. Or so it was, when limited solely to documenting every little personal detail knowing only close friends were paying attention. After September 11, the popularity of blogs exploded as "warbloggers" like Instapundit, Daily Kos, and Talking Points Memo voiced political opinions that main media outlets would never touch. With over 10 million blogs currently in existence, it's a good bet that almost any subject or interest matter—no matter how obscure—is being covered. But only a tiny fraction build an audience and keep people informed, educated, and most of all, entertained. The best blogs possess a strongly distinct voice and a unique outlook—similar to what propels a writer to the bestseller list.

In the case of those who cover literary matters—"litbloggers"—the most popular sites, such as The Elegant Variation, Old Hag, and Maud Newton, present breaking news with a mix of commentary and personal musings in a way that traditional media simply cannot do. Other blogs like Gawker and Defamer serve up New York and L.A. gossip with a healthy dose of irony and individuality, while The Minor Fall, The Major Lift pseudonymously skewers media and culture as only a well-read intellectual could. And you can't get more offbeat than the Detroit-based Whatevs.org, which has single-handedly introduced a new kind of blogging dialect that's seeped into blogs the world over.

It was this sort of anarchic sensibility that I wanted to tap into when I launched "Confessions of an Idiosyncratic Mind" in October 2003. I'd become a huge fan of several blogs (including those mentioned above) over the course of the previous few months, loving how they kept me in touch with New York–centric matters as well as more literary ones. But I was also growing frustrated that my main book-related passion—crime fiction—wasn't covered in depth, or at least to the depth of my liking. I realized that what was missing was something that covered the mystery beat in a way that other literary blogs covered mainstream fiction or nonfiction—but with a slightly off-center viewpoint and a heavy dose of humor.

Thus, the blog. If there's one reason above all that it's regarded as the go-to site for crime fiction happenings, it's due to timing. In late 2003, the world was really only waking up to the potential of blogs beyond politics. But by early next year, millions more were streaming aboard the blog train. And many of these new converts included crime writers, a development I'm especially ecstatic about. It's a chance for the writer's voice to reach fans old and new in an informal and interactive way, getting instant feedback and generating spirited discussions.

Ultimately, blogging is as individual an act as writing,

and the voices emanating from the most memorable blogs are as unique as those who write them. What follows is my attempt to highlight the most notable: who they are, what they focus on, and why they work.

Much as any crime writer believes his or her blog attracts an undue amount of attention, all of us pale in comparison to the readership attracted by Roger Simon. With well over a million page views per month, his political transformation from the ardent leftism espoused in his earlier novels to a Bush supporter has attracted a serious following—and a passionate one. The blog often boasts over one hundred comments per post, all vociferously debating how the former avowed socialist could support the Iraq war and President Bush in the previous election. And the media has taken notice, too—he's a frequent guest on the *Hugh Hewitt Show* and wrote a semiregular column for the *National Review Online.* The irony, as Simon has said, is that he created his frequently-updated blog to promote his then-latest novel, *Director's Cut* (2003). Instead, he's become a major political voice, and is no longer writing the Moses Wine series. Many people wonder if blogging detracts from writing, but what they don't think about is that it can change your perspective and what you write about.

Another major controversy-courter is Lee Goldberg, TV writer, producer, and novelist. His "A Writer's Life" blog has the requisite posts about his own career and is especially insightful about the media tie-in world, but more often than not it's served as a back fence for heated, often circular arguments about two major topics: fan fiction and self-publishing. Goldberg's long on the record as being heavily critical of those who appropriate characters, but that doesn't stop angry fans from challenging him. Same goes for those clueless enough to venture forth with scamming publishers promising instant success, and Goldberg is quick to tell them exactly where they erred.

Another Goldberg—younger brother Tod—got into the blogging game more recently but quickly established himself as one of the most amusing voices in the literary blogosphere. Every week one can tune into his "Letters to Parade" where he skewers the hapless columnist responsible for the magazine's epistolary column. But especially potent and wickedly hilarious are Goldberg's points about wannabe writers he meets at the classes and conferences he's taught. In other words, if Tod's your teacher, you better go in prepared.

Laura Lippman's Web site has always had the form of a blog, what with its monthly, link-heavy updates. Long a fan of the form, she launched "The Memory Project" as a means to document important (and not-so-important) memories of her personal and writing life. The response she hoped for, and received, was to incite commentary from readers and other writers who offered up their own memories of the same subject.

David Montgomery's "The Crime Fiction Dossier" bills itself as an outpost for news, commentary and reviews. It's especially illuminating about the last point, as Montgomery is a frequent book reviewer who offers up compelling insight about how he chooses a book for review and what a writer can or can't do to influence his potential choices.

Blogs are an equivocal form; it doesn't matter if you're old or young, Web-savvy or not. As long as the content's worth coming back to, then your audience will do so. And on the crime fiction front, blogs have enabled several younger writers—published or on the verge—to get the word out. They include Dave White (whose story "God's Dice" is included in this anthology), Ray Banks, Bryon Quertermous, and John Rickards, twentysomething writers whose influences favor film and graphic novels more than the usual diet of Chandler, Hammett, and the MacDonald boys. But their energy allow them to do inspired activities; in early 2005, White and Quertermous co-edited "Junk in the Trunk," the first anthology of short stories written exclusively by bloggers.

The form has also allowed more established types to find a readership they might not have been able to in the age before the Internet. 2004 saw the reissue of *Texas Wind*, James Reasoner's very first novel—and only foray into private detective fiction. But his blog showcased how Reasoner how far he has come in the twenty-five years since that book was published. He famously blogged about how he'd finished twelve novels and over 4,500 manuscript pages during the last calendar year. If that's not an astonishing pace, I don't know what is. Other vets getting deserved due thanks to their blogs include Texas-based Bill Crider, whose dry wit and fond recollections infuse his posts with warmth and nostalgia; Sandra Scoppettone, one of the early pioneers for female crime writers; and Ed Gorman, always the outspoken advocate for the genre.

Not all blogs are permanent, or belong to a singular voice. A recent trend in "tour blogs" prompted Lawrence Block to chronicle his 2004 tour for *The Burglar on the Prowl* and Lee Child to document his travels for his latest

Jack Reacher novel. S. J. Rozan, on top of the personal blog she maintains, documented the process from completion to publication for her 2004 stand-alone novel *Absent Friends*. The group blog is also becoming more popular, evident by the growing audience for the Girlfriends Cyber Circuit (featuring well known crime writers and bloggers like M. J. Rose) and the Lipstick Chronicles (co-authored by Nancy Martin, Harley Jane Kozak, Sarah Strohmeyer and Susan MacBride). Other writers, like Olen Steinhauer, make use of the content management capabilities of blogging to replace the customary "What's new" page on the author website. That he also adds anecdotes about drinking during Edgar Week and reflections on being an American ex-pat in Prague only adds to the charm.

As of this writing, there are thousands of writers who have taken up blogging, and the number looks to keep on increasing. Will the bubble burst anytime soon? As long as each new voice offers up something slightly different to say, he or she will be heard over the volume of noise. Not unlike trying to break in as a mystery novelist these days . . .

## A list of notable crime fiction blogs

Confessions of an Idiosyncratic Mind:
*http:// www.sarahweinman.com*

The Crime Fiction Dossier:
*http:// www.crimefictionblog.com*

The Lipstick Chronicles:
*http:// thelipstickchronicles.typepad.com*

The "Junk in the Trunk" blog anthology:
*http:// www.bryonquertermous.com/junk.html*

Ray Banks:
*http:// www.thesaturdayboy.co.uk/news/index.html*

Lawrence Block:
*http:// www.lawrenceblock.com/content_blog.htm*

Bill Crider:
*http:// billcrider.blogspot.com*

Victor Gischler's World's Worst Blog:
*http:// www.victorgischler.com/_wsn/page3.html*

Lee Goldberg:
*http:// leegoldberg.typepad.com/a_writers_life*

Tod Goldberg:
*http:// todgoldberg.typepad.com*

Ed Gorman:
*http:// www.edgorman.com/edgormanandfriends*

Laura Lippman's Memory Project:
*http:// www.journalscape.com/LauraLippman*

Stuart MacBride:
*http:// halfhead.blogspot.com*

Bryon Quertermous:
*http:// bryonquertermous.blogspot.com*

James Reasoner:
*http:// jamesreasoner.blogspot.com*

John Rickards:
*http:// johnrickards.blogspot.com*

S. J. Rozan:
*http:// www.journalscape.com/ sjrozan*

Rozan's progress blog:
*http:// www.journalscape.com/ progress*

Sandra Scoppettone:
*http:// sandrascoppettone.blogspot.com*

Roger L. Simon:
*http:// www.rogerlsimon.com*

Olen Steinhauer:
*http:// olensteinhauer.blogspot.com*

Charlie Stella:
*http:// www.charliestella.com/ knucks*

Duane Swierczynski's Secret Dead Blog:
*http:// secretdead.blogspot.com*

David White:
*http:// jacksondonne.blogspot.com*

James R. Winter:
*http:// jamesrwinter.typepad.com*

Many more fine blogs are listed in the blogroll of *Confessions of an Idiosyncratic Mind.*

*(Ed. Note: portions of this piece appeared in the Sept/Oct 2004 issue of* Mystery Scene *magazine as "Mystery Writers Who Blog: The Latest Trend Examined.")*

# The Adventure of the Missing Detective

Gary Lovisi

Gary Lovisi has been a Sherlock Holmes fan and collector for thirty years, he has written three Holmes pastiches and the nonfiction books *Relics of Sherlock Holmes, Souvenirs of Sherlock Holmes,* and *Sherlock Holmes: The Great Detective* in paperback on which he is working on a new, expanded edition. He is the editor of *Paperback Parade* and *Hardboiled* magazine, and the publisher of Gryphon Books. His Web site is www.gryphonbooks.com.

***Here is a strange tale*** *for you, gentle reader, one that is perhaps the most fantastic adventure of Sherlock Holmes's entire career. I have left it for posterity, secreted with my special papers at Cox & Co., to be opened in the future, and done with as my heirs deem best.*

*Here now are the circumstances of that story as I heard them from Holmes's own lips . . .*

* * *

As you know, Watson, my return to London after the happenings at the Reichenbach Falls was not in 1894 as you have written in your amusing account of the Moran case for the popular press. I will relate to you now the actual story of what occurred during those missing years when you, and the world, thought me dead.

It was during the affair at Reichenbach. Moriarty was dead, destroyed by the furious power of the Reichenbach Falls. I had seen his body dashed to the jagged rocks below. I had seen his head crushed on those very same rocks. Then I had unaccountably lost my own balance, taken by some strange sudden draft of wind, no doubt, which caused me to plummet into a mysterious vortex of whirling fog and roiling mists below. It was a cold and supercharged atmosphere that I entered, quite unlike anything I had ever experienced before. My fall seemed to descend almost in stages, slowly, staggered, even sluggish. I could not comprehend it at all. It was a most unnatural affair, and nothing at all in the manner of which the Professor met his timely demise barely minutes before. My descent was somewhat transcendental in nature. It may have even been miraculous, for it was unusual in the extreme and seemed to bypass what I know of our laws of physics and gravity.

That final encounter with Moriarty, and my resulting injury, had caused a long convalescence. If not for the kind ministrations of an isolated hill folk couple, I surely would have passed on from a comatose state to death. As it was, I spent much time in that near-death dream state, lost in a miasma of thoughts, my mind playing tricks, nightmares wracking my brain, even as my body lay still and silent in an apparent total vegetative existence.

After some time, I came out of my coma, and as I slowly recuperated, was eventually well enough to question my Swiss rescuers. As you can well imagine, I had many questions. Hans and Gerda were a simple farm couple who had a small parcel of land below Interlaken. They told me of how Hans had found me at the bottom of a lonely ravine, apparently uninjured. Initially he thought I was merely asleep, but he soon discovered that I was in the grip of some deliberative state and summoning Gerda, the couple took me into their small cabin to care for me.

Once I regained consciousness I found I had lost much weight and was extremely weak. After I had regained some strength, I listened with great interest to Hans and Gerda's story. I did not tell them about Moriarty or my tumult over the ledge near the Great Falls. That would have seemed incongruous with the fact that the few minor bruises I had sustained were much too insignificant injuries for one who had gone through such a violent fall. It did not make sense, but you will see that this was just the beginning of a series of incidents and activities that made little sense to me at the time, but by the end of this strange narrative will all be explained.

In fact, quite early on I began to believe there might be a more significant mystery here than met the eye. You see, just as Moriarty met his death from going over the falls—and I saw him with my own eyes meet his doom before I myself plunged downward—I also should have been killed from my own incredible fall. However, there was something about that mist, the wind, perhaps various air currents and updrafts? I do not know for certain, but something saved me and seemingly with great gentility set me down upon the lush green sward of the ravine bottom where Hans later found me.

I make no explanation for it at all. I can not explain the lack of injury or my comatose state. I am no man of science, save where the criminal element is concerned. Perhaps my friend the distinguished Professor Challenger would make something more of it. Sufice it to say that I was at least satisfied with the results of the situation. Moriarty was dead and I was alive.

Before I left the area below Interlaken, I asked my kind hosts if they or those in the nearby village remembered anyone having come around looking for me. I also asked them if any tourist had gone missing, or if there were reports of anyone killed in an accident off the falls. Hans and Gerda told me they had no such knowledge, but when I told Hans to ask around the village, he returned with interesting news indeed. While I was apparently not missed at all, it appears an Englishman, perhaps on holiday at the time, had in fact died going over the falls on the very same day that I had my own descent. I was told the body had been claimed and was buried in the local cemetery by a visitor friend from London.

I sighed with relief. Moriarty, no doubt. I only thought it strange that you, good Watson, or my brother, Mycroft, had not yet found me.

Months later as I took my leave from Hans and Gerda I decided to book a small room at an inn of the lower village for a few days. It was a robust little place, one of those lively alpine respites, and I began to feel more in tune with the world I had been so long estranged from since my injury. Hans and Gerda, the souls of propriety and generosity lived a private and lonely life in a secluded area. Now I was back in a village among people and activity and beginning to get back to my old self again. Why, I was even able to find an English newspaper to catch up with events in the world and back home. It was a copy of the London *Times* and I began to peruse it nonchalantly.

It felt good to feel the *Times* in my hands again, to smell the newsprint, to see the well-remembered large lettering of the headlines and the many narrow columns of small and tightly packed print for the various news items from all around the world.

However, one item below the fold caught my attention as no other has in my life. I read it with shock and dismay. The horror I felt, the alarm and confusion was something I had never experienced before. I grew dizzy, weak-kneed, my heart raced. I read it once again, very carefully. The news item was rather simple and matter-of-fact. In essence it said this: *The British Monarch, King Albert Christian Edward Victor, former Duke of Clarence and Avondale, and grandson of the late Queen Victoria, will bestow the honour of a knighthood upon Mr. James Moriarty. The well-known and respected professor of mathematics, formerly at one of our most prestigious universities, is the author of various noted scientific works, including, "The Dynamics of An Asteroid," which has been well-received in academic circles. He is being honoured for his invaluable service to the Crown. The ceremony is to take place upon the 24th day of April in the year of Our Lord 1892, at Buckingham Palace.*

I thought this must be some bizarre type of joke or even

a misprint, or perhaps suddenly I had become deranged and entirely lost my mind from my injury. Victoria, dead? Eddy, the new king! Why, was it not rumored in dark circles, that he was under suspicion in the Ripper murders? But more so, Moriarty, *alive!* It was incomprehensible! I had seen him die! His body had been buried. Now, if this news item was to be believed, he was not only alive, but to receive a knighthood of all things! It was preposterous, outrageous, and the news left me totally astonished, perplexed and nonplused. Yet it gave me much food for thought, and it was food that would *not* stay down.

Immediately I perused that newspaper closely from front to back. It was a chilling experience, let me tell you, my friend. The brunt of it all seems to be that it appears as if the entire world I have known all my life had gone irrevocably and incomprehensibly mad. All was upside down and *wrong!*

Here then, is some of what I gleaned from my perusal of that one issue. Our Gracious Majesty, Queen Victoria was, in fact, dead, as was her son and heir, Edward. I found an article that spoke of a Court of Inquiry which had recently cleared their deaths of any but natural causes in a carriage accident, even though rumors and questions apparently abounded that it had been no accident at all! No autopsy had been performed upon the royal personages. A disturbing turn of events under the circumstances. In other areas news items leaped out at me and they were the most incongruous with the facts that I knew. One of the most bizarre was that a military dictatorship was assuming control in the United States and that there was the threatened succession of five western states from the Union. It appeared to be civil war all over again. Russia was in turmoil, the government of France had fallen, and a united Germany had suddenly risen from the ashes of Bismarck's Prussia and appeared to be making ready for world war.

There was more, but I'll not bore you with the details of the many seemingly trivial items that in and of themselves appeared insignificant, but to my trained eyes and historical knowledge were no less disturbing and fantastic by their very existence.

Something very big and far afield was happening throughout the world. Things were very wrong. I could not fathom it, but if I did not know better, I would be pressed to admit that this might be some trick, set into motion by Moriarty. A fantastic thought, surely, and utterly unfounded, for he was dead. Nevertheless, while logic told me what was true, my intuition told me differently. You know I seldom listen to emotions; they are not to be trusted in my line of work. Nevertheless, one question nagged my thoughts. That newspaper said Moriarty was alive. How could that be? How could Moriarty be *alive*—and have been knighted—when I *knew* he was dead?

A chilling thought suddenly grabbed me—could it have been someone else entirely who plummeted over the falls? Someone disguised as Moriarty? Even as I considered the thought I knew it just could not be possible, nevertheless some investigation seemed warranted.

Now I knew that I must seek out that grave here in the village and determine that which was within.

The next night was cloudy and moonless, an alpine version of those evenings you may remember that shrouded the moors around Baskerville Hall so many years ago in dire gloom. It was the perfect evening for the dark business I had that night with my nemesis—who now seemingly dogged me in death, even as he had in life.

I enlisted the help of good Hans in my nocturnal investigation, telling him just enough to let him know how important it was for me to see the body in that coffin. He was somewhat concerned about such activities, but being a former medical student, agreed to help when I made clear it was important to me.

Now I had to be sure that Moriarty's casket held *his* body!

It was after midnight and the village was wrapped up tightly for the evening as Hans and I stole out of the back door of my little inn and he lead me to the small cemetery on the outskirts of the village.

We quietly walked through a carved wooden arch, and entered a small fenced in area of burial plots topped with memorials and statues in stone and wood. Hans brought me to one such lonely grave at an isolated spot in the end. The marker was a simple wooden cross, its inscription Hans translated for me.

"It says, 'English Man, Died, May 1891,'" Hans whispered.

I nodded. I looked around us carefully. There was no one. All was quiet and peaceful. Hans and I began to dig.

I can not express to you the excitement that surged through me as my spade cut into the hard cold earth, and once it finally hit the lid of the pine box that contained that with which I was seeking.

Now was the moment of truth. Hans and I quickly cleared away the last of the dirt so as to make the top of the plain wooden casket accessible. Hans looked at me and I nodded, then he began using a crow bar to pry open the casket.

With a loud screeching of rusted nails, the lid finally came off and we saw that a tall male body wrapped in shrouds lay before us. I motioned Hans away. I quickly knelt down before the corpse. Deftly, I removed the shroud cloths, until I had a full view of the face.

There had been some decay and natural parasite activity upon the flesh of the face, but the cold climate ensured there was more than enough left for me to make a very definite determination. I froze with astonishment and some fear, my blood ran cold, for the face I now looked upon was not that of Professor James Moriarty at all. It was the face of Sherlock Holmes! It was my very own face!

Hans asked me if everything was all right. He said that I did not look well. Hans would not look closely at the face of the corpse, while I could not take my eyes away from it. You can imagine my reaction. I hardly knew what to make of this at all. At first I thought it might be some trick or joke. I was here after all, and alive, was I not?

You know my methods and I never theorize before I obtain all the facts. I have said so over and over again, that solving cases is a matter of eliminating the impossible—and then whatever remains, however improbable, must be the truth. I felt that what I was viewing now created implications that would soon test that maxim to the very limit. You see, that corpse before me bore silent witness to the truth of this strange event and I vowed it would tell me all it knew before this dark night was over.

"Hans," I ordered. "Bring that lantern closer, I must examine the body."

Then I began what can only be described as a very methodical and detailed search of the corpse to rule out all suppositions until I could get to the truth of this matter.

What I discovered was even more bizarre and shocking than anything you could have ever put into your little accounts of my cases for the popular press. First of all, the corpse was that of an actual human being, not any statue or manikin. By all accounts the man appeared to have met his death sometime within the last year. There were severe bruises and a few broken bones from his fall that I immediately noticed. However, it was the physical characteristics that were interesting to me in the extreme. The corpse appeared to be my age, my height, my weight, wore my own clothing, and had my exact physical appearance in every category. I was shocked and dismayed. Needless to say I examined the body as detailed as possible under the lantern light held so steadily by my trusty Hans. And the more I looked, the more I could only come up with one determination. It was me! There was no doubt. I even examined the sole of the right foot of the corpse. There I found the scar, an exact duplicate of which was on my own right foot. I had acquired it as a young boy. No one but Mycroft and I knew of it. I tell you, it was uncanny. The corpse was not just someone who looked like me, or was made up to look like me. It was not some copy, but an original. It was me! I was looking upon the dead body of Sherlock Holmes!

This was a discovery that set my world reeling in more ways than one. It allowed, even demanded, that my thoughts now entertain a multitude of questions that I had hitherto ignored. Surely something mysterious had befallen me at the Reichenbach. That mist, my fall, the coma, now it began to make some sense. But what indeed, did it portend? Something strange, no doubt, perhaps supernatural. The very thought surprised me greatly.

Although perplexed at this discovery and the questions it raised, I had to put them all aside. For all I knew for certain now was this: with Moriarty apparently alive, I must get home to London, immediately.

For I was sure everyone I knew there was in great danger. The world I knew did not exist any longer, and somehow I was in a new world, or a different, perhaps alternate one. Here I had died at the Reichenbach, while Moriarty had somehow lived and has been free to make his plans and schemes.

I feared for Mycroft now.

I feared for you, Watson.

I feared for England, the Empire, the world.

The boat train took me into Victoria Station in London's center on schedule as always. I noticed the familiar building but it was now draped with black sashes and bunting in mourning and remembrance of our dear deceased queen. It was a somber homecoming.

I was in disguise as an old sailor. I knew it would be best to get the lay of the land, so to speak, and then decide on a course of action before I made my presence known.

Quite honestly at that moment, I was not sure what to do. For the first time in my life I was far out of my depths, but I knew there was one sure anchor in my world, or worlds, and that was you, good Watson, and our rooms at

221B. So I headed for Baker Street, an apparent elderly sailor on pension, a bit taken with drink and fallen on hard times. That latter part of my disguise was more true than I'd have cared to admit.

Baker Street came into view and appeared the same as always, but as I approached the building that housed 221B my heart sank and a great feeling of gloom overtook me. The building was closed and boarded up. It appeared a massive fire had gutted the entire structure many months back.

I ran to our lodgings and looked with disbelief at the boarded up building and then at the people passing by on the street, desperately seeking a friendly or recognizable face. Mrs. Hudson, Billy, Wiggins, anyone!

"My good man!" I shouted to a neighbor. "Can you tell me what happened to this house and the people who lived here?"

"Aye, Pops," he replied, shaking his head sadly. "Not much to say, big fire last year, a real shame."

"What of the doctor?" I blurted.

"Oh the doctor? The doctor went off, no one knows where. The lady what owned the house I hear tell is living with a sister in Kent."

I sighed with relief. At least you, and Mrs. Hudson, were alive. But where?

"And what of Mr. Sherlock Holmes?" I asked with more trepidation than I realized I possessed.

"Aye, the detective? Dead this past year. It broke the doctor's poor 'eart, I tell you."

I nodded, feeling as if I was in a dream. Or a nightmare. This just could not be. I took one last look at the rooms we had shared for so long in happier days, and then went on my way.

I am afraid that I received even worse news at the Diogenes Club. After Baker Street I immediately hailed a hansom cab and made my way to Pall Mall. There I entered that venerable establishment, only allowed into the environs of the Visitors Room, where I was informed by a liveried butler that Mr. Mycroft Holmes was no longer a member of the Diogenes Club.

"Why is that?" I asked, still in my disguise as the old retired sailor.

The butler looked at me with obvious annoyance from being asked to explain such things to one of the lower classes, but then shrugged and added, "Murdered he was, last May, not soon after his famous brother died on holiday in Switzerland, I hear."

"Assassinated," I whispered. "Oh, Mycroft, now I see . . ."

"Sir?" the butler inquired.

"Nothing," I replied. "I will be leaving now."

On the street before the Diogenes Club I stood frozen, stunned, it surely seemed all was lost. Mycroft my brother, dead? Murdered? Murdered no doubt by Moriarty's henchmen no sooner he returned to London from the Reichenbach. Watson, you were gone. Where? The world in turmoil, while Moriarty had since received a knighthood and was now Sir James! I balked at the effrontery of it all.

I knew now Watson, that I must find you, and together perhaps, we could make something of this most strange and disastrous turn of events. I tried to locate you at the usual haunts, at St. Barts Hospital, your office on St. Anne's Street, even at your old regimental stomping grounds. No one had seen you for months. Some told me a sad story of how you had fallen on hard times, that you had taken the news of my death badly, that you had fallen to drink. I was shocked. Astounded, really. It was most unlike you, old boy, to overindulge in spirits at all. To allow yourself to become so wedded to drink as I was being told was quite incomprehensible to me. At first I did not believe it at all. However the rumors I heard in my travels told me of a once proud doctor of medicine who had descended deeply into the dubious comfort afforded by the bottle.

And so it necessitated a change of tack, and I began to seek you out in those more retched establishments frequented by denizens of our grand city who look to drown the past, and their own place in it, with drink.

I tell you, dressed as I was as a hapless old salt of the seven seas, I was able to fit in quite well with those who frequented such establishments and find out many interesting tid-bits as I tracked you down. The most disturbing of which is that the common folk believe Good Queen Victoria had been murdered and the crime covered up. The people hate King Eddy, and they are restless and fearful. Many believe he seeks to restore the monarchy to its full power, and that soon now he will disband Parliament and ask for the resignation and abolishment of the office of Prime Minister. That is surely incredible, and I put these rumors to the superstitions of the common folk and less educated classes. Yet they believe them firmly, I can tell you. A dark pall seems to have descended upon our city—a dark pall, I would wager, by the name of Moriatry.

But first things first. I had to find you, Watson, and in this most effective disguise it was but a day later that I was to stumble into the Cock & Crow, a shabby East End pub. There I saw a sight I thought I would never see in my life. There I saw a familiar figure seated at a lonely table, slumped down and obviously unconscious from too much drink.

I approached carefully, and nudged you awake.

You looked up annoyed, your eyes red with drink and barked, “Move on! Move on! Can’t you see I want to be left alone in my misery!”

My heart broke to see you like that, old friend, rank and disheveled, bleary-eyed and forlorn. Nothing but a hopeless drunk. You’d have hardly fared worse had you sunk to the opium pipe.

I sat down opposite you and looked you over. You had not changed much in my absence and yet you had changed significantly, and for the worse. You looked terrible, but I hoped it was nothing a bath, shave, and good food would not cure.

“Barkeep! Barkeep!” I ordered, “Bring us a pot of your strongest coffee!”

“Aye, mate, coming right up,” the barman replied.

Then your head rose off the tabletop and you made a valiant effort to focus your eyes across the small table to see who I was.

Of course I was in disguise and you did not recognize me.

“Be gone! Leave me alone!” you barked. Then your head dropped back to the tabletop barely conscious.

The barman brought over a pot of steaming coffee. I poured a large cup and set it down in front of you.

"Drink," I ordered.

You looked up at me again, let out with a curse, moved to grasp the nearby whisky bottle on the table, which I promptly dashed to the floor in a dozen pieces.

"Hey! What the . . . ?"

"Drink the coffee, Watson!" I said firmly. "I need you sober and keen of mind."

Well that got your attention. Your head rose off your hands and you took a second look at the old salt in front of you. Your head swayed with the affliction of too much drink but you steadied your gaze long enough to see through my disguise.

"Holmes?" You whispered in a low and fearful gasp. "Can it be?"

"Yes, good Watson, it is I, but keep my disguise in order, I do not want to be found out yet." I said.

"But . . . but you are dead?" you stammered.

"Not quite yet," I tried to reassure you.

"Then you must be some hallucination?"

"Watson, really!" I replied sharply.

Then your eyes grew wide as saucer plates, and a tiny smile broke through your cracked lips. Tears streamed from your eyes.

"Holmes." You whispered, "Holmes."

"Sssshh!" I warned.

"Yes, I understand."

I had found you, my good Watson, my anchor in the world!

After half a dozen cups of the barman's strong but brutal brew, your demeanor and state of mind slowly came back to that which I know and love.

"Holmes! I can not believe it!"

"Keep it low, my friend. It is to both our advantages that certain people continue to believe me dead. Call me . . . Sigerson."

You nodded, tried to clear your mind and finally asked, "But you are alive. So tell me, what has happened?"

I smiled, "That is what I hoped you could tell me?"

You were quiet for a long moment, thoughtful. Then said, "Yes, much has transpired since you left. But how can this be? You are dead! What happened in Switzerland?"

"Obviously I am quite alive, Watson. Nevertheless, that is an adventure I will relate to you in its entirety some other time. Right now you have to answer me this one question."

"Anything."

"Watson, I have been gone long by some standards—but surely not long enough that such fantastic events should transpire in the world. In London."

"I take it you have been to 221B?" you said sheepishly.

"Indeed, what is left of it."

"So you saw . . ."

"I saw the results of a fire. I also know of the murder of Mycroft."

"I am sorry."

We were silent for a time.

"Now, Watson," I asked, "tell me truly. What has been going on here while I have been gone?"

You steadied your hand as you took another reassuring drink of the hot coffee. "It's terrible. The queen is dead, the new King, Eddy is a lascivious libertine. You should hear the rumors about him, if but half are true, he is a monster."

I nodded.

Then you looked around, carefully, whispering to me, "Have a care. The king has agents everywhere. Secret police agents."

"Really?" This was news. That certainly smacked of Moriarty.

Then you whispered fearfully, "England, the world, we seem to be in the grip of some dread dilemma and I fear where it all may lead."

"Moriarty is the source of this particular dilemma," I said in a low tone. "With my absence and supposed death no one could stand against him or his plans. With Mycroft murdered, our enemy was left to indulge his boldest and most devious devices. He apparently has done so quite well, and on a worldwide scale."

"What do you want me to do . . . Sigerson?"

"Do you still have your revolver, Watson?"

"Of course," you replied, perking up at the prospect of action.

"Where are you living now?" I asked.

"I have a small room at the Whistle and Thump, four blocks away."

"Good, go to your room now and rest. I will meet you there tomorrow," I said, "And Watson, stay sober."

"You have no need to worry about me now, seeing you here and alive is the one true medicine for my sick and tortured spirit."

"Good old Watson, together we shall work through this conundrum."

Seeing you again, old friend, had done much to revive my own sagging spirits, but to see the state to which you had sunk with drink had not only saddened me it had surprised me as well. It also got me to thinking. It really was most unlike you.

In fact, it seemed to me now there were many events, even given Moriarty's unrestricted activity, that did not add up. Mycroft dead? Assassinated? Once I got over the shock of that, the more I thought about it, the more it seemed quite impossible. Our rooms at 221B burned and boarded up? Well that was a shock, but it was always a real possibility. What was not a possibility was that I was apparently both alive *and* dead. Then there was the Queen's death, was it murder? Moriarty's knighthood, the turmoil in America and elsewhere. My body in Moriarty's coffin! All most incongruous events as far as the facts I knew in my world.

It just didn't add up. These things I have mentioned could never all have happened in the world I knew. Something was amiss, and I fear that you are a factor as well, Watson, one more piece of evidence for the thesis I have reluctantly come to put on the table as a probable explanation for these strange events. Until this moment I had been loath to seriously mention my thesis in this narrative. You see, I know you. I know there is no way that the man I know would become a hopeless drunk. Not in my world. Therefore, you are *not* the man I know. You may be Watson, but you are not *my* Watson. You are . . . *another* Watson. And therefore, with the evidence of my body in that grave, and Moriarty alive, I must be *another* Holmes!

Following this reasoning, I knew that Moriarty was not *my* Moriarty either. I also knew I must exercise extreme caution now. I had much to think upon. This was certainly becoming quite the three-pipe problem.

When you and I met next morning at your room, you looked much improved and I explained most of this to you. I told you my theory. I added, "I now believe that my falling through the mists at Reichenbach had somehow transferred me into a different world. Your world. A world that is almost exact to that which I know, but with jarring differences."

Your response, at first, was entirely expected. "It seems preposterous, Holmes, utterly, and incredibly unbelievable. I am sure it was your body I had buried."

"Not my body, but *another.* I tell you, somehow I have entered your world, which is separate from my own. If you do not believe it, Watson, at least believe that such a thing can be possible. For how do you explain that I am here before you?"

You thought this over knowing I was serious about it. I could see that even if you did not entirely believe my fantastic tale, you *wanted* to believe it.

"Nevertheless, old friend, when you eliminate the impossible, whatever remains, however improbable, must be the truth." I said. "I put it to you, your world and my world being the same place, that is impossible. It can not be. Therefore these worlds exist *separately.*"

"I do not know, Holmes. Truly, I have seen and heard many strange things in my service in the medical field and during my war service in Afghanistan and the Far East. This however, is simply incredible."

"Yes it is, but mere incredibility does not negate the

truth of the matter. Something strange happened at Reichenbach. Moriarty and I fought. In your world *and* mine. In mine, *he* fell and died. In yours, *I* fell and died. At the same time, in my world I fell into the mist but did not die, instead I was somehow transferred here, to your world. A parallel world, or an alternate one, Challenger would surely be able to explain it better than I. That has to be why when I exhumed the body of the Englishman who died at Reichenbach, it was not Moriarty as it *should* have been—as it *must* have been if I was in my own world. It was myself! I tell you I was quite shocked at the time, but I knew that it was a very significant fact. It was my body in the coffin! It should by all accounts and logic, have been Moriarty's! That was the key that set me upon this course and raised many strange questions. Events since have only forced me to consider this thesis more seriously." I concluded.

"I hardly know what to say."

"Then don't say anything, but think about it," I continued. "However fantastic, my thesis must be true. As improbable as it sounds, it is the only one that fits all the facts. The icing on the cake was seeing you, old man. Seeing to what depths you had fallen after my 'death' alerted me to one simple but incontrovertible fact. While you are surely my good friend, John H. Watson, you can not be *the* John H. Watson I have known for so many years. Hence the corollary, that this world is *not* the world I have known for so many years either. Therefore I am the outsider here, lost, stranded in *your* world."

"Holmes, but if what you say is true, then . . ."

"Yes, Sherlock Holmes did indeed die at the Reichenbach.

It was his body I saw, it was his body you saw—and let me tell you, there can be no mistake—it was the corpse of Sherlock Holmes. *Your* Sherlock Holmes."

There was a long silence.

You nodded final acceptance, and I noticed a deep sadness creep into your features once again. Finally you looked at me with determination and even managed a wan smile.

"You are a doppelganger of my own Watson, or I of your Holmes, if you prefer. It does not matter much now so long as we understand it and what it means. Buck up, all is not lost. Quite the contrary, in fact. For instance, I believe your descent into drink may have actually worked in our favor, for it certainly saved your life."

"How so?" You asked.

"Simply put, Moriarty held back on his revenge against you for I am sure he reveled in your self-destruction. Such would fit his warped ego and sense of justice, and it saved you from his henchmen. So now, here we are, both alive, and none the worse for wear."

"Well, Holmes, It is good to have you back, where ever you are from," you said, managing a good-hearted smile.

"Good man, Watson. It appears the game is afoot once again. And the name of this particular game, is Moriarty. I accept the fact now that this is not my world and I do not belong here. More than anything else I want to find a way to get back to my own world. But first, I can not in good conscience leave this world to its own devices with Moriarty unleashed without doing something to restrain or stop him. Are you with me?"

"You know I am, Holmes."

"So now we must determine what Moriarty's game is. That is what we must ask ourselves, for only then can we thwart those plans and bring him to justice," I said.

"More crime?" you suggested, rather lamely, I am afraid.

"Not merely crime. It's rather beyond that now, if you keep up with what is being written in the popular press. I study the papers every day. It is rather amazing. The worldwide turmoil, and worse on the horizon, indicates some worldwide controlling factor. That can only be Moriarty. I really must say that the Moriarty of your world, has far eclipsed the Moriarty of my own in his boldness and in his accomplishments."

"Well, I certainly never expected you to compliment him, Holmes."

"And why not? He has achieved much in a short time. I am afraid we have our work cut out for us."

"It certainly sounds that way." Then you gave me a determined look and said, "I am ready to help you any way I can."

"Bravo!" Then I added, "But we must take care here. Moriarty and I seem linked in some way I can not yet understand, but it has to do with how I came here. I must be sure that whatever I do to stop him will not interfere with my being able to get back to my own world."

"I do not understand, Holmes."

"Simple enough," I replied. "Moriarty and I are linked, simply killing him may stop his plans, but I am afraid it might strand me here forever. That will not do. I fear if I kill him, it must be in a very specific manner. Perhaps I must draw him out somehow, for one final encounter."

"Then what shall we do?"

"First, I have a little errand for you to perform," I said.

It was not soon thereafter that you were off to Scotland Yard, while I sat down and wrote a letter to a mysterious Far Eastern visitor whom the papers told me had lately arrived in London.

It was with dire alarm that I listened to the news upon your return from Scotland Yard two hours later. You looked bleak and were reticent to speak and I had to prompt you a bit impatiently.

"Well, come out with it! What of Lestrade and Gregson?" I said. We were seated in your small East End room. It was a pale replacement for our luxurious lodgings at 221B, but it would have to do. "Did you see them and ask them to come here?"

Well, you were evidently quite upset by what you had learned. I had a bad feeling about the entire business from the looks of you.

"Watson?" I prompted. "Are you all right?"

"Holmes," you replied, "I never saw Lestrade, nor Gregson. They were not at the Yard. When I inquired, I was told they had both been sacked."

"Sacked!" I blurted, the surprise even affected my normal level demeanor.

"Yes, the new administration, Holmes . . . "

"What *new* administration?" I began pacing the small room now, longing for my pipe, or even the cocaine needle.

"You see, I made certain inquires, very discreet, never mentioning your name or mine. It is incomprehensible! His Majesty the King has appointed a new commissioner of Scotland Yard. At first I found out that the new man was a war hero, a retired Army officer, even a big game hunter, and I thought . . ."

"Yes, well, out with it now, Watson!"

". . . but no, they told me his name was . . . Colonel Sebastian Moran."

I had to sit down. "Moran?" I whispered. "There's Moriarty's hand in that for certain."

"It gets worse. Moran has shaken up the entire Yard, he has sacked Lestrade, Gregson, and others that you have had good relations with over the years. I heard he is expanding the force of secret police agents and giving them special powers. I fear he has doomed the Yard."

"Indeed, now for certain the wolf is guarding the hen house and I am fearful for the good people of our fair London."

There was not much more to say. For a long moment we were quiet, thoughtful.

"What do you want me to do, Holmes?"

"I will seek out Lestrade and Gregson. Now that they are unemployed, they should be at their residences. I'll try Lestrade first." I said. Then I handed you the envelope that contained the letter I had written but an hour before. "You shall hand deliver this message to our distinguished foreign visitor. He is in Room 600 of the Grand Hotel, and I want you to await his response."

You nodded and looked dubiously at the envelope and the strange name written upon it, saying, "*Thubten Gyatso, Ocean of Wisdom?* What does it mean, Holmes?"

"Deliver it, Watson, then meet me back here this evening."

Inspector Giles Lestrade had a small flat off Great Russell Street. I made my way there through the streets of London.

I continued wearing my disguise; gray beard, stringy gray lock wig, a bulk suit that made me appear to have 50 pounds of additional weight. For all intents and purposes I was an old retired sailor who had seen better days. I walked with an unsteady gait. No one on the street approached me, or paid me even the least attention, just as I wanted it. Carefully I made my way from your tiny East End room to central London and the Great Russell Street environs.

Greater London seemed not to have changed at all since I had been gone, at least on the surface. However underneath all the fine buildings and statuary, the busy crowds and traffic of hansom cabs, and the bustle of big city life, I noticed with great trepidation those small and disturbing items that made up that dark pall I felt had enshrouded the city.

While there had not been any substantial change, changes were evident to me. There was a new meanness in the people and fear I could see in their eyes. I had never seen such before in the good people of London. To be sure, people went about their daily business as they always have, but more than ever, they did so without paying attention to anyone else around them. Like horses with blinders on, they did not talk to strangers, they did not ever look in another's eyes. And the police and constables—well, I could see that people feared them now as they had never done so before—and even more so the plainclothes detectives of the Yard. As you said Watson, these seemed to have been organized into some form of secret police.

I saw it all with my own eyes as I walked the streets of London. The police now take people off the streets at all hours for questioning if it is even suspected they have made some negative remark against the King. I hear tell some of them do not return. The Tower of London has been reopened and is being used for a special type of prisoner—so-called 'enemies of the Crown.' Another special edict which the King has so directed. I have been told the dungeons below the Tower are full with malefactors who have been imprisoned for political crimes against the Crown without charges filed or any trial. Something our Good Queen Victoria would never sanction in all her years as our sovereign. Our new King seems to be seeking an expansion of the powers of the monarchy. With Moriarty an advisor behind the throne, it appears he and King Eddy are beginning a program that will strangle our nation. I fear where it will finally lead.

Another item I heard in my travels through the city today; there will be a rally in Hyde Park to seek a redress of the people's grievances with the monarchy. It seems this could be the beginning of much civil unrest in our city. I was determined to attend that rally later in the day and see for myself what the situation was in this other London I now found myself a part of.

Meanwhile, upon reaching Lestrade's rooms at Great Russell Street I was surprised to see through the front window that the former Scotland Yard inspector was already ensconced with a visitor. I smiled at my good fortune when I noticed his guest was none other than Inspector Tobias Gresgon, also now formerly of the Yard. Here indeed, was an opportunity to score two birds with one stone, so to speak.

Once more I relied upon my disguise as the old sailor,

Sigerson. I could not give away my identity yet, and neither of these men would scarcely believe my identity in any regard. To them, like this entire world I found myself in, Sherlock Holmes was dead. I would leave him dead for a while longer.

I had to keep reminding myself that indeed, I was not *their* Sherlock Holmes, but was from another world, a different one than this, and that while my sympathies ran with the problems I had observed here, my heart yearned to be back in my true home. For in fact, this world was becoming more and more of a nightmare to me.

But now, first things first. Lestrade and Gregson were about to have a visitor.

Lestrade answered the bell, the little man looked as ferret-like as ever, his small mustache and nose crinkling up with distaste as he saw me.

"I do not accept solicitations, my good man. Now be gone." he said as he made to slam the door in my face.

My foot in the breach prevented that nicely, and I responded with a powerful growl, "Lestrade, I bring word to you from an enemy of your enemy. Be you interested?"

"Here now! What?" Lestrade muttered, perplexed, but it was Gregson who standing close behind put his hand on his companion's shoulder saying, "I think we should hear what this man has to say."

Lestrade shrugged and moved away from the door. "Very well." Then to me he said, "You may enter, old man, and explain yourself forthwith."

I smiled and said calmly, "I serve the enemy of your enemy. My Master must remain anonymous until a time in the future when it is safe for him to reveal himself."

"Sherlock Holmes is dead, old man," Lestrade said boldly.

"That, my good inspectors has yet to be determined," I growled forcefully. "But that is not a question to be answered now. What is important now, is that we confront Moriarty and his organization. He must be defeated or England and the world are doomed!"

"Moriarty?" Lestrade said, "but he is the King's man now."

"And the man behind the King's oppression of the people, and your own problem, Lestrade" I replied boldly.

Both men stood quiet for a long moment.

"Fine words, whoever you are, old man, but we have been sacked, the King has appointed Moriarty's henchman, Moran, Commissioner of Scotland Yard, and we no longer have any official capacity," Gregson offered gruffly.

"Nevertheless, there are ways," I said plainly. "What I and my master want to know is this. Are you interested?"

"Aye," Lestrade barked. "I tell you at this point I care not for reinstatement to my previous position so much as I would like to wreak revenge upon those who brought this atrocity upon me. Gregson and I were discussing this very matter before you showed up, but we were at a loss what to do."

"I believe that I can remedy that situation, with a course of action," I said with a smile.

Then I told Lestrade and Gregson what I had in mind and they promised to meet me later that evening.

On my way back to your East End room, Watson, I passed by Hyde Park. It was but a couple of blocks from our old lodgings at Baker Street and there I saw throngs of people listening to speakers from various political parties publicly airing their grievances against the Crown and King. Such has been a custom in London and the Park for generations and often times it was merely the venue of fools or the unstable. But not today. Today there were thousands of citizens present from all classes and social positions who had felt the cruel yoke of oppression from this new monarch over the last year. In a rare effort, members of the Labor and Tory parties had united to seek redress against the Crown. I walked over to the speaker's platform in order to hear some of the grievances and listened with intense interest to one firebrand after the other describe acts that flied in the face of our good English law. I could scarce believe what I was hearing, but then I must remember that this for all its symmetry and exactness, was not my England, not my world.

I was harshly reminded of that fact when companies of stout London Bobbies, whom I noticed now uncharacteristically carried firearms, had been brought in to break up the crowd.

"This is an unlawful assembly and you are hereby ordered to disperse immediately by order of the King," the Captain of Police demanded of the crowd.

Well, the speakers began to incite those assembled to taunt the police and soon the crowd was booing and telling them to leave. To my consternation, I noticed light cavalry that could only be from the Royal Household Guard forming up at the edge of the lake. This was not a positive development.

There was alarm and concern growing now in the faces of the crowd as well. The police captain demanded once more, "You have been ordered to disperse immediately, or face the consequences."

Well, this was a fine pickle I can tell you, but matters got far worse when some in the crowd went from booing the constables to throwing objects. What happened next can only go down in the history books as a day of bloody murder. For the Household Guard drew their sabers and moving upon the crowd suddenly burst into a wild charge with points down and out. The effect was dramatic and disastrous, and after ten minutes of chaos, I could see there were dozens killed and hundreds wounded.

The remnants of the crowd along with the various speakers had become a mob and its members were being herded forward and arrested. I was able to make my way to safety along the lake. Many others were not so lucky. God knows where those arrested were taken or what was done with them.

As I walked the streets of London on my way back to your room, I could not fathom the nightmare world this was. With Moriarty unchecked, it appeared that civilization itself might be doomed.

When I returned to your room you were there waiting for me.

"Holmes! My God! What has happened to you? You look like you have gone through the Battle of Waterloo!"

"Not Waterloo, Watson, the Battle of Hyde Park. I suspect you will read about the massacre at the hands of the King's troops in tomorrow's *Times*," I said, as I began to clean myself and change my clothes. "But tell me, my friend, did you see Thubten Gyatso and deliver my letter to him?"

"Yes, I did. He is a very old man and had to have the boy at his side read and translate your message to him."

"Indeed, that is most interesting." I could not help but raise my eyebrows in curiosity at that inconsistency.

"Holmes?"

"Never mind," I replied. "But tell me, what was his reply?"

"His reply was one word, 'Yes' "

I sighed deeply, in truth I had hoped it would not be so, but knowing the facts as I knew them to be, I had to discover what part our faraway visitor played in this strange series of events.

"We must leave at once, for I believe he may be in danger. Thubten Gyatso may also be the one person in the world who can answer my questions and perhaps help me return to my own world. We must speak with him immediately."

We had to walk a number of blocks before we could acquire a growler with a driver who would deliver us across town to the Grand Hotel. The hotel was an imposing pile, one of the tallest buildings in London with six floors. We took the new "lift," or as the Americans are calling it these days, the "elevator," to the top floor. That floor was actually taken up by an entire suite of rooms for the express use of His Holiness and his rather large retinue of monks and servants.

We were led by one monk, apparently acting as a major-domo, to wait in a small anteroom while our request for an audience with the Ocean of Wisdom, as he was reverently called, was being considered.

"Ocean of Wisdom, Holmes? Who is this strange man?"

"Not man, Watson, for he is but a boy of sixteen years. His

name was Thubten Gyatso in his mortal form, but he is better known as His Holiness the Dalai Lama of Tibet. He is the thirteenth in a line of Dalai Lamas said to be reincarnated from that first of the line back in the fifteenth century."

"But what of the old man I was introduced to?"

"That old man presented to you as His Holiness was but a stand-in. He was obviously assuming the role for purposes of protection, assuming the target for any assassination attempt to save his master's life."

"I see. Rather mysterious, is it not?"

"To be sure. That sixteen-year-old boy has traveled thousands of miles here to London. That is an extremely unusual journey for one of his vaulted status and implies great danger in some manner or form. I believe he knows something about my situation here. I do not know how that can be, but I feel he may be able to help me."

"How so, Holmes?"

"The Tibetan form of Buddhism is a powerful force for peace and love, as well as the spirit of harmony and justice in the world. They have a long history of spiritualism and knowledge in many esoteric matters, and can detect changes in the flow of worldly events," I added.

"Well, what was in your note to him? Did you ask him if he knows how you can get back to your own world?"

"No. When I read in the *Times* that His Holiness had come to London, I knew it could be no mere coincidence. After all, Moriarty and I are in London. This entire scenario of events has London as its nexus. So I asked him, was his reason for coming here because he had detected certain anomalies in the flow of worldly events? As you say, his answer to that question was 'Yes.' That is an admission I find very interesting. I also wrote that if that was his answer, then he should take precautions because his life might be in danger. That is why we are here this evening."

"What can we do, Holmes?"

"Fear not, we have allies, and I have placed them surreptitiously to unmask any danger. But hello, here is the major domo returned and he is indicating that we are to follow him for our audience with His Holiness."

The central room of the hotel suite was large and set up as a richly appointed audience chamber in the Far Eastern style. Large and luxurious *thankya* tapestries hung from the walls bearing colorful images of Buddha. At the end of the room was an elegant but empty throne, and off to the side standing in front of the large windows stood a young man, shaven pate, dressed in a fine yellow *namsa* silk robe. Around him buzzed a dozen Tibetan monks, in orange saffron robes, bald of pate as was their master, discussing heated issues as we approached.

Thubten Gyatso saw us and motioned his followers to silence. They quickly formed up in two long rows on either side of The Presence, as he was also known, while we walked forward to meet him.

"Your Holiness, I am Sigerson, and this is my friend, Doctor John H. Watson, who delivered to you a note earlier today." I said. We shook hands in the western form of greeting. I had read that His Holiness was very much interested in the modern world and Western customs.

His Holiness the Dalai Lama smiled graciously, he was but a boy, but there was a depth to his face, and most notably his eyes, that made you feel you were in the presence of a much older and wiser man. He was purported to be the reincarnation of the last Dalai Lama, in a line that stretched back to the first master, and I could almost believe it true.

He surprised us by speaking English with a decided British accent, "Welcome, my friends. Yes, I speak English, Mr. Sigerson, a teacher at the monastery in my youth. I find myself fascinated by all things British and modern and so thought it best to learn the language of the modern world so as to experience it first-hand. But, to get to your question, the answer is, of course, 'Yes.' You are correct. You see, for centuries my people have observed visions of the future in the sacred Lake of Lhamo Lhatso at Chokhorgyal. It was on one such vision quest where I viewed all that has transpired and much that will transpire." The Dalai Lama suddenly stopped speaking. He turned to his retainers, motioned to them, and quickly they began to file out of the chamber. It was not long before we found ourselves alone with the Dalai Lama.

Once we were seated facing each other at the other end of the room, Thubten Gyatso looked at me intently and said, "You are one of the two men I saw in my vision. Your actions at the exact same time in both worlds caused a breach, a doorway to open between these worlds."

Well, here seemed more verification of my theory, and even if I did not entirely believe, I knew this had to be the truth. Nevertheless I asked, "How can that be?"

"Better you might ask, how can such a thing *not* be?" His Holiness replied answering my question with one of his own. He was silent for a moment before he continued, "Two exact events, happening simultaneously in different worlds—but with opposite outcomes—may open a doorway between those two worlds. Then, it could be possible to fall through from one world to the other. Sigerson, as you call yourself here, you see far, so much farther than most. What does your reason tell you? what do your facts tell you?"

"That what you say may be true." I replied quietly.

"*May* be true?" he prompted.

"*Must* be true," I amended.

The Dalai Lama nodded his youthful head, smiling graciously, then added, "The other I saw was your nemesis. I have seen all this and more in my visions, and fear for our world with your nemesis unchecked. My visit here, aside from a most selfish desire to see the modern world, was to see if I could alert those involved to correct this error."

"What, error?" I asked.

"In your world, Sigerson, you slew your nemesis. In my world, here, he slew you. That should never have happened. The combination of his living, with your death through that encounter, has caused turmoil in my world. Which has caused his evil to exert itself to its fullest. The equilibrium has shifted. You must set it level again."

"I want to get back to my own world, Your Holiness, but if what you are saying is true, I can not in good conscience let my enemy destroy your world. I know what he is capable of, I have seen the results of his handiwork. I agree with you, I must do something to stop him," I said.

"Then there is only one way to do that *and* for you to be able to return to your rightful world. You both are connected by the doorway. It is still open, waiting for you to return . . ."

"The Falls! That must be it!" you blurted, Watson, adding, "Sorry, Holmes."

"Correct, Doctor," the Dalai Lama continued. "Your friend must replay the passion of that original encounter once more, and this time you must be victorious. Seek the mist, that is your doorway."

I looked into the weary eyes of Thubten Gyatso and there was an almost beatific smile on his face. Most incongruous, that young face, with such worldly old eyes.

"And now, Sigerson, tell me, what does that far vision of yours tell you about me?"

I was taken aback by his request, but I automatically replied, "Ocean of Wisdom seems an appropriate name, and if your youth is any indication, I see great things in store for you and your people in the coming years. You will have a long reign. You are wise. You are good. You understand evil."

The stoic look on the Dalai Lama's face never changed as he stood up and said, "The audience is over, may you be successful in your quest, Signerson."

As we got up to leave, His Holiness added, "Doctor Watson, please stay one moment."

Both men saw the look of surprise on my face. But I left you, Watson and exited the room to await you in the small anteroom we had been in earlier.

The monk who was acting as major domo came in, said, "Your friend will be returned to you presently."

I thanked him and waited patiently. I was left wondering just what the Dalai Lama would need to speak to you about privately, out of my presence.

As I waited, I heard a ruckus in the outer hallway and

suddenly Lestrade and Gregson entered the room and behind them were four brace of stout London bobbies. They held none other than Colonel Sebastian Moran in irons, as Lestrade hefted a peculiar looking rifle in his hands. It was Moran's notorious airgun.

"Just as you said, he was across the street, aiming to get another shot off at the old man by the window." Lestrade offered, "The old man you said would be the target."

"Is the old man all right?" I asked.

"Flesh wound, but it is enough to tie Moran and his gun to alleged murder," Gregson offered with a smile.

"You can not arrest me! I am the Commissioner of Scotland Yard!" Moran demanded with substantial pomp.

"Not quite," Gregson said triumphantly, "We may not have official authority any longer but there are still laws against murder. This is a citizens arrest, all quite legal. You have been arrested for the attempted murder of His Holiness the Dalai Lama of Tibet. The crime may not get you gaol at the assizes because of powerful friends, but your days as Commissioner of The Yard are quite over!"

"Take him away!" Lestarde ordered the constables and soon Moran was gone.

"Things will go badly for him, and better for Lestrade and me now," Gregson said. "Who knows, perhaps there will even be a reinstatement?"

Once Lestrade and Gregson had left it was not long before you returned to me, Watson, from your private audience with the Dalai Lama.

"Well? I must admit, I am intrigued. What did he have to say?" I asked, full of curiosity.

You seemed strangely reticent, but finally you simply smiled at me, putting your hand on my shoulder in a very touching brotherly fashion. “Fear not, Holmes. His Holiness explained it all. He really does see almost as far as you do. We must find a way to make Moriarty return to the Reichenbach Falls.”

I nodded, “There is something you are not telling me.”

You ignored my question and so I did not press it. Instead my thoughts turned to the problem at hand.

I was thinking about that link between Moriarty and I. It made sense, and Thubten Gyatso’s words seemed to validate the facts that I knew. However, getting Moriarty to the Reichenbach once again, and by himself without henchmen, could prove difficult, if not impossible. He was powerful now, he had a seat beside the King, and he was a brilliant criminal. My plan would be near impossible, but I would have to find a way to make it happen.

“Can it be done, Holmes?” you asked me, seemingly reading my thoughts.

“I do not know,” I replied. Then I told you of the events that had transpired in the last half-hour with Gregson and Lestrade arresting Moran.

“Moran?” you said, showing evident surprise.

“Yes, Moran with his airgun, the perfect, silent, assassination weapon,” I replied sharply.

“But why, Moran, Holmes? Does Moran know something?”

“No. Not Moran, Watson, Moriarty. He must suspect. I wonder what it could be? Well, whatever the case, he will surely be alerted now that Moran has been taken out of the picture.”

"That seems a key move," you ventured.

I looked at you, standing there, the Watson of another world and yet, so very much like my own true friend. "Indeed, you are correct. Moran being taken out of the game is a key event. A move Moriarty will not be able to accept lightly. If I know my Moriarty's, and I think I do, this event will disturb him no end. Perhaps we can play on that to good effect."

"Well, Lestrade and Gregson made the pinch . . ."

"Moriarty knows Lestrade and Gregson would never be able to pull such a coup on their own. He will suspect something, see the hint of my hand in the action. He will send his agents to ask questions about the old sailor who calls himself Sigerson. That is good also. Perhaps we can nudge those suspicions a bit into fears he can not ignore."

"How so, Holmes?"

"I feel the rumors of my demise have been greatly exaggerated and too long gone uncorrected." I said with a smile. I had an idea, one that might not only solve the problems of this world, and my own, but yours as well. You had lost your honor and taken to drink for my death. Now you shall be vindicated.

"Watson," I said, "I shall cause Moriarty to suspect through certain circles that I may, in fact, be alive. It will draw him out. He could not resist finding the truth out for himself and settling this once and for all."

"Bravo, Holmes! That will set them up in Piccadilly! But how do we do it?"

I was silent for a long moment. There was much to consider. I began to miss my pipe and the swirling clouds of helpful tobacco smoke that always offered surcease in such matters. I knew this had to be done just right. I could not overplay my hand by being too bold, nor be scant in my approach. Finally, I took out pen and paper and wrote three letters. The first two were almost identical. One each were addressed to Lestrade and Gregson at their residences. I told them that I was indeed alive, that it had been I who had directed them under disguise, as the old sailor, Sigerson. Then I explained your part, Watson, in my plan. I told them you had always been acting under my direct orders.

Next, the third and most important letter, addressed to Professor James Moriarty. The missive was short, simple and direct. It said, "If you seek the truth, then seek that which is in the grave of Sherlock Holmes." It was unsigned.

Then I gave you these three letters, and asked you to deliver the first two to Lestrade and Gregson. The third letter I instructed you to leave at a West End pub in the hands of the barman, Reynolds. I knew the message would not fail to get to its intended addressee and pique his interest. Then, over your objections, I solicited a promise from you that you would stay in London and await my return.

Immediately after, I took the boat train once more, to the Continent and Interlaken, alone.

The evening of the first day I arrived at the small village below the mighty falls and took a room at the local inn. There I set my plan in motion. I contacted good Hans, and that night we stole to the cemetery, opening a grave. We moved the body within to another location and closed the grave. It was empty now, save for one small item.

The next night, from a place of concealment using my spyglass, I kept constant vigil on the grave of Sherlock Holmes.

As I expected, I spied a tall, thin figure furtively approach the cemetery with an enclosed lantern after midnight. He was alone and he carried a shovel. I watched with interest as he dug the dirt away from the grave of an "English Man, Died, May 1891." The more he dug, the faster he dug. Once he hit the wood of the simple coffin, he stopped, brought his lantern closer, and deftly cleared away the remaining dirt. Finally he was able to open the casket lid, and after he did so, he stood motionless and silent as a statue. I could well imagine his consternation, for there was no body in the coffin now. It was certainly shocking, but then, that coffin was not entirely empty either. Slowly, the tall figure brought the lantern closer to the coffin and he peered down to look at something within. Suddenly he reached down and pulled out a small envelope. It was the one I had left there the evening before. It said simply, "Moriarty" on the outside. On the inside was a small note, which he pulled out, carefully unfolded, and began to read. That too was short and simple. It read: "Meet me at dawn, upon the heights overlooking the Reichenbach Falls." It was signed with the initials, "S. H."

Moriarty crushed the note and envelope and in anger threw them into the empty coffin. He looked around him into the darkness, quickly extinguished his lantern, and suddenly let out a loud menacing yell of sheer animal rage. I have never heard anything quite like it in my life. It brought a grim smile to my face.

It was now far after midnight and I gathered my things

together and began my trek up to the heights overlooking the Reichenbach Falls, where I would await Moriarty, and our destiny.

Dawn at the Reichenbach is a beautiful sight, Watson, and I was surely sorry that you missed it this time. In my own world you had accompanied me to the falls, but then at the last minute had been called away upon some pretext by Moriarty, so that he and I would be alone. Now, no such subterfuge was necessary, for it would just be Moriarty and Holmes, as it was intended all along. Two primal forces engaged in the eternal struggle between good and evil.

I was out of disguise now, it was no longer necessary and I was dressed in my usual clothing, along with heavy hiking boots and jacket. It was quite chilly upon the Reichenbach, even with the sun having just come up.

I looked over at the falls below in order to discern the whereabouts of that strange mist I had encountered upon my first visit here, more than one year ago. To be sure, it was still there, a misty fog, that seemed to shimmer and shift as it moved to different locations along the falls edge. I began to surmise that if the strange mist encompassed properties of movement—or at least of being able to change location—then that might be the reason why in our original encounter in my own world, Moriarty had died in his fall, while I had fallen into the mist and been transported here. The mist had to be the doorway. It seemed quite possible and I found myself enjoying the evident logical solution to this most strangest of problems once and for all when I suddenly heard a footstep behind me.

It was Moriarty! He was instantly upon me, wrapping me

tightly in his arms, pinning my own arms to my sides, as he quickly dragged me to the ledge.

"Now, Mr. Holmes, I know it can not be, but it is! You seem to plague me unto forever. Can I never be free of you? Well, I shall be free of you, Holmes. I killed you once, of that I was certain, and I'll kill you again, and this time you shall stay dead!'

"Moriarty!" I growled, shocked now by what I could see of him. For this Moriarty was not the old, bent over, bookish professor I knew from my world. This man appeared to be younger, and certainly much stronger. I was at a loss to understand why—but then why should it not be so? The Dalai Lama had told me that while this world was similar to my own, it was also different from my own world. Had I not seen so for myself? Suddenly I realized that this Moriarty had killed the Holmes of this world in their first encounter. He could easily do so to me as well. He was bigger, stronger than the Moriarty of my own world. I felt myself being inexorably dragged to the ledge. I heard the churning, roiling waters crashing below, felt the spray from the cliff, the sun blinded my eyes, as I was pulled closer to my doom.

"You'll not escape this time, Holmes! This time you go over the cliff and die!" Moriarty growled these words into my ear.

I tried to fight him off but he was stronger and held me tightly. I could not free my arms from where he had them pinned to my sides. I could not break his hold over me. It was then that I realized I *was* going to die. He was going to do it again! He was going to hurl me over the ledge into the falls to my death on the rocks below.

And then I felt a heavy blow, as if from some mighty collision and we were entirely spinned around. Then, good Watson, I saw your face, and you fought with Moriarty.

"Holmes, I'm here, the Dalai Lama knew you would need my help!"

"I told you to stay in London!" I blurted as I tried to free my arms.

"Hah!" you laughed, pummeling Moriarty with blows from your fist as you tried to pull us apart.

Then I broke Moriarty's hold over me and I was free. Immediately I stepped in to shield you from his blows. You hit him again, and once again, causing him to move away backward, where he seemed to hesitate, to lose his balance. Then as Moriarty slipped over the falls, I watched in horror as he suddenly grabbed your coat, and you followed him over the cliff.

"Watson!" I cried.

"Holmes, no need, I'm glad it ended this . . ." and your voice diminished as you fell down to the rocks below.

I stood at the abyss, as you and Moriarty plunged down to the falls and instant death below.

It was over. I looked down and saw that Moriarty and you lay mangled upon the stones of the falls and were soon pulled under by the furious water of the river. Both of you were gone a moment later.

"Moriarty finally dead," I whispered, shaking with sorrow, "but at what price? My good Watson, dead! What am I to do now?"

And then the words of Thubten Gyatso came back to me, *"Seek the mist, that is your doorway."*

I looked over and saw that the mist was about twenty

yards away and I walked towards it as if in a dream. It was shimmering in a most unnatural manner, and I could well believe now that it might in fact be some form of transcendental, or supernatural, doorway between the worlds as the Dalai Lama had told me.

Moriarty in this world, and in my own world, was dead now. I had accomplished my mission. I wondered, had I been brought here for this very reason in the first place? It was a question I had no way of answering. Perhaps Thubten Gyatso knew more than he was saying? Perhaps he had told you, Watson, and that is why, stout fellow, you had disobeyed my order to stay behind in London? Yet, your disobedience had saved my life, and enabled me to accomplish that mission.

Now it was time for me to go home to my own world, where I belonged. The gate awaited me. Sadly, I was leaving behind a world where not only Moriarty and Holmes were dead, but so was your own other self. Yet now, more than ever, I yearned to be free of this nightmare world and be back home in my own London, with my own good Watson, at our own 221B, with Mycroft, Mrs. Hudson, and even dour-faced old Lestrade.

I made for the mist. Once it was stationary below me I looked carefully down upon it. I knew what I had to do. I could not live in this world. Not with my best friend dead—who had given his life to save my own. But what I was considering was incomprehensible as well. If I was wrong, I would be doing myself what Moriarty had just been unable to do. I could be killing myself, committing suicide.

I looked into the roiling mist below. I took a deep breath. The shimmering seemed to call to me. I thought of you, good friend, and home, and all the people I desired to see again, and I dove down into the roiling mist and into my destiny.

"Are you all right, Mister?" I heard a voice saying from above me.

I was coming back to consciousness slowly, breathing the chill mountain air, feeling the dirt and grass under my body, I felt my shoulders and body shaken. I opened my eyes and there I saw good Hans.

"Are you all right? A strange place to fall asleep, no?"

"Hans?" I asked.

"Yes, that is my name. But how did you know it?" he replied carefully.

"You do not know me?"

"No, Sir. Should I know you? I have never met you before this moment."

I nodded, "No, of course not, you would not know me."

On my way to London, I bought a copy of the *Times* and read it with a renewed sense of joy as I learned of the plans being set in motion for the Birthday Celebration for Good Queen Victoria. She was to be joined in the celebration by her son Edward, heir to the throne. I sighed with relief, the world I knew, the world I belonged in was here, and I was in my rightful place in it. I read with interest where a new American president had recently been elected, and there was nary a peep of military insurrection or succession; where the government of France was still in the usual turmoil but had not yet fallen; and where Germany and Russia were quiet. It appeared now that all was as it should be.

I also noticed a small item tucked away in the back pages about Eddy. He wasn't king here, just a minor royal. It said simply that Albert Christian Edward Victor, Duke of Clarence and Avondale, and grandson of Queen Victoria, had been hospitalized for a severe illness, previous to his sudden demise. Now it was rumored the notorious libertine had contracted syphilis and that it had been the disease that had slowly driven him mad. It appeared the disease had taken its ultimate toll on the young royal. Now, there was no way he would ever become king.

I closed the paper and put it away. The train was pulling into Victoria Station. I can not express the joy I felt. I had been gone a long time. Now I was home again. Immediately I hired a hansom cab to take me to Baker Street and our rooms at 221B.

## Epilogue

I watched as you entered our old rooms so quietly, Holmes. I knew that you did not want to startle me. You eased yourself down into your favorite armchair, the comfortable one, and allowed a long sigh to escape your lips. I could not fathom that you were back.

"Holmes, is that you? Holmes! You're back!" I shouted, from the other room. In spite of what my eyes told me I entered our sitting room and stopped in the doorway as if I had seen a ghost.

"Watson, it is so very good to see you again, old fellow," you said, and it appeared you were trying to keep your voice even and unencumbered by the emotion you felt.

"Holmes! I can not believe it!" I blurted, rushing over to you. We shook hands and then embraced. There were tears of joy in my eyes as well as your own.

"I thought you were dead! I looked for you, for your body, for weeks, but it was nowhere to be found," I said whipping away a tear.

"It's a long story, my friend." you replied.

"I can not believe it! It really is you!" I said squeezing your arms, hardly believing you were not some type of ghostly apparition.

"Believe it, good Watson, it is I. I am back!"

I took your hand again and shook it vigorously.

"You know I wrote of your death in a story in *The Strand* last year. It caused such alarm and sadness in the public that . . . Well, Holmes, you should know, you are very much loved."

"Thank you, Watson."

"But what of Moriarty?" I asked.

"Moriarty is dead, Watson. Both of them."

"*Both* of them?"

Then you laughed mildly, "It was quite the three-pipe problem, let me tell you. Some day I must write it up for you for publication—though I am sure no one would believe it. But for now, it is just good to be back home."

"Oh, Holmes, this is wonderful, you are alive! I can not wait to spread the good news."

"Whoa, Watson! If the world thinks me dead, who am I to dissuade them. In fact, this might be just the opportunity we need to wreak havoc with the criminal classes. I for one, will not allow it to pass us by; let's not alert the public to my return just yet. Oh surely, you can tell brother Mycroft—whom I am really keen to visit—and Lestrade and Gregson at the Yard—but as for the general public and the popular press, let them believe for a year or so that I perished at the Reichenbach. It will do them no harm."

"Well, if you say so, Holmes. I am just happy that you are back and apparently in good health. We should celebrate! Shall I have Mrs. Hudson make us a grand dinner?"

"Ah, Watson, yes, how is good Mrs. Hudson? But why put her to toil?" you said, sighing as if indeed all was now right with the world. "No, let us go out for an evening in London. There is that restaurant I've had a mind to try at the Grand Hotel for a long time now. Then perhaps, we can take a brisk walk to visit Mycroft at the Diogenes Club. I've missed that portly fellow, more than you or he could ever know."

"Sure, Holmes, a night on the town sounds fine with me," I said. "I will get my coat and call down for a cab."

You nodded and looked with great satisfaction over our familiar rooms. Mycroft and I had kept them the same as you had left them so long ago; your slipper with the tobacco, your beloved pipes, even the cocaine needle hidden away where you had secreted it from me. I put on my coat and walked over to you, then the downstairs bell rang.

"I say, Holmes, the cab is here. Are you ready?"

"Yes, Watson, let's be off. A fine meal, a good vintage, and I think I can promise you the details of a very strange story, if you have a mind to hear it?"

# The Westphalian Ring

Jeffery Deaver

Former attorney Jeffery Deaver is perhaps best known for his several books about Lincoln Rhyme, a quadriplegic who solves crimes using his computer and the able help of Amelia Sachs. He is noted for his encyclopedic knowledge on a wide variety of subjects as well as his use of various types of forensics, combining them both into plots with several twists and turns along the way. He has been an international bestseller for a decade and his audience increases in size and enthusiasm with each book. Under the pseudonym William Jeffries, he also writes a series featuring John Pellam, a location scout for a movie studio. His most recent novel is *The Twelfth Card.*

**The Charing Cross burglary had** been the most successful of his career.

And, as he was now learning, it would perhaps be the one that would permanently end this vocation. As well as earn him a trip to a fetid cell in Newgate prison. Sitting in his chockablock shop off Great Portland Street, wiry Peter Goodcastle tugged at the tuft of wispy hair above his ear and below his bald head and nodded grimly at his visitor's words, just audible amid the sound of Her Majesty's Public Works' grimy steam hammer breaking up the brick road to repair a water main. "The man you robbed," his uneasy companion continued, "was the benefactor to the Earl of Devon. And has connections of his own throughout. Parliament and Whitehall Street. The queen speaks highly of him."

The forty-four-year-old Goodcastle knew this, and considerably more, about Lord Robert Mayhew, as he did all his burglary victims. He always learned as much as he could about them; good intelligence was yet one more skill that had kept him free from Scotland Yard's scrutiny in the twelve years since he'd returned from the war and begun plying his trade as a thief. He'd sought as much data as he could about Mayhew and learned that he was indeed well regarded in the upper circles of London society and among the royals, including Queen Victoria herself: Still, because of the man's massive wealth and obsession for amassing and hoarding rare jewelry and valuables, Goodcastle assessed the rewards would be worth the risk.

But in this estimate he'd clearly been wrong.

"It's the ring he's upset about. Not the other pieces, certainly not the sovereigns. No, the ring. He's using all his resources to find it. Apparently it was handed down to him by his father, who received it from his father. It's of great personal value to him."

It was, of course, always wiser to filch items to which the

owners had no sentimental attachment, and Goodcastle had decided that the ring fell into such a category because he'd found it sitting in a cheap, unlocked box on Mayhew's dressing-counter, covered by a dozen pieces of worthless costume jewelry and cuff links.

But the thief now concluded that the casual treatment was merely a clever ruse to better protect the precious item—though only from thieves less skilled than Goodcastle, of course; he had inherited the family antiquities business ten years ago and of necessity had become an expert in valuing such items as music boxes, silver, furniture . . . and old jewelry. Standing masked in Mayhew's dressing chamber, he'd frozen in shock as he uncovered the treasure.

Crafted by the famed goldsmith Wilhelm Schroeder of Westphalia early in the century, the ring featured bands of gold alternating with those of silver. Upon the gold were set diamonds; upon the silver, deep-blue sapphires. So astonished and delighted was Goodcastle at this find that he took only it, a diamond cravat pin, a modest broach, and fifty gold guineas, eschewing the many other *objets d'art,* pieces of jewelry, and gold and silver coin cluttering Mayhew's boudoir (another rule of thievery: The more modest the take, the more likely that weeks or months will pass before the victim discovers his loss, if indeed he ever does).

This was what he had hoped had occurred in the Charing Cross burglary. The incident had occurred last Thursday and Goodcastle had seen no reports of the theft in the *Daily Telegraph,* the *Times,* or other papers.

But sadly, such was not the case, his informant—a man well placed within Scotland Yard itself—was now explaining.

"What's more," the man whispered, fiddling with the brim of his homburg and looking out over the cool gray April sky of London, "I've heard that the inspectors have reason to believe that the thief has a connection to the furniture or antiquities trade."

Alarmed, Goodcastle whispered, "How on earth can they have found that? An informant?"

"No, the coppers discovered in Sir Mayhew's apartment certain clues that led them to that conclusion."

"Clues? What clues?" As always, Goodcastle had been meticulous in leaving nothing of his own behind. He'd taken all his tools and articles of clothing with him. And he never carried a single document or other token that would lead the police to him or to Goodcastle Antiquities.

But his confederate now chilled the burglar's blood further with the explanation. "The inspectors found bits of various substances on the ladder and in the bedroom and dressing room. I understand one was a bit of cut and desiccated horsehair, of the sort used in stuffing upholstered divans, sofas, and settees, though Mayhew has none of that kind. Also, they located some wax unique to furniture polishing and of a type frequently bought in bulk by craftsmen who repair, refurbish, or sell wooden pieces. . . . Oh, and they discovered some red brick dust, too. It was on the rungs of the ladder. And the constables could find no similar dust on any of the streets nearby. They think its source was the thief's boots." The man glanced outside the shop at the reddish dust from the pulverized brick covering the sidewalk.

Goodcastle sighed angrily at his own foolishness. He'd replaced the ladder exactly as he'd found it in Mayhew's carriage house, but had not thought to wipe off any materials transferred from his shoes.

The year was 1892 and, as the world hurtled toward the start of a new millennium, one could see astonishing scientific advances everywhere. Electric lighting, petroleum-driven vehicles replacing horse-drawn landaus and carriages, magic-lantern moving pictures . . . It was only natural that Scotland Yard, too, would seek out the latest techniques of science in their pursuit of criminals.

Had he known before the job that the Yard was adopting this approach, he could have taken precautions: washing his hands and scrubbing his boots, for instance.

"Do you know anything more?" he asked his informant.

"No, sir. I'm still in the debtors'-crimes department of the Yard. What I know about this case is only as I have overheard in fragments of conversation. I fear I can't inquire further without arousing suspicion."

"Of course, I understand. Thank you for this."

"You've been very generous to me, sir. What are you going to do?"

"I honestly don't know, my friend. Perhaps I'll have to leave the country for the Continent—France, most likely." He looked his informant over and frowned. "It occurs to me that you should depart. From what you've told me, the authorities might *very* well be on their way here."

"But London is a massive city, sir. Don't you think it's unlikely they will beat a path to your door?"

"I would have believed so if they hadn't displayed such diligence in their examination of Mayhew's apartment. Thinking as we now know they do, if I were a Yard inspector, I would simply get a list of the queen's public works currently underway or ascertain the location of any brick buildings being demolished and compare that with lists of furniture and antiquities dealers in the vicinity. That would indeed lead very near to my door."

"Yes, that would, make sense. . . . Frightful business, this." The man rose, putting his hat on his head. "And what will happen to you if they arrive here, Mr. Goodcastle?"

Arrested and imprisoned, of course, the shopkeeper thought. But he said, "I will hope for the best. Now, you should leave, and I think it wiser if we don't see each other again. There is no reason for you to go to the dock at criminal court as well."

The nervous man leapt up. He shook Goodcastle's hand. "If you do leave the country, sir, I wish you the best of luck."

The burglar gave the informant a handful of sovereigns, a bonus well above what he'd already paid him.

"God bless, sir."

"I could most assuredly use His assistance in this matter." The man left quickly. Goodcastle looked after him, half expecting to see a dozen constables and inspectors surrounding his shop, but all he observed were the public-works laborers in their grimy overalls, carting away the shattered brick from the powerful chisel of the steam hammer, and a few passersby, their black brollies unfurled to fend off the sporadic spring rain.

The shop deserted at the moment and his chief craftsman. Boyle, in the back, at work, the shopkeeper slipped into his office and opened the safe hidden behind a Turkish rug he'd mounted on the wall and further concealed behind a panel of oak constructed to resemble part of the wall.

He extracted a cloth bag containing several pieces from recent burglaries, including the cravat stickpin, the broach, the guineas, and the magnificent Westphalian ring from Mayhew's apartment.

The other items paled in comparison to the German ring. The light from the gas lamp hit the gems and fired a fusillade of beams, white and blue, into the room. The Frenchman to whom Goodcastle had arranged to sell it would pay him three thousand pounds, which meant, of course, that it was worth many times that. Yet Peter Goodcastle reflected that as marvelous as this creation was, it had no particular appeal to him personally. Indeed, once he'd successfully executed a burglary of an abode or museum or shop he cared little for the object he'd made off with, except as it provided income and thus the means to continue his felonious vocation, though even regarding his recompense, he was far from greedy. Why, receiving three thousand sovereigns for the ring, or its true value of perhaps thirty thousand, or merely a handful of crowns wasn't the point. No, the allure to Goodcastle was the act of the theft and the perfection of its execution.

One might wonder how exactly he had chosen this curious line of work. Goodcastle's history revealed some privilege and a fine education. Nor had he rubbed shoulders with any particularly rough crowds at any point in his life. His parents, both long deceased, had been loving, and his brother was, of all things, a parish priest in Yorkshire. He supposed much of the motivation propelling him to steal could be traced to his terrible experiences during the Second Afghan War.

Goodcastle had been a gunner with the famed Royal Horse Artillery, which was among the detachments ordered to stop an enemy force of ghazis intent on attacking the British garrison at Kandahar. On the searingly hot, dusty day of July 27, 1880, the force of 2,500 British and Indian infantry, light cavalry, and artillery met the enemy at Maiwand. What they did not realize until the engagement began, however, was that the Afghans outnumbered them ten to one. From the very beginning the battle went badly, for in addition to overwhelming numbers of fanatical troops, the enemy had not only smoothbores, but Krupp guns. The ghazis pinpointed their weapons with deadly accuracy, and the shells and the blizzard of musket balls and repeater rounds ravaged the British forces.

Manning gun number three, Goodcastle's crew suffered terribly but managed to fire over one hundred founds that day, the barrel of the weapon hot enough to cook flesh—as was proven by the severe burns on his men's arms and hands. Finally, though, the overwhelming force of the enemy prevailed. With a pincer maneuver they closed in. The Afghans seized the English cannon, which the British had no time to spike and destroy, as well as the unit's colors—the first time in the history of the British army such a horror had occurred. As Goodcastle and the others fled in a terrible rout, the ghazis turned the British guns around and augmented the carnage, with the Afghans using the flagpoles from the regiment's own flags as ramming rods for the shot!

A horrific experience, yes—twenty percent of the Horse Artillery was lost, as was sixty percent of the 66th Foot

Regiment—but in some ways the worst was visited upon the surviving soldiers only after their return to England. Goodcastle found himself and his comrades treated as pariahs, branded cowards. The disdain mystified as much as it devastated their souls. But Goodcastle soon learned the reason for it. Prime Minister Disraeli, backed by a number of lords and the wealthy upper class, had been the prime mover in the military intervention in Afghanistan, which served no purpose whatsoever except to rattle sabers at Russia, then making incursions into the area. The loss at Maiwand made many people question the wisdom of such involvement and was an instant political embarrassment. Scapegoats were needed, and who better than the line troops who were present at one of the worst defeats in British history?

One particular nobleman infuriated Goodcastle by certain remarks made, to the press, cruelly bemoaning the shame the troops had brought to the nation and offering not a word of sympathy for those who lost life or limb. The shopkeeper was so livid that he vowed revenge. But he'd had enough of death and violence at Maiwand and would never, in any case, injure an unarmed opponent, so he decided to punish the man in a subtler way. He found his residence, and a month after the improvident remarks the gentleman discovered that a cache of sovereigns—hidden, not very cleverly, in a vase in his office—was considerably diminished. Not long after this, a factory owner reneged on promises of employment to a half-dozen veterans of the Afghan campaign. The industrialist, too, paid dearly—with a painting, which Goodcastle stole from his summer house in Kent and sold, the proceeds divvied up among those who'd been denied work. (Goodcastle's experience in his father's antiquities business stood him in good stead; despite the veterans' concern about the questionable quality of the canvas, done by some Frenchman named Claude Monet, the thief was able to convince an American dealer to pay dearly for the blurred landscape.)

The vindication these thefts represented certainly cheered, him—but Goodcastle finally came to admit that what appealed most deeply wasn't revenge or the exacting of justice but the exhilaration, of the experience itself. . . . Why, a well-executed burglary could be a thing of beauty, as much so as any hand-carved armoire or Fragonard painting or William Tessler gold brooch. He tamed his guilt and began pursuing his new calling with as much vigor and cunning as was displayed by all men, in whatever profession, who were counted successful.

Once he inherited the familial shop on Great Portland Street, he found that he and his workers had unique access to the finest town homes in metropolitan London, as they collected and delivered furniture—perfect hunting grounds for a refined burglar. He was too clever to rob his own clients, of course, but he would listen and observe, learning what he might about these customers' neighbors or acquaintances—any recent valuables they'd purchased, sums of money they'd come into, where they might secrete their most precious objects, when they regularly traveled out of London, the number and nature of grooms and waiting-servants and guard hounds.

A brilliant idea, and perfectly executed on many occasions. As on Thursday last in the apartment of Sir Robert Mayhew.

But it is often not the plan itself that goes awry, but an entirely unforeseen occurrence that derails a venture. In this case, the unexpected cleverness of Scotland Yard inspectors.

Goodcastle now replaced the Westphalian ring and the other items in the safe and counted the cash inside. Five hundred pounds. At his home in London he had another three thousand sovereigns, plus other valuable items he'd stolen recently but hadn't yet found buyers for. In his country house was another five thousand quid. That would set him up easily in the southern provinces of France, where he spent time with Lydia, the raven-haired beauty from Manchester he often traveled with. She could join him there permanently when she'd settled her own business affairs.

But living forever in France? His heart sank at the thought. Peter Goodcastle was an Englishman through and through. For all its sooty air from the dark engines of industry, its snobbish elite, its imperialism, his shabby treatment after Maiwand, he still loved England.

But he would not love ten years in Newgate.

He swung the safe door shut and closed the secret panel, letting the tapestry fall back over it. Caught in furious debate about what he might do, he wandered out into his shop once again, finding comfort in the many fine objects offered for sale.

An hour later, having come to no decision as to a course of action, he was wondering if perhaps he'd been wrong about the prowess of the police. Maybe they had hit on some lucky initial conclusions, but the investigation had stalled and he would escape unscathed. But it was then that a customer walked into the shop and began to browse. The shopkeeper smiled a greeting, then bent over a ledger in concentration, but he continued to keep an eye on the customer, a tall, slim man in a black greatcoat over a similarly shaded morning suit and white shirt. He was carefully examining the clocks and music boxes and walking sticks with the eye of someone intent on buying something and getting good value for his money.

As a thief, Peter Goodcastle had learned to be observant of detail; as a shopkeeper he had come to know customers. He was now struck by a curious fact: The man perused only the wooden items on display, while the inventory consisted of much porcelain, ivory, mother of pearl, pewter, brass, and silver. It had been Goodcastle's experience that a customer desirous of buying a music box, say, would look at all varieties of such items, to assess their value and quality in general, even if his intent was to acquire a wooden one.

Goodcastle then noted something else. The man was subtly running his finger along a crevice in the seam of a music box. So, his interest wasn't in the wood itself but in the wax covering it, a sample of which he captured under his nail.

The "customer" was not that at all, the shopkeeper understood with dismay; he was one of the Scotland Yard inspectors his informant had told him about earlier.

Well, all is not lost yet, Goodcastle reasoned. The wax he used was somewhat rare, due to its price and availability only in commercial quantities, but it was hardly unique; many other furniture and antiquities dealers bought the same substance. This was not any means conclusive evidence of his guilt.

But then the policeman took a fancy to a red overstuffed chair. He sat on it and patted the sides, as if getting a feel for its construction. He sat back and closed his eyes. In horror Goodcastle noted that the man's right hand disappeared out of sight momentarily and subtly plucked a piece of the stuffing-out of the cushion. The substance was desiccated horsehair, which surely would match the piece found in Robert Mayhew's apartment.

The inspector rose and prowled up and down the aisles for some moments longer. Finally he glanced toward the counter. "You are Mr. Goodcastle?"

"I am indeed," the shopkeeper said, for to deny it would merely arouse suspicion at a later time. He wondered if he was about to be arrested on the spot. His heart beat fiercely. "You have a fine shop here." The inspector was attempting to be amiable but Goodcastle detected the coldness of an inquisitor in his eyes.

"Thank you, sir. I should be most glad to assist you." His palms began to sweat and he felt ill within the belly.

"No, thank you. In fact, I must be going."

"Good day. Do return."

"I shall," he said, and walked outside into the brisk spring air. Goodcastle stepped back into the shadows between two armoires and looked out. No!

His worst fears were realized. The man had started across the street, glanced back into the store, and, not seeing the proprietor, knelt, presumably to tie his shoelace. But the lace was perfectly secured, already; the point of this gesture was to pinch up some of the brick dust from the construction currently being undertaken—to match against similar dust Goodcastle had left on the rungs of the ladder or inside the apartment in Charing Cross, he thought in agony. The policeman deposited the dust in a small envelope and then continued on his way, with the jaunty step of a man who has just found a wad of banknotes on the street.

Panic fluttered within Goodcastle. He understood his arrest was imminent. So, it was to be a race to escape the clutch of the law. Every second counted.

He strode to the back door of the shop and opened it. “Boyle,” he called into the back room; where the round, bearded craftsman was putting a coat of lacquer on a Chinese-style bureau. “Mind the shop for an hour or two. I have an urgent errand.”

Bill Sloat was hunched over his cluttered, ale-stained table at the Green Man pub, surrounded by a half-dozen of his cronies, all of them dirty and dim, half-baked Falstaffs, their only earthly reason for being here that they did Sloat’s bidding as quickly and as ruthlessly as be ordered.

The gang man, dressed in an unwashed old sack suit, looked up as Peter Goodcastle approached and pierced a bit of apple with his sharp toadsticker, eating the mealy fruit slowly. He didn’t know much about Goodcastle except that he was one of the few merchants on Great Portland Street who coughed up his weekly ten quid—which he called a “business fee”—and didn’t need a good kick in the arse or slash with a razor to be reminded of it.

The shopkeeper stopped at the table and nodded at the fat man, who muttered, “What’s brought you ’ere, m’lord?”

The title was ironic, of course. Goodcastle didn’t have a drop of noble blood in his limp veins. But in a city where class was the main yardstick by which to measure a man, more so even than money, Goodcastle swam in a very different stream than Sloat. The gang man's East-End upbringing had been grim and he'd never gotten a lick of boost, unlike Goodcastle, whose parents had come from a pleasant part of Surrey. Which was reason enough for Sloat to dislike him, despite the fact he coughed up his quid on time.

"I need to speak to you."

"Do you now? Speak away, mate. Me ear's yours."

"Alone."

Sloat harpooned another piece of apple and chewed it down, then muttered, "Leave us, boys." He grunted toward the ruffians around the table, and, snickering or grumbling, they moved away with their pints.

He looked Goodcastle over carefully. The man was trying his hardest to be a carefree bloke but he clearly had a desperate air about him. Ah, this was tidy! Desperation, and its cousin fear were far better motivators than greed for getting men to do what you wanted. Sloat pointed toward Goodcastle with a blunt finger that ended in a nail darkened from the soot that fell in this part of town like black snow. "You'll come a cropper if, you're 'ere to say you don't 'ave me crust this week."

"No, no, no. I'll have your money. It's not that." A whisper: "Hear me out, Sloat. I'm in trouble. I need to get out of the country quickly, without anybody knowing. I'll pay you handsomely if you can arrange it."

"Oh, me dear friend, whatever I do for you, you'll pay 'andsomely," he said, laughing. "Rest assured of that. What'd you do, mate, to need a 'oliday so quick like?"

"I can't tell you."

"Ey, too shy to share the story with your friend Bill? You cuckold some poor bloke? You owe a sack of lolly to a gambler? . . ." Then Sloat squinted and laughed harshly. "But no, m'lord. You're too bald and too skinny to get a married bird to shag. And your cobblers ain't big enough for you to go wagering more'n a farthing. So, who's after you, mate?"

"I can't say," he whispered.

Sloat sipped more of his bitters. "No matter. Get on with it. It's me dinnertime and I 'ave a 'unger."

Goodcastle looked around and his voice lowered even further. "I need to get into France. Nobody can know. And I need to leave tonight."

"Tonight?" The ruffian shook his head. "Lord love me?'

"I heard you have connections all over the docks."

"Bill's got 'is connections. That 'e does."

"Can you get me onto a cargo ship bound for Marseilles?"

"That's a bleedin' tall order, mate."

"I don't have any choice."

"Well, now, I might be able to." He thought for a moment. "It'll cost you a thousand quid."

"What?"

"It's bloody noon, mate. Look at the clock. It ain't easy, what you're asking, you know. I'll 'ave to run around all day like a chicken without its 'ead. Blimey. Not to mention the risk. The docks're lousy with guards, customs agents, sergeants at arms—thick as fleas, they are. . . . So there you 'ave it, gov'nor. A thousand." He skewered another brown apple wedge and chewed it down.

"All right." Goodcastle said, scowling. The men shook hands.

"I need something up front. 'Ave to paint some palms, understand."

Goodcastle pulled out his money purse and counted out some coin.

"Crikey, guv'nor." Bill laughed. The massive hand reached out and snatched the whole purse. "Thank'ee much. . . . Now, when do I get the rest?"

Goodcastle glanced at his pocket watch. "I can have it by four. Can you make the arrangements by then?"

"Rest assured I can," Sloat said, waving for the barmaid.

"Come by the shop."

Sloat squinted and looked the man over warily. "Maybe you won't own up to what you done, but tell me, mate, just 'ow safe is it to be meetin' you?"

The shopkeeper gave a grim laugh. "You've heard the expression 'giving somebody a taste of their own medicine'?"

"I 'ave, sure."

"Well, that's what I'm going to do. Don't worry. I know how to make sure we're alone."

Goodcastle sighed once more and then left the Green Man.

Sloat watched him leave, thinking, *A thousand quid for a few hours' work.*

Desperation, he thought, is just plain bloody beautiful.

At five minutes to four that afternoon, Peter Goodcastle was uneasily awaiting Bill Sloat's arrival.

While he'd made his arrangements to evade the law, Goodcastle had kept up the appearance of going through his business as usual. But he'd continued to observe the street outside. Sure enough, he'd noted several plain-clothed detectives standing well back in the shadows. They pretended to be watching the construction work on the street, but in fact it was obvious that their attention was mostly on Goodcastle and the store.

The shopkeeper now put his plan into action. He summoned Boyle and one of the men he regularly used for transporting furniture to and from clients' houses. Purposely acting suspiciously, like an actor in a one-shilling melodrama, Goodcastle slipped the young deliveryman a paper-wrapped package, which contained a music box. He gave instructions to take it to Goodcastle's own house as quickly as possible. Witnessing the apparently furtive mission, and probably assuming that the box contained loot or damning evidence, one of the detectives started after the young man as soon as he left the shop.

Goodcastle then dismissed Boyle for the day and gave him a similar package, with instructions to take it home with him and make sure the music box mechanism was dependable. The remaining detective observed Boyle leave the shop, clutching the parcel, and, after a moment of debate, appeared to decide it was better to pursue this potential source of evidence rather than remain at his station.

Goodcastle carefully perused the street and saw no more detectives. The workers had left and the avenue was deserted except for a married couple, who paused at the front window, then stepped inside: As they looked over the armoires, Goodcastle told them he would return in a moment and, with another glance outside into the empty street, stole into the office, closing the door behind him. He sat at his desk, lifted aside the Turkish rug, and opened the secret panel and then the safe. He was just reaching inside when he was aware of a breeze wafting on his face, and he knew the door to the office had been opened.

Goodcastle leapt up, crying, "No!" He was staring at the husband of the couple who'd just walked into the shop. He was holding a large Webley pistol.

"Lord in heaven!" Goodcastle said, gasping. "You've come to rob me!"

"No, sir, I'm here to arrest you," he said calmly. "Pray don't move. I don't wish to harm you. But I will if you give me no choice." He then blew into a police whistle, which uttered a shrill tone.

A moment later, beyond him, Goodcastle could see the door burst open, and in ran two Scotland Yard inspectors in plain clothes, as well as two uniformed constables. The woman—who'd obviously been posing as the first inspector's wife—waved them toward the office. "The safe is back there," she called.

"Capital!" called one inspector—the lean, dark man who'd been in the store earlier, masquerading as a customer. His fellow officer, wearing a bowler, was dressed similarly, a greatcoat over a morning suit, though this man differed in his physique, being taller and quite pale, with a shock of flaxen hair. Both policemen took the shopkeeper by the arms and led him out into the store proper. "What's the meaning of this?" Goodcastle blustered. The white-faced inspector chuckled. "I warrant you know right well."

They searched him and, finding no weapons, unhanded him. The inspector who'd entered with the woman on his arm replaced his Webley with a notebook, in which he began taking down evidence. They dismissed the woman with effusive thanks and she explained that she'd be back at the police precinct station house if they needed her further. "What is this about?" Goodcastle demanded. The pale officer deferred to the lean one, apparently a chief inspector, who looked Goodcastle over carefully. "So you're the man who burglarized Robert Mayhew's apartment."

"Who? I swear I don't know what you're speaking of."

"Please, Mr. Goodcastle, don't malign our intelligence. You saw me in your shop earlier, did you not?"

"Yes."

"During that visit here I managed to collect a sample of furniture wax from several wooden pieces. The substance is identical to the wax we found traces of in Lord Mayhew's dressing chamber—a material that neither he nor his servants had ever been in contact with. We found, too, a horse hair that matched one that I extracted from your chair."

"I'm at a loss—"

"And what do you have to say about the fact that the brick dust in front of your store is the same as that which we found on the rungs of the ladder used to break into Lord Mayhew's first floor? Don't deny you are the thief."

"Of course I deny it. This is absurd!"

"Go search the safe," the chief inspector said to a constable, nodding toward the back office. He then explained, "When I was here earlier I tried to ascertain where you might have a hiding place for your ill-gotten gains. But your shop boasts far too much inventory and too many nooks and crannies to locate what we are seeking without searching for a week. So we stationed those two detectives outside on the street to make you believe we were about to arrest you. As we had anticipated, you led them off. . . . I assume in pursuit of two parcels of no evidentiary value whatsoever."

"Those deliveries a moment ago?" Goodcastle protested. "I sent one music box home for myself to work on tonight. Another, my man was taking with him to do the same."

"So you say. But I suspect you're prevaricating."

"This is most uncalled for. I—"

"Please, allow me to finish. When you sent our men on a goose chase, that told us that your flight was imminent, so my colleague here and a typist from the precinct house came in as customers, as they'd been waiting to do for several hours." He turned to the policeman who'd played the husband and added, "Capital job, by the way."

"Most kind of you."

The chief inspector turned back to Goodcastle. "You were lulled to incaution by the domestic couple and, prodded by the urgency of escape, you were kind enough to lead us directly to the safe."

"I am, I swear, merely an antiques merchant and craftsman."

The pale detective chuckled again, while the "husband" continued to take everything down in his notebook.

"Sir," the constable said as he stepped from the office. "A problem."

"Is the safe locked?"

"No, sir. The door was open. The trouble is that the ring is not inside."

"Ring?" Goodcastle asked.

"What is inside?" the lean officer asked, ignoring the shopkeeper.

"Money, sir. That's all. About five hundred pounds."

"Are they guineas?"

"No, sir. Varied currency, but notes mostly. No gold."

"It's the receptacle for my receipts, sirs. Most merchants have one." Frowning, the head detective looked into the office beyond them and started to speak. But at that moment the door opened again and in strode Bill Sloat. The ruffian took one look at the constables and inspectors and started to flee. He was seized by the two coppers and dragged back inside.

"Ah, look who we have here, Mad Bill Sloat," said the bowlered inspector, lifting an eyebrow in his pale forehead. "We know about you, oh yes. So you're in cahoots with Goodcastle, are you?"

"I am not, copper."

"Keep a respectable tone in your mouth."

Goodcastle said uneasily, "By the queen, sir, Mr. Sloat has done nothing wrong. He comes in sometimes to view my wares. I'm sure that's all he's doing here today."

The chief inspector turned to him. "I sense you're holding back, Goodcastle. Tell us what is on your mind."

"Nothing, truly."

"You'll be in the dock sooner than we have planned for you, sir, if you do not tell us all."

"Keep your flamin' gob shut," Sloat muttered.

"Quiet, you," a constable growled.

"Go on, Goodcastle. Tell us."

The shopkeeper swallowed. He looked away from Sloat. "That man is the terror of Great Portland Street! He extorts money and goods from us and threatens to sic his scoundrels from the Green Man on us if we don't pay. He comes in every Saturday and demands his tithe."

"We've heard rumors of such," the flaxen-haired detective said. The chief inspector looked closely at Goodcastle. "Yet today is Monday, not Saturday. Why is he here now?"

The villain roared at the shopkeeper, "I'm warning you—"

"One more word and it'll be the Black Maria for you, Sloat."

Goodcastle took a breath and continued. "Last Thursday he surprised me in my shop at eight A.M. I hadn't opened the doors yet, but had come in early because I had finished work on several pieces late the night before and I wanted to wax and polish them before I admitted any customers."

The chief detective nodded, considering this. To his colleagues he said, "The day of the burglary. And not long before it. Pray continue, Goodcastle."

"He made me open the door. He browsed among the music boxes and looked them over carefully. He selected that one right there." He pointed to a rosewood box sitting on the counter. "And he said that in addition to his extortion sterling, this week he was taking that box. But more, I was to build a false compartment in the bottom. It had to be so clever that no one examining the box, however carefully, could find what he'd hidden in there." He showed them the box and the compartment—which he'd just finished crafting a half-hour before.

"Did he say what he intended to hide?" the senior Yarder asked.

"He said some items of jewelry and gold coins."

The villain roared, " 'E's a flamin' liar and a brigand and when—"

"Quiet, you," the constable said, and pushed the big man down roughly into a chair.

"Did he say where he'd acquired them?"

"No, sir."

The detectives eyed one another. "So Sloat came here,"

the senior man offered, "selected the box and got wax on his fingers. The horsehair and brick dust attached themselves to him as well. The timing would allow for his proceeding directly to Lord Mayhew's apartment, where he left those substances."

"It makes sense," the third offered, looking up from his notebook.

The pale detective asked, "And you have no criminal past, Goodcastle? Don't lie. It's easily verified."

"No, sir. I swear. I'm a simple merchant—if I've done anything wrong, it was in not reporting Sloat's extortion. But none of us along Great Portland Street dared. We're too frightened of him. . . . Forgive me, sirs, it's true—I did send the police across the street on a merry chase. I had no idea why they were present but they seemed like detectives to me. I had to get them away from here. Mr. Sloat was due momentarily and I knew that if he noticed the law when he arrived he would think I'd summoned them and might beat me. Or worse."

"Search him," the pale-visaged detective ordered, nodding toward Sloat.

They pulled some coins, a cigar, and a cosh from his pockets, as well as the money purse. The white-faced detective looked inside. "Guineas! Just like the sort that Lord Mayhew lost."

The Royal Mint had stopped producing gold guineas, worth a pound and a shilling, in 1813. They were still legal tender, of course, but were rare. This was why Goodcastle had not taken many from Lord Mayhew's; spending them could draw attention to you.

"That purse is not mine!" Sloat raged. "It's 'is!"

"That's a lie!" Goodcastle cried. "Why, if it were mine, why would you have it? I have mine right here." He displayed a cheap leather pouch containing a few quid, crowns, and pence.

The constable holding the pouch then frowned. "Sir, something else is inside—hidden in a pocket in the bottom," He extracted two items and displayed them. "The cravat pin, like the one Sir Mayhew reported missing. Most surely the same one. And the ruby broach, also taken!"

"I'm innocent, I tell you! Goodcastle 'ere come to me with a story of 'aving to get his arse to France tonight."

"And what was the motive for this hasty retreat?" the inscribing detective asked.

" 'E didn't say," Sloat admitted.

"Convenient," the pale detective said wryly. It was clear that they didn't believe the ruffian.

Goodcastle tried to keep a curious and cautious expression on his face. In fact, he was wracked by anxiety, wondering if he could pull off this little theater. He'd had to act fast to save himself. As he'd told Sloat, he was going to treat Scotland Yard to a taste of their own medicine—but not to forsake his homeland and flee to France, which he'd decided he could never do. No, he'd use evidence to connect Sloat to the burglary—through a fabricated story about the music box with the hidden compartment on the one hand and, on the other, making certain Sloat took the incriminating money purse from him at the Green Man. But would the police accept the theory?

It seemed, for a moment, that they would. But just as Goodcastle began to breathe somewhat easier, the chief inspector turned quickly to him. "Please, sir. Your hands?"

"I beg your pardon?"

"I will examine your hands. One final test in this curious case. I am not yet completely convinced the facts are as they seem."

"Well, yes, of course."

Goodcastle held his palms out, struggling to keep them steady. The detective looked them over. Then he looked up, frowning. After a moment he lowered his head again and smelled Goodcastle's palm. He said to Sloat, "Now yours."

"Listen 'ere, coppers, you bloody well ain't—" But the constables grabbed the man's beefy hands and lifted them for the chief inspector, who again examined and sniffed. He nodded and then turned slowly to Goodcastle. "You see, the Westphalian ring is of a unique design—silver and gold, unusual in metal craft. Gold, as you know, needs no polishing to prevent tarnish. But silver does. Mayhew told us that the ring had been recently cleaned with a particular type of silver polish that is scented with perfume derived from the lily flower. It is quite expensive, but well within Mayhew's means to buy liberally for his staff to use." Then he turned toward Sloat. "Your hands emit a marked scent of lily and display some small traces of the off-white cream that is the base for the polish, while Mr. Goodcastle's do not. There's no doubt, sir. You are the thief."

"No, no, I am wronged!"

"You may make your case before the judges, sir," the light-haired policeman said, "from the dock." Goodcastle's heart pounded fiercely from this final matter about the polish. He'd nearly overlooked it, but had decided that if the detectives were now so diligent in their use of these minuscule clues to link people to the sites of crimes, Goodcastle needed to be just as conscientious. If a burglar could leave evidence during the commission of a felony, he might also pick up something there that might prove equally damning. He thought back to the ring and Mayhew's dressing chamber. He recalled that he'd recognized the scent of Covey's Tarnish-Preventing Cream in the velvet-lined boxes. On the way to the Green Man, he'd bought some and slathered it liberally on his palm. Shaking Sloat's hand to seal their agreement had transferred some to the ruffian's skin. Before returning to his shop, Goodcastle had scrubbed his own hands clean, with lye soap and discarded the remaining polish.

"Cooperate, sir, and it will go easier on you," the hatted detective said to Sloat.

"I'm the victim of a plot!"

"Yes, yes, do you think you're the first brigand ever to suggest that? Where is the ring?"

"I don't know anything of any ring."

"Perhaps we'll find it when we search your house."

No, Goodcastle thought, they wouldn't find the ring. But they would find a half-dozen other pieces stolen by Goodcastle in various burglaries over the past year. Just as they'd find a crude diagram of Robert Mayhew's apartment—drawn with Sloat's own pencil on a sheet of Sloat's own paper. The burglar had planted them there this afternoon after he'd met with the ruffian at the Green Man (taking exemplary care this time to leave no traces that would link him to that incursion).

"Put him in darbies and take him to the hoosegow," the pale officer ordered.

The constables slapped irons on the man's wrists and took him away, struggling.

Goodcastle shook his head. "Do they always protest their innocence so vehemently?"

"Usually. It's only in court they turn sorrowful. And that's when the judge is about to pass sentence," said the pale officer. He added, "Forgive us, Mr. Goodcastle, you've been most patient. But you can understand the confusion."

"Of course. I'm pleased that that fellow is finally off the streets. I regret that I didn't have the courage to come forward before."

"A respectable gentleman such as yourself," offered the detective with the notebook, "can be easily excused on such a count, being alien to the world of crime."

"Well, my thanks to you and all the rest at Scotland Yard," he said to the chief inspector.

But the man gave a laugh and turned toward the pale detective, who said, "Oh, you're under a misapprehension, Mr. Goodcastle. Only I am with the Yard. My companions here are private consultants retained by Sir Robert Mayhew. I am Inspector Gregson." He then nodded toward the dark, slim man Goodcastle had taken to be the chief detective. "And this is the consulting detective Sherlock Holmes."

"A pleasure," Goodcastle said. "I believe I've heard of you."

"Indeed," Holmes replied, as if a shopkeeper should most certainly have heard of him. The man seemed like a don at King's College, brilliant but constantly distracted by complex thoughts.

Gregson nodded toward the man who had portrayed the husband and introduced Dr. John Watson, who shook

Goodcastle's hand cordially and asked a few more questions about Bill Sloat, the answers to which he jotted into his notebook. He explained that he often wrote accounts of the more interesting cases he and Holmes were involved in.

"Yes, of course. That's where I've heard of you both. The accounts are often published in the newspapers. So that is you! An honor."

"Ah," said Holmes, managing to summon a look simultaneously prideful and modest.

Goodcastle asked, "Will this be one adventure you write about?"

"No, it will not," Holmes said. He seemed piqued—perhaps because, even though a villain was under arrest, his reading of the clues had led to the wrong suspect, at least in his perception of the affair.

"But where, Holmes, is the ring?" Gregson asked.

"I suspect that that Sloat has already disposed of it."

"Why do you think so?" Watson asked.

"Elementary," Holmes said. "He had the other ill-gotten, gains on his person. Why not the ring, too? I deduced from his clothing that the blackguard lives in the company of a woman; both the jacket and trousers of his sack suit had been darned with identical stitching, though in places that wear through at different rates—the elbow and the inseam—suggesting that they were repaired by the same person, though at different times. The conclusion must be that a wife or female companion did the work. His request of Mr. Goodcastle here regarding the secret compartment makes clear that he does not trust people, so he would be loathe to leave the ring in an abode where another person dwells and would have kept it on him until the special music box was ready. Since he doesn't have the ring on him any longer, we can conclude that he has disposed of it. And since he has no significant sums of cash with him, other than Lord Mayhew's guineas, we can conclude that he used the ring to settle an old debt."

"Where did he dispose of it, do you think?"

"Alas, I'm afraid that the piece is on its way overseas."

When the others glanced at each other quizzically, Holmes continued, "You observed, of course, the fish scales on Sloat's cuffs?"

"Well," said Gregson, "I'm afraid I, for one, did not."

"Nor I," Watson said.

"They were scales unique to saltwater fish."

"You knew that, Holmes?" the Yarder asked.

"Data, data, data," the man replied petulantly. "In this line of work, Gregson, one must fill one's mind with facts, but only those that may perchance bear on a criminal venture. Now, the scales could mean nothing more than that he'd walked past a fishmonger. But you certainly observed the streaks of pitch on his shoes, did you not?" When the others merely shook their heads, Holmes sighed, his visage filled with exasperation. He continued. "You gentlemen know the expression, 'devil to pay.' "

"Of course."

"The figurative meaning is 'to suffer consequences.' But most people don't know its literal derivation. The phrase has nothing to do with handing money over to fallen angels. The devil is that portion of a sailing vessel between the inner and outer hulls. To 'pay' it is to paint the outer seams with hot pitch to make them watertight. Obviously climbing between the hulls is an unpleasant and dangerous job, usually meted out as punishment to errant sailors. The pitch used is unique and found only around the waterfront. Because of the fish scales and the tar, I knew that Sloat had been to the docks within the past several hours. The most logical conclusion is that he owed the captain of a smuggling vessel some significant sum of money and traded the ring to him in exchange for the extinguishing of the debt." Holmes shook his head. "The ring could be on any one of dozens of ships and all of them out of our jurisdiction. I'm afraid Lord Mayhew will have to look to Lloyd's to make himself whole in this matter. In the future, let us hope, he will use better locks upon his windows and doors."

"Brilliant deductions," said Gregson of the white face and flaxen hair.

Indeed it was, Goodcastle noted, despite the fact that it was completely incorrect.

Holmes pulled a cherrywood pipe from his pocket, lit it, and started for the door. He paused, glanced around the shop, and turned back to Goodcastle, his eyebrow cocked. "Sir, perhaps you can help me in another matter. Since you deal in music boxes . . . I have been on the lookout for a particular box a client of mine once expressed interest in. It is in the shape of an octagon on a gold base. It plays a melody from 'The Magic Flute' by Mozart and was made by Edward Gastwold in York in eighteen fifty-six. The box is rosewood and is inlaid with ivory."

Goodcastle thought for a moment. "I'm sorry to say that I'm not familiar with that particular piece. I've never been fortunate enough to come upon any of Gastwold's creations, though I hear they're marvelous. I certainly can make inquiries. If they bear fruit, shall I contact you?"

"Please." Holmes handed the shopkeeper a card. "My client would pay dearly for the box itself or would offer a handsome finder's charge to anyone who could direct him toward the owner." Goodcastle put the card in a small box next to his till, reflecting: What a clever man this Holmes is. The Gastwold music box was not well known; for years it had been in the possession of the man who owned the massive Southland Metalworks Ltd. in Sussex. In doing his research into Sir Mayhew's life in preparation for the burglary, he'd learned that Mayhew was a major stockholder in Southland.

Holmes had asked a simple, seemingly innocent question, in hopes that Goodcastle would blurt out that, indeed, he knew of the box and its owner.

Which would have suggested that he might have delved, however subtly, into Mayhew's affairs.

Surely Holmes had no such client. Yet still he knew of the box. Apparently he'd taught himself about music boxes just in case facts about such items came in useful—exactly as Goodcastle did when preparing for his burglaries. ("Data, data, data," Holmes had said; how true!)

Goodcastle said to them, "Well, good day, gentlemen."

"And to you, sir. Our apologies." It was the amiable Dr. Watson who offered this.

"Not at all," Goodcastle assured them. "I would rather have an aggressive constabulary protecting us from the likes of Bill Sloat than one that is remiss and allows us to fall prey to such blackguards."

And, he added to himself, I would most certainly have a

constabulary that is candid in how they pursue wrong-doers, allowing me the chance to improve the means of practicing my own craft.

After the men had left, Goodcastle went to the cupboard, poured a glass of sherry. He paused at one of the jewelry cases in the front of the store and glanced at a bowl containing cheap cuff links and shirt studs. Beside it was a sign that said, Any Two Items for £1. He checked to make certain the Westphalian ring was discreetly hidden beneath the tin and copper jewelry, where it would remain until he met with his French buyer tomorrow.

Goodcastle then counted his daily receipts and, as he did every night, carefully ordered and dusted the counter so that it was ready for his customers in the morning.

# The Hit

Robert S. Levinson

Robert S. Levinson is the best-selling author of the Neil Gulliver and Stevie Marriner series of mystery-thriller novels, including *Hot Paint, The John Lennon Affair, The James Dean Affair, and The Elvis and Marilyn Affair,* which has been optioned for development as a film and a possible television series. His most recent novel, *Ask a Dead Man,* has received a coveted starred review from *Publishers Weekly:* "A novel that not only stands alone but stands tall. Writing with considerable invention, grace and energy, [Levinson] tells an intricate and emotionally potent tale of murder and double cross." Presumably Hollywood will turn it into a good movie soon.

**First things first, double-checking to** make sure it was Dickinson he had found, had not traveled two thousand miles to score the wrong woman again. Another miscue and he'd be off-track for keeps, they'd said as much, in a way that told him check and be sure he was current on his life insurance premium.

He got directions to the sheriff's substation from the mush-faced gas jockey at Phillip's Garage and Self-Serve Fill-Up, who checked him out with the curious, brow-squeezed look the question always drew, but didn't ask why a stranger straight off the freeway had need for the law. They never asked, like *curiosity* wasn't a word in their dictionary. He was as sure of that as he was that they would never think to connect his question to the hit, once the hit was history and he was long gone, which also sat fine with him.

*Out of sight, out of mind.*

Words to live by.

The substation was a half mile down Main Street, to the overhanging stoplight, a half block north after turning left, a freestanding single-story brick building not about the size of a McDonald's. He wouldn't have been surprised to find the hand-painted RIPLEY COUNTY SHERIFF'S SUBSTATION sign hanging above the double-door entrance also proclaiming: "Millions Upon Millions of Criminals Caught."

It was almost nine o'clock, the quarter moon lost behind layers of rain-fat black clouds. He eased the boosted SUV into an open diagonal spot and didn't bother chirping the door locks.

The only deputy around was at the reception desk, half-asleep, his chair tipped back against the wall, a *Sharp-shooters Monthly* on his lap. The elaborately-carved name plate by the log-in sheet said he was Bill Grange. His eyes snapped open to the clang of the service bell and did a bewildered zigzag to check his whereabouts. Satisfied, Grange adjusted his seat upright, drew an indifferent smile across his sun-baked baby face, and wordlessly wondered the reason for his visitor.

"Franklin Bachardy," he said. He drew an ID case from an inside jacket pocket, flipped it open, and proffered it to the deputy sheriff.

Grange relocated a pair of wire-framed lenses from the desk to his lineman's nose and pushed them up tight against the break in his unruly auburn eyebrows. "FBI, huh?" The man calling himself Franklin Bachardy nodded agreement. The deputy said, "I once thought serious about going FBI. You guys have the best-looking badges ever." Bachardy accepted the ID case back and returned it to his pocket. "The knock-knock joke got in the way."

"The knock-knock joke?"

"As in, *Knock-knock, who's there?* Go ahead."

"Knock-knock, who's there?"

"The stork and guess what I brung with me." The deputy sheriff wheezed a sigh. "Lesson in that, Agent Bachardy, is never knock-knock up your girlfriend before you got yourself a career set in stone." He shook his head. "So, what brings you way out here to the Nowhere Capital of the World?"

"Tracking somebody." The man calling himself Franklin Bachardy dipped into another pocket and this time pulled out a five-by-seven color photograph. "She look like anyone you know, Deputy? We have reason to believe she's resident here in Ripley."

"Believe it or not."

"What?"

"What people usually add on the first time or two they say *Ripley*. That was the name of some comic strip some guy named Ripley did a hundred years ago, but folks still remember it from somewhere—believe it or not." The deputy laughed at his joke. Franklin Bachardy contributed a friendly squeak of a grunt. "Not how this got it's name though. Got it from a land speculator who squatted out here in what was then wasteland waiting to happen and is still a leading contender for the title . . . What'd you say her name is?"

"Didn't. From the sound, though, you can put one to her."

"Two names," Grange said. "A first name and a last name. That's Lizzie Morrow, as sure as God made little green apples." His head bobbed in vigorous agreement. "You are not going to tell me Lizzie committed some crime, are you? Or, anything that'll cost Ripley probably the best damn church organist we ever had . . . Not the only organ hear tell she's damn good around, but you didn't hear it from me."

Bachardy thinking, *Who's this deputy think he is, Jay Leno? Letterman?* Popping an appreciative laugh and saying, "Which church might that be?"

Grange gave him the name and, after checking the wall clock, directions. "You're of a mind, the nightly prayer meeting shouldn't be over for another half to three-quarters. Reverend Kiel, he really knows how to give the Bible a good workout . . . You never did say what you're wanting with Lizzie."

"That's right," Bachardy said. He put a finger to his lips and winked.

The deputy made like he understood.

* * *

Blessed Samaritan was in the middle of Wellington Road, a well-lit block full of nondescript two-story tract homes of recent vintage, their lawns neatly-groomed, flower beds and hedges well-tended; unblemished white picket fences. The moon playing peek-a-boo with the rain clouds, making a dance of the shadows cruising the neighborhood.

Bachardy caught parking across from the church, about a half block up the street, close enough to hear the drifting sound of the organ and mixed voices on undecipherable lyrics to a hymn he remembered from when he was growing up, but couldn't immediately give a name. He stayed behind the wheel, aiming smoke out the window while he waited for the prayer meeting to end, mentally reviewing the options he had with the Dickinson woman. A.k.a. Lizzie Morrow. Soon to be the late Ellen Dickinson a.k.a. Lizzie Morrow.

He didn't have to wait long. He was chain-smoking his fourth when the organ quit abruptly and, after a few minutes, the church doors swung open and people began passing onto the cement portico, engaging in random chatter punctuated here and there by laughs as they moseyed down the broad steps to their cars or away on foot.

The one who had to be Dickinson was among the last, lingering just outside the entrance with someone Bachardy guessed to be the minister, Reverend Kiel. He was dressed in black and sporting a clerical collar, a Bible tucked under his arm, his hands clasping hers. About her age. Mid-thirties. Almost as pretty as Dickinson. Whatever the minister was telling her drew a nod of acknowledgment and a reluctant smile in the tricky light. He released his grip and studied Dickinson as she hurried down the steps, then retreated inside the church.

Dickinson beeped open the relatively new red Mustang parked a few cars down from the Toyota he'd paid cash for at the chop shop. He started the ignition and gave her half a block before switching on the lights and pulling after her. Five minutes and two-and-a-half miles later, she turned onto Buckingham Road, a pretty-as-a-picture street not much different from Wellington Road. She curved left into the driveway eight homes up as the garage door rose. A minute later, it closed behind her.

With no idea who else might be inside, Bachardy called it quits for the night.

Tomorrow would be soon enough to take her out.

The day after, it came to that.

He'd find a motel and phone to let them know it was Dickinson, for real this time. They wouldn't care if it was done tomorrow or the day after, just so it got done, clean and simple or down and dirty. Either way. Just so it got done. What he was paid for, the *what*, not the *how*.

The rap-a-tap-tap on the door woke him and had become a louder buhm-badda-boom-boom by the time he got to spy hole, figuring to see it was housekeeping ignoring the Do Not Disturb hanging from the knob and ready to shout them a piece of his mind, even though the bedside clock was reading ten, three hours past the time he'd requested for his wake up call. No matter which direction he was traveling or for how long, jet lag always did that to Bachardy.

It was the deputy, though, Grange, smiling back at the peep like he knew he was being checked out. He retreated a step to better show off the two paper cups of Starbucks.

Bachardy opened the door the length of the chain and gave Grange a questioning look.

"Morning, Agent Bachardy. You had a block on your phone or I would've called ahead," Grange said. "Besides, the snack room coffee machine here at Ida's Cozy Motel delivers somebody's idea of a joke, where what I got here for us is the kind of he-man caffeine that could jump start a cadaver."

"Something else?"

The deputy's head did a combination nod and shake. "To do with Lizzie Morrow. Something I figured you should know."

Bachardy slipped the chain.

Grange settled at the desk, blew on his coffee and checked out the room while Bachardy threw on his robe, grabbed for a cigarette, lit up, and came after the other cup of Starbucks, Grange telling him, "Watch those first sips. Hot as blazes."

Bachardy removed the lid and excused himself to the bathroom. Back in a few moments to say, "My little trick. Add some tap water, just enough to cool, and no worry about burning your mouth." He settled on the edge of the bed, the side closest to Grange, his .38 under the pillow and an easy reach. There was something discomforting about a lawman showing up unannounced this time of morning. Any time. "What's this you have to tell me about Lizzie Morrow?"

Grange adjusted his wire-frames on his face. "She knows you're on her case."

"How's that?"

"Not you, exactly. Somebody. She called the station last night, sounding scared, saying how she was certain she'd been followed home from prayer meeting. Looking out her window and telling me she had a feeling whoever it was now was outside, lurking in the dark. Lizzie's never been one to see the sky falling, so I played along with her. Went on over to her place and made like I was checking after her safety, all the while knowing it was you."

"You didn't say anything, did you? Tell her?"

Grange gave him a *What do you take me for?* kind of look. "I'm not one to get in front of a federal operation, no sir, not me, Agent Bachardy." He gentled off the lid of the cup and finger-tested the coffee. Took a sip; then another. "Told Lizzie to try and have a decent night's sleep and we'd be running some patrols. Call for any reason, which she did this morning—sounding tired—to say she spent half the night at the window, but it must've been her imagination playing tricks, and thank you." A gulp of coffee, which he used as a mouth rinse. "With all due respect, if it were up to me, I'd think seriously about getting on with whatever business brought you here after her."

"Does Ms. Morrow share her home with anyone?"

"Nothing on two feet, at least, nothing permanent, and nobody inclined to stay on to sunrise, if you catch my drift. A giant mutt she found wandering the street, deaf and a mute, what loves to be scratched behind the ear. Two Siamese cats what live in their own world, come and go as they please."

"You sound like you know her well."

"Never after sunrise," the deputy said.

"How about now? You tag along with me?" The suggestion seemed to please the deputy. "Her seeing a familiar face at the front door would ease any alarm she might still be feeling about last night. Make my job that much easier."

Grange gave Bachardy a thumbs up. "How about this? I

call her to say how I'm dropping by to check up on her welfare?" He was already reaching after his cell phone. "Make sure she'll be there waiting for us."

Bachardy answered with his own thumbs up.

Grange, so pleasant, so eager, so close to being dead Bachardy almost wished the option was to let the deputy live, but he'd learned years ago, the hard way, trial and error, that leaving no witnesses was the only way to guarantee less opportunity to be identified, caught and convicted. Poor Geller. Geller always came to mind at times like these. Geller the one who taught him caution, then went and blew it himself over some woman, not so much as a looker, as someone who reminded him of his sainted mother. Not that it would have made a difference, but nothing about Ellen Dickinson a.k.a. Lizzie Morrow spelled m-o-t-h-e-r. Under different circumstances, he would have enjoyed riding the merry-go-round with Dickinson. Might even have stayed past sunrise.

Something made Bachardy flash on the gas jockey from last night. The look the gas jockey had given him. *Out of sight, out of mind.* No reason to think it would go any differently this time. Except—the feeling. He'd had the feeling once or twice before and he'd played off it: *Better safe than sorry.* No chance his getting directions to the sheriff's substation would come back to haunt him if he deep fried the gas jockey. The lesson of Geller. So, okay. First things-first: Dickinson. And second-things-second: The deputy sheriff. Then, third, his farewell to this hiccup of a town: The gas jockey.

"Done," Grange said, snapping the cell closed. "She's putting the pot on to go with her gingerbread muffins, says she may be out back in the garden pruning her roses, so the door'll be unlocked and to just barge right in. How's that for easy, Agent Bachardy?"

"I'd say you're in for some special recognition, Deputy."

"Suits me fine. This business has me thinking I might yet try out for the FBI. My knock-knock joke nowhere around to point me otherwise anymore, us gone our separate ways and that badge, still a real winner. You think, if I do—apply—you might sign off on me?"

"Count on me for that," Bachardy said.

Grange banged out notes with the knocker, a second and third time, before there was the clacking sound of the door handle depressing and the door swung open. Instead of Ellen Dickinson, Bachardy found himself staring back at Reverend Kiel from last night. If there'd been any question at all about who he was, Kiel's clerical collar resolved that. He was better-looking in daylight, except for two rows of canary-colored teeth that formed a welcoming smile for Grange. The smile surrendered to curiosity when he realized Grange was not alone.

"Lizzie didn't mention you were bringing a friend, Billy."

Grange tossed his palms into an oh yeah gesture. "Sure there's enough coffee in the pot and muffins to go around, wouldn't you say, Jerry?"

"Lizzie's never been one to prepare for less than an army," the minister agreed, and both men laughed. "Come in, come in, come in, Mr.—?"

"Bachardy." He took Reverend Kiel's outstretched hand, large and calloused, not what he would have figured for a minister. "Franklin Bachardy." A solid hold, a hearty pump that Kiel seemed almost reluctant to quit.

"Franklin, what a wonderfully old-fashioned name. It fits you, Franklin. It fits you." The minister stepped aside. He ushered Bachardy and Grange inside; closed and locked the door behind them. "Two steps and a right turn gets you to the living room, Franklin. The couch, any chair will do. Lizze likes that one"—pointing—"for herself. Says it's best for her back, but it looks gosh darn uncomfortable to me. To you, too, Billy?"

"Looks like it gives more backaches than it cures, Jerry. You fellas go on. I'll go on out back and fetch her."

"Remind her to leave the fresh cuts out for now, Billy." The minister settled in the chair across the coffee table from the one Bachardy had chosen. "They inspire my asthma when they're fresh cut," he said, ruefully. "Not only roses. How's your respiratory system, Franklin? You one of the lucky ones don't know what allergies are all about?"

"Some hay fever now and then," Bachardy said, struggling to find a comfortable position, crossing one leg over the other; patting himself like he was after his cigarettes, but actually needing a comfort feel of the .38 packed under his left arm; thinking how he now had to consider popping the minister if he was going to bring off this hit at all, right now. Three scores here, the gas jockey on his way out of town—four pops where he was only being paid for one, the woman, Ellen Dickinson a.k.a. Lizzie Morrow. Maybe wait for a better time? he thought, at once answering himself: *No. Get it over and done with. Scram the town. Let the clients know. The extra pops no charge, with my compliments. An investment in my own survival. Get the clients off my back once and for all. Collect the balance due and then maybe a couple months R&R, the* QE2 *cruise I've been thinking about, or maybe just to Hawaii.*

Bachardy found the pack. He lit up. Pushed a jet stream at the ceiling. Gave his thigh an anxious rub, psyched out the room for a game plan that would let him take care of business wham-bam-thank-you-ma'am, with the least effort.

Sound might be a problem, he decided. One shot, neighbors were likely to figure it for a car backfiring. Same with the second shot. The third shot, that was going to bring puzzlement and maybe someone dialing nine-one-one. The sofa was loaded with throw pillows. Heist one of them, use it as a muffler. Not the best solution, but it would have to do in a pinch.

The minister was saying, ". . . cigarettes don't bother me, personally, although I am concerned about secondhand smoke. I do two sermons a year about the evils of tobacco, lung congestion and other long-term problems. Franklin, did you know cigarettes cause more deaths from heart attacks than from cancer?" Nodding in accord. "An absolute fact. Studies in the *New England Journal of Medicine* and all. You can find out for yourself up on the Internet."

"Heard it said," Bachardy said, wishing the minister would shut up and wondering what was keeping Grange and the woman. He pulled the cancer stick from his lips, gave it a fast study, and checked around for an ashtray. No ashtray. He extinguished the cancer stick on his sole and field stripped it inside the jacket pocket where he kept his backup, a short-barrel .22. Thinking: *The .22, less noise, so maybe better to use than the .38?* Only that before he was momentarily startled by the door chimes.

Reverend Kiel bounced up, motioning Bachardy to stay put, and padded out.

Bachardy put the time to use. He shifted onto the sofa and stored the .38 under a throw pillow he repositioned closer to his right hand. On reflection, he returned the .38 to his shoulder holster and substituted the .22, with not a second to spare.

The minister was back, and he wasn't alone.

Bachardy remembered the black woman from last night, leaving the church. She was impossible to miss, her three or four hundred pounds on a frame that could not be more than five-one, five-two, but carried with a ballet dancer's grace underneath a multi-hued muumuu that defied anyone not to notice her and she glided down the steps.

"Mr. Bachardy, say hello to Alice Jefferson. Alice is my star vocalist, the choir nothing without her. Dropped by to work with Lizzie on her selections for next Sunday's services. Lizzie's our wonderful organist, or did Billy tell you so already?"

"So," Bachardy said.

"Oh, go on, pastor," Alice Jefferson said, her robust voice feigning modesty. "Oh, go on . . . I'm pleased to meet you, Mr. Bachardy." Searching the room. "Where is that girl? We got some serious rehearsing to do . . . Let me guess. The garden. Her and them roses of hers. A thorn in my side, it comes to keeping enough time for rehearsing." Her laugh did not trill true.

Reverend Kiel said, "Settle down; relax, Alice. Someone's already gone to fetch her."

Alice Jefferson mumbled another thought and moved in the direction of the sofa. Bachardy, fearing she would pick a spot that obliged her to move the throw pillow under which he'd hidden the .22, quickly shifted over and patted the space to his left. Using the armrest for support, the woman made a soft landing. She deposited the songbooks she'd brought with her on the coffee table, wheezed a comfort sigh and settled her arms along the back of the sofa.

Bachardy reassessed the situation while she recited a catalog of song possibilities for the minister. So, now he had another complimentary corpse to create. Ellen Dickinson a.k.a. Lizzie Morrow, as originally bought and paid for. The deputy sheriff, the minister and the choir singer, three on the house in the house. The gas jockey before leaving town. Five for the price of one. How's that for a bargain? Man, would the newspapers and the TV ever have a field day, all sorts of speculation about some devil-possessed killer with a grudge against the church, probably all of mankind, before the story made it onto *Law & Order* and finally wore out its welcome. He didn't even want to think about what special guest they'd hire to play him, at the same time hoping it wouldn't be Christopher Walken, somebody like him, who would turn Bachardy into a sick, psychopathic, perverted prick of a human being. Walken, he was good at that, where somebody like that Macy guy or that Reilly guy could make him the victim of circumstance he was, only trying to do his job and get on with his life.

With an apologetic look for him, Reverend Kiel began evaluating the songs proposed and dropping in a few personal choices.

Bachardy looked anxiously at the archway and thought about strolling out to the garden to see for himself what was keeping Dickinson and the deputy. He decided to give it a few more minutes and began drafting a new scenario for the hits.

Latch onto the throw pillow and the .22 rising to greet Dickinson. *Blam.* Drop Dickson. *Blam.* Drop the deputy. A shift to the left. *Blam.* Send the minister to Heaven. Wheel around. *Blam.* Send Alice Jefferson to that great choir in the clouds. What? Four seconds? Five? A minute to check his handiwork.. Possibly the need for a *coup de grace*, although that was doubtful; his accuracy was as good as Nowitzki at the free throw line, Bowen on three-pointers, Kobe on anything. Better, actually. He'd been at it longer and no scars to show for time served. *Bachardy's Greatest Hits* and not a clinker in the bunch.

The mutt Kiel had mentioned, a blimp of a dog, wandered into the room and over to Bachardy. Sniffed his leg and satisfied, backed off and did a slow merry-go-round with his tail before settling down on the rug.

The minister interrupted his conversation with Alice Jefferson to explain, "That's Ludwig. Deaf as a stone."

"I heard," Bachardy said.

"More than Ludwig could say," Reverend Kiel said, earning a laugh from Alice and a play smile from Bachardy while Ludwig found a spot on his hairy paw to gnaw.

Reverend Kiel resumed lobbying for some hymn called, best he could tell, "God Be With You Till We Meet Again," and instantly earned enthusiasm from Alice Jefferson, who began singing the lyrics in a voice that started low and slow and was soaring by the time Bachardy realized she'd been joined by a younger-edged soprano singing harmony.

He trailed the sound to the archway.

The girl addressing her singing to the Siamese cat she was stroking was a junior-sized version of Alice Jefferson, maybe ten or eleven years old, decked out in a fluffy pink dress and matching ribbons braided through pigtails that stood up from her head like antennas.

The two of them finished the hymn in perfect harmony, to generous applause and shouts of "Bravo!" from the minister. The Siamese, having heard enough, slipped out of the girl's arms and disappeared.

"Mama, you coming yet? I don't want to be late for Ruthie Mae's birthday?"

Alice Jefferson glanced from Reverend Kiel to Bachardy explaining, "It's Ruthie Mae's birthday today. She's best friends with my Sally over there . . . Any minute now, Precious. I still need to be having a conversation with Miss Morrow about Sunday. You like for us to sing that one on Sunday?"

Sally Jefferson shrugged.

Her mother said, "You go on back to the car, Precious. Only be another minute or five."

"Wait here with you, Mama," Sally said, and skipped over to the baby grand piano that dominated the area immediately in front of the picture window. She tucked her skirt and settled on the bench with a super-sized smile for Bachardy, began one-fingering "God Be With You Till We Meet Again" and humming along.

The sound transcribed in Bachardy's mind as a TV newscaster saying: *The killer's victims also included a sweet, adorable little girl named Sally, maybe ten or eleven years old, with a beautiful voice, looking forward to her best friend's birthday party and every reason to believe she'd have a long, happy, healthy life and—*

No, no, no.

No way.

Bachardy knew he was a lot of things, all of them rotten,

but one thing he wasn't, never could be, was a kid killer. Bachardy drew the line at kids. He'd do Ellen Dickinson a.k.a. Lizzie Morrow, but not here and now. Later. He'd come back later and do her, but not the dog, either. Kids and dogs. People, one thing, but kids and dogs? He had one of each back home, two more kids with his ex, and that one in Santa Fe with—He couldn't remember her name. It was being crowded out of memory by some fast, fancy thinking.

Bachardy checked his watch, slapped his forehead like he'd had a sudden thought, and pushed himself off the sofa. He threw up his hands and shared a concerned look with the minister and Alice Jefferson. "Didn't realize the time . . . Another appointment in town I can't be late for. Explain and apologize to Ms. Morrow for me, will you? And to Deputy Grange . . . I'll make it back here another time."

He started quick-stepping to the hallway, but was halted by the minister saying, "Aren't you forgetting something, Franklin?" Reverend Kiel was pointing at the sofa.

Bachardy turned and saw Alice Jefferson with the .22 in hand and aimed at him, a flash of reality before the weapon disappeared underneath the throw pillow that was now on her lap and before little Sally had been able to turn from the keyboard and see what the minister meant.

Alice Jefferson converted her firm stare into a smile and called to her, "Precious, go to the car and wait for your mama."

"But, Mama."

"Just do what Mama says, Sally. Now. Scoot. You listening? You hear me? Don't see you moving any, Sally."

Sally made an eleven-year-old face of discontent and

worked off the piano bench, headed out of the room with her shoulders hunched, her fists clenched, muttering what to Bachardy sounded like, *I never get to watch.*

Once satisfied she was gone from the house, Alice revealed the .22 again, telling the minister, "Let's hurry up on this, Jerry. My baby needs to get to her birthday party."

The minister advanced on Bachardy, cautiously, careful not to enter Alice's line of fire. He reached around and dug the .38 out from Bachardy's shoulder holster. He pressed the .38 between Bachardy's shoulder blades. "That chair there will do just fine, Franklin," he said. "Sit down and take a load off."

Alice said, "You still need me anymore, Jerry?"

"I know. The kid's birthday party. You done good for us. Go on out back and pass the word to Lizzie and Billy and take off." The minister inched backward from Bachardy and into the seat across from him, the .38 primed to excavate his chest. "Lizzie and Billy will be with us any minute, Franklin. Then, it'll be time for show-and-tell. You can spill your guts or I'll have to spill them for you."

Bachardy stared at him hard and said, "You'd really kill an FBI agent?"

The minister hooted. "As if the FBI has anything at all to do with you, Franklin, or whatever your real name is."

Ellen Dickinson a.k.a. Lizzie Morrow working over the piano keyboard, "God Be With You Till We Meet Again" sounding a hundred times better than when little Sally was tinkering it out. "It's a good choice for Sunday, Jerry, and isn't that girl a marvel, the way she picks up so fast on music? Carnegie Hall, I wouldn't *not* predict it."

"A damn sight better'n her winding up in juvenile hall," Deputy Bill Grange said, admiring his own sense of humor. He was standing alongside Bachardy, the throw pillow in one hand, the .22 in the other. "Jerry, can we get this show on the road?"

The minister settled back in his seat, one hand across his belly, using it as a perch for his gun hand. "This for certain, Franklin or whoever you are, an FBI agent you're not or you'd never have come after Lizzie or here in the first place. So, what's it all about?"

"You're the wise guy, you tell me," Bachardy said, toughing it out until he had the situation measured.

"Me? I think you're the wise guy here, Franklin. Me? I'm the ex-wise guy. Same way Billy's an ex-wise guy. Here in the witness protection service, same as Lizzie here's in the witness protection program, only for different reasons." Dickinson struck some dramatic chords on the piano. "It was the same only different with Alice. You could say the same only different for every member of my congregation. For the whole town. Yes, Billy?"

"Affirmative, Jerry. What the Attorney General went and did after they chopped his operating budget to ribbons. He had the U.S. Marshals Service gather us up from all over the country and deposit us here in Ripley. A ghost town in the middle of nowhere, but you see what rehab can accomplish over a few years. The AG figured it cheaper having us under one roof and sharing the secret. Cheaper the long run and safety in numbers, us policing ourselves, taking care of ourselves people like you ever came along."

Bachardy, meanwhile, thinking: *Move fast enough and get my hands on the .22. Use Grange as a shield while taking out Kiel. Pop Grange; then, the woman.* Thinking: *I'll have surprise working for me. It could be enough. I've been in tighter spots than this and lived to tell . . .*

The minister saying, "Billy read you the minute you pulled the FBI gag on him."

"Before then, Jerry. Why I got on the phone to you pronto."

"He wasn't the first, either. Phil at the garage also smelled trouble when you pulled in."

"You do me, they'll send someone else after her."

"Lizzie will be gone from here by nightfall, like she never was here in the first place."

Dickinson began playing that song from *The Sound of Music* with all the goodbye words in different languages.

"You're saying there's another Ripley?"

"Believe it or not," the deputy answered Bachardy, and followed with a hoot and a howl.

Bachardy deciding the moment had come.

Deciding: *On the count of ten . . .*

He was at "six" when Ellen Dickinson a.k.a. Lizzie Morrow switched back to "God Be With You Till We Meet Again."

Bachardy heard a dull pop. Understood it was the sound of a .22 shell cracking through a pillow. Felt his head disintegrating. Was aware of the minister bending over to whisper in his ear, "God be with you till we meet again."

Three weeks later, Deputy Billy Grange was explaining to the stranger who had come calling, "The knock-knock joke got in the way."

# The Last Case of Hilly Palmer

Duane Swierczynski

Duane Swierczynski is the author of *The Wheelman*, from St. Martin's Minotaur, as well as other books about crime and vice. He's also the editor in chief of the *Philadelphia City Paper*, where his writing ranges over a wide field of topics, sometimes including the mystery field. He is one of the new voices of crime fiction, taking the field into places it's never been before. If he isn't already, he will soon be a major player in his generation's world of mystery fiction.

**I met Hilly Palmer in** a bar on 15th Street. James Roy set it up. At the time, he was *Metropolitan* magazine's star crime writer, and I was the magazine's fact checker. But a fact-checker with ambition. Since joining the staff that previous May, I had been peppering my editor in chief with story idea after story idea.

Finally, in early November, I pitched a winner: an interview with one of Philadelphia's last hardboiled private eye. My editor loved it. Little did I know he was a big-time Hammett and Chandler junkie. Just like me.

However, I'd pitched that idea directly out of my ass. I didn't know any private eyes, let alone "Philadelphia's last hardboiled" one.

I said I was ambitious. Not smart.

Fortunately, James Roy was around to save me. I guess he thought he owed me a favor. I had fact-checked his big summer crime story, "The Cop Who Hated the Police," and caught a major fact lulu—one that surely would have gotten us sued. (Or least that's what our magazine's lawyer told us.) Since it was nothing that ruined his story, and since I'd approached James about it first, he'd taken a liking to me.

After the idea meeting, I rushed back to my office, closed the door, and prayed to God that the editor in chief wouldn't stop in on his way back from the conference room. I speed-dialed James and explained the situation.

"I happen to know just the man," James said. "I can't say he's exactly hardboiled—I mean, he is seventy-five, and does a lot of gopher work for lawyers these days. But back in the day, you couldn't find a better P.I. in Philadelphia."

I made a mental note to start attending church again. "James, you just saved my life. What's his name?"

"Hilly Palmer. He has an office downtown—right around 16th and Spruce. Tell you what. I'll set up a time when we can all have a beer, and you'll get your story. I'm sure he'll be up for it."

"I owe you my firstborn child for this."

"You're kidding," James said. "Women actually have sex with you?"

"Enough chloroform, anything's possible."

James ended the call with a hearty laugh and a promise to get back to me with word from Hilly Palmer. I felt like a million bucks. There's nothing better to an ambitious staff member than making a senior staffer—let alone someone as legendary as James Roy—laugh. You savor those moments, because just for a short while, you feel like you belong. They aren't going to find you out. They aren't going to laugh at you. They might even let you enter their club.

Seconds later, there was a knock at the door. My editor's head popped in without waiting for a response—editors do stuff like that. "By the way," he said. "Who's this P.I.?"

"Hilly Palmer," I said, trying to not to smile like a goof. "An old friend of James Roy's. They worked on a bunch of stories together."

My editor gave a tight-lipped nod. "Have it in next week?"

"Sure," I said.

Fuck the million bucks. Make it a billion.

A week later: $2.39.

At first James was apologetic; Hilly Palmer was sick with a hideous cough. He wasn't up for a beer, or anything. I asked, as politely as possible, when Palmer might recover enough to grant me a thirty-minute interview. James got annoyed fast. Like he usually did when I asked for something twice.

"What do you want me to do, Andrew? Go over there, tell him to accept Jesus as his personal savior, and cure his lungs with the power of my fucking hands?"

I begged James to try Palmer again in a few days.

The next day, at the staff production meeting, my editor asked about the hardboiled dick. I lied. I said Palmer was out of town on a case and wouldn't be back for a few days, but he promised to sit down with me the moment he set foot on Philadelphia soil.

Right after, I called James to cover my bases. "Whatever," he said, and quickly got back to work on his own story.

"I really appreciate you trying, James," I added.

"Uh-huh. Gotta go."

Another week passed. The tension mounted. Not a day would go by without my editor popping his head into my office and asking, "Hardboiled dick?" Soon, it was twice a day. Then the snide jokes in the bathroom, whenever I had the misfortune of being there the same time as my editor. "You know, I bet a reporter from the *Gay News* would find dick with no problem. Maybe I should reassign this story to someone there."

I went home every night, drank a six pack, ate slightly-heated pre-fab chicken patty-things on increasingly stale hamburger buns and looked at my wrists, trying to decide which one to cut first.

*"Dick?"*

*"Got Dick yet?"*

*"No Dick? How about Jane?"*

Finally, Jesus accepted me back into his bosom: James Roy called, saying that Hilly Palmer had come back from the dead, and we were to meet at McGlinchey's on 15th Street for a beer this coming Wednesday, the day before Thanksgiving.

I practically skipped into my editor's office to update him with some version of the truth.

He didn't fire me on the spot, which was a good sign.

We opened the door to McGlinchey's, and the stale odor of beer, cigarettes and human lives smacked us in the face.

I secretly rejoiced when James told me that this was the bar Hilly had chosen. Even though I was only twenty-one, I had been coming to McGlinchey's for well over three years now.

The bar hadn't seen a paintbrush or broom since Carter was running the country. The previous Halloween, I remember looking up and smiling at the cobweb decorations that someone had strung across the stamped tin ceiling of the bar. Three months later, I realized they weren't decorations.

Hilly Palmer was perched at the edge of the bar closest to the bathrooms. Like most things in life, he wasn't what I'd expected. I had expected one of two extremes: either a tall, muscular Phillip Marlowe–type, or short fat Nero Wolfe–type that had only grown more rotund over the years as cases eased up and the Italian dinners kicked in.

Hilly Palmer was neither. On the short side, maybe 5'7", medium build. He looked like a college professor, with a brown tweed jacket and a dress shirt without a tie, opened at the collar. His hair was on the short side, but not military. And not as gray as I'd expected; there was still some brown pigmentation left in his head. He vaguely resembled Jack Lemmon.

"Dr. Palmer," James said.

The old detective looked up and smirked for a brief second, then resumed his Sphinx face. "Dr. Roy."

“Hilly, meet R. Andrew Panico, researcher at the magazine and rising editorial star.”

I approached to shake Palmer’s hand. Instead of his paw, he gave me an exaggerated once over, a bit of mugging that warped the pentagram slightly. “This is *Metropolitan’s* rising star? Looks like Northeast Philly white trash to me.”

“That’s Dr. White Trash to you,” I said.

Palmer didn’t laugh. I couldn’t blame him. I performed an autopsy of the joke in my head; it hadn’t been funny.

James stepped in before I made a complete ass of myself. “How about a few drinks? First round’s on me, the rest is on *Metro* mag.”

That sounded fine to me. But I hoped that James planned on being *Metro* mag for the later rounds. The editor-in-chief had a funny policy with expenses: Well-paid senior staffers received corporate American Express cards. Struggling junior staffers had to lay out the cash in advance, submit receipts, then wait a month for the expense check to kick back from accounting. This particular junior staffer—actually, sub-junior staffer—had only $90 in my checking account at the time. This was to last me until next Friday. Nine days away.

In addition to being Northeast Philly white trash, I was also bad with money.

After ordering a round of Yuengling Black and Tan pints—and a Courvoisier for the old dick—James turned to Palmer. “What’s new, gumshoe?”

Palmer made a sour face. “Right now? I’m trying to choke a lousy $400 out of those pigfuckers at Rent-a-Kings. I did the job over a month ago, and I’ve had to have my girl send them three invoices.”

"By the way," James said. "How is Margaret?"

"Fine. She's been going on about getting her nose pierced."

James chuckled. "So what was that Rent-a-Kings job again? Did you tell me?"

The detective grunted, then took a hard pull from the glass in front of him. "Sure as hell told you. The one where my Buick got the crap shot out of it?"

Now this sounded interesting. I caught James's eye and gestured down to my handheld tape recorder. He gave me a curt shake. *Not now.*

"I remember now. Why don't you bring Andrew up to speed?"

Palmer gave me one of those *oh-you're-still-here?* looks, then resigned himself to the task of speaking to me.

"I had to deliver papers to some hophead up in Spring Garden. Simple job, but he made me wait it out. I sat in my Buick for three hours before he showed his face. Now I just had a prostatectomy last spring . . . you know what those are, don't you?"

"Removal of the prostate gland," I blurted, as if I were on a game show.

"That's one way to put it. Another way to put it might be that a group of overpaid meat-monkeys flipped me over, shoved knives up my ass, hacked out a glob of flesh, then sewed my winkie to my pee-sack again."

James laughed. "Pardon the medical jargon, Andrew."

"And now my pee-sack has fun with me, especially if I'm sitting in an uncomfortable position for a while, or move my leg one inch further than I'm supposed to. So there I was, trying not to wet myself wondering if I had enough time to bleed the lizard into a mayonnaise jar, when boom. My man arrives. Only, I didn't know he was my man at first. He was wearing a ski mask and gloves, and in his hand was one of those AK-47 deals. And he starts firing at me."

"*At* you?" I asked. "Jesus, what were those papers?"

"The dickhead rented a living room set, then decided he didn't want to pay for it."

"He must have loved his coffee table," James said.

"You're kidding," I said.

Palmer ignored both of us. "Something told me to duck. Halfway down, the pigfucker opened fire. Blew out the windshield. Shredded the hood and front tires. But not one bullet hit me. Then I hear this boom. Then this thump against the front of my car. Rocks the whole thing. And then somebody whining, right outside my car."

"Where in Spring Garden was this?" I asked. At the time, I lived in a tiny apartment on Green Street, in the heart of that neighborhood.

Palmer ignored my question. "I took a chance and took a peek. There was another guy walking toward the car, with a three fifty-seven in his hand. I ducked back down and reached for Bud and Lou . . ."

"His pistols," James added.

I took a sip of my beer and remembered my tape recorder. Shit. I should be getting this down. I hoped James would help me piece it together later.

"The guy with the .357 starts talking to me," Hilly said. "*Yo, G, what y'all doing in there,* that kind of thing. *You and me got bid-ness to discuss*. Blah blah blah." Hilly finished his drink, then summoned the bartender with his fingers. "I didn't care. My hands hit the cement first. I pulled the rest of my elderly butt out of the car, then felt around for a weapon. Something. Anything. Though maybe I'd find a pamphlet from the Jehovah's Witnesses so I could bore the bastard to death."

James chuckled, then so did I. We were Palmer's studio audience.

"Instead, I found a chunk of curb. Thank God the city doesn't give two fucks about street repair north of Spring Garden Street. I got myself a piece of curb about the size of a regulation softball, then pulled a notebook out of my shirt pocket. I flicked the notebook up and behind the car. I heard the new guy start for it, which is when I stood up and nailed him square in the head with the chunk of curb."

"I love this part," James said.

"Unfortunately," Palmer said, and then paused to swivel his stool around to look at me. "Unfortunately, this guy was a *monster.* His mother probably fed him steroid-laced breast milk and let him wrassle alligators in the sewers. Huge. Wearing this ridiculous black suit—and by suit I mean the jacket and pants, and some kind of a clod-hopper shoes—and nothing else. Black tattoos. At least he matched."

James chuckled, and I did too, more out of politeness than genuine mirth.

"My little piece of Philadelphia did nothing to that Godzilla-sized bastard. Nothing. He just smiled at me, then pointed his gun my way. And you know what he says? He says, '*Lu-ceee! You have some s'plaining to do!*' I'm not kidding. Just like that."

James was crying and laughing and wiping his face. "I love that part even more."

"So we started talking, and it turns out to be a classic case of mistaken identity. The idiot who stiffed Rent-a-Kings also stiffed one of South Philly's most powerful drug lords. The brick wall in the suit was hired to scare him, while I was hired to hand him some papers. The dickhead got us confused, and tried to wipe me out with his Howitzer."

I made the appropriate awestruck sounds and took a sip of my beer.

Impossibly, Palmer's drink was already gone. He waved his thick fingers at the bartender again. This time I watched the bartender pour. Palmer was drinking Courvoisier. I wondered if it was expensive.

"So we get to talking, and decide that it's better off that Tomb—that's his street name, Tomb, as in final resting place of mummies—that Tomb not have the police talking to him about what happened. I spin some story about being in the crossfire, the cops buy it, and I make a new friend."

"He forgave you for the facial bruise," James said.

"He did," Palmer said. "That was a plus. On the minus side, I discovered later moments that my bladder had given up on me. I hadn't even noticed. My pants were soaked right through. I'm thinking it was the act of hurling that piece of sidewalk—strained the pee sack too much. And even worse, I still haven't been paid."

"Did the guy die?" I asked.

"Who?"

"The guy with the living room set."

"Ah, him. No, he didn't die. Tomb aimed for the knee. I hear he's doing fine. He's taken up pottery. He writes to his mother every week and thanks her for the chicken soup. Who gives a fuck how he is? I'm out four hundred dollars."

We continued drinking. James and Palmer made idle conversation—how's this guy, have you hear from that guy, hey I might have some work for ya, some election fraud stuff, oh yeah, great. Then James excused himself, leaving Palmer and me by our lonesome. It was time to start some reporting.

"Do you mind a tape recorder, Mr. Palmer?"

"What are you, Nixon?"

I fished it out of my bag anyway, pressed the RECORD and PLAY buttons, then placed it on the bartop.

"Care for another drink?"

Palmer looked as if I'd asked him, *Care to continue breathing?* I waved for the bartender. Nothing. Palmer twitched on index finger. His Courvoisier was refilled within thirty seconds. My beer, too. A courtesy to Palmer, I suppose.

"So what's this article you're doing about me?"

That was my cue, but I fumbled. "Yes. I want to know what it was . . . er, is, like . . . . Uh, being Philly's last private eye. One of the old-style ones, I mean."

Now I knew better than this. Even at this early point in my journalism career. But I fucked it up anyway.

"You mean to say, What's it feel like being an old dick?"

"That's not quite how I'd put it . . . ."

"That's a horrible question. Listen, I've gotta shake the dew off my lily. You sit there and drink some beer and try real hard to think up a good question."

With that, Palmer slid from his stool and pushed his way through to the bathrooms.

For a man who'd been sitting down for who-knows-how-long drinking who-knows-how-many glasses of Courvoisier, he walked fairly straight, with a determined kind of step. Maybe it was annoyance. Maybe his pee sack was ready to burst.

Maybe I'd better start thinking of some better questions.

There was no such luck. For the next half-hour, no matter the question, Palmer would be annoyed, hurt, angered or bored. After each offensive question he'd drain more of his drink and curse under his breath. After nearly thirty minutes of desperate attempts, I was reduced to the most inane questions I could think of.

"How about your favorite color then."

"My favorite color?"

"Yes. Your favorite color."

"Ah!" he said. "Finally a question worth answering. A chance to share the *real me* with thousands of suburbanites who buy your fine publication. I have two favorite colors, actually. Tape running, young Andrew? The first is dysentery green—a.k.a. infectious snot green. The other is very light brown, the color of diseased shit. How's that? Green snot and brown shit and bright little roses. These are a few of my favorite things."

I was feeling drunk, and not in the mood anymore. Fuck him, fuck it. I hung up my cub reporter's hat.

"You'd like my car then, you old goat. It looks like shit."

Palmer looked like he swallowed a carpet tack. "What did you say?"

"Actually, I prefer to describe the color as 'dietary chocolate' rather than human feces. But it runs like shit, so I guess the description is accurate."

A pause. "Did you call me an old goat?"

"Yeah."

"That's what I thought."

We proceeded to get shitfaced, not saying a word to each other. I would have thought he was mad, but he had the bartender keep refilling my glass.

He was probably waiting me out.

I scanned the rest of the bar, just to do something with my eyes. I didn't have to look far. Standing on the other side of Palmer was an extremely cute blonde—cute in the best possible sense. College-girl-almost-grown-up cute. Cute enough to get away with smoking clove cigarettes and wearing a Weezer T-shirt emblazoned with words HIP, HIP yet probably two years away from marrying a thick-necked jock fresh out of law school and moving out to Bryn Mawr. She was blonde in the best way imaginable.

Just as I was working up the courage to feed her a lame line, Palmer tapped me on the shoulder.

"What the fuck is the 'R' for?" he asked.

"R?"

"When Jimmy introduced you, he said R. Andrew whatever-the-hell-your last-name-is. What's it stand for? Or is that a piece of pretense right out of the Harry S Truman school?"

"Raymond. The R stands for Raymond."

"Big Ray! Why didn't you tell me your name was Ray? I love Ray. Much better than Andrew. Andrew's kind of a pussy name, you know? But not Ray. Name of champions and two-fisted thugs alike. You look like a Big Ray. I think that's what I'll call you."

"Sure, Hilly."

"Fuck you, *Ray*. It's still Mr. Palmer."

I had long since broken the seal, so I found myself with the urgent need to hit the head again. There are no urinals in the McGlinchey's men's room—instead you piss into a large piece of porcelain that resembled a feeding trough.

There was some writing on the ceiling just above the trough: IF YOU CAN READ THIS, YOU ARE PROBABLY PISSING ON YOUR SHOES. Nice motto. They should put that on the *Metro* mag masthead.

I zipped up, and wondered if I should try again with Palmer, or decide to forget about him for the night and go talk to the blonde. I had enough booze in me to make the latter seem much more desirable. I splashed water on my face, smoothed out a few errant hairs on top of my head, then returned to the bar.

The old goat had made up my mind for me.

He was gone.

I couldn't believe it. The old dick couldn't even hang around long enough to give me the polite brush-off? Was I that miserable a reporter? Scratch that—human being? I walked up to my barstool and kicked my foot at the darkness beneath, just to make sure my bag was there. My bag, with my tape recorder and blank tape sitting inside of it. Useless. What did I have to work with? Little more than a collection of choice epithets from a grumpy old man with a slightly fucked-up face and an voracious appetite for booze. I could almost picture the story I would turn in Monday morning: LOCAL P.I. REVEALS 37 USES OF THE WORD "PIGFUCKER."

"Buddy."

I looked up. "Yeah?"

It was the bartender, a burly freckled thickneck with a head full of curly red hair—kind of like Irish dreadlocks. "I need you to take care of this." He slid me a slip of paper.

I didn't have to look. It was the tab. So James Roy hadn't been running a tab on his credit card, and Palmer hadn't ponied up anything for the endless tumblers of Courvoisier he'd downed. Now I didn't *want* to look.

I did anyway. $87. Not including a tip for Mr. Irish Dreads.

Things just kept getting better and better. In addition to pissing away my fledgling magazine career, I would also have to figure out how to survive on $3 for the next nine days. Even Ramen noodles didn't go that far.

I reached down for my bag and put it in my lap. I wanted desperately to chug the rest of my beer, but I had less than two centimeters in my mug. With . . . oh look. A sprinkling of cigarette ashes on top. My beer looked like a watery plane crash site.

Okay, I told myself, not the end of the world. Really. Tomorrow was Thanksgiving, and that meant I had at least one free hot meal coming to me, courtesy my mom and her new boyfriend George, who both were shacked up an hour away in Vineland, New Jersey. I wasn't sure my car had enough gas to make the trip, but I could worry about that later. South Jersey was relatively flat. I could coast on fumes for a while.

I was so amped with enthusiasm, I almost didn't feel the tap on my shoulder.

"Hey."

I spun around on my bar stool. It was the blonde in the Weezer T-shirt. I had been wallowing so deep in my own despair, I'd forgotten I planned to hit on her.

"Hey," I said.

"Where's your friend?"

"The old guy? I guess he went home to watch *Matlock*."

She didn't laugh, but I did see the beginnings of a smirk on her lips. Her red bee-stung lips.

"If you'd like his phone number," I continued, "I could hook you up. Granted, he has a bladder-control problem, he drinks like priests pray, and he's generally the crankiest bastard alive, but you two might hit it off."

The blonde didn't miss a beat. "We might. But it would be a purely physical thing."

"It's the wrinkles, isn't it?"

"Oooh yeah," she cooed. "You don't have any acne scars on your back, do you?"

Now it was my turn to smile. I stepped back, took a look at the situation, and found myself pleasantly surprised. Here was an attractive woman not only chatting *me* up, but apparently on the same warped wave length. Either I was drunk, she was drunk, or I'd slipped in the bathroom and snapped my neck.

She held out her hand. "Name's Rineheimer. Maggie Rineheimer."

"Andrew."

Maggie had a very nice hand—soft yet strong.

"Andrew's kind of a pussy name, isn't it?"

My jaw almost dropped, but then I clued in: she must have overheard Hilly. "You can call me Big Ray."

Maggie leaned in conspiratorially, touching my shoulder lightly with her fingertips. "How big, Ray?"

Before I had a chance to react, she bumped me with her hip. "Buy a girl a drink."

*Why, sure—*

Nuts.

I should have known this was too good to be true. Couldn't Maggie have caught me last Friday, when I was still flush—well, relatively speaking—from payday? Hell, couldn't she have caught me a couple of hours ago, before Hilly Palmer drank away my food money for the week?

But there I was, with no way to buy her a drink without blowing the bank or risking the ire of Fergus, the bartender with a chip the size of County Kerry on his shoulder. So, I did the honorable thing.

I lied my ass off.

"Here's the thing," I said. "That old guy? That was my grandfather. He was here, and he promised to pick up the tab. Thing is . . ." And here I realized that I had said "thing" twice, and that made me nervous. ". . . thing is he forgot about it, and I didn't bring my wallet."

Without warning, Maggie patted my ass—the part that wasn't attach to the bar stool.

"What's that?" she asked. "Adult undergarment?"

"My other wallet," I offered, feebly.

"That's either weird, cheap or pathetic," she said.

"Okay," I said. "God's honest truth? I'm stuck with a bigger tab that I thought. And I'm not great with money."

Too much information, Panico. You're gonna spook her.

"Hmm."

I said nothing, clutching the bag in my lap like a security blanket.

"Tell you what," she said, sliding her purse strap from her shoulder. "Tab's on me. I can write it off."

"You can what?"

"Expense it. I'm in the insurance game. I'm supposed to take people out all of the time. You're doing me a favor. That leaves you free to buy me a drink. A gin gimlet. Tell Fergie not too sour." She removed an American Express Gold card from her purse.

I suddenly found myself beginning one of those half-hearted financial wrestling matches. On one hand, this would save my ass for the next nine days. On the other, there was no way in hell I could let her pick up this tab. What the hell would that say about me? What, was I to be a kept boy, and she, my *Sugar Mamacita*?

I had to admit—the first hand had a good point. Still, I said, "I can't let you do that."

"You're not going to stop me."

"Maggie, really . . ."

"We can argue about this for a while, or we can quickly have our drinks and then you can show me your apartment."

"But . . . what?" I'm sure I did one of those classic movie double-takes.

She turned away from me. "Fergie babe!" she called, waving her card and my tab in the air.

*And then you can show me your apartment.*

I sat there, clutching my bag and pondering the odd turns of recent events: the lucky story break, the diss, the murder and gunfight stories, the shitty interview, the drinks, the diss, and now this. What ever this was. But who cares? Maybe this is the way life is supposed to be when you're at twenty-one. Maybe I shouldn't ask so many questions. Why fact-check my own life?

Somebody tapped me on the shoulder, jolting me from my mild fugue state.

Hilly Palmer.

"Big Ray."

"Hilly?"

"Fuck you, *Ray*. It's *Mr.* Palmer."

"What . . . ?" That's all I could manage. I was still in shock. Did the old man and I pass each other en route to the bathroom? Where the hell had he come from?

Maggie turned around from the bar, the tab and credit card still in her hand. "Oh. Grandpa Munster's back."

"Grandpa?" Palmer asked, his face scrunched up like a troll. "Who the fuck is this?"

"Hilly Palmer, Maggie Rineheimer."

The two locked eyes. Neither of them flinched. It was a weird battle of wills, the rules of which I couldn't begin to comprehend.

Finally, the old man gave up. "Send this wench home to her mama in South Philly," Palmer said, jerking his thumb toward Maggie. "We need to get down to business."

Maggie's jaw unhinged from the rest of her pretty face. "Excuse me—Grumpy Old Guy? Won't the Home be looking for you by now?"

Inside, I cringed.

"Why don't you peddle your ass down the street and leave the paying customers alone?"

Inside, I cringed an epileptic fit.

"Oh, yeah," Maggie said. "I'm a hooker with an AmEx Gold card."

"What, you don't take Mastercard?"

"Guys, guys . . ." I said, trying to play the peacemaker.

"Who is this guy, Andrew—really? I hope to God he isn't your grandfather, otherwise you've got a long swim from the shallow end of the gene pool."

"Maggie . . ."

"I'll make it simple for you, Big Ray. Ditch the ditz and let's do this interview thing now, or you can forget about ever seeing my good name and your byline on the same page. Ever."

That was it. I shut down. I decided not to say a word that might be held against me in the court of law that sentenced me to this oddball alternate universe in which I was being fought over by a cranky old man with dentures and a wise-ass hottie with an AmEx Gold card. I hugged my leather bag tighter. My mommy had given it to me as a college graduation present. I rubbed one of the metal buckles with my thumb. It felt nice. Safe. Reassuring.

Then both Maggie and Palmer started laughing.

I looked up, my eyebrows surely askew.

"I've gotta say," Maggie said, smiling at me. "You really must be dedicated. I was practically in your lap." She turned to Palmer. "Wasn't I, Uncle Hilly?"

"I'll say. I was ready to reach for Bud and Lou, in case Big Ray here got any funny ideas."

I exhaled the air that had been slowly gathering in my lungs for the past sixty seconds. "For fuck's sake."

A set-up. Big time. Maggie had Fergus cue up another round of drinks, and the truth came out. Maggie Rineheimer was Palmer's great niece, and worked for him at his office. She was the "girl" he'd mentioned earlier in the evening.

James had called her "Margaret."

It was mostly for fun, she explained—Palmer wanted her to drop by and get a "read" on me, to see if she thought I was going to write a hatchet job on her uncle. He trusted James Roy . . . to a point. After he saw I was harmless ("toothless" was more like it, in my opinion), Palmer waved Maggie over during one of my later trips to the head. A plot was hatched. A great laugh was had by both. I felt like a complete weenie.

"So, Maggie, I guess that trip to my apartment is out," I said, only half-joking.

"Yo, Big Ray," Palmer warned. "Don't give me a reason to cut off your scrotum and use it as a candy dish."

The drinking continued, and the interview picked up again. Having Maggie there made a world of difference. Gone was the obstinate old fuck who wouldn't answer a straight question. In his place was a guy who clearly still enjoyed what he did, even if he pretended that he was awfully bitter about it. He launched into one anecdote after another, and I laughed and drank and stole glances at Maggie, who would occasionally return a glance and smile sweetly. The liquor and warmth and euphoria burned strong on all levels.

I remember feeling especially pleased that this story was going to work out after all, and that I was actually going to have fun reporting it.

That's when the guy in the black suit and tattoos approached Maggie.

"How are ya, baby?"

Maggie turned around, and gave him a cocked eyebrow.

"Been a long time," he continued.

"Nope," Maggie replied, running her finger along her bottom lip and giving the stranger the once-over, from bottom to top. "Try again. Maybe something along the lines of, 'I like your pants . . . on my floor.' Well? What do you think, big guy?"

Hilly finally looked up and turned white.

The stranger flipped open the folds of his coat to reveal a pistol. He turned to face Hilly and said, "Yo, G. You been doing some *'splaining*, haven't you?"

Then I got it. *Tomb.* The guy from Hilly's Rent-a-Kings case.

And now that he was pointing the pistol at Hilly's face, I got the joke.

What's the old expression? Fool me once, shame on you?

I reached out and pressed my palm against the barrel of the gun. "You're going to have to shoot through me first," I said. Tomb gave me a sideways glance. Which confused me. Tomb was supposed to belly-laugh, drop the pistol and then wrap his arm around the old man. We'd order another round of drinks, piss away the rest of the night, and then I'd file my first magazine story, all about the surly-yet loveable private eye with a hottie for a niece and a tattooed-yet-loveable killer for a sidekick.

It wasn't until the bullet had blasted its way through my hand and into Hilly's face that I realized:

Not everything's a fucking joke.

# Everybody's Girl

Robert Barnard

Robert Barnard was born in 1936 in Essex, England, and has served as lecturer and professor at universities in Australia and Norway. His innovative novels are well-plotted solutions of murders, but are also noteworthy for their wit, social satire, and the author's depiction of human nature at its best, worst, and everything in between. Besides his more than thirty novels, Barnard is also the author of nonfiction works about Agatha Christie and Charles Dickens, as well as *A Short History of English Literature.* He is one of those writers who has never written the same book twice, finding new ways of turning old forms into contemporary crime fiction of the highest rank.

**When the sound came of** mail pushed through the letter box and plopping on to the front doormat, Hannah Lowton saw a gleam of hope come into her husband's eye. He pushed aside his plate.

"At least it's come before I go to work," he said.

Hannah was already in the hall, and he heard her pick up the post and slit open an envelope.

"It's from her, from Ruth," she said, coming back into the dining room and extracting a letter from the envelope. Peter looked at her hopefully. He could not fail to see her mouth drop. "Oh dear. She doesn't seem any happier . . . She seems more confused than ever . . . 'Dearest Mum and Dad. I'm sorry I sounded so depressed and scatty in my last. I do try to get more settled, do want to make a go of it . . .' Then she blames herself that she can't settle down."

"Typical Ruthie. Protects everyone except herself."

"Says she can't fit in because she won't go along with the crowd. The history course doesn't help. The Dark Ages—I ask you!"

"I think it's only dark because there's not much known about it.'

"She says her only friend is this boy called George, the one she's mentioned before: "He's a friend because he's lonely and mixed-up like me."

"Poor, poor Ruthie!"

"Oh dear—then she says, 'I don't see the point in a life that's going nowhere.' "

"Right. That's it." Peter Lowton pushed his chair back from the table and stood up. "That's the second time she's said something like that. I'm going to Leeds to talk to her."

"Oh Peter, is that wise? Shouldn't she sort it out for herself?"

"It's six weeks since she started there. If she feels there's no point in her life, something's gone terribly wrong."

"Do you want me to come, Peter?"

"No—you stay here in case she rings. And tell the office I won't be in." The look on his face was wild with anxiety. The next thing she heard was his pulling on a coat and banging the front door.

Across the road at number 18, Sheila McCartney saw Peter dash out to his car. She registered the panic in his face and body movements.

"God, Peter looks desperate," she said. It was the first time she had spoken to her husband in ten days. He merely grunted. "He's reversing the car into the drive. He's not going into work. He's going towards Leeds. It must be something to do with Ruth, They've been getting worrying letters from her."

Neville McCartney muttered: "You got too involved with that girl—"

"*I* got too involved with her?" Their eyes met, it seemed for the first time in months. *I* did?"

"She was never more than a sweet girl across the road to me."

"Well? *Well?*"

"You were in love with her."

"Oh, and you weren't? Well, at least I admit it. At least I know myself. All right, I loved her. *Love* her. Why these past tenses?"

"Because she's gone to university. Gone out of your life."

"Our lives. Maybe she has, maybe not. It doesn't alter the fact that I love her." Her voice raised itself to a shout. "Do you think I'm ashamed of it? I need some love. God knows I need some love."

When she had washed up and heard her husband leave

the house she went next door to her father, now over seventy and increasingly immobile.

"Everything all right, Dad?"

He turned a troubled gaze in her direction.

"Shouldn't I be asking you that?"

"Oh, did you hear?" She made a gesture of dismissal. "Just the usual."

"Couldn't you both make an effort? He's not a bad man, Sheila."

"I never said he was. He's a nothing man."

"It wasn't about Ruthie, was it, Sheila?" He saw at once in her face that it was. "Oh, I am sorry. The pair of you like that, quarrelling over a sweet young girl. It's disgusting."

"It's not disgusting, Dad. She's just a good friend to me."

"I should hope so. But what about Neville? A man of forty-five."

"Can't we forget about Neville? I do all the time. Now what do you want at the shops, Dad?"

Ruthie's bedsit in Kirkstall, three miles out of Leeds, was in Cannock Road, and Peter and Hannah had seen it when they brought her from Barnsley in September. He turned the car upwards from Kirkstall Abbey and found the right road without difficulty. Ruth's was in the middle of a set of named bells, a first-floor room, but three rings produced no response. Peter had been conscious of a shape moving around in the bay-windowed room to his right, and he pressed one of the lower bells on spec.

"Yes?"

The name, apparently, was Kit Wakeham. He was a big young man in tracksuit bottoms and T-shirt, and he clearly felt himself in control. Peter had to repress a sense of being menaced.

"I'm trying to make contact with my daughter, Ruth Lowton. There's no answer when I ring."

"I'd say she was out, wouldn't you?"

"Yes. I'm sorry to trouble you, but we had a letter this morning that worried us. She sounded at the end of her tether."

"News to me if she is."

"When did you last see her?"

"Two or three days ago. And I think she was supposed to be going out with a friend here last night. Beyond that—"

"You see, we're afraid she might commit suicide." The young man looked at him.

"Frankly, I think you're barking. Look, if you want to talk to someone who's close to her, try George Carlson, three doors up."

"Oh yes, she mentioned someone called—"

But he was speaking to a closed door.

On his way to work, Neville McCartney stopped at the newsagent's for a *Guardian* and a packet of cigarettes. He frowned when he saw Isobel Franklin at the counter.

"Something the matter, Mr. McCartney?"

"Oh, nothing . . . Well, you were her history teacher. It seems the Lowtons are very worried about Ruth not settling. We think he's gone to Leeds today."

"Oh, really? Surely he should have left her to sort things out for herself. She's a *very* bright girl. No reason why she shouldn't settle down, left alone."

"Perhaps you pushed her too hard."

"I didn't push her at all. I was very conscious she was more intelligent than me. Perhaps you involved her too much in your domestic affairs."

"I didn't involve her at all. *She* came to *me.* She wanted to make peace between us. She Was so sweet, so understanding."

"A teenager can hardly understand a twenty-year marriage that's gone wrong."

"She tried so hard to. She didn't realise that by being there, by being so sweet—"

But Neville thought better of it, and walked abruptly out of the shop. Mrs. Franklin walked slowly toward the Bygrove Comprehensive School where she taught, thinking of how often Ruth Lowton had shown how much quicker and brighter she was than the teacher who had been forced back into teaching when her soldier husband died and she was left with a family to support. Of course Ruthie didn't know she was doing it, but she made her teacher feel so inadequate, so dull, so middle-of-the-road. Every lesson with Ruth had made Isobel feel she was on trial.

The bedsitter was shabby and sad, but the saddest thing about it was its total lack of character. George Carlson did not apologise for it. He was too worried by the arrival of Ruth's father.

"I was beginning to wonder," he said. "I hadn't seen her, and normally I'd . . . I was *worried.*"

"When did you last see her?"

"It was Tuesday morning. We were at a lecture on King Alfred."

"How was she?"

"Well, much as usual . . . She wasn't happy with the course."

"I know. She told us you were her only real friend here."

"Oh, I don't know about . . . She said she might be going out on Thursday, that's last night. Clubbing, I suppose. She didn't ask me along because she knows that's not my kind of place."

"Not hers either, from what she said. Where is your kind of place? Where do you talk together?"

"Oh, anywhere. The lecture room, the Brotherton Library, in the queue at the bank, down at the Abbey."

"Kirkstall Abbey?"

"Yes, it's one of her favourite places. We go there quite often. It's only five minutes away. It really gives me a lift, talking to Ruth. She's so . . . understanding."

"You're not happy here either, she says."

"I don't know about *either* . . . Ruth seemed . . . It's a wonderful university of course, but I don't fit in. I thought it would be different from school, but . . ."

Peter felt that if he was not careful he would have to sit there for hours listening to Carlson's problems, as poor Ruthie so obviously had done, so he interrupted: "Kirkstall Abbey—you said it was one of Ruthie's favourite places."

"Oh it is. So peaceful. It puts things into perspective, she always says."

"Do you think we could walk there? Just in case?"

On the way down George got back on to Ruth—himself and Ruth.

"Ruth is so good with people. She'll do anything for anyone, not just me. She'll go clubbing with the people from her house, even though from what you said she couldn't have enjoyed it. I know she hates some of the things going on there. I think she feels they need someone honest to be there and warn them, stop them going on drugs or sex binges."

"Ruth is always there for people who need her."

"She and I walk around Kirkstall on a fine day, and she'll tell me a little about herself, but mostly she listens to me, and I tell her about school, how out of things I always felt there, and how my parents are always bullying me and pushing me to stand up for myself. One time, when we'd been walking for nearly two hours, she had to go and get an essay done, and she said, 'Doesn't time fly when you're having fun?' and I thought she might have been making fun of me, but I just looked in her eyes and I knew she wasn't."

They had passed the Abbey Museum and its car park and had reached the Abbey Road. Suddenly Peter became aware that further up, on the way to Horsforth, three police cars were parked. For a second he was stunned. Then he heard the siren of another police car approaching. Ignoring the crossing he weaved his way through the heavy traffic and ran through the Abbey grounds in the direction of the police activity.

The body had lain underwater, visible but trapped, just under the weeds and dead leaves up beyond the Abbey grounds and edging Kirkstall rugby pitch. A strong current had released it, and it came down a hundred yards, to be trapped again by vegetation just beside a little bridge where many people and their dogs passed. It was wearing a skirt of dark blues, purples and clarets—Laura Ashley colours—and a charcoal-grey top. It had been quite warm until the frosts came on Thursday night, so perhaps she had gone in before that happened.

Charlie Peace looked down at the fragile body and the blond hair and shuddered. The corpse was suddenly his daughter's, anyone's daughter's.

"What are you thinking?" said Superintendent Oddie, coming up.

"Thinking maybe she went in before the weather turned cold."

"Haven't you noticed how little clothing young people wear these days, even when it's freezing? They seem to have some sort of internal heating."

"Eh oop," said Charlie, feigning broad Yorkshire. "Who's this then?"

From the direction of the Abbey two men were running towards them, the older man easily outstripping the younger. When they got near, the uniformed policeman tried to bar their way, but the older man turned to Oddie: "Please. You've got to let me through. Is it a girl? My daughter is missing, and she loved this place."

Oddie looked at Charlie Peace, then taking the man firmly by the arm he led him through the cordon of policemen. The body was just being eased on to dry land. The face was uppermost. When he saw it the man fell on his knees and sobbed his heart out. Oddie left him for a minute, then raised him and led him back to the little group.

"It's what we feared, my wife and I. We had a letter this morning. It sounded as if she was thinking of suicide."

But Oddie and Charlie Peace had seen the back of the body's head, and the wound at the crown that did not look like suicide to them.

Half an hour later the pair were driving up the hill towards 13 Cannock Road and Ruth Lowton's bedsit. Oddie had talked to her father. Through his tears Peter had told them how Ruth had somehow failed to fit in at the university of her choice, had been increasingly unhappy, and had sounded suicidal in the letter he and his wife had received that morning. He said that Ruth was someone who always felt deeply for people in trouble, and he thought she was saddened and upset by many of the aspects of Leeds student life she saw around her.

Charlie had talked to George Carlson, who had told him—also with sobs—much the same as he had told her father earlier. Charlie had a strong impression of a loner, an outsider, an unhappy young man who entirely lacked the capacity to change the conditions of his life. If anyone was a potential victim, it was Carlson, Charlie thought.

Both men were beginning to get the faint outline of a picture of the dead girl: the first stage in getting a picture of her killer. Ten minutes later they were in armchairs in the airy front room of Kit Wakeham.

"I'm sorry I swore at you," he was saying. "It's been one of those days. Her father was here earlier. I should never have taken a ground-floor room. But this is awful . . . horrible."

"Was she a popular girl?" Charlie asked. Kit shrugged.

"It was early days. She'd only been here a few weeks. She went around with some of the gang in these houses. Half of the places on this street are student residences. She went clubbing, to films, things at the student union. She mixed in all right, so far as I could see . . . I'm third year, and I've done all that. I didn't have a lot to do with her."

"When did you last see her?"

"Couple of days ago, maybe three. I didn't notice. She wasn't interested in me, probably because I *didn't* notice."

"You didn't like her, did you?" Oddie asked.

"Like I said, I didn't notice . . . She spent a lot of time with that miserable specimen George Carlson up the road. On the surface it was very good of her . . . too good, I thought. It didn't ring true, not to her other self, the clubbing, good-time girl. I felt she used people, or led them on, tried to bring out their worst side, their unhappiest side . . . I dunno . . . Ignore me. I'd make a rotten psychiatrist."

But would he? After two hours of interviewing friends and acquaintances in the Kirkstall area and the history department, Oddie and Charlie were far from sure. Ruth seemed to be a girl who presented a different face to different people, took on a new identity whenever it suited her. What was not clear was *why* it suited her, what she was trying to do. It certainly went beyond just trying to fit in, chameleon-like, to any environment she happened to be in. Sometimes it did seem as if she was trying to bring out the worst in the people around her, or to encourage behaviour likely to lead them into disaster and unhappiness.

Her movements began to be clearer after a time.

"She was supposed to be coming out with us on Thursday, yesterday," said Edwina Faye, the other girl on the first floor of number 13. "It was all arranged. We were going together—into town around nine, then on to the Jurassic Club when things began to liven up there. Only she wasn't around here all evening, and. finally I went on my own."

"When did you last see her?"

"I heard her singing in the bathroom that morning."

"You're sure it was her?"

"I know her voice, and I know what she sings."

"What sort of girl was she, to your way of thinking?"

"Liked having a good time. Up for anything." Edwina thought for a moment. "But sly with it. She never let herself get out of hand, but she didn't mind at all watching while other people went over the edge. Got a kick out of that, I sometimes thought. And as far as I know she hadn't slept with anyone all the time she'd been here. I mean, that's six weeks. It just wasn't natural, not first time away from home."

One of the men in the house had had a brief talk with her in the kitchen on Wednesday. She had been very full of herself because she'd written what she called "a great work of fiction." It was in the form of a letter, which she put down briefly on one of the surfaces of the kitchen, but the man had not tried to see the addressee. Charlie concluded that students were too wrapped up in their own selves to have any natural curiosity about others.

Talking it over, Charlie and Oddie felt they were beginning to get a picture, but were still a long way from finding out anything about Ruth that could suggest a reason for anyone wanting to kill her.

"I could imagine George Carlson committing suicide if he found out she'd been having him on to have a laugh at his expense," said Charlie. "But not committing murder—no way. She would have had to have been playing games with a really strong character, someone with deep feelings that she'd trodden on. Kit Wakeham might fit the bill, but I believed him when he said he didn't care for her."

"A letter suggests someone back home, and having it with her in the kitchen suggests it was posted that day. Posts are unpredictable, but on balance the letter to her parents would have been posted on Thursday, to get there today. So who was it she posted that one to on Wednesday?"

"Strong feelings suggest long-matured ones," said Charlie.

"Middle-aged people," said Oddie. "That surely means Barnsley."

"Someone there who she had driven mad over the years," agreed Charlie, as Oddie started the car.

When they got to the suburb of Barnsley where Ruth had lived they found the street without difficulty. They stood outside her house for a moment or two, but registered there was no sign of life within. Peter, her father, had been driven home some time ago, and they were reluctant to pressure him for a second time so soon after the devastating discovery. Standing indecisive in the street, and looking at the neighbouring houses, they saw a middle-aged woman at a window, watching them. A moment later she appeared in her front door, and they went over. Crying had made rivulets down her make-up, and her lipstick had been smudged around the edges. She looked a mess.

"Will you come in?" she said, as Oddie showed her his ID. "I guessed you were policemen. Hannah rang me and told me of Ruthie's death, and I've been telling those who were close to her. Hannah's grief-stricken, of course, and so am I. She meant so much to me, to all of us."

"Are you a relative?" Charlie asked.

"No, just a friend. Such a *good* friend—I mean she was

to me, more than I to her. She was so understanding, such a wonderful support."

"Support in what?" Oddie asked.

"Oh, you know, personal troubles. My husband is a pig. Tell me something new, I hear you say. Let's not go into it. The point is that Ruthie was always interested, always listened, really helped, even when she was hardly more than a girl."

"You know she'd told her parents she was unhappy in Leeds?"

"Yes. Hannah just told me that. I can't understand it. She had so many friends here. Everyone at school, in the neighbourhood, loved her."

"Your husband too?"

"Well . . . yes, she was nice to him. Nicer than he deserved. She was to my father too. He's chairbouiid, with nothing much to do all day. She did little bits of shopping for him, but mostly just talked. He thought the world of her."

Oddie nodded.

"Can you think of any reason why Ruth should be unhappy at Leeds University, if she was?"

"Oh, she was. She made that quite clear in letters home. I think she felt she had been pressured to go there by her history teacher. You know how teachers live alternative lives through their pupils. In fact Mrs. Franklin wanted her to try for Oxbridge, but Ruth wasn't willing to go so far from home. People who are pressured like that—not that Ruth put it like that, or felt anything other than grateful—often develop a sense of resentment, don't they? Almost *want* things to go badly. She'd have been so much better off staying at home and going to Sheffield or the nearest poly-that-was."

"I suppose what you say makes sense," said Oddie cautiously. "Maybe we should have a word with Mrs. Franklin."

So it was that the last talk of the day took place two streets away from Ruth Lowton's home, in a postwar semi which periodically erupted with the sounds made by teenagers coming in or going out, and the incursion of loud music suddenly hushed as they remembered Charlie's stern injunction to keep the noise down.

"I'm glad you've come, but I'm afraid you'll find me a sadly muddled witness," said Isobel Franklin, serving them instant coffee. "I've been thinking about Ruth all day, and of course talking about her at school, and I've been forced to look at her and wonder about my assessment of her."

"In what ways?" asked Oddie.

"In every way. My headmaster talked to me this afternoon, and he said: 'I think she robbed you of confidence in yourself.' And that I know was true, though I always believed it was the reverse of what she intended." She paused, and took a draught of her coffee. "My husband was a regular army officer, killed on winter exercises in north Norway. I went back into teaching on the basis of a teaching certificate, and a general interest in history. I found myself teaching it further and further up the school because they couldn't get anyone properly qualified. I was always perfectly confident about facing a class. What I had doubts about was whether I was knowledgeable enough, sophisticated enough in my approach to teach at O and A levels."

"And Ruth Lowton?"

"She once said to me: 'I think you're wonderful, being able to teach history so well without a degree.' There were lots of other remarks to similar 'encouraging' effect."

"And you never saw through her?"

"No. I don't think anyone she targeted did. Something Neville McCartney said to me in the newsagent's this morning suggested that he was wondering whether Ruth's 'sweet' and 'understanding' attempts to bring peace to his marriage weren't really sexual teasing designed to make matters worse. And the headmaster reminded me this afternoon of a boy who left school, didn't find work, and sank further and further into apathy, staying in bed all day, losing all his friends. Ruth visited him, over and over, trying to get him to snap out of it and make an effort, she said. But his mother asked her to stop coming, and privately she said she thought she was driving him to suicide."

"What happened to him?" Charlie asked.

"He met a girl, got a job, everything turned out okay. Typical teenage phase. But . . . it seems like there's a pattern."

Yes, it seems like there's a pattern, Charlie and Oddie said to themselves.

The next morning they did not set out from Leeds until after ten, wanting the day to have settled down before they arrived in Barnsley. They went first to Fred Mortimer, Sheila McCartney's old and chairbound father, then to the local PO sorting office to see if they could get on to the scent of Ruth Lowton's Wednesday letter. They didn't feel they should hurry to report progress to Ruth's parents, and it was nearly lunchtime when they rang the doorbell of number 15. Hannah Lowton's eyes were red, and she was near to tears when she explained that they couldn't talk to her husband.

"I had such a night with him," she said. "She was the

apple of his eye. The doctor's just been and given him a sedative."

"We do understand," said Oddie. "I wonder if we could see the letter from your daughter, the one that made him go to Leeds yesterday."

"Of course," she said, and fetched the cream pages from the sideboard.

It was what they had expected: her unhappiness, her inability to settle, her doubts about the activities of her fellow students, her feelings of desperation at the pointlessness of her life in Leeds. It ended with love to her 'dear old stepmum' and the assurance that they had both 'done all you can for me.'

"You're her stepmother then?" asked Charlie.

"Her mother died of breast cancer when she was one. I married Peter when she was three. To everybody I am her mother."

Except to Ruthie apparently, thought Charlie. He felt that that 'step' could have been left out.

"Have you got the envelope?" asked Oddie.

"The envelope? I don't think so. I've probably thrown it out."

"Never mind. The postmark wouldn't have proved anything."

"What do you mean?"

"You see, Mr. Mortimer opposite says he saw you come out of this house on Thursday, soon after the postman had been, with a letter in your hand, in a cream envelope. You got into your car and drove away."

"I expect he got the day wrong. You would, being there all the time."

"I don't think so. Because on Friday morning your

husband's car was parked in the road and your car was in the garage. That all depended on who was home first, didn't it? And on Friday you stayed home in case there was a call from Ruth. Your husband told me that."

"I expect Mr. Mortimer mistook something I was holding for a letter. My husband can tell you it arrived on Friday."

"He heard you tearing open a letter, and saw you come in with this one. That doesn't prove it arrived yesterday. It may be that you wanted him to think it arrived yesterday."

Hannah Lowton looked from one face to the other, from, the middle-aged white man to the young black one, both faces filled with professional certainty: they knew. They thought they knew. But how could they really know?

It had started so long ago, when Ruthie was about seven and, like so many children, learning the art of playing off one parent against the other. She soon realised that, whatever she wanted, her father would eventually give her, however strong the opposition from her stepmother. As soon as these contests began to be a struggle for Peter Lowton's heart, Hannah gave in. Constant victories of that sort would be bad for Ruthie, bad for all three of them.

But as the child grew older it became clear that victories she must have, that emotional dominance was a sort of drug to her. Time after time she would work her way into people's lives, let them attach themselves—and all their hopes, fears and fantasies—to her, and then bring disaster, chaos, disruption to their lives. Hannah only once tried to bring her understanding of what Ruth was doing into the open.

"I'm just trying to do my little bit to make the world a better place," Ruth had said, looking at her with a smirk on her face. The smirk seemed to Hannah to say: "Your turn is coming."

The tone of disillusion and discontent had begun to enter her letters almost as soon as she had moved to Leeds. "She doesn't lose much time," Hannah said despairingly to herself. If she had questioned the truth of the letters, Peter would have called her heartless, jealous of his love for his—and only his—daughter. She knew Ruth was playing with them, driving her father to desperation, and getting from it the same pleasure she had got from fostering despair among her neighbours and schoolfellows in Barnsley. When the letter came on Thursday, her first thought was gladness that Peter had gone to work: the suggestion of suicide was new, and something had to be done before he returned home.

She left the car at the Woodhouse Lane multi-storey and walked up to the University. It was easy to find out where the history lectures were, and she lingered and mixed in with the students when they came out, leaving Ruth a little to the front. She could see the girl was happy, carefree, and already knew most of her year. She waved, smiled and made plans.

"We're out tonight at the Jurassic," she shouted to someone. "If I don't see you there, see you at the Majestic on Saturday."

To another person in the crowd she shouted that he should make sure he had plenty of the white stuff. Ruth, Hannah had no doubt, was in her element at Leeds, and was busy spreading chaos and desperation.

Nothing could be done until classes and library work were over. She drove down to Cannock Road, had lunch in a nearby pub, then waited. At one point in the long wait she got out of the car, went to the boot, removed the monkey-wrench, then put it in her capacious string bag. It was said at the trial that this was for self-protection. It was not believed.

When Ruth arrived back in Cannock Road Hannah got out of the car and met her as she was alighting from a bus. Her expression was one of satisfaction rather than surprise. When Hannah asked if they could talk, Ruth said: "Let's go down to Kirkstall Abbey. I talk to a lot of people there. It's such a peaceful, spiritual place."

And she had smirked. Hannah had kept her anger bottled up until they were in the Abbey grounds, then it burst out.

"You are just playing with your father. Driving him mad with pain and worry because that's what you do best. I've seen yon with your friends here. You're perfectly happy!"

"Haven't you heard of the clown with the broken heart, step-mama? I smile even though their dreadful deeds and habits break my heart. Dad knows what a caring person I am." The voice oozed with sneer.

"He's deceived by your disgusting games with people. What has he done to deserve this? He's always given you what you demanded."

"Yes, he has, hasn't he? In spite of you. But I think he was always pleasing himself, don't you? He wasn't thinking whether I ought to have those things: he was thinking of the pleasure he would get in letting me have them. We're all selfish at heart, aren't we?"

"I don't know of a less selfish person than your dad."

"Have it your own way." Ruth shrugged. "I suppose

you'd know. He only married you to provide a mother for me. Pity you never did."

They were under the weeping willows, near-leafless now, by the rugby pitch. Hannah's hand had been on the wrench for some time. As Ruth came out with those last words she smirked again and turned towards the flowing river. Hannah gripped the wrench, took it from the bag, and with all her strength bashed it into Ruth's skull. As her stepdaughter fell into the water Hannah put the wrench away and composedly walked back to the car.

Hannah looked at the two men opposite. Professional men, men whose business was crime. It would be so easy to tell them what they already knew, to confess. But to do that would be to hand Ruth her last victory, to give her on a plate the ruin of her own and Peter's fragile marriage. She couldn't do it. She had to fight back.

She stood up.

"Could we continue this at the police station?" she asked. "I need to have a lawyer to advise me, don't I? Do you think you could ask Mrs. McCartney opposite to come and sit with Peter till he wakes. He'll be lonely and upset, and I may be gone a long time."

And she started with them out to the police car.

# Imitate the Sun

Luke Sholer

Luke Sholer was nominated for the Edgar Allan Poe Award for his story "Imitate the Sun," which appeared in *Ellery Queen's Magazine.* Recently he has places stories in *Crimewave* (UK) and *Eureka Literary Magazine.* His poems have appeared in *Analecta, Better Than a Stick in the Eye, Laughing Dog, Veil,* and *Zeniada.* After earning his bachelor's degree from the University of Arizona, Luke relocated to Madrid, Spain, where he writes and teaches English. He will be starting a master's degree at the Universidad Complutense de Madrid in fall 2005.

**Tokyo. This is where it** started and this is where it ends. The elevators ring faintly as they rise and fall in the shafts.

This Akasaka hotel room. I can still see the oil mark where you rested your forehead on the glass. You stood there confessing for two nights straight while forty-two stories below limousines and taxis drew patterns on the street.

But now, the third night, I'm only watching for one car. The long black one we saw Kumi tumble lifeless out of. Long and black and old, like the cars generals used in World War II.

And from the bathroom, moments ago, came a gunshot.

The elevators ring faintly, going up and down the shafts. Any minute those doors will slide open on the forty-second floor.

They will be coming for you.

But you, you're already gone. You're already someone else.

Madrid, several months ago. I saw them, back under the porticoes, but pretended I didn't.

I went on spraying the cobblestones of the Plaza Mayor. When I looked again they were gone. I tilted the nozzle back. The water punched in an arc and washed ringing down the lamppost.

I finished my shift and headed home. The sun was rising on a Madrid that had been rinsed new, like a miracle, in the night.

They were on the sidewalk outside my building. Four, in identical black suits. Four Japanese men.

"Major Inman," said the one in front. His red silk tie matched his red silk pocket square. He had sharpened fingernails.

At first I didn't react. It had been over a year since anyone addressed me in English.

"Major Inman," he repeated. "We would appreciate a moment with you."

* * *

I led them into my living room. The other three stood back as the man with the fingernails sat with me. He mentioned Tokyo, grieving families, an unpunished criminal.

"As you can imagine, Major, the families—"

"Don't call me that. I'm not in the service anymore."

"Ah, I had forgotten. You are a streetcleaner now." He smiled. "The night shift."

I twisted my wedding band, said nothing.

"The families need to put this to rest. You find the criminal, return him to Japan. Then—" he caged his palms as though trapping a fly "—there can be justice."

"Why don't you try the police?"

"This," he said, "is a personal affair. As much for us as for you."

"This has nothing to do with me."

"Do you like being a widower, Major Inman?"

I got up. I was about to throw them out.

Then he talked about death on the Tokyo subway, and about you.

I told him I had to think it over.

By night I worked in Old Madrid, spraying down the cobblestones and columns, pressure-blasting posters off the walls. It was calming, repetitive. The waterproof suit swished as I moved.

But by day, insomnia. I lay half-dressed in the bed my wife had never slept in, in an apartment she had never even seen, and thought of that morning on the Tokyo subway.

It was spring, 1995. I'd been granted two weeks' leave. We went to Tokyo on our second honeymoon.

The morning of March 20, 1995. Five members of the terrorist cult Aum Shinrikyo released sarin nerve gas on Tokyo's rush-hour trains.

That morning she got up early; she was going to observe the cherry blossoms before the parks got crowded. I slept in.

She died alone.

At St. Luke's International Hospital, surrounded by people vomiting and screaming in a language she didn't understand.

Cardiopulmonary arrest, the doctor said.

Sarin gas. Before that I didn't even know it existed.

Seven years passed.

Then the man with the sharpened fingernails came. He explained: Your role was crucial. Without you, Aum Shinrikyo never would've pulled off the attack.

I'd thought it was behind me, but it wasn't.

I couldn't sleep.

I saw her body in the hospital bed, her name omitted from all the newspapers. I thought of the people who had taken her from me. I thought of you.

This, every day, for a week.

Then I told him yes. I would hunt you.

We were at the Universidad Complutense rugby fields. I went there often in the afternoons, when I was waking up. It was good to drink coffee from the snack bar while the men in white shorts collapsed in piles.

This time the tie and pocket square were lime green. His fingernails were still sharpened.

He was explaining: After the attack you went missing. You hadn't been back to Japan since. Meanwhile you'd lived everywhere, been a dozen different people. You even spent a few years in the states. Once near my hometown.

"If you knew that, why didn't you go after him?"

"Because we didn't know. Not then. We hadn't made our contact yet."

One team advanced on the field, each player shunting the ball behind him.

He continued: Madrid was the last place you'd been. They'd come to catch you themselves, but they were too late. You'd already changed identities, fled.

"Where to?" I asked.

"La Paz, Bolivia."

I thought cocaine fields, revolutionaries.

"No," he said. "He'll be making his money a different way. An invisible way."

"Meaning?"

"He specializes in passports, fraudulent identities."

"And when I find him?"

"If you try to bring him back to Tokyo, he'll struggle. So you will disguise your purpose. You will tell him his father is very sick, on the verge of dying. His last wish is to see his son."

"And why will he buy that?"

"Because it's true."

La Paz then.

I quit my job and my plane touched down at El Alto International.

I left my suitcase at a hotel on the Calle Loayza, asked the concierge for a map, and walked.

I walked all day.

And saw: a sky cluttered with electrical lines and sun-bleached signs, street vendors amid stacks of colorful wool, disintegrating sidewalks, grim bars with only men in them, Indian women in bowler hats and layered skirts, gutters lined with refuse, infants' faces caked in saliva and dirt. And in the background, giant and white, the triple peaks of Illimani.

I would give you time. I would survey the city, follow the black market goods. I would learn the playing field.

Then engage you.

But that first afternoon it hit me.

On the Avenida 16 de Julio, in the snarl of cars and trucks trailing paper streamers, I started hyperventilating and sat dizzy on the sidewalk coning my hands over my mouth as horns and catcalls shrieked all around me.

*Soroche*, the Bolivians call it. Altitude sickness.

My whole body felt like it was suffocating. The vomiting and diarrhea chained me to my hotel room. At night I watched the high plaster ceiling.

I could do nothing but rest and drink coca leaf tea.

I was losing ground.

You took my wife and even my vengeance from me.

My silhouette on the dark glass. Beyond it, red lights wink on the skyscrapers. It's so the helicopters don't slap into them, you said.

This Akasaka hotel room. We spent two nights holed up in Tokyo luxury. Floor to ceiling windows, down duvets, teak hangers from the Cambodian rainforest.

That one sudden shot behind the bathroom door. He just went in. There was no reason to think he had a gun.

The elevators chime as they rise and fall in the shafts. You're gone now.

But for two nights you stood here, overlooking the city you spent seven years running from. You against the glass, narrating.

"It was Kumi," you said. "She was the start."

You met her at a stand-up noodle bar in the Shinjuku district. You looked like you'd walked straight out of a music video. So did she: pink hair, a camouflage wristband. She wasn't even eating. She just leaned on the metal counter, ignoring even the cigarette between her fingers.

You made eye contact. The air started to scrape. You thought once, then went over. She acted like you weren't there. You stole the cigarette from her and inhaled as the elevated train scraped a long curve overhead.

You mouthed something in the roar.

"What?" she said.

"Do you know anything fun to do around here?"

She waited for the train to pass.

"You don't look like you need my help to find fun."

You grinned; then stopped. "How's your luck?"

"Alarming," she said, snatching the cigarette back. The tip hissed orange. "I always win."

Your eyes locked with hers.

"Let's go," you said.

And you went. To a pachinko parlor in East Shinjuku. You were gambling, both of you, with your money, giddy like winners of a shopping spree. You sank it into the machines until nothing was left.

"Come here," she said, slipping her hands into your

jeans. You trembled; you were close enough to bite her. She pulled the last coin out.

"That's for the subway home."

"No it's not," she said.

And she put it in and slammed the button and the shower of coins that followed clinked throughout the parlor for several minutes straight.

"Here." She handed you one from the overflowing tray. "For the subway."

Then she wrote ten numbers on a napkin. "Ask for Kumi."

El Mercado Negro.

Anything undocumented, anything stolen or bootlegged, can be found in La Paz's black market. Including identities. When I got better it was the first place I went.

In stalls and on the sidewalk people were selling mobile phones, tin pots, dubious Levi's, bright crumbling pigments, Japanese film, cassettes with photocopied covers, imitation French handbags.

A mestizo vendor who recognized that I spoke with a Castillian accent said, *"Tengo algo que le puede interesar."* He led me down an alley to a dim workshop and in the back room unstrung a pouch full of sixteenth-century colonial coins. They were large and silver; the edges were wiggly.

"Straight from the mines at Potos"," he said. "There was enough silver there to underwrite the Spanish economy for two hundred years."

I held all that forced labor and rape and history in my hand.

And traded him a fan of U.S. dollars for two colonial coins.

"Maybe you can help me with something else," I said.

He couldn't but he knew who could. He led me back through the market to a man sitting in a folding chair.

"He wants a passport," my vendor said.

The man nodded. He had the letter *S* tattooed on his neck. "What kind?"

"Canadian," I said. At that time a Canadian passport was the most coveted: it raised the fewest suspicions and had the friendliest visa agreements. With it you could travel, and get residence, almost anywhere.

He clicked, shook his head. "Nobody has one."

I told him what I was willing to pay.

"My name is Santi." He wrote down a phone number. "This guy doesn't have any, but he knows someone who does. A new kid. Japanese."

I went to an Entel phone booth.

An Indian woman squatted on the sidewalk in front of me. Her multiple skirts ruffled out around her like a hen. She got up, leaving a puddle.

*"Dígame,"* said a man on the fourth ring.

"*Buenas tardes.* Santi said you know about Canadian passports."

*"No sé nada."*

"That's a pity," I said. "Because my friend lost his."

He didn't respond.

"He needs a new one. And if he likes it, he'll need twenty more."

I could hear nothing but the line static.

*"De acuerdo,"* he finally said. "I know somebody. He'll meet you on the Calle Sagárnaga tomorrow at noon. Be drinking a lemon Fanta."

* * *

Back in my hotel on the Calle Loayza. A crack as faint as a spider strand ran across the high plaster ceiling. On the nightstand, under the handcuffs and the gun, were pictures of you.

I closed my eyes and tried to see my wife. Tried to see her sleeping, her hair dark and flowing as a diver's. Tried to see the weekends we spent in Sevilla, her on tiptoes pulling oranges off the trees. I tried, even, to see her in Tokyo, collapsing as she stepped off the subway. Then at St. Luke's, not responding to CPR, her pupils shrunken with nerve gas.

But I only saw your face.

Only saw those pictures of you.

The man with the sharpened fingernails gave me an assortment, all of them old, from when you still lived in Japan. There was one, from a yearbook. You went to Tokyo's best international school, where you learned flawless English. You're wearing a blazer, your hair is parted. Each student says what he wants to be as an adult. There are surgeons, diplomats. You put: *street magician.*

And he also gave me the terms.

He said: *Justice can be a delicate matter, Major Inman, and so you have a choice. You may hand him over to us in Tokyo, or you may send us clear proof of his death. Upon completion of either condition, you will receive the second half of your payment.*

And I said yes.

Because I could let your countrymen judge you. Or I could leave you nameless and dead in a foreign country.

Like how you left my wife.

When I saw you the next day on the Calle Sagárnaga I would decide.

In the beginning you lived with your parents and so did she. Which meant you had nowhere to yourselves. Nowhere except the love hotels of Kabuki-cho or Dogenzaka. How many afternoons spent in spotless rooms you would never return to? Just two or three hours at a time, the length of a film.

You remember one afternoon in particular, you described it several times. Everything was sky blue: the Jacuzzi, the comforter, the curtains. That and the white carpet. Like a model home, a place people could visit but never live in.

She was sitting cross-legged, sheets up to her navel. Everything else was bare.

"When I was a girl," she said, blowing smoke out, "I used to rollerskate."

You were in the bathroom, washing your genitals in the sky blue sink. "Could you do any tricks?"

"I could jump." She inhaled and thought for a second. "They were professional skates."

You suddenly thought she was lying. You watched her in the mirror.

She was caressing her arm. "I used to be left-handed."

"What?"

"We were in the park, it was Sunday."

You moved to the doorway.

"I was skating backwards around my parents. I wanted to impress them. There must have been a pebble, a twig. Suddenly I was falling. Backwards. My head was going to crack open. That's all I saw: my head cracking open like a purse being dumped out."

"But you didn't—"

"My father caught me just in time. By the arm," she said, still caressing her left arm. "And tore it out of socket. I started screaming. He slapped me."

She eyed you, removing the cigarette from her lips.

*"I saved you,* he said. *You should be grateful."*

You knelt naked on the bed.

"They put it in a sling. After that I did everything right-handed."

You knocked her back. The lit cigarette fell onto the sheets.

"That's what men do," she said. "Save you and hurt you at the same time."

And you devoured her neck as the smell of burning linen filled the room.

The Calle Sagárnaga is the Artisans' Market.

I arrived early. I had the handcuffs in the small of my back, the gun in my coat pocket.

Stands and shops, vivid shawls and blankets. Indian women knelt weaving on heddle looms, spinning wool with drop spindles. From beneath their bowler hats hung long black braids.

I was supposed to be drinking a lemon Fanta, that's how you'd recognize me. But that's not what I wanted.

I moved past a stand, pushing the embossed leather purses out of my eyes.

And saw: you, among the craftsmen and tourists, hair disheveled, wearing a black duffel coat. You walked slowly, your head at a tilt, musing.

The gun in my pocket.

But something wasn't right.

You were young, too young. More like a student than a terrorist.

I loosened my grip and turned around. I picked up a wool blanket, feeling the weave.

"It's typical of the Jalq'a region," the woman said, indicating the black and magenta bands. I nodded, sensing you pass behind me.

You entered a music shop displaying pan flutes and charangos made from armadillo carapace. You complimented the craftsman. I clenched the gun, and saw my wife up to her stomach in the Mediterranean. She smiled, glistening, and I was thinking: the sea changes a woman, it rinses away the years and compromises, it shows her as she wants to be.

You came out of the shop.

I could have shot you then, but I never would've got any closer. I never would've learned more.

I let the gun fall loose in my pocket.

And shadowed you, your black head bobbing on the river of black heads, all the way down the Calle Sagárnaga.

I followed you all over the city.

First to a Banco Sol branch office, where you spoke to a manager but made no transaction.

Next, up into the canyon-rim slums of El Alto where naked children played tag around the potholes and their mothers pounded laundry in streams, carefully avoiding the feces. At an auto repair shop you spoke to a waiting group of Indians, passed them envelopes, and shook their hands.

Then back down the steep dirt streets of El Alto into the lower city, to your apartment on the Calle Indaburo.

You spent entire days with the Indians in El Alto. Entire days out.

The doorman of your building had the curved back and tiny hands of a watchmaker. His pocket was full of keys. I passed him some American bills and he escorted me up the stairwell.

Yours was a studio with only one window. The shutters were drawn.

I touched the light switch.

Laid out like a card game on your desk were dozens of *cádulas de identidad*—Bolivian national ID cards. There was a stack of papers to go with each name: credit histories, bills, paystubs.

But that wasn't what caught my eye.

Scattered on your bed, in a kind of puzzle, lay hundreds of pictures of you and Kumi. Phoenix, Miami, San Francisco, Bucharest, Madrid. All the cities where you ran your scams, your Cayman Island accounts growing ever vaster. Your goal was to retire at 30, anonymous and wealthy. No longer running. Kumi would be at your side, always. Your fortune would make you legitimate, stable.

There were photos of Tokyo too. You're no older than twenty; she's even younger. There's one with the date in orange numbers: *19-02-95*. You and her on a lookout platform of Tokyo's imitation Eiffel Tower. She's wearing sunglasses; the wind's got her hair. You look extremely proud to be with her.

My wife was still alive the day that photo was taken. She

might have driven to the beach, the Costa de la Luz, while I was at the Rota base processing codes. I would come home sometimes to find an arrow of silt in the bathtub.

I told you, in the hotel: "There are things you can't forget even though the memory is gone."

And you said: "There are memories you can't recreate even though the evidence is there in front of you."

Those photos scattered on your bed, like pieces dumped out of a puzzle box. Cities, expressions, years. It was harder and harder for you to fit them together in a way that made sense.

One afternoon you went to the airport, carrying just a day bag. My taxi followed yours through the nameless streets and mudbrick chaos of El Alto and I told the driver to wait as you got out at international arrivals.

Twenty minutes later the glass doors opened and you and Kumi stepped onto the sidewalk. She was svelte, fluid. Her body spoke ambition. You pushed her baggage on a trolley. And I didn't realize—until you were entering the hotel you'd rented for her visit, on the Calle Jaén—that she was taller than you.

The Calle Jaén, the façades white and smooth, black iron balconies. The whole quarter was like something out of Andalucía, half a millennium away. Built from memory, the nostalgia of conquistadors.

Kumi had eaten on the plane, between naps.

"What I want now," she said, "is a bath."

White towels on the floor and wall. The mirror opaque.

She stepped out dripping, like a sculpture in the rain. And you could taste the bath gels as you knelt in front of her.

* * *

These were things I didn't see. Things you told me later, in Tokyo.

You were in a restaurant. Kumi had discovered *tucumanas*, little pastries filled with meat, olives, raisins. It's all she would order.

"You know all those commercials I had to do when I was a kid?" she said. "In one of them, I couldn't get the smile right. The director kept shouting to re-shoot. I had to eat these wafer crackers. It got so dry I started choking."

She sipped her water.

"I choked so hard I vomited."

"Did they pay you?"

"No," she said. "Well, yes. But my dad kept it, like always. You remember. That was one of the first things you did."

"The first thing—"

"The first time you helped me," she said. "You raided the account he kept all my money in."

"He'd spent a lot of it."

"But there was a lot left. You gave it back to me."

"That was a long time ago."

"That was eight years ago," she said.

It was quiet.

"Are you making a lot of money here?"

"Starting to," you said.

She nodded, and another silence came.

"When are we finally going to live together?"

"Soon." You took her hand. "Soon."

But you knew, and she did too. You were just talking. Indulging in impossibility, because the truth was too bitter.

They were hunting you, and they were close.

* * *

In those days you were studying International Banking Law at Tokyo University. You wore a suit and tie to class, but at night you sported piercings and spiked hair. Your father was the director and controlling shareholder of one of Japan's biggest banks. It had taken him decades of dedication and ruthlessness to build it; growing up you barely saw him. There were no family vacations and he never paid you allowance. *In life there are no favors,* he said. *You get what you work for.*

Another dictum: If you failed even one class he'd kick you out of the house. So you studied what he wanted, and kept your grades high.

For pocket money you resorted to small-scale credit card fraud and identity theft.

Then you met Kumi, and life suddenly got expensive. There were dinners, hotels, taxis. She liked concerts, imported clothes.

"There are certain things I need," she said. And you understood the omitted, *If you can't give them to me, I'll find someone who can.*

You stepped up your operation. You started working with fellow university students, shipping illegal credit card orders to empty apartments all over the city, manufacturing work and residence permits for the Filipinos and Chinese.

On your twentieth birthday you invited her to your house. You asked your father for only one thing.

"What?" he said, you and Kumi in front of him. She was wearing safety pins as earrings.

"That you give us your blessing to date."

He took one look at her and left the room.

You told Kumi to wait in the kitchen and even she could hear him shout that his son would not be seen dating that Shinjuku gutter-cat. Your response was muffled, but the sound of a hand connecting with flesh was unmistakable.

You came out with your suitcase and laptop. Your cheek was already swelling.

"Come on," you told her. "I don't live here anymore."

You moved into a hotel until you could find an apartment. Kumi stayed those first few nights with you, telling you her dreams and making them yours.

"To travel everywhere," she said, kissing your chest. "To have our own place. To never be judged by anyone."

You had to take your operation another step up. One of the students you worked with had a contact in Aum Shinrikyo.

"Who are they?" you asked.

"A group of scientists and technicians who believe the world is ending. They have," he spread his hands, "unlimited funding."

You were nodding.

"They need people with your skills. And they pay."

You didn't care about their beliefs. You wanted an apartment you'd be proud to take Kumi to. You wanted to never crawl back to your father.

The sarin gas had already been developed. Aum Shinrikyo hired you to create false identities and offshore bank accounts for their key members. It gave them the confidence to conspire, to dream; if things went wrong they had escape routes.

You worked well. You got your apartment.

Two months later, my wife and I landed in Tokyo. It was our second honeymoon. We'd been married five years. The first night we couldn't sleep. Jet lag and crisp white sheets. She whispered: "I'm ready to conceive. I want to. Here."

The subway attack provoked a massive police investigation. The man who hired you said wait, they can't do anything. But you jumped. You took one of the identities and secret accounts, and vanished. The man who hired you—he was sentenced to death by hanging.

For six months not even Kumi knew where you were. Not until you placed a re-routed call from the other side of the earth. You were in Miami, involved in identity theft and bank fraud, working with a con team who bought, mortgaged, and resold luxury homes. You didn't explain it, not over the phone. You just told her that you missed her, and that you'd booked her a flight. The tickets were in the mail.

And I was back in Spain, where nothing felt mine anymore. I was a code-breaker at the Rota military base. American spies on Spanish soil. Our antenna could sweep communications up to a 3,000-mile radius. I spent my days with numbers and signals, looking for meaning. The desolation came at night. Alone in our bed, remembering her breath like a soft bellows on my skin. The emptiness overwhelmed me. So I moved to the couch, watching the television static fall in patterns until dawn.

Mid-morning. You were taking her to see the Witchcraft Market.

You could have blended in, but there was nobody—out of all the vendors, barterers, and witch doctors—that looked like Kumi.

She was wearing a Lufthansa Airlines jacket and black tank-gunner pants. Her hair was spiky, dyed yellow. Her sunglasses cost more than the average Bolivian made in a year.

On the sunbaked asphalt people sold herbs and seeds, animal fragments and folk remedies, enigmatic liquids in bottles. Meanwhile the witch doctors stitched in and out of the crowds, their heads full of coca and other people's futures.

You were so wrapped up in her I didn't even have to keep my distance.

At a little stand selling llama fetuses Kumi covered her mouth and pointed.

Then. I wasn't sure what I was waiting for but suddenly it happened.

Two men hustled off through the throng. Kumi let out a shout of amazement then anger when she felt for her vanished purse.

They separated and you chased the one with the purse all the way down the Calle Santa Cruz to the Avenida Baptista and pulled him to the ground in the middle of the Flower Market, petals and cut stems everywhere. He rolled over knife-side up and you gave no sound, just a look of surprise, as the blade went across your palm. That's when my boot crossed his face and I closed the handcuffs, slippery with your blood, around your wrists.

*"Quién coño eres?"* you shouted as I steered you, shoving your head down, past the flowersellers.

"Your father is dying," I said. "His last wish is to see you. I'm making sure that happens."

You didn't resist. As we walked, I began to relax.

Suddenly you fell and kicked back with the agility of a tumbler and before I could breathe again you'd already got the handcuffs around in front of you. I drew my gun and leveled as you dashed past the wicker baskets and flower-women but the colors and screams got in my eyes and I put it back.

Sprinting after you, knocking into things I didn't even see.

We crossed into the cemetery. A maze of mausoleums several stories high, little glass windows covering the niches: apartment blocks for the cremated.

I crashed through devoted family members and a string of professional mourners and when I stopped to apologize the mausoleum walls were still spinning and nobody could tell me which way you'd gone.

I left the cemetery. *"Señor,"* I heard. *"Disculpe, señor."*

It was a small boy, a beggar. He had something to sell.

"Show me," I said.

He held out a pair of handcuffs. They still had your blood on them.

She was where I thought she'd be. Back at your hotel on the Calle Jaén. I called from the lobby.

"Meet me at the café three doors down," I said. "It's about your boyfriend."

Her face was a little less beautiful. She'd either been sleeping or crying.

She ordered a Coca-Cola and the waiter looked at me. *"Lo mismo,"* I said.

He brought two scuffed glass bottles.

"Is he okay?" she asked. Her accent was unquestionably Japanese.

"He can be," I said, placing the bloody handcuffs on the table, "if you tell the truth."

She was quiet for a long time.

"He's been away for seven years. Why do they suddenly want him back?"

She put her fingertip to the blood. A tear came.

Kumi told me everything. That your father was extremely ill; the doctors gave him a few weeks. That his bank was one of the most important in Japan. He'd spent his life expanding and defending it and now a group of rival shareholders wanted to take it over. The old man's wish, it was rumored, was for his vanished son to replace him. He would forgive everything, like a king passing his throne to the errant prince.

At the end I asked: "How do you know all this?"

"The man who hired you," she said, "he have pointy fingernails."

"How—?"

"You and me," she said, "we work for same people. Rival shareholders."

Kumi stayed in La Paz for three more days, waiting for some sign of you. Then flew home. It was the last time she or I would see you in the Southern Hemisphere.

"What were you doing there?" I asked. "Other than hiding out."

You turned to me, all the lights of Tokyo behind you.

"Making money."

"You were using the Indians," I said, "to do something with Bolivian banks."

"I was giving them work," you said. "And paying them well."

"To do what?"

"To take out loans."

"Loans?"

You faced the glass again. A helicopter landed on top of a skyscraper.

"Banco Sol was giving out collateral-free microcredit loans," you said. "It was an initiative of the Bolivian government, to help poor people set up small businesses. The vast majority of these loans were being repaid. Banco Sol got careless."

"And you tricked the Indians. You told them it was free money."

"No," you scoffed. "They knew better. I drew up business plans, gave them false identities, told them how to dress. They took out the loans, and gave me two-thirds."

"What about the identities?"

"They burned them. And disappeared back into El Alto."

You disappeared among mausoleums and reappeared in Lisbon.

That warehouse where you lived and worked. The River Tejo lapped vast and opaque, and at night you watched semi-trucks and buses cross the Vasco da Gama Bridge. All those nights you couldn't sleep, knowing Kumi had sold you, and needing her anyway.

Now, not even she knew where you were.

You lay on a mattress, surrounded by plastic envelopes full of stolen and counterfeit passports, birth certificates, national identity cards, work permits.

On the floor, next to the photos of Kumi, the brick-red cover of your new passport. This time you were Spanish. Your name was Ignacio Onoda.

You repeated and repeated it but it didn't ring true. It was a life without her.

The procession of headlights across the Vasco da Gama Bridge. The emptiness gave you vertigo.

You held out as long as you could, and then called.

You sent the tickets but she never came.

I did.

Lisbon is a labyrinth of red tile roofs. A labyrinth laid out over seven hills, intercut by uneven stairways and deteriorating castle walls.

You were in the port, they told me that. Finding you was a matter of patience.

I rented a car and drove the Avenida Infante Dom Henrique, exploring all the service roads and side streets. I parked, watched. Corrugated warehouses, dockside cranes. And beyond everything, the container ships riding enormous on the estuary.

It took a week.

You slid open the red iron door of a warehouse and chained it behind you. You were carrying a leather Puma bag. I watched you walk into the white afternoon, direction the Baixa.

Then got out of the car.

Inside.

Dim, spacious. Your mattress on the polished concrete floor, the photos of Kumi spilling from their pile. Nearby were all those plastic envelopes full of passports, work permits, national ID cards.

In the corner glowed a black light. On industrial shelves

and picnic tables you had card printers, scanners, laptops, laser printers, an embosser, a tipper, and a hologram replicator.

I got the idea, which you confirmed later.

Lisbon was a port city, and an entry point to the European Union. Every day—from the economic freeze of the Ukraine, from the arid misery of Algeria and Morocco, from the murder and famine of black Africa—arrived scores of immigrants looking for new lives.

You were selling them those lives, and making a fortune at it.

I went back to the photographs of you and Kumi. Her hair and wardrobe changed with each city. It was as if she was running from some version of herself, or trying to invent another.

"Both," a voice said.

I turned and you were there, fifteen feet behind me.

"You spend too much time alone," you said, "You've started to think out loud."

I drew my gun.

You dropped the Puma bag.

"Don't move," I said.

You took a step towards me. "You're a long way from Bolivia."

You took another step.

"Don't move!" My gun aimed, and I was seeing the secret military plane they flew my wife home in.

"Listen. Whatever my father is paying you, I'll double it."

You took another step.

We carried her casket across the runway.

"It's easy," you said.

Her in the Tokyo sheets, whispering she wanted to be a mother.

"Just forget you found me."

You took one more step, and my gun erupted.

You stood, stupefied.

"You missed."

"On purpose," I said, and struck blood from your mouth with the gun butt.

So I took you home.

At Portela Airport your passport raised no questions. I led you to the gate with my hand around your elbow, like a coach escorting a player off the field.

That eighteen-hour flight to Tokyo. You at the window seat, your ankles handcuffed. You were nursing a cracked tooth.

Eighteen hours. We spoke once.

You asked: "What did you do before this?"

"Before what?"

"Before you hunted people."

At that moment I didn't know if the clouds I saw were part of Europe or Asia.

"I was a streetcleaner."

You glanced over.

"And before that?"

"Before that," I said, "I had a life I loved."

Home.

"This is what I remembered," you said, "when I was away."

At dusk and at dawn, the skyscrapers gleaming like lenses. Monorails full of sleeping office workers, phonebooths wallpapered in sex leaflets. You saw manga comics, Shibuya crossing. There were suburban homes with eaves and tiled roofs, homeless men in boxes and blue tents. And the night: the punks, salarymen, and hookers all colliding on the neon sidewalks of Shinjuku.

"This is what I remembered, when I lied. When I tried to pretend Tokyo was more than just her."

This Akasaka hotel room.

I lay on the bed, my shoes on. The gun rested on my chest.

"How'd they know I was in Madrid?" you asked. "How'd they know about La Paz?"

I shrugged.

You said one word: "Kumi."

"Why?"

"She felt trapped, in her life. She wanted a new one. But that one cost a lot."

You were at the window, facing your reflection.

"When I was on the run, trying to get rich, it's all I thought about. Building us that life. Acquiring enough money to make it permanent. But I wasn't fast enough. She got sick of waiting."

"But she'd been doing it for years. Why stop?"

"Out of nowhere," you said, "a man offered her more cash than she would make in her working life, just to say where I was."

You shook your head. There was sadness, scorn.

"And she took it."

Several months earlier. Her last visit to Madrid.

She'd sold you.

No one had moved yet, but you already sensed the trap to be laid. You flew her into Barajas and had her take a taxi to your hotel on the Castellana.

The city mute beyond the glass. The Iberia sign blazed red and gold atop an apartment tower. Roses lay across the bed.

She said: "Why didn't you meet me at the airport?"

And you said: "There wasn't time."

"You always had time before."

"I wanted to finish everything up. To be able to concentrate on us."

You left the lights off, carried the roses to the table. By the end of it you felt her tears on your face, and the silence between you was recognition enough.

The next day you went shopping. Serrano, Ortega y Gasset, Goya. You bought her everything she wanted and you paid cash. You remembered something she'd said once, when these trysts and long absences were still novel to her. *My friends all envy how international my wardrobe is.*

In prison, you thought, you can't wear any of it.

Twilight. Indigo clouds blown across the sky.

You came out of a six-story department store and were starting to cross the street. The alarm went off. Suddenly a kid knocked into you, hard, so hard you felt his breath, and sprinted down the Calle Narváez. A team of security guards swarmed out of the department store and sprinted after him.

You looked at Kumi and all those shopping bags, and shivered. As you were waiting for a taxi, the guards escorted the kid back into the store. His sweatshirt was black from the asphalt.

She said: "I wonder what he stole."

And you said: "I wonder who he stole it for."

I said yes, because your voice was sheer yearning. I said yes, because in two days you'd be dead forever.

"But both of you," I said, "will speak only English. You have thirty minutes. And you'll be handcuffed to me."

We took a taxi to a sushi restaurant in Harajuku.

Kumi showed up late. Her hair was blue-black, thrust forward.

She greeted you in Japanese. As you stood, I jerked down on the handcuffs. "Uh, we have to speak English," you said. You kissed her.

She was gorgeous, nervous. She made no sign of recognizing me.

The waiter brought tuna and salmon sashimi. We made small talk, lifting the pink and orange filets with our chopsticks.

"She finishes her degree this semester," you said.

Kumi nodded.

"What are you studying?"

"Design," she said.

"I told her she had to," you said. "I never did. I regret it."

"Never what?"

"Finished university."

"Yes, but say him why," she interjected bitterly.

You looked at her, then looked down.

"Yeah, well, it's one of the things I hope to do now that I'm back."

We all fell quiet.

Kumi stood up. She was crying. "Excuse me. I go to bathroom."

You tried to get up. I shook my head.

And your voice had that same sheer yearning. And you'd be dead soon anyway.

"Fine," I said, unlocking the handcuffs. "But I'll be waiting outside the bathroom door."

You talked fast, jerky, in Japanese. You kept repeating something.

You came out a few minutes later, alone.

We sat down. I locked your wrist to mine.

"Did you get that resolved?"

You nodded, not looking at me. "She's going to stay in there a bit longer. She's pretty shaken up."

"All right," I said. "Time's up. Ask for the check."

In the taxi you said something to the driver. We went around the block.

"What's going on?" I said.

"Just, hold on. I need to see something."

We went around two more times and then Kumi came out of the restaurant. Her mascara was running. She got into a car. It was long and black, an antique. The kind generals used in World War II.

We followed.

At a red light, in the Ginza shopping district, the passenger door opened. And Kumi, with no more life than a Ginza mannequin, tumbled out.

This Akasaka hotel room. Maybe the last time.

You were at the window, your hair damp. You'd just

taken a shower and even over the water I could hear you crying.

"What did she tell you at the restaurant?" I asked.

"What I already suspected."

Below you, the city lights spread uncountable.

"That there's a power struggle inside my father's bank. That she was working for his enemies."

Neon signs hung vertically from the buildings, with characters you could decrypt, and that I couldn't.

"That's all?"

"She was sorry."

I nodded.

"I've employed a lot of people," you said, "and I can tell when someone's doing a job just for the money. You're not. Why?"

For a long time it was quiet. Then I spoke.

"You never finished university."

"What?"

"You never finished university."

"I left," you said. "I told you that."

"But you didn't say what term."

You turned to face me.

"Spring, 1995," I said. "The same time as the terrorist attack."

You stiffened.

"They carried nerve gas, in double-lined bags, onto subway trains."

I moved close to you.

"My wife died that day."

Your voice came hollow. "Who?"

I said her name.

You were thinking. You were whispering names.

"No," you said. "She wasn't—"

I moved closer.

"Twelve people," you said, "died. But nobody with that name."

"She was the thirteenth. Her name was never published."

"What, what are you talking about?"

"She was Spanish. She was the wife of a U.S. Marine officer. Me. I was a code-breaker, top secret. That kind of international coverage would have compromised everything. My government suppressed it."

You crammed yourself against the glass. I leaned in over you.

"You killed her. You and that cult."

"I didn't—"

I put the gun to your abdomen. I pushed.

"No," you said. "That's not what you want. That won't bring her back."

I pushed so hard that a knife would have gone through you.

You gasped, falling burdensome into me.

"To destroy a man," you panted, "destroy the thing he loves. They've already taken Kumi. There's nothing else you can do to me."

You slid down the glass, and we crouched there, exhausted as lovers.

It happened faster than I thought possible.

The room service waiter knocked. He had acne on his forehead. He placed a bottle on the table, bowed to you, and left.

"It's over," I said. "Your father's men will be here any minute. We're both going home."

"To going home," you said.

Your glass clinked mine and we drank our whiskey.

But you knew I was lying. Your father had no idea you were here. The man with the sharpened fingernails—it was his men who would step out from the elevator with garrotes and calfskin gloves.

"I'm sorry about Kumi," I said.

"Don't be. It's the only thing that could have happened."

You watched a jet, taillights flashing, rise into the night.

"Loyalty"—you waited for your voice to get steady—"is priceless. It's what my father looked for, in his employees. He wanted samurai."

"What?"

"The samurai were so loyal they would commit suicide rather than serve another lord." You paused. "They did it for other reasons too."

"Like?"

"To save one another. To avoid falling into the hands of the enemy."

I set my glass on the polished table. I thought you were in shock.

"I'm going to the bathroom," I said.

You grunted, watching that jet rise.

And when I came out you weren't there. Just your oil mark on the window.

The hallway was long silent carpet. The ice machine hummed in a recess.

A movement.

I crept. Behind the ice machine a young man was putting your clothes on but he wasn't you.

I rammed him into the machine and a batch of ice fell rumbling inside.

"Who are you?"

He gasped something. Then I noticed the acne on his forehead.

"Read," he said.

He handed me a note with your handwriting.

I read it.

So that's why they killed Kumi, I thought. When she cried in the sushi restaurant. She repented. She warned you. And you told her—before she did anything else, before she even left the restaurant—to call your father. He placed an employee in the hotel.

Then I did what the note said, because both our lives depended on it.

I pushed the young man into the room.

And you, dressed as a room service waiter, walked into the Tokyo night.

In your clothes he actually resembled you. I didn't think to search him.

"Where is bathroom?" he said.

I pointed.

He closed the door behind him.

A melting cube shifted in my glass. Then I heard the gunshot.

The elevators ring, and this time it's our floor.

I'm at the window, where you were. The skyscrapers reflect other skyscrapers.

Footsteps in the long silent hall. They're coming for you.

My head rests the same place yours did. The shot's replaying in my ears.

A knock. Four men stand distorted in the eyehole.

“Good evening, Major,” he says as I open. His fingernails are sheathed in calfskin. “I hope you’ve enjoyed the city.”

The man with the garrote closes the door. They all have gloves.

I tilt the bottle. It comes out amber.

“He’s in the bathroom,” I say, turning my back.

Their shoes echo on the tile.

“My god,” calls the one with the sharpened fingernails. “He shot himself in the face.”

I swallow, the whiskey sweet on my lips.

“He didn’t want to fall into the hands of the enemy.”

“Understood.” He gives an order in Japanese. Shoes move on the tile.

I wipe your oil mark from the window. The lights of Tokyo are as numberless as stars.

“You may leave now, Major,” he calls from the bathroom. “By noon tomorrow your account will be credited.”

I nod.

Down there, amid the lights, you’re already in one of your father’s limousines. You’re going home.

The elevator opens and I step in.

In a month your father will be dead. By then you will have changed your name a final time, fabricated the perfect résumé, been handpicked by the dying director. Older employees will think, only to themselves, how like his vanished son the new director looks. And the rival shareholders, their power play blocked, will be unable to do anything. The errant prince has returned, and become king.

# Father Diodorus

Charlie Stella

As Crime Scene Scotland puts it: "For those of yous unfamiliar with Mr. Stella (or Knucks, as he signs off on his blog), he's a New York–based writer whose tales of mobsters and lowlife are among the freshest and most deliriously compulsive being written today." His four novels so far are *Jimmy Bench Press, Eddie's World, Charlie Opera,* and *Cheapskates.* We've described him before as before as being like Elmore Leonard writing the *Sopranos* while being hit about the head by George Pelecanos. Others have described him as "the best damn crime writer you've never read" (*Mystery Ink*), and even his mum says, "It was good sonny . . . But do you have to put all that dirty stuff in there like that?" Sounds like a perfect introduction to us.

**Aristo Diodorus washed his mouth** out with Scope and warm water before rigorously brushing his teeth. When he was finished, he stared at himself long and hard in the mirror. He had planned a full day with Raymond; a morning of sex followed with a late lunch on the boardwalk. They would nap into the afternoon. If they were into it, they would have good-bye sex instead of dinner, or maybe both, until they met again. Afternoon sex or not, Aristo would offer to buy Raymond dinner. He would then drop him off at the train station and head back to the parish.

Of course, those were his plans prior to his discovery of the betrayal.

Now he looked up and could see Raymond's reflection in the bathroom mirror. The Judas was sitting up in bed clipping his toenails.

Aristo frowned at the sight of Raymond grooming himself so soon after sex. Why hadn't he thought of clipping his thick, ugly toenails earlier? Why hadn't he cleaned his ears while he was at it?

Raymond's ears were always dirty.

It had been a tough few hours since Aristo first discovered the tape recorder under the bed. His immediate reaction had been rage. He had chipped a tooth from clenching his teeth so hard. It was a glance up at the crucifix that had stopped him from committing an act of passion.

Once he was calm again, Aristo worked at the problem logically. Raymond wasn't an intelligent man. He was a spoiled and impressionable child. He had found someone to lean on, a therapist, who was as much the culprit as the betrayer himself. Aristo turned to the cross again for guidance. Who better to lean on than him?

As was his way, Aristo had hung the cross above the bed

when he first arrived. He had blessed the room, said prayers, and burned incense to dilute the smell of marijuana. The cross was more a gesture of sincerity than religious ritual. It was Aristo's way of humbling himself before God.

He looked at the cross and wondered if it had been divine intervention that had caused him to fumble a matchbook to the floor in the first place. It was how he had spotted the recorder under the bed. The marijuana he had scored on the street outside the hotel had helped to mellow him. He wondered if that, too, had been a gift from God.

Instead of losing control, Aristo had quietly dropped to the floor and examined the tape recorder without moving it. He had traced the white wire up over the mattress under the top sheet. When he stood up, he realized that Raymond's pillow had covered the tiny microphone.

He closed his eyes and remembered how Raymond had moved the pillow from under his head when Aristo went down on him.

*Or the recorder would've been muffled?*

Aristo also remembered Raymond being more vocal than usual. He remembered being prodded to speak while he performed fellatio.

Totally out of character, Raymond had said, "Suck that cock. Tell me you love to suck it."

"I do," Aristo had replied, both surprised and turned on by the exchange. "I do love it."

"What do you love?" Raymond had asked between gasps of ecstasy. "What do you love?"

"Your cock," Aristo had told him. "I love your cock."

Raymond had moaned loud and long when he came. It had excited Aristo and he had moaned along with his lover.

The more he thought about it now, the more violated Aristo felt. He had never suffered a fool so gladly. Raymond was beautiful, but he was also a simpleton. The sin of pride had surely visited Aristo. It unnerved him still.

He opened his eyes to examine himself in the mirror again. He squinted as he reminded himself that the subterfuge had been but a temporary victory, for it was after Raymond fell asleep that Aristo had gone to light the joint and dropped the matchbook.

He smiled at the thought.

*Who was the fool now?*

Aristo turned off the cold water and opened his mouth in front of the mirror. He tried to spot the remnants of Raymond's cum under his tongue. He dipped his head as he lifted his tongue. He turned his head from side to side, but there were shadows inside his mouth he couldn't see through. He closed his eyes and imagined a pool of his saliva under his tongue with *spermatozoa* swimming in it playfully, like tiny dolphins jumping for joy.

Aristo opened his eyes again. He had left the hot water running. The mirror was fogged with condensation. He could barely see Raymond through the steam. He heard the snap of a toenail being clipped and frowned at an image of the tiny shards littering the sheets.

He closed his eyes one more time, but the happier image from a moment ago was gone; the aftertaste had turned sour.

Aristo turned off the hot water and returned to the bedroom.

"You have a cigarette?" asked Raymond, without looking up from his feet.

Aristo grabbed his open pack of Marlboros from the

dresser. He pulled one from the pack, lit it, and brought it to the side of the bed.

Raymond looked up. “Thank you.”

Aristo held the cigarette out for Raymond to take between his lips.

“I wish you’d do that in the bathroom,” he said. “I’ll wind up sticking myself with your nails.”

“I’ll clean them up in a minute,” Raymond said.

Aristo sat naked in the armchair facing the bed. He glanced up at his crucifix and searched for a smile on Christ’s face. Aristo liked to believe it was there when the sex got especially steamy and he and Raymond were lost in their lust.

*Or was the smile more of a smirk?*

*And what did Christ think of the tape recorder?*

Aristo did his best to ignore what he had found since swallowing his lover’s release. He preferred to remember how their wanton energy covered them with sweat, and how it ended with Raymond’s tears.

Raymond always cried after he came.

Aristo glanced at his watch on the dresser and frowned. There was little time left to ignore what had happened.

“Zillah thinks I should stop seeing you,” Raymond said. “She thinks it’s unhealthy. She says it’s gone on way too long.”

“Our relationship or your clipping your toenails in bed?”

Raymond looked up from his feet. “Why don’t you just tell me to stop if it bothers you so much?”

“Because if I do, you’ll become petulant and put a puss on. You won’t let me go down on you again. You won’t let me ream you later.”

Raymond put the nail clipper on the night table to his left. "Okay?"

Aristo feigned applause.

"Frankly, I didn't think you missed going down on me or reaming me. I didn't think you missed me at all. How long has it been now since the last time? Two months? Three?"

Aristo sighed.

Raymond crossed his legs on the bed. He pointed at Aristo's crotch. "You're still leaking."

Aristo used a tissue to wipe himself.

"Anyway, Zillah says it's time I open myself to a real relationship," Raymond said. "One I can enjoy outside of a hideaway like this place."

"Zillah will say whatever she needs to say to keep you paying her. I think her biblical name is paying dividends on suckers like yourself. You think it's some kind of signal from on high when she tells you to wipe your ass."

"That's disgusting," Raymond said. "And it's not true. And she's highly recommended by fellow priests."

"Former fellow priests."

Raymond ignored the correction. "And she doesn't tell me what to do."

"Actually she does, but you can't accept that."

"She helps me make decisions."

"And why is that? Are you too stupid to make your own?"

"Don't be cruel."

Aristo smiled. "You know what, three biblical letters up front of her name and it sounds like a monster."

Raymond had to think about it. When he finally got it, he frowned. "That isn't funny."

"No, but it's popular. Look at what the Japanese did with it."

Raymond ran a fingertip across each of his toenails. “Anyway, she thinks this has to end, that I should leave you. For my benefit.”

“Is that what she told you or she suggested it?”

Raymond rolled his eyes.

Aristo said, “I'm curious, does she ever tell you it's time to leave her?”

“You have to admit this is going on a long time,” said Raymond, instead of answering the question.

Aristo nodded. “Ten years.”

“It's a long time.”

“It's ten years. The blink of an eye in the grand scope of things.”

“I'm going to be forty-three in two years,” Raymond said. “You're going to be sixty. We don't have many blinks of the eye left between us.”

Aristo lit his own cigarette. “Now you're being pragmatic.”

It was the way Raymond sometimes became; forcing arguments he really didn't believe just to be contrary. Today, though, it was probably for the recorder.

“Zillah says you should leave the church. She said you would if you really cared about me.”

“Forget it. I'm not doing that. Not for you or for her.”

“It would be for me.”

“It would be for you for her. Like I said, you haven't figured that out yet. That's not my problem.”

“Except I left the church.”

“For me?”

“Because of you.”

“Because you were sloppy, Raymond. Don't go near blaming me for that.”

It had long been a bone of contention between them.

Aristo had always been the careful one. Raymond had too often yielded to carnal desires. Eventually, an affair he had been careless with cost him his priesthood.

"It isn't fair the way it is now," Raymond said.

*No, Aristo was thinking, and so you're betraying me.*

"We only meet when it's convenient for you," Raymond added. "We come to places like this, remote and dumpy. And you cancel at a moment's notice. I'm the one left wanting. You're the one who's content."

Aristo sighed again.

"Well?" Raymond said.

"You won't fill the void, Raymond, I'm sorry."

"And what is that supposed to mean?"

"There's more to life than sex. There is for me. You know that. The church fulfills my life. You don't."

"Now you're just being cruel again."

Aristo shot Raymond a hard look. "Cruel to be kind, Raymond. Don't ever forget that."

Raymond frowned. He said, "According to Zillah, I—"

"Ah, the gospel according to your therapist. Now we'll learn something."

"Now you're being sarcastic."

"Yeah, I guess. I'm sorry."

"I don't want to be hidden anymore. I don't want to play hide-and-seek. I feel like something less than myself every time we leave each other. I want to be introduced to your friends in and out of the church."

*And how should I feel knowing you brought a tape recorder with you, Aristo was thinking. What do you intend to do with it? What are you getting out of this betrayal? What constitutes your thirty pieces of silver?*

"I have no church friends," Aristo said instead. "I have my flock, such as they are, and our relationship is none of their fucking business."

Raymond waved Aristo off. "Oh, that's just your way of lying to yourself, saying that, that it's none of their business. That's like some politician who hides money he's stealing."

It was irksome to Aristo the way Raymond sometimes generalized. He was handsome and sexy and extremely good in bed, but he could also be embarrassing at times.

Aristo smiled at him now.

"You really are in denial over this," Raymond added. "You're just another politician hiding money he's stolen."

Aristo wasn't going to pursue it, but now Raymond had annoyed him. "How?" he asked. "How am I like some politician that hides money he's stealing?"

"Huh?"

"How is it like that, our relationship. How is it like some politician hiding money that he's stealing? What the hell do you mean by that? Explain it to me."

Raymond was caught off guard. He held up a finger. "Don't be a bully."

Aristo smiled. He held up three fingers and spoke softly this time. "For the third time. How is our relationship like some politician hiding money that he's stealing? Did Zillah say something like that and now you're misquoting her? You should get it right, what she says, since you're so devoted to her."

Raymond did his best to ignore the sarcasm. "When you say it's none of their business, what you are, what we are, it's only because you don't want them to know. You're hiding it."

"And how is that stealing?"

"Because that's what I feel, like you've stolen my time and love. Because you take it whenever you want and never give back."

"I'm sorry you feel that way. And how is it illegal?"

"What?"

"Us, what we do."

"In God's eyes it is."

"Oh, really? Is that what you really think?"

"In the church's eyes, yes, and you know it is or you wouldn't hide it."

Aristo shook his head.

Raymond moved closer to the end of the bed. "What?" he asked. "What?"

Aristo shook his head again. He slumped in the chair and let his head lay against the back. He closed his eyes. He remembered happier times.

They had met nearly eleven years ago when a young Father Raymond Joseph Bruno was first transferred to Our Lady of Fatima Catholic church in Port Washington, New York. Father Aristo Diodorus was pastor at the time. He was to train Father Bruno to take over pastoral duties the following year.

It was the middle of a steamy summer the actual day they first met. A church outing to Jones Beach included a volleyball game on the hot sand. Fathers Bruno and Diodorus played against a group of high school seniors who had just graduated from the parish school. After a long game, which they eventually lost, the two priests ran into the surf to cool off. They swam out a ways to where they could tread water and talk privately.

Father Bruno commented on how much the children seemed to like Father Diodorus.

"We're in a position of power," the older priest explained. "They'll like you just as much. So long as you don't abuse your power with kids they'll respect you. We're idols to many of them. Not as priests as much as adults that try and understand them without judging."

"Very well put," Father Bruno said.

Father Diodorus inched closer in the water. He asked, "How are your accommodations so far?"

"The room is great, really," Father Bruno said. "It's much more than I expected. A television and air conditioner. It's wonderful."

"Port Washington is a money town. They'll take care of you here. If you don't ruffle feathers, they'll make your stay paradise."

"I noticed some of the homes the day I arrived. It certainly isn't a poor town."

Father Diodorus was inches away. He had been drawn in by the young priest's handsome face, tanned skin, blue eyes, and dark hair. He swallowed hard when Father Bruno combed back his wet hair with both his hands.

Father Diodorus said, "If you want me to stop, just say so."

He reached under the water and placed his palm flat against Father Bruno's crotch. He felt the erection through the younger priest's trunks.

Father Bruno didn't respond. He glanced toward shore instead. Father Diodorus continued to rub the full, thick erection through the swimming trunks. Father Bruno bit his lower lip until he couldn't restrain himself. He moaned a moment before he came.

Afterward, Father Bruno ducked his head under the

water, swam a few strokes, and came up splashing water on his face. He used his hands to comb back his hair again. Father Diodorus thought he was beautiful.

"Should I reciprocate?" Father Bruno asked.

"Not here, no. Not now."

"I don't know what to say."

"Your face said it all."

"How did you know?"

"I didn't."

"My God, it was wonderful."

Father Diodorus smiled.

The two priests swam back to shore where they set up a tug-of-war with the same seniors that had beat them in volleyball. It was a long and anxious afternoon for both of them. The week that followed was no different.

The next time they were alone together they were on their way to a conference in the city. Father Bruno was excited at their opportunity. Father Diodorus was more hesitant.

"Can we stop somewhere?" Father Bruno asked. He had turned on the front seat so his back was flush against the passenger door.

"I'm not sure we should," Father Diodorus said.

"I'd like to repay you."

"Repay me?"

"You know."

"I took as much pleasure as you received."

"I'd like to do the same."

Father Diodorus chuckled. "A hand job?"

"Are you teasing me?"

"No, I'm sorry, I'm not. I don't mean to."

"I've thought about us in the water that day a dozen times a night since."

"I was afraid of that."

"Why afraid? It was wonderful. I can't thank you enough. I was dying for something like that."

Father Diodorus tried to joke. "Been a while?"

"Two years."

"Are you kidding?"

"I mean I masturbate all the time, but it's been two years since I've been with somebody."

"Another priest?"

"Yes."

"No children, I hope."

"Never."

"Good. It isn't right. I hope you understand that."

Father Bruno crossed himself. "Never."

Father Diodorus was excited. He turned the radio on to clear his mind.

They attended the conference and returned to Long Island in the early afternoon. Father Diodorus was driving through the Midtown Tunnel. It was one-way traffic in the tube with cones separating the traffic.

Father Bruno said, "I can take care of you while you drive if you want."

"Not in the car, no."

"Then we should stop someplace. It's only right."

"I'm afraid of moving too fast, to tell you the truth. That we'll become careless."

"I saw you looking at me this morning."

"Yes, I know. And I saw you. It's what I'm most afraid of."

"We'll make sure we're careful. Drive someplace remote."

"I'm talking about lust. It isn't easily controlled. I've seen it before. I've seen priests touch each other inappropriately when they thought nobody was watching. I know two who were outed and eventually excommunicated. One killed himself."

"Then we'll be extra careful. I want to please you, Aristo. Please let me."

Father Diodorus lit a cigarette. "Living in the same house won't make it easy, once we've become intimate. I'll want you in the middle of the night sometimes."

"And I'll want you. Probably in the middle of the day, too."

Father Diodorus smiled. "You're very charming, Raymond, but I'm serious. It won't be easy to restrain ourselves. And we'll have to, make no mistake. I don't want to lose what I have. I live for the priesthood. I can't imagine not having the church in my life. I can't imagine not being a priest."

Father Bruno turned silent. Their conversation was over until Father Diodorus turned off the Long Island Expressway onto the Cross Island Parkway. He drove to one of the exits for Belmont Race Track and parked in one of the empty lots near the stables. Horse racing was between meets up at Saratoga. The parking lots were empty.

Father Diodorus got out of the car and walked around to the other side. He opened the passenger door and unzipped his pants. He put his hands on the roof of the car and let Father Bruno take him in his mouth.

"Are you asleep?" Raymond asked.

Aristo opened his eyes. "No," he said. "I was getting a

nice slow blow job from a good-looking priest almost twenty years my junior."

Raymond waved it off. "That again? You should stop living in the past."

"Is that a sermon from Zillah, too?"

"That's from me."

Aristo nodded.

"She says you won't let me go because you like to be in control," Raymond said. "That you want to keep me where I am."

"You're where you are, Raymond, because you like it."

"I don't like it anymore."

"Then don't do it."

"Are you serious? You're saying you don't care if I leave you?"

Aristo reached for his cigarette and saw it had burned out. He lit a fresh one. "I'm saying I can't stop you if you do. I'm saying your therapist doesn't know her ass from her elbow. I'm saying if you really want to take charge of your life, you should start with telling Zillah to fuck off already. And if you want to leave me, if you want to stop seeing me, then do it. I promise I won't kill myself."

Raymond was insulted. "You know what I think, Aristo? I think you're full of shit."

"Because you want to be needed."

"And who doesn't? What the fuck is that supposed to mean?"

Aristo held up a hand. "Why don't you smoke a joint and calm yourself down. I didn't mean to insult you. You're right, everybody wants to be needed. Even me."

"And you have Him," Raymond said with resentment. He

pointed to the crucifix. "You have the church." He nervously grabbed a joint off the night table and lit it.

Aristo wondered if he would've guessed now what was going on if he hadn't spotted the recorder earlier. Raymond had been goading him to talk all along. Was there a point, Aristo wondered, when it would have become obvious that a trap had been set?

He watched Raymond take a long hit on the joint. He refused the joint when it was offered to him.

"No, thanks."

"I miss the church, Aristo," Raymond said.

"I can't get it back for you. I'm sorry, but I also warned you a long time ago about losing it."

Raymond spoke while holding the smoke in his lungs. "You warned me? You fucking introduced me to the man who ruined it for me." He let the smoke out of his lungs and coughed a few times. "You did that, Aristo. That was as much your fault as mine."

Aristo offered Raymond an ashtray. "And that's what this is really all about, isn't it?" he asked. "You and Zillah and me. This is about you losing the church. You need someone to blame. You need me to blame."

Raymond waved the ashtray off. "Fuck you," he said, squinting hard at Aristo. "Fuck you," he repeated, before he stormed into the bathroom. He slammed the door shut behind him.

Aristo took a long drag on the joint Raymond had left behind and looked up at the crucifix again. This time it was Christ's cynical smirk staring back at him.

When Father Bruno first came to Port Washington, Father Diodorus had already been involved with a local policeman. He had met officer Ronald Jasnow at a Turkish steam bath in Coney Island during a church outing. The two men had talked a while before masturbating one another under towels in a sauna.

The relationship slowly blossomed, but Officer Jasnow had sexual hang-ups that precluded anal sex. They maintained a clandestine affair that suited both of them. It rarely required a room or a bed. One would do the other, or they'd do each other, in a car, a shed, a garage, or a private bathroom. They would use their hands or their mouths, although kissing wasn't permitted.

Aristo had long assumed that he was the wrong partner for Officer Jasnow. At the risk of ending what little they had together, he had tried to talk the policeman into therapy to deal with his homosexual issues. He didn't do it so much out of love as his own desire to seek someone new and more open to intercourse.

It was why Aristo eventually introduced Officer Jasnow to Father Bruno, after a particularly long and heated argument about finding someone new that might help the policeman overcome his sexual hang-ups.

"I'm not letting anything inside my asshole and that's just the way it'll have to be," the cop had yelled at Aristo. "Let it the fuck alone already."

Aristo had just tried to bugger his partner using the middle finger of his right hand. The cop had grabbed Aristo's finger and bent it back until it was nearly broken.

"You're gay and you're depriving yourself!" Aristo had yelled at him.

"You mean I'm a perverted faggot and I'm trying to keep myself from going all the way," the cop retorted.

Aristo had mocked laughing.

"Maybe if I kick some of your teeth out, you won't think it's so funny," the cop said.

Aristo let go of his wounded finger. "You'll suck my cock and lick my balls, and kiss them even, you'll do that sometimes, when you're not thinking so hard, when you're not stopping yourself, you'll kiss them, my balls, but you won't fuck."

"Not in the ass, no, I won't."

"Not me."

"Not you or anybody else?"

"And how do you know that?"

"What?"

"About anybody else? If I'm your first male experience, how do you know you won't let it happen with someone else?"

The cop grew frustrated and waved Aristo off. He was twenty-nine years of age and powerfully built. He had won local bodybuilding competitions throughout his police career. Most of his entire adult life had been spent denying what he was.

"I have someone I want you to meet," Aristo had said.

"Another fag? No, thanks."

"He's my lover."

The cop wheeled on him. "I hope you use a condom, he's your lover."

Aristo ignored the comment. "He's my lover and he's really quite submissive. I think he'd be perfect for you."

"Why, so I can feel like I raped him afterward? I can feel like twice the pervert I already am."

"So you can learn to enjoy what you are, you dumb shit. So you can free yourself from this bullshit you're choking yourself with."

"I'm a cop, padre, in case you fucking forget."

"You're a gay cop."

"Which means I'll be fired if they find out."

"Which means they can't anymore, and so what if they can? We're talking about your sexuality, for God's sake, what will make you happy versus a salary. How can you equate the two? How can you let the one outweigh the other?"

The cop went silent until he finally left Aristo alone. Two weeks later he agreed to meet with Father Bruno. A week after that, Officer Jasnow finally engaged in anal sex. Father Diodorus ended his relationship with Father Bruno and left the new couple alone.

The cop and the young priest weren't careful. They saw each other too often and too carelessly to keep their affair secret. They were eventually found out when the wife of a local veterinarian discovered them while having her own affair with a man twenty years her junior. They were in cars parked at opposite ends of a local beach parking lot. It had just turned dark. The young man had just ejaculated inside the woman. She was heading for the public bathroom to clean herself when she spotted the police car and thought it odd the way the officer's head was resting. She moved closer to the car and saw a head moving over the officer's lap. She moved closer still and was just feet from the car when she heard the officer moan and saw the other man spit a mouthful of semen into his cupped hands. She saw the collar at the same time Officer Jasnow and Father Bruno saw her.

The next morning the woman made an anonymous phone call to the police department. A secret surveillance investigation ensued. The priest and the cop were exposed.

Officer Jasnow was transferred a few months later. A detective with two boys in the Catholic school where the priest taught brought surveillance pictures to the diocese. Because of recent high-profile pedophilia cases involving priests, Father Bruno was convinced to resign his position with the church.

The priest and the cop would never engage in sexual relations again. Officer Jasnow eventually met a gay detective with the NYPD who lived on Long Island. No longer a priest, Raymond Bruno turned to teaching within the New York City public school system. After a long break he eventually resumed his secrete relationship with Father Diodorus.

Because he was afraid of Raymond's instability, Father Diodorus asked for an assignment in New Jersey. It was his token sacrifice to Raymond's loss. He would give up his quest to become bishop someday. He would maintain a clandestine relationship with Raymond, but the two lovers would rarely see each other over the next several years.

The last year had been the toughest for Raymond. Their relationship had been reduced to a few hours of lust every few months at remote short-stay hotels. Today they had met in Asbury Park, New Jersey; a forty-minute drive from the Parish Aristo had transferred to the previous year in Fords, New Jersey.

Aristo knew that his lover was reaching an emotional breaking point. Raymond had been living with his humiliation for a decade. Because Aristo hadn't encouraged him to stay or offered to help in his defense, or even come out himself to denounce the antiquated church policy that had caused so much emotional pain to so many, Raymond had felt abandoned.

Now he wanted revenge. Aristo wasn't sure in what form the revenge would come, but the tape recorder suggested it would be public.

If his time as a priest was running out, Aristo wanted control of it. He had earned his way to heaven. He had never seduced or lured a child into his bed. He had never even been attracted to one. His relationships had all been with consenting adults. He had performed his duties as a priest with total conviction and sacrifice. He had ministered to the poor and sick as if they were his own. He had given his life to the charity of the church.

And so it was just that he would protect now what he had treasured all his life. He would lay his own trap and bring the waters down on his pursuers the way Moses had drowned the Egyptians.

Raymond couldn't help himself. The therapist behind it all wouldn't stop until the damage was done. It was up to Aristo to protect himself and to never worry about either again.

If he was to be abandoned at this late date, if God's shelter had run its course, or if it was just Aristo's time for the most unfortunate of random coincidences—that Raymond's crisis and his had crossed wires at just the wrong moment in time—he was . . . willing to leave a little bit of hell in his wake.

Judas Iscariot had hung himself. Raymond would need help.

Afterward, if the pain was too great, Aristo thought he might kill himself.

With pills, he guessed, or he could buy a gun and shoot himself. He saw himself searching the street outside the motel for the black kid that had sold him the marijuana.

*"Can you get me a gun?"*

*"A what?"*

*"A gun."*

*"The fuck for?"*

*"I want to kill myself."*

*"Why not drown yourself. The ocean's right across the street."*

He chuckled. There was no way Aristo would kill himself.

Raymond was still angry when he came out of the bathroom. He was stubborn and refused to talk. When he glanced at his watch and mentioned he had to leave soon, Aristo pleaded with him to sit on the bed. Raymond grudgingly did so.

Aristo kneeled behind Raymond on the bed and massaged his shoulders.

"That feels good, but I'm still angry with you," Raymond said.

Aristo smiled at Raymond in the small mirror hanging on the wall to their right. He applied more pressure and Raymond moaned. He altered the massage, switching from firm kneading to lightly touching Raymond's neck with his fingertips.

Again Raymond moaned.

Watching Raymond's submission in the small mirror, Aristo grew excited. He stood up on the bed and let his erection brush against Raymond's left ear. He left it there until Raymond turned on the bed and took it in his mouth.

Aristo lasted all of two minutes before he felt his orgasm building. He had already removed the white wire from under the sheet at the head of the bed. He pulled it now from his mouth, where he had hid it.

Raymond's right hand moved to Aristo's penis to help pump the ejaculation into his mouth. He moaned again when he tasted the hot semen.

Aristo began to whisper a prayer as Raymond swallowed.

Aristo stopped to moan.

Raymond swallowed again.

Aristo felt his knees buckling and grabbed Raymond's shoulders to steady himself.

Raymond moaned louder.

Aristo stretched the wire by its ends under Raymond's chin. He felt the last spasms of orgasm as Raymond looked up, his right hand still clutching Aristo's penis. Aristo coiled the wire around Raymond's neck and pulled tight in opposite directions. Raymond's eyes opened wide as he gagged. His tongue wiggled left to right as his hands flailed in front of him.

Aristo silently mouthed his prayer as he continued to pull. He bent at the knees for leverage and lifted Raymond's head up with the wire.

Raymond grabbed at the wire around his neck. Aristo tugged harder and Raymond's hands reached up over his head. Using Raymond's weight to hang him, Aristo continued to lift. Gurgling sounds filled the room.

Aristo prayed in a forced whisper as Raymond's eyes rolled up and spittle drooled out one corner of his mouth.

Aristo pulled the wire as tight as he could. His arms began to shake as sweat rolled down his face. Raymond's body went limp and Aristo guided it down to the bed.

He let go of the wire and took deep breaths before finishing his prayer.

"And the prayer of faith shall save the sick man. And the Lord shall raise him up: and if he be in sins, they shall be forgiven him," Aristo said aloud. "Amen."

Raymond had died with a mixture of semen and saliva in his throat.

Aristo could see the image in his head. "Amen," he repeated as he reached down and closed Raymond's eyelids.

His fingers were sore. He rubbed them a moment until he saw himself in the small mirror. He was covered in sweat.

He stepped down off the bed and took a quick shower. When he was finished, he gathered his things and packed Raymond's recorder.

There was just enough time to drive to Raymond's therapist and catch her at her office before she left for the day. He might not have time to strangle her, but he could use Raymond's pocket knife. Either way, he wouldn't need to spend time praying over her body. He could do that now as he removed his crucifix from the wall above the bed.

"For I have slain a man to my wounding," he whispered, "and a young man to my hurt."

# A Nightcap of Hemlock

Francis M. Nevins

Francis M. Nevins is a professor at St. Louis University of Law, where he has taught since 1971. In addition to his writings on legal subjects he is the author of six mystery novels, his most recent being *Benediciaries' Requiem.* He has also written about forty short stories which have appeared in *Ellery Queen's Mystery Magazine, Alfred Hitchcock's Mystery Magazine,* and leading mystery anthologies. He has edited more than fifteen mystery anthologies and collections and has written several nonfiction books on the genre, two of which—*Royal Bloodline: Ellery Queen, Author and Detective* (1974) and *Cornell Woolrich: First You Dream, Then You Die* (1988)—have won him Edgar awards from Mystery Writers of America. He has also written articles, book reviews, and similar short pieces on mystery fiction for newspapers, magazines, and reference works.

**She sat forward in the** roomy leather seat of the Starco corporate jet and squinted out the plexiglass window at clouds pure as sea foam and, as the plane began its descent, at tracts of lush forest and the river glistening in spring sunlight. She saw none of it. *Never again*, the jet's motors seemed to hum, *never again*. The unseen pilot touched down at the small private airport, taxied along a runway to a smooth stop. The motors shut down and she unbelted herself and retrieved her bag from the luggage bin.

A man was waiting for her at the foot of the wheeled staircase she descended. Blocky, buzz-cut, bundled in a bomber jacket against the March chill. "Lieutenant Holt? Bill Nodella. I guess you could say I'm your counterpart in this neck of the woods."

His bullfrog voice was all too familiar from the call she had taken at her condo that morning. She blinked through her spectacles and held out her hand. "Oh yes, you're the one who called me about Paul's. . . ." She couldn't make herself complete the sentence.

"General Anderson's death," he finished for her. She let him take her carry-on bag and lead her to a county police sedan parked in a No Parking slot outside the airport administration building. Once ensconced in the back seat she noticed in the rear vision mirror that the uniformed man behind the wheel chewed gum.

"I can't say I enjoyed the ride terribly much," she said, twisting her awkward body around to study her counterpart's jowly face, "but it was good of you to arrange with Starco to bring me."

"Not a problem," Nodella replied. "Starco's vital to the regional economy and I don't have to tell you the General was a legend at Starco." He paused, cleared his throat as the sedan swerved into a two-lane blacktop that thrust between tracts of lush woodland. "I, ah, know a little about you and the General, like how you and his daughter were buddies in college, but it might help if I knew more before we get to the scene."

*You'll never know more about it than you need to know,* she said to herself.

He was the only man in her life. They first met when she was in college and Lynn Anderson her roommate and dearest friend had brought her back on spring break to meet her widower father. Paul was a full colonel then, and chief legal adviser to the commandant at Fort Monmouth in New Jersey near the Atlantic coast. She liked him. Before meeting him she could never have imagined a career soldier who could talk intelligently about art and literature and music and philosophy. She knew that Lynn and her father had never been terribly close and that the raging Viet Nam war had made their relationship worse than ever. Lynn was a firebrand and an activist, she marched against the war, she cheered Jane Fonda's visit to Hanoi while her mousier roommate kept her subversive thoughts to herself and read literature and went to chamber music recitals and thought about getting an MLS degree after graduation and then finding a librarian's job in some quiet liberal arts college. By the time Lynn had vanished Paul was a brigadier general and commandant of the Judge Advocate General's School in Charlottesville, while she in the wake of the women's movement had wound up not a librarian but a plainclothes detective and eventually the newest member of her city's Major Case Squad. Paul had left the military and become CEO at Starco, shaping that corporate colossus as a potter shapes moist clay until on his seventy-fifth birthday he retired. That was when he had begun calling her.

Two or three times a year, usually late in the evening, she would receive a phone call inviting her for a visit, and in the morning she would arrange for some leave time, and a few days later she would take a cab to the private airport on the edge of the county where a Starco jet would be waiting. She would be flown four hundred miles diagonally across the state to another private airfield where the jet would touch down and a cab would be waiting to take her along two-lane blacktops through gently rolling hills to a high flagstone wall bordered by the sign STARCO CONFERENCE CENTER. There was a golf course on the left side of the road, tennis courts and the starting points of hiking trails on the right, and eventually the cab would stop under the porte cochere and a Conference Center attendant would take her bag and lead her along a walkway through densely forested hills to the long low house in the center of a clearing in the woods where one could almost imagine the world could not intrude. Paul would be waiting for her at the door with his shock of white hair and wild thatchy eyebrows and thick cane and they would hug and she would stay there with him for three or four days and they would play chess or Scrabble before the vast fireplace in the central room and talk about music and literature and the world and quietly mourn his lost daughter and sip wine and watch old movies on his DVD player connected to a video projector so that the images were almost as large as in a regular theater.

Her visits had been the brightest part of her life for more than a dozen years now but recently she had found herself wondering how much longer they could go on. Wouldn't he soon be ninety?

The county car wove past a huge and all but empty parking lot. "They've just finished a major remodeling job," Nodella explained. "The place won't be open to groups again till the first of next month but there's a skeleton staff on duty and Starco's putting you up here gratis." He pronounced the last word graytis. "For now we're treating the General's house as a crime scene so you can't stay there." The gum-chewing driver braked under the porte cochere and Nodella scrambled out ahead of her to open the massive wooden entrance door of the Conference Center. Inside the vaulted atrium she peered around as if she had never seen the place before. "Lieutenant Holt," Nodella told the double-chinned blond woman behind the registration counter. A slight young man with hair dark as midnight and a nametag JORGE above the breast pocket of his white mess jacket materialized from nowhere. After a whispered colloquy with Nodella he took her bag and led the way to the elevator and pressed the button for the lower level. He stopped at a large corner room with a glass rectangle in its door, unlocked it with a key from a ring in his hand, switched on the overhead fluorescents. It was designed for small group meetings: clusters of leather chairs and couches, low tables, unobtrusive art prints on the paneled walls "Mr. Nodella say he'll talk with you in here. You should phone front desk when you like him to come down." Leaving the door ajar he led her down a cross corridor to another door, this one without a window in it, and keyed it open and set her bag down and, while she was fumbling in her purse for a tip, took a few steps backward with his palm raised. "No no," he said. "No money. The General he was good man and you were his friend." He eased out of the room and closed the door gently between them.

"Doesn't it remind you of Robert Frost?" she asked an hour later in the small meeting room.

"What, this room? Georgie said it was a good place for us to powwow but I don't see. . . ." Nodella looked blankly around him, reminding her once again of the sad state of the younger generation's cultural literacy. Her inner nanny nagged at her to make a sweetly cutting comment, like "The name is pronounced Hor-hay, you poor dear," but she repressed the urge and opted for something kinder.

"Two roads diverged in a yellow wood," she said, hoping against hope that the quotation wouldn't be Greek to him. Two roads, two scenarios: suicide or murder? They didn't know yet which road they should take so like good detectives they would try to travel both at once.

The evidence so far seemed inconclusive. Paul's body had been found when the waiter, a young man from India whose multisyllabic name Nodella had turned into hash, had come over from the conference center bringing the General's usual breakfast on a wheeled serving cart. From Nodella's description and the reports he had given her to read she could visualize the scene as clearly as if she had found the body herself. Paul slumped over the desk in his study, a half-empty bottle of Bushmill's Black Bush and a thermos bucket of ice cubes on the wet bar across the room, tumbler with residue of the Irish whisky upset on the carpet at his feet. No suicide note. Nothing on the desk but his will.

"You're sure he was prepared to commit suicide under the right circumstances?" Nodella asked in turn.

"He was something of an old Roman," she told him. "He wanted to go neatly and without pain. Although I don't think he would ever have slit his veins in the tub like some of them did. More like the old Greeks perhaps." *Socrates,* she thought. *Hemlock.* "He never learned how to use a computer but even without going online it's not hard to learn the best combination of pills."

"And I found a stash of them in his house," Nodella said, "and the medical examiner found them in him. But that doesn't prove he took them himself. Somebody else could have taken them from his stash or brought their own. We don't know how many he had to begin with. Like you said, two roads through the woods. First road: he decides it's time, takes the pills with the booze and sits down and waits to die. Second road: Someone drops in for a nightcap with him, laces the General's with the pills, hangs around for him to die, then cleans up so it looks like he died alone. The gates are locked and a security guard comes on at eleven every night but it's only a short walk to the house from the service road behind the property and we've already found some cronies of the General who knew about it. So how do we decide which is the right road? One thing we do is look at motive. You knew the General was worth a bunch of money, right?"

"Yes," she admitted. "And we talked once or twice about what would happen to it after he died. He wanted to leave much of it to me. I begged him not to."

"And he talked with you about the mess at Madison University, right? That being his alma mayter and a couple of hours' drive from your bailiwick."

"Naturally," she said. "He was furious at Mad U. Apoplectic."

Paul had gone to law school on the GI Bill after World War II and before being recalled to active duty for Korea. He had made the military his life but retained a great fondness for old Mad U and, once convinced beyond a reasonable doubt that Lynn was dead, had set up his estate plan so that after his death the bulk of his property would be left in trust to Mad U to fund one or more chairs in international law. Then, at the height of the 1990s political correctness boom, Mad U Law School had made its stand against the military's "don't ask, don't tell" policy regarding gays and lesbians by banning recruiters from the Judge Advocate General's offices of the various armed services from interviewing students on its property. The Law School had been forced to reverse itself only when Congress threatened to retaliate by denying all government grants to any part of Madison University. That brouhaha had made Paul angry enough but it was like a puff of smoke in comparison with his fury earlier this year. For twenty years the law school's policy had been to forgive the student loans of those who after graduation opted for low-paying public service jobs. Less than six months after 9-11, the law faculty had voted by the narrowest of margins to deny access to its Loan Repayment Assistance Program to any graduates who accepted commissions in JAG.

"Paul called the Dean at Mad U," she said. "He gave them a month to change their policy, otherwise he said he'd cut the law school out of his will. He told me about it a few weeks ago. It was—the last time I spoke with him."

"Well, we know what the Law School did," Nodella said. "Dean Corrigan sent his Associate Dean down here to try to reason with the General. Guy named Mark Stern. I get the sense his main job is keeping potential donors happy. He's staying here at the Conference Center. Checked in the night before last. He told me he saw the General yesterday morning and was supposed to see him again today."

"Something's wrong with that picture," she said. "He agrees to see this man, arranges a room for him here, meets with him once, then kills himself the night before their second meeting? That isn't the Paul I knew."

"You might see it as a suicide that was timed to sort of give Mad U a dope slap," Nodella suggested. "Especially when you connect it with the changes he made in his will before he killed himself."

"You didn't tell me about any changes," she said. Nodella said nothing. "Do you mean that he revoked the bequest to Mad U before he took those pills?" Nodella still said nothing. "But you said changes," she added then. "More than one?"

"Three if you include the codicil." Nodella rummaged in the slender attache case at his feet, pulled out a sheaf of blue-backed papers and extracted one document which he handed her. "These are photocopies of course, the originals are evidence." She peered through her bifocals at the single page. "That dates back to a year and a half ago," Nodella explained. "When he changed executors."

"I see," she murmured. "From Joseph W. Dengler to Joseph W. Dengler, Jr." She had a vague recollection of

Paul explaining to her at the time. Dengler Senior, who was Paul's protege at Starco and about twenty years younger, had become CEO when Paul retired. Two years ago he had contracted brain tumors and gone into an assisted living facility. His son had taken over as Starco's CEO and Paul had substituted the son as executor of his own estate.

"Not that that has any bearing on what happened yesterday," Nodella told her. "But here." He handed her the much thicker sheaf of papers he had taken from the attache case. "This is a photocopy of the will itself. This has one hell of a bearing on what happened."

She took the document and held it close to her eyes. It seemed a perfectly proper, formally executed will, dated several years ago. There were several pages of relatively small bequests to various charities and acquaintances, then just above Paul's signature and those of the witnesses a paragraph leaving most of his estate in trust to Madison University for the purpose of creating one or more chairs in International Law. The first words of the operative sentence—"The rest, residue and remainder of my estate I bequeath to"—remained intact on the page. Lines had been drawn through every word after those, lines so straight and precise she knew they must have been drawn with the help of a ruler. In the space left after the end of the original sentence she saw two words, handwritten. Words that made her blink in disbelief.

Jean Holt.

She felt faint. There was a whistling noise like an angry teakettle in her head. "This is insane," she protested. "He could never have. . . ." The whistling was replaced by an insidious little voice inside her saying

*You're rich you're rich nothing can hurt you again* and she began to tremble.

Nodella's voice broke into her roiling thoughts. "The pen that seems to have made the changes was found on his desk."

She pressed her lips together, forced herself to function like a professional. "Paul didn't write this," she said, handing the document back to him.

"Both Jody Dengler and the head of the legal department at Starco tell me it looks like his handwriting," Nodella said.

"I don't care a damn what they tell you!" She dug into the purse on the carpet at her feet, hauled out her badge case and thrust it at him. "Look! Look!" She removed from various compartments of her wallet her Social Security card, credit cards, AAA card, library card, membership cards in the art museum and the botanical garden and the chamber concert society. Nodella's thick brows lifted as he scanned them.

"My birth name is Eugenia Holt," she said. "I've gone by Gene since I was a girl. Don't tell me Paul forgot how to spell my name! Whoever made this change in the will, it wasn't Paul."

"You visited the General here regularly," Nodella pointed out, and Gene reluctantly nodded. "You knew his feelings about suicide. It wouldn't have been hard for you to find out where he kept his pills and his will. I'm told his residuary estate is worth around seven million dollars. You're human just like everyone else, let's suppose for a moment that you were tempted. Write your name into the will, feed the General either his own suicide pills or duplicates you got hold of yourself, you're rich. Of course, being a detective and I'm told a damn good one, you would have known that you'd come under suspicion. You might have thought to divert those suspicions by misspelling your own name. Legally I don't think the wrong spelling would stop you from claiming under the will. Umm—can you prove where you were yesterday evening?"

The question made Gene feel shamed and violated, gave her a sudden swift insight into the feelings of the countless suspects she had questioned in her years with Major Case Squad. Many of them were innocent too, under suspicion because they were in the wrong place at the wrong time or had said the wrong thing to the wrong person. "As chance would have it," she replied, "I can. I was at the retirement banquet for the man who until very recently was my boss. At the head table on a dais, in plain view of the mayor, the chief of police and approximately two hundred fellow officers. I gave a little speech." She cleared her throat. "Is that alibi enough for you?" she asked meekly.

"You could still have hired it done," Nodella said. But Gene saw an impish gleam in his eyes that told her he wasn't serious, that he was playing a cop game. Then suddenly he seemed to tire of the sport. "Oh hell, I know you didn't," he said. "You might have been tempted to change his will if you happened to come across it, but if I read you right that's the limit. Prudence is your middle name. Anderson was in his late eighties and in poor health. You wouldn't have killed him and risked everything, you would have sat back and waited for nature to take its course."

Gene was far from certain that this was a compliment but she felt the tension between them seem to vanish in an instant and her mind began working again. *But why would someone else change Paul's will that way?* she asked herself. *Do I have a secret psychotic admirer who decided I should be a rich lady?* The instant the question was formed in her mind she answered it No. *Couldn't be. Too much like a TV Movie of the Week.*

Nodella grunted and lifted his bulk out of the deep leather chair, then offered a hand to help Gene out of the depths of her own. "Come on," he said. "We have time for a bite before our evening appointment. I'm buying. You like falafel?"

Almost before she knew it the two of them were in the center of the city and bolting a quick supper at the al-Tarboush deli around the corner from police headquarters. Then they drove out in Nodella's official sedan to the other end of town and passed a security checkpoint and parked in an all but empty lot and walked along broad pathways through a setting whose twilight serenity reminded her of an idealized college campus, dotted with flowerbeds and ponds and statuary. Just beyond a clocktower surrounded by jetting waters Nodella turned into a three-story red brick building with LAW CENTER over the entranceway and a security guard who unlocked as soon as Nodella displayed his badge case. "Law Library's on the second floor," the guard told them. "Mr. Dengler and Mr. Foley and the judge got here a few minutes ago."

When the elevator door slid back on the second floor a slender blond man in a cashmere suit signaled to them from across the corridor. Gene guessed his age as early forties. There was a look of smug and somehow perverse power about him. In a drama about Roman history he might have been cast as Caligula. "Th-this way," he said, and opened the door behind him. "Y-you must be L-Lieutenant N-Nodella." The stutter altered Gene's perception of him, made him seem not so much a Caligula figure as a Claudius. He held out his hand to the guests. "I'm J-Jody Dengler."

Nodella introduced Gene and they followed the supreme poohbah of the Starco empire into a vast room surrounded by shelves full of law tomes and dominated by a rosewood conference table which could seat twenty people comfortably even if they each had a pile of books beside them. At the moment only two persons were sitting there, a bald sharkskin-suited man of about fifty with the smell of pipe tobacco about him and a black woman roughly the same age who wore her gray-streaked hair in a pixie cut. She closed the hefty green-bound volume in front of her and beat the bald man to his feet as the three approached. "Lieutenant Holt," Nodella said, "The Honorable Artemisia Wellston, probate judge of this county. I got to know the judge last year," he explained to Gene, "when my mom died and we had to probate her will." Gene shook her hand.

"Alex Foley," the bald man introduced himself in a deep baritone. "Starco General Counsel."

"J-Judge W-w-wellston has agreed to c-confer with us about Gen-general Anderson's w-w-will," Jody Dengler explained as all five took seats.

"Hypothetically only," the jurist cautioned. "The will has not been offered for probate yet and I cannot give an opinion on any matter that I might have to officially rule upon a few months from now." She sat and folded her hands on the gleaming table surface. "Show me the will, sweetie," she said.

Gene and Nodella sat in silence at her right and Dengler and Foley at her left as she read the document. A few minutes into her perusal she began to react, shaking her head slightly as if in disapproval, murmuring "Uh-uh, uh-uh" as if it were the strangest paragraph she had ever encountered. She set the will down and folded her hands again. "Someone got troubles here," she said.

"On this side of the table we're just cops, Your Honor, not lawyers," Nodella said. "I'd appreciate it if you could explain in layman's, er layperson's language."

"That's simple enough," Judge Wellston said. "Now this will, this hypothetical will I should say, seems to comply in all respects with the formal requirements for a valid will. Signed by the testator, proper number of witnesses etcetera. Was General Anderson of sound mind when he executed it? Are there any issues of testamentary incapacity or undue influence? Of course from the will itself there is no way I or anyone else can tell." She cleared her throat. "The problem here is what happened to this will after he executed it. I am to assume he made these changes himself?"

"You can assume that for our purposes here," Nodella said.

"Well, let's take the earliest first." She looked up from the will into the ice-gray eyes of Jody Dengler. "Eighteen months ago, when he changed executors from your father to you. No legal problem there, but you should all thank your lucky stars he didn't die within thirty days of making that change." Dengler and Foley nodded slightly as if they knew what she was talking about but Gene and Nodella looked blank. "Any codicil to a will," she explained, looking at the nonlawyers in the room now, "has an effect on the will that we call republication. This means that all words and concepts of time that apply to the will are sort of moved forward from the date the will was executed to the date the codicil was executed. With me so far? Now this is our probate code." She tapped the green-bound book in front of her. "One of its provisions was designed to prevent religious and other scoundrels from terrorizing people on their deathbeds into leaving money to their group. It invalidates any charitable bequest in a will if the person dies within thirty days of executing the will. Now, if you'll connect the dots between that and what I said about republication. . . ."

Nodella at least made the connection. "The thirty-day clock started running again from the date he signed the codicil changing executors?"

"Very good! Maybe you should consider going to law school. If General Anderson had died within a month of executing that codicil, the residuary clause of his will would have been invalidated and all that money would have gone by intestate succession."

Gene cast her thoughts back. Wasn't it just about eighteen months ago that Paul had flown to Europe? Yes, he had talked to her on the phone a few days before leaving; said he wanted to revisit the places he'd been stationed while he was still able to travel. He must have changed executors very shortly before his departure. Well, Gene told herself, in any event he came back and survived the execution of that codicil by far more than thirty days.

"Now for the changes in his will he apparently made just before his death," Judge Wellston continued. "First he drew a line through the original residuary bequest. That would seem to constitute a valid partial revocation of his will." She smiled at Gene. "You see, sweetie, executing a valid will requires certain formalities but revoking a will in whole or in part is much simpler." She leafed through the green-bound tome until she found what she needed. "Under our law and the laws of every other state I am familiar with you can revoke a will in whole or in part by physical act. Each state's probate code has, well, you might call it a laundry list of the physical acts that count. In this state the acts are burning, canceling, tearing or obliterating. If any of those acts is done either by the testator or in his presence and by his consent and direction, it counts as revocation. Of course you also need *animus revocandi.*" She stopped and emitted a low giggle. "Oh, I'm sorry, I promised no law talk, didn't I? That just means the act must have been done with the intent to revoke. Assuming those requirements were met, General Anderson revoked the residuary clause of his will. The body of his will would be given legal effect but the residuary would pass by intestate succession."

"But, Judge," Nodella protested, "remember that after the General lined out the original residuary clause he wrote in Ms. Holt's name."

"I do remember," Judge Wellston assured him. "Ms. Holt takes nothing. You see, holographic wills and holographic codicils aren't recognized in this state. You can revoke a will or any part of a will without witnesses but you do need them to add new matter to a will. This handwritten addition to the will was not attested. The General may have intended Ms. Holt to be the new residuary legatee but he did not comply with our Probate Code. The residue of his estate will go to his intestate successors, which means to his nearest relatives within the ninth degree of kinship as determined by the civil law method of counting. My oh my, there I go again! Sorry, sweetie," she said to Gene.

"Paul had a daughter," Gene said, "but she vanished back in the seventies." Softly and without mentioning aspects that were too personal she explained to the judge her college friendship with Lynn and how it had led to her friendship with Paul.

"He was always hoping she'd come back," Alex Foley said. "I remember that several months before he retired from Starco he hired a big private detective firm to try and find her. The search took more than a year. Jody, didn't your dad put you in charge of supervising the detectives when he took over as CEO?"

"Th-that's right, Al-Alex," the younger Dengler said. "It was a w-waste of time and m-money. A c-court declared her legally d-dead about f-f-fifteen years ago and th-that was wh-when the G-general had the w-will drawn up that left m-most of his estate to M-Mad U."

"He had no other relatives?" Judge Wellston asked. "Brothers, sisters, cousins?"

At that moment a horrible scenario sprang full-grown into Gene's mind. *Lynn is alive. She's around here somewhere incognito. She fed Paul his suicide pills and monkeyed with his will so that the seven million dollar residue would wind up hers.* She struggled to keep her face and voice neutral as she answered the judge's question. "He was an only child. I never heard him mention any relatives."

"No adopted children?" the judge asked. "They're treated the same as biological children for succession purposes, you know."

"He never adopted any children," Gene said. *If Lynn is around somewhere, would I know her after thirty years? Would she know me?*

"If there are no relatives within the ninth degree of kindred the residue goes to the state," the judge said. "Hypothetically of course. That is known as escheat. Unless—well, there is another legal concept that may come into play here if Madison University wants to bet on a long shot."

"Are we in for more lawyer talk?" Nodella asked glumly, and at the judge's nod he and Gene grimaced at each other and reached for legal pads from the stack at the center of the table.

She slept poorly that night. Distant thunder rumbling in the mountains, thoughts churning in her head. Alternative accounts of Paul's death and the changes in his will, versions that required her to turn on the bedside lamp and reread the notes she'd taken as Judge Wellston lectured. After a while, when she realized how deeply she was engrossed in the technique of legal analysis, she shuddered like Lon Chaney Jr. when he saw himself turning into a werewolf but she didn't stop thinking. Finally she drifted into a fitful doze, waking with a start to find her room flooded with sunlight. She bathed and dressed and went up to the main floor and the registration kiosk, behind which the double-chinned blonde who had checked her in sat at a computer terminal. *Could that be Lynn?* Gene turned away and entered the dining room, which opened off the lobby and was bereft of patrons except for one man tackling an omelet in an alcove. She recognized the attendant who escorted her to a window table and took her order as the same young man who had taken her bag yesterday. Jorge brought her orange juice and hot tea with lemon and, a few minutes later, a basket of muffins. She had just finished spreading marmalade on one of them when she saw the man across the dining room push his chair back and saunter casually in her direction as though he had seen a deer through the window and wanted a closer look. “Ms. Holt, I presume?”

“I'm Lieutenant Holt,” she corrected him gently.

“We do seem to have the place to ourselves,” he smiled. “I'm Mark Stern.” He reached for a cardcase in his hip pocket.

“I thought you might be,” she said without looking at the card. “You're the Associate Dean at Mad U School of Law, yes?”

“Precisely. So you're the lucky lady whose name was written in as residuary legatee in General Anderson's will.”

*How did he come to know that?* Gene wondered. The fact was not included in what Nodella had released to the media. Her best guess was that Mad U had some kind of pipeline into either the Department or Judge Wellston's chambers. “Well, yes,” she replied, hoping to test how good a pipeline he had, “but not by General Anderson.”

“Er, well, hm hm,” Stern coughed, “I imagine it will be our position that it was.”

Gene needed no more to sense the drift of the conversation. Her mind went back to Judge Wellston's impromptu lecture of the evening before. “Oh, I see,” she said. “Mad U is going to argue Dependent Relative Revocation. I'm familiar with the doctrine,” she went on brightly. “If a testator revokes a bequest in his will and replaces it with another that after his death is held to be invalid, his revocation is deemed to have been contingent on the efficacy of the substitute and, that contingency having failed, the revocation is disregarded."

Associate Dean Stern's jaw dropped and he stared goggle-eyed at her as if she were the Medusa with legalisms rather than snakes coming out of her mouth. Gene half-rose in her chair and signaled to Jorge across the dining room.

"There are two reasons why the plan won't work." She seated herself again as the young waiter approached her table. "One of them is legal. The majority of courts apply the doctrine only where doing so seems in line with what the testator would have preferred. In this case that clearly isn't so."

"And the other reason?" Stern asked.

"Jorge," Gene said, "I want you to listen carefully to what we say." The waiter gave her a look of polite blankness and positioned himself warily between the standing man and the seated woman. "Spell my name," she told the associate dean, and glowed with delight when she saw a frown of puzzlement etch his brow.

"H-O-L-T," he replied. "I guess."

"And my first name?"

He hesitated for perhaps three seconds. "J-E-A-N," he ventured.

"I hoped you'd say that." Gene reached into her clutch bag, extracted badge case and wallet and displayed the same cards she had shown Nodella the day before. "That is how it was spelled in the handwritten addition to Paul's will. Now Paul knew me for more than half my life. He knew how to spell my name. Whoever added my name to his will spelled it wrong—precisely as you just did!"

Stern's complexion went dead fish gray. He began to

sway as he stood over her and for a moment Gene was afraid he'd keel over. Jorge stepped back in alarm.

"You were staying here at the conference center the night Paul died," she went on. "Suppose for whatever reason you slipped out and over to his house that night, and discovered him dead, and saw the will on his desk with the residuary bequest to Mad U lined out? Now you, sir, are responsible for buttering up potential donors to the law school. That means you probably knew a little bit about Paul's relationship with me. Suddenly the words Dependent Relative Revocation flash into your legal mind. You take Paul's pen and write my name in as close to his style of handwriting as you could. But you had the bad luck to spell it wrong."

"I didn't . . ." he gasped. "I didn't. . . ."

"Perhaps not," Gene smiled, "but can you prove you didn't? Whoever is on the other side of the lawsuit you have in mind, whether it's I, or the state, or someone else—well, you can be sure I'll testify to this little interlude between us, and Jorge here will confirm it."

Stern turned on his heel and stalked out of the dining room, without waiting for his check and leaving the rest of his omelet uneaten. Gene felt a warm serenity inside her. It wasn't every day that one had the chance to out-lawyer a lawyer.

Crossing the atrium on the way back to her room, she paused for another unobtrusive look at the double-chinned blonde behind the registration counter. *No way,* she told herself. The lean and dynamic Lynn she remembered from college could never have morphed into this pudgy frump. *But what if. . . .* She cleared her throat loudly and the blonde looked up from her computer terminal.

"Excuse me." Gene took the badge case out of her bag and held it open. "I'm working with Lieutenant Nodella on General Anderson's death. Would you happen to have a list of the Conference Center employees?"

"Certainly, ma'am," the blonde said. She slipped into an office inside the registration area and returned with a roster of several dozen names which she handed across the counter. "Only the ones with asterisks next to them are working this month," she said. "The rest were furloughed while we were doing renovations."

Gene counted eleven names with asterisks and recognized a few of them from the interview reports Nodella had shared with her. JONES, DEMETRIUS was the night security guard on the front gate. NARAYAN, RADHAKRISHNAN was the waiter who had found Paul's body. SOTO, JORGE had just served her breakfast in the restaurant. Some of the unfamiliar names on the roster were foreign and she couldn't be sure of their gender. "How many of these are women?" she asked.

Frowning as if she feared Gene might be a compliance officer with the EEOC, the blonde took the roster and returned it with red pen marks beside four names. "The one at the top is me," she said.

"And the other three—would you say any of them were, well, in my own age bracket?"

"They're all young enough to be our daughters," the clerk laughed. Gene silently buried the Lynn-is-among-us theory in the well-stocked boneyard of her speculations, thanked the other woman and turned away.

Halfway across the atrium she froze in her tracks and for a moment her heart stopped. She was Prince Gautama under the bo tree, she was Newton watching the apple fall, she was Beethoven touching piano keys to produce the first notes of the Fifth Symphony. *It all fits! It all rhymes!* With stoic calm she took the elevator down to her room, sat on the unmade bed for a while as silent and motionless as a statue, then reached for the stenographic pad she had used the previous evening and began filling the clean pages with fresh notes. At one point she stopped, found the local phone directory in a night table drawer, tapped out the Probate Court number and was lucky enough to find Judge Wellston free. She asked three questions, received the answers she had expected, hung up and wrote in her steno pad some more. Then she reached for the phone again and called Nodella's extension.

"Come see me," she said. "I need your undivided attention for an hour or two."

Nodella stopped pacing Gene's room and dropped to the edge of her still unmade bed. "I can't believe it," he muttered. "My God, it goes back so far!"

"If I'm right," she said, "it goes back to Paul's last months as CEO of Starco, when he decided to make one final all-out effort to find Lynn. Remember what Mr. Foley told us last night? Paul gave Dengler Senior the job of hiring and supervising detectives. When Paul retired and Dengler Senior took over as CEO, he delegated the job to his son."

"Yes, but the detectives struck out," Nodella reminded her. "And the General gave up and had his daughter declared legally dead. That was what, fifteen years ago?"

"You have no idea what those detectives found and neither do I," Gene said. "If my theory is right, they either didn't find Lynn at all or found evidence she was dead, but they also found something else. *That she had either had or adopted a child.* Remember what Judge Wellston said last night? Biological and adopted children are treated the same for succession purposes. So Paul had a grandchild but didn't know it. He planned his estate so that most of it would go to fund chairs of international law at Mad U. But meanwhile Jody Dengler had made some kind of devil's bargain with the grandchild that would put those millions into their pockets if they played their cards right and were lucky.

"What happens next? Dengler Senior contracts an incurable disease and Jody takes over as CEO. In due course Paul has a codicil added to his will, replacing the older Dengler as executor with the younger. Now, suppose Paul had happened to die within thirty days of executing that codicil."

Nodella rubbed his chin and scowled.

"Judge Wellston told us last night," Gene said. "The Probate Code's restriction on charitable bequests would have kicked in and the residuary, meaning the vast bulk of Paul's estate, would have passed by intestate succession to his nearest relative within the ninth degree of kinship. *The grandchild he never knew he had!*"

"Well, but nothing happened to the General within thirty days after he changed executors," Nodella pointed out.

"Only because almost immediately after signing the codicil he took off for a long trip to Europe! That happenstance added a year and a half to Paul's life and frustrated Jody's scheme. But he didn't give up. He sat back and ran Starco and waited for another opportunity. Which was offered to him recently when Mad U adopted the anti-military policy that sent Paul up the wall with anger so that he threatened to cut the school out of his will. Now I knew Paul for a long time and he was not a man to make idle threats. I don't know whether he did it before his meeting with Mark Stern or after but I'm convinced that he lined out that residuary clause himself—and that he told Jody Dengler. Can you imagine Jody's ecstasy when he heard the news? Now if Paul would only die before he decided on a new residuary legatee, the residue would pass by intestacy to his unknown grandchild just as it would have if he'd died within thirty days after changing executors! And this time Paul obliged—with a great deal of help from Jody."

Nodella was silent for a few minutes, then looked up. "It's a beautiful theory," he admitted. "You can't prove a word of it but it seems to account for everything we know. . . ."

"And while you were coming out here Judge Wellston confirmed that the legal steps of it are sound," Gene cut in.

"Except for one little thing," Nodella went on. "The will we found wasn't the way it needed to be for this scheme to pay off. Your name, misspelled, was handwritten in as the residuary legatee! Now why after killing the General would Dengler have done that?"

"He would have been insane to do it," Gene agreed. "Therefore he didn't. Paul must have written in my name himself, probably while Jody was busy cleaning up the evidence of his visit. He was dying, he knew he'd been poisoned, he sensed that the reason must be connected with his having cancelled the Mad U clause in his will, so he wrote in my name. Not knowing it was legally invalid."

"And misspelling it?"

"I think he meant that as, well, as a signal to me that there was something amiss about his death." Gene rose from her chair and Nodella from the edge of her bed. "Let's go see if we can find some evidence." She held the room door open and shut it behind them. "We need to locate the reports of the agency that was hired to trace Lynn. Then we'll see the head of the agency and demand copies of all their files on the case and we look for gaps. We'll interview all the investigators who worked on the case. If someone found a biological or adopted child of Lynn's and took a bribe to keep it under wraps, they might prefer to talk rather than be charged as accessory before the fact in a murder."

"So where do we begin?" he asked. "If you're right, and if we go to Starco and ask to see those detectives' reports, Dengler's going to know we're getting warm."

"The subject of those reports was Paul's daughter," Gene said. "He would never have kept them at Starco after he retired and probably not even while he worked there. He must have kept them somewhere in his house. And that's excellent because the place is sealed off as a crime scene and, unless Dengler managed to find them when he poisoned Paul, there's no way he can make them disappear now. Come on, let's start looking."

She had walked this paved footpath so many times before, through twilight shadows when she and Paul would stroll over for dinner at the conference center, through the night songs of cicadas and toads when they would return home. With Nodella as her companion the pace was much faster. Once beyond the conference center the path curved through thick woods that shut out most of the sunlight. The only sounds she heard were their footsteps. Then off in the woods she heard something else. A thrashing and a soft moaning. Nodella held up his hand for them to stop.

"A deer?" she whispered.

"I'm a hunter," he told her. "That's no deer. Wait." He stepped off the path and into the woods, slowly, cautiously. In less than a minute she lost sight of him amid the trees. Then she heard him cry out her name. "Over here!" he shouted. "Careful where you step!" She made her way around sprawling roots, following his voice until at the edge of a clearing she saw him. On his knees. Bending over another man who was lying in a twisted position on his side. Even in the gloom she could see the blood all over his clothes. Nodella slowly rose, looked around as if to make sure he wasn't disturbing anything, then came close to her. "Dengler," he breathed. "Stabbed five or six times. I think he just died in my arms but I'm not a doctor. Damn, I left my cell phone in the car!"

"Oh God," Gene breathed. "Did he say anything before he died?"

"I asked him who did it."

"And?"

Nodella looked stunned and shaken, as if his best friend had just punched him in the solar plexus.

"He laughed in my face!"

They trotted back to Nodella's sedan in the conference center parking lot. With his cell phone he ordered the officer on duty at Paul's house to secure the new crime scene, then called in for backup. Gene crossed to the rear entrance of the conference center, found her way to the atrium, spoke to the frumpy blonde behind the registration desk and came away with the name, address and phone and license numbers of the murderer. Sirens screamed and tires squealed as two black-and-whites and a boxy EMS truck braked within a few feet of Nodella's car and four plainclothesmen with sidearms and two medical technicians in white with a stretcher emerged from their respective vehicles. Nodella sent them off along the path with preliminary instructions. Gene waited until he was through before she showed him the paper.

"This is who you want," she said.

She looked out the window of Major Case Squad headquarters at the midnight lights of the city below as Nodella thanked the cop at the other end of the line and hung up. It was over. The wild auto chase had begun at a truck stop three counties south and ended forty minutes later in a collision between the murderer's car and an eighteen-wheeler he had thought he could pass at ninety-five miles per hour. He had been thrown clear but with a broken neck and back and in the emergency hospital he had made two statements, the second to police officers who had taped it and faxed a transcription to Nodella's office while he and Gene were out grabbing a quick supper at al-Tarboush. The first had been to the hospital's chaplain. During the call that had just come in Nodella had mouthed two words to Gene across the room. "He's dead." Now the lieutenant joined her at the window and gazed out empty-eyed at the light-dotted canyons of downtown.

"I can't get over how quickly you knew," he said after a space of silence.

*You would have known too if you could pronounce the man's name right,* Gene thought but politely declined to say. "It was so easy," she replied instead. "Why would Jody laugh in your face when you asked who had killed him? Well, if this were a detective story I suppose we could come up with some outlandish reason or other, but there's such a simple explanation—*when you remember that he stuttered!* He was trying to say 'Jorge Soto' but just couldn't get beyond the first syllable!"

"And knowing who did it you right away knew why?"

"Well, there didn't seem to be more than one possibility," Gene said. "Lynn has been dead for years, we know that now, but Jorge is the child she adopted long ago. The detectives found him but Jody kept the news from Paul and made a private deal with Jorge. The young man came out here a few years ago on what the British would call a watching brief. He took a job at the conference center and spied on Paul as best he could. We know from his statement that he was afraid to come out and tell Paul who he was because then Paul could rewrite his will so as to leave him either nothing or a relative pittance. Jorge was something of a gambler. He was playing for the big jackpot."

"But you don't think he was the one fed the General his nightcap of hemlock?"

"Paul was a military man," Gene said. "He had a sense of rank. I don't see him offering a tot of his whiskey to a menial. No, it was Dengler who was his last drinking companion. Not that we have to prove him guilty of anything now. Remember, it was Jorge who suggested that meeting room for us yesterday. I think he must have eavesdropped on some of our conversation and learned about my misspelled name having been added to Paul's will. He had no idea what that meant but he saw his dreams collapsing and hit the panic button and arranged a meeting with Jody in the woods near the conference center and they fought and Jorge killed him and ran. I wouldn't be surprised if he still dreamed of coming back someday to claim Paul's estate on his own. We all have our dreams. So," she finished, "I suppose most of Paul's money will wind up escheating to the state."

"Suppose somebody crawls out of the woodwork," Nodella asked, "claiming the estate through Georgie? After all it wasn't Soto who poisoned the General, so maybe a relative of his could argue. . . ."

"In that unlikely event," Gene said, stifling a wince at Nodella's rendition of the name, "I expect the state would try to show Jorge was somehow complicit in Paul's murder in a way that would bar any relative of his from profiting from the crime. And it would be a civil proceeding so the state would only need to prevail by a simple preponderance of the evidence, not beyond a reasonable doubt."

"Are you sure you're not a lawyer?" Nodella scowled.

She gazed unseeing out the plexiglass window of the Starco jet at cloud wisps in a bright blue sky. Alex Foley and the gray-bearded black man who had been appointed acting CEO sat in their dark suits across the aisle from her, heads bent close, talking business in low voices drowned out for her by the plane motors. They were on their way back from seeing Paul laid to rest in Arlington National Cemetery. For want of any family member in the party the folded flag had been given to her at the ceremony's end. That and a flood of memories was all she had of him now. If she had played her cards differently with him, what would she be today? His widow perhaps? Two roads diverged in a yellow wood and part of her knew she had taken the one right for her and part of her wished she had taken the one she hadn't.

*Never again*, the jet's motors seemed to hum. *Never again.*

# The Best in Online Mystery Fiction in 2004

Sarah Weinman

**Ask several well-regarded mystery professionals** and it's likely you'll get the same answer: short story markets are dwindling. Once it was possible to make a decent mint by submitting to all sorts of print publications. Now, at least in the mystery public's consciousness, there's *Ellery Queen*, *Alfred Hitchcock*, and year-end anthologies like this one—and that's about it. But if you're a writer and your voice and style doesn't fit *EQMM* or *AHMM*'s guidelines, or if you're still not known enough to be picked up by one of the themed anthologies sponsored by the major crime writing associations, where do you go?

For the last few years, the answer is online.

Like any new medium, the Web was greeted by publishing industries with skepticism and scorn, and often for good reason: poor presentation, questionable editing, and seeming instability. Many heralded early players such as *Blue Murder* and *HandHeldCrime* no longer exist. And even as several online publications did create their own distinct presence, adopt strict editorial guidelines and produce quality fiction, what still remains a sticking point is the lack of cash. Writers trade greater exposure and the opportunity for a story to stay in print in perpetuity for, if they are lucky, the equivalent of two Starbucks lattes.

So why go online?

Several reasons. First, it gives undiscovered writers a wonderful opportunity to get their unique voices heard and distributed to, potentially, a bigger audience than a tiny print magazine that goes out of print after a month. Second, because of the dwindling print markets, more publishing professionals are looking to the Web for talent and quality—think of Scott Wolven, whose stories have almost exclusively been published online, being included in four consecutive editions of the *Best American Short Stories* and getting a collection published by Scribner. Or Allan Guthrie, who went from publishing his first story online to having two books published by major presses and acquiring books for Point Blank Press—all in under two years' time.

The Web has become a haven of experimentation and risk—of stories that don't quite fit a particular mold. It's inspired a new wave of noir and allowed younger writers to have their voices heard. And it's allowed fiction editors like myself (for *Shots UK*), Gerald So (for *Thrilling Detective*), Anthony Neil Smith (of the late, lamented *Plots with Guns*), Megan Powell (for *Shred of Evidence*), Dave Zeltserman (for *Hardluck Stories*), and Russel McLean (for *Crime Scene*

*Scotland*)—just to name a few—to open up our inboxes every day and discover some of the best stories we've ever read. In 2004, the StorySouth Million Writers Award awarded several crime stories with a Notable mention, not only increasing the presence of these particular writers, but of the genre itself.

And so, as a writer, editor and passionate supporter of online fiction, I was honored that Ed Gorman and Marty Greenberg asked me to pick three of the best stories published online in 2004. Not surprisingly, it was an exceedingly difficult task—how to pick between so many quality stories? But in the end, I picked the three that stuck with me weeks, if not months after I first read them.

The first, I will admit, I selected for its original publication. But when Martyn Waites submitted "Just Pretend," to me as part of the UK Noir Issue of *Plots with Guns,* he just wanted it to find a home. I read the story—all 7,000 words of it—in one shocked sitting, marveling at the honesty and emotion of the lead character as he slowly reveals his brutal life story and the circumstances that landed him in prison for many years to come. It's a story that confirms Waites as one of the finest crime writers to emerge from the UK in recent years.

Aliya Whiteley's "Geoffrey Says," is a little different. *Very* different. How else to describe a tale that hinges on the narrator following orders of an emerald green penguin, and then following it up with a hilarious twist at the end? Whiteley's deadpan humor makes the reader swallow the surrealism that underscores some seriously nasty business.

Finally, one can't have a feature like this without mentioning David White, certainly one of the rising stars in the crime fiction short story world. A Derringer award winner and twice a notable for the Million Writers Award, White's stories offer excellent plot, strong characterization, and a thoughtful voice. I've chosen "God's Dice," which features the New Jersey–based PI Jackson Donne investigating a woman's disappearance on behalf of a local priest. Donne visits confessional booths, casinos, and seedy hotel rooms to discover the woman's whereabouts and confront larger issues of personal accountability and faith. And like all good stories, it leaves the protagonist in a different place from where he began.

Consider these three stories as a taste of what's out there in the online fiction realm. Once you've partaken, you'll be back for more.

## Links to Chosen Stories

Martyn Waites, "Just Pretend"
*Plots with Guns,* issue 30, Summer 2004
*http:// www.plotswithguns.com/pretend.html*

Aliya Whiteley, "Geoffrey Says"
*Shred of Evidence,* Vol. 2, issue 4, November 2004
*http:// shredofevidence.com/nov04/geoffrey_says.html*

David White, "God's Dice"
*Thrilling Detective,* Spring 2004
*http:// www.thrillingdetective.com/fiction/04_04.html*

# Just Pretend

Martyn Waites

Martyn Waites is the author of five novels, most recently *Born Under Punches* (2003) and *The White Room* (2004). A native of Newcastle-upon-Tyne, he has turned his hand to many occupations: market trader, bar manager, stand-up comic, actor, and teacher of drama to teenage ex-offenders. He lives with his family in Essex.

**I keep having this dream**. I suppose you could call it a recurring one cept I don't have it often. Only when I'm stressed an unhappy lie. Like me first night in prison.

In it I'm with me dad. Me real dad. We're in the car together, goin somewhere, an the sun's out, the sky's blue, there's not a cloud to spoil etc., an we're in the country, all leafy an green. An we're laughin. He says something an looks at me an I laugh. An when I laugh, he laughs. An when he laughs he looks at me an I see somethin there in his eyes an it makes me feel good. Me belly feels all warm an full.

Then we turn off the road to where we're goin. An the sun's still shinin an that bu the green's gone. We go down this road an it gets more an more bumpy the further it goes on. An then we're in this quarry an it stretches for miles, just rock an sand an dust. In the middle there's these buildins from corrugated metal with lots of old machinery lyn around them an we head for them.

Me dad says he's got to see someone an smiles an when he smiles there's something in his eyes but it's not like it was before. It doesn't make me feel warm. Then before I can say anything he gets out of the car an goes inside the buildins, leavin me there.

I sit there for a while an at first it's all right. But then these clouds start to roll over the sun, sendin shadows over the rocks. Then it starts to get cold an I shiver. I'm only wearin a t-shirt. Then I realize me dad's been gone an long time an I start to get worried. At first I do nothing, just sit there, then I wind down the window an shout but all I hear is me own voice comin back at me. I'm getting really scared now. I open the car door an get out. I go inside the building, the same way me dad did. Inside it's all old an dusty an fallin apart, like no one's been there for years. An there's no sign of me dad.

I run round all the buildins shoutin Dad! Dad! Until I can't shout anymore. But there's no reply. I run back outside an now the car's gone, just disappeared. An it's got cold now, really cold. An the clouds are turnin the sky grey. Soon the sky'll be black. An the stones stretch on forever.

I wanna run everywhere an scream everythin at the same time. But I don't. I just sit down an hug me knees into me chest an cry. An cry an cry an cry. An then I wake up. An I'm still cryin.

An that was me first night in prison.

I suppose you want to facts an things now. What I'm here for an that. Well, no point beatin around the bush, it's armed robbery. What happened was, me an me co-de, well half-brother really, but we say co-de in prison, short for co-defendant, we knocked over this petrol station. We did it properly, masks an that, balaclavas an shotguns. Paralysed the bloke in there. But we still got caught. Known to the police we were. Or me brother was, anyway. I wouldn't care, but we only got four fuckin grand, for fuck sake! Hardly worth goin out, was it?

Anyway, we got sent down. An split up. Sean got Hollesley Bay. I got here.

So where's here? Well I can't tell you that, can I? Like I can't tell you men name. Cos I'm underage. So pick a prison, any one, they're all the same, an that can be it. Same with me. Pick a name an I'll answer to it.

It's okay here, I suppose, once you get used to it. Not a fuckin holiday camp, but then it shouldn't be. But I can ride it. My wing's not bad. I'm in with the Section 52s, the long termers. Not just armed robbers like me, but street robbers, murderers an that. Rapists an sex offenders too, but they try an hide that. Make up stories about what they're in for. The other lads are all right, really. You all get on if you've got respect. When you first go in they all wanna know ya. Wanna know your history, sus you out.

See if you're a threat. So I tell them things about me. Just bits, though. What I'm in for, who me co-de is an where he's at. Stuff like that. An stories. Things I want them to hear. Some are real some are pretend. But I don't tell them my history. My real story. I carry that with me.

Sometimes, lookin at the other kids, I feel so old. I'm seventeen. The youngest are about fifteen. When we're eighteen we get shipped out to an adult nick. There's a big gap between fifteen an eighteen. A big fuckin gap.

But I just keep me head down. I watch, I smile. I ride it. You have a lot of time to think in here. I think about me family. About me dad. He's great, me dad. I've got pictures of him on the wall of me cell. There he's standin in our front room laughin, there he's with Marie, me stepmum. There he's down the Cross Keys doin his karaoke. Fuckin loves his karaoke. The Karaoke King, we call him, an he laughs. But he's really good. He does all the old stuff, Frank Sinatra, Moon River an that. Says his dad, my gandad used to play all that. He got it from him. Me dad could've done this for a livin. He's that good. You can tell by the photo. See the way his eyes are screwed tight shut, the way the veins in his neck are poppin out. An all the people in the audience are starin at him like they can't take their eyes off him. I look at that photo a lot. Makes me proud that he's me dad.

An then there's Kayleigh. She's me girlfriend an she's standin by me. I met her through me stepmum. I think she's her niece or somethin. She's got a flat of her own now, lives there with Tod. Haven't told you about him, have I? He's me son. Nearly six months old now. An I love him too. See this tattoo? Just above me wrist. There. I ain't rollin me sleeve back too far. There. Says Tod with a heart round it. I had that done whe he was born. That's how much I love him. I know I'm gonna miss out in him growin up an that, but he'll be with his mum. An me dad an Marie'll help. An she can tell him about me.

I don't think about Sean much. I know he's alright cos I hear things. Boys are comin in or bein shipped out. Word gets back. He's doin all right. An I don't think of mum much. Me real mum. She's alive an that, but I just don't think of her much.

No, it's just me dad, Kayleigh an Tod. They're me family now. An me dad's always sayin that families are important. Families are about love. An he's so right. Now I sit or lie in me cell an think about when Tod's older. I can do things with him me dad did with me.

Like boxin. An football.

When me dad come an got me from me mum's an took me to live with him, one of the first things he did was to join me up with a boxin club. Teach you to hit an hit hard, he said. Teach you to fight back.

I looked round the place. Lads about me age were skippin an doin weights, punchin bags an in the ring punchin each other. The boys in the ring were wearin the shorts an boots along with those padded helmet things an vests. I didn't like the vests.

I don wanna do it dad, I said.

He looked at me. Why?

I don wanna wear no vest like, I said not lookin at him.

I heard him sigh. But it was a good sigh. Like he was on my side an wanted to help. Not like he was pissed with me an wanted to hit me. I tried to help him out.

What about a T-shirt? I asked.

I think he smiled. Yeah, that should be okay. Just tell them.

An I don hafta take a shower with them?

Just wait till they're done, then you go in, he said.

I felt that warm glow again in me belly. Like I get in me dream when it's all goin well.

Yeah I'll join then, I said.

He smiled. I saw it this time. Good.

I joined then. An I loved it. It was difficult at first, I thought it would be just hittin. But Tommy the trainer showed me different. You have to keep your guard up, not let your opponent get a shot in, hurt you. Block them, keep them out. Then hit back. But don't let them see you comin. Make them think you're gonna go one way then go another then BAM! you've got them. You've hurt them.

I wish I'd met Tommy earlier. I wish my dad had brought me here earlier. I wish I'd been with my dad all the time.

Anyway, like I was sayin, I loved it. I did everythin Tommy told me. I kept me guard up. I hit back. I didn't let them see me comin. An I hurt them.

I got so good Tommy put me in fights. An I won. Seven fights, seven wins. Four knock-outs, three on points. I used up a lot of energy in my fights. A lot of anger. A lot of hate. They sometimes had different faces but that just made me hit them harder. That was good, Tommy said. Use it. Channel it. Be in charge of it. I was. An it felt fuckin good.

But I wanted to do somethin else as well. So one of the lads suggested football. So I went to play for a youth team. I was a bit wary at first but I used to turn up with me strip on underneath me clothes an after the match wait until they'd all been in the shower before I went in. They thought that was a bit weird but I didn't care.

An I found out I was good at that too. They made me striker. An I had a run where it seemed I couldn't stop scorin. I ended up havin a trial at Spurs. I did, honest. I thought it was goin really well but when I got called in to see George Graham an Stefan Iverson came out before me smiling I knew it wasn't goin to happen. I was pissed off at the time but I got over it. The boxin helped. Me dad helped.

There's a funny thing about prison. The names. They all sound like prisons. Feltham. Glen Parva. Huntercombe. Dartmoor. Frankland. They all sound bleak an grey, like even before there was a prison there they were just names waitin for prisons to be built. An then there's ones like Swinfen Hall, Bulwood Hall, Maidstone. Palces that should sound prietty, but even they sound sinister. Then there's the big one, the daddy of them all. Wormwood Scrubs. Makes you fuckin shudder just to say it.

But like I said, mine's not that bad. You learn which screws are safe an which wanna fuck you up. Some of them do that, y'know, just for the hell of it. One kid on my landing once complained that this screw had kept him awake all night by kickin his door in. This kid makes stuff up, so the mornin screw didn't believe him. But when he tried to open the door he couldn't. The bolt was bent an jammed tight in. They pay a bit more attention to what this kid says now.

But some of the screws are okay. You can have a laugh with them. Like the teachers. Some of them are there cos no other place'll have them, some of them are really good, there cos they wanna be.

An it's like learnin a new way to talk. Prison's got its own language. If you wanna fit in you gotta learn it. They all wanna be gangsta rappers. Not just the black kids but all of them. Black, white, Asian, whatever. They all talk like that an they all act like that. An they all love rap. Especially Tupac. We all love Tupac. They ask me about it, an I talk back like they do an they say that's cool. That's real. But really I'm just pretendin. I like the old stuff. Sinatra, Moon River, stuff like that. Proper songs. Me dad's songs.

There is one thing, though. I won't take a shower. Haven't had one since I've been here. Not that I don't wanna be clean. I just don't wanna take a shower. Not with them. Not with anyone. An I won't. The other kids on the wing are startin to say things. Fuck em. Let em.

Anyway, I've got a job now. That takes me off the wing. Car maintenance. Fuckin love it. I love cars. I was training to be a mechaninc before I came here.

But listen. I'm in a good mood today cos guess what? I've got a family visit! Fuckin great, eh? They try an do this for the lads who've got kids, who wanna keep in touch. It's an incentive to behave. An I've been good. I've been a model fuckin inmate.

So yeah, Kayleigh, Tod, Marie an me dad! Fuckin great, eh? Next Wednesday in the chapel! I can't fuckin wait!

I'm in the Educational Psychologists office an she's just made me a cup of tea. She's just turn round to get some biscuits, bent down an I can see her arse against her jeans, see the line of her knickers underneath. Some lads would say something, try an hot her up, but not me. Victoria helps me. Talks to me like a friend. I try not to think about those things too much with her.

She's found the biscuits, sat down, is offerin me one. Her tits are nice too, but I try not to look at them. Custard creams. I take one an say thank you.

I asked to see her after the visit an she knows I'm upset, but I just don't know how to start.

Tell me about the visit, she asks.

I dunk my custard cream an suck it. I tell her about the visit.

My dad looked pale when he came in. Like he'd shrunk or something. He must've seen me lookin shocked because he said, Haven't been well. But don't worry, I'm getting better. An he smiled. When he did that I saw his teeth, all yellow, an the black rings under his eyes. I gave him a huge an tried to smile back.

Then I hugged Marie. Then Kayleigh. She pulled away.

What's that smell? She said.

I said, I haven't had a shower since I've been here.

She said, You should.

I said, They can't make me.

She said they should, an sat down opposite me. Away from me.

An then there was Tod, sittin in his pushchair. He didn't pull away when I picked him up. He looked confused for a bit, then he smiled.

Look, he still remembers me, I said.

No he doesn't, said Kayleigh lightin a fag, it's cos you're smilin at him. He's smilin back.

I put him down then, on the mat they'd put out. There

were some toys there, old ones, worn ones an Tod wanted to play with them. My dad gave me a fag. Then we talked.

I told Victoria all of this. I talked till me tea went cold.

Oh no, she said. She looked like she meant it.

Yeah. My dad's got lung cancer.

Oh no.

She talked for a bit longer, tryin to cheer me up, tryin to help. There was nothin she could do to help, I knew that an she knew that, but she kept talking. The sound of her voice made me feel better. It made me feel like she was my friend.

It was time for me to go. I didn't want to go back on the wing. I knew I had to, though. The screw was waitin outside with his portable metal detector, makin sure I hadn't nicked anythin.

Look, Victoria said as I was nearly out the door, this is nothin to do with your dad, but d'you wanna try havin a shower?

No I can't, I said.

It would help.

It wouldn't. Believe me, it wouldn't.

I left. The screw ran his metal detector over me an led me back to the wing.

After dinner I was supposed to have soch. Association time. But I didn't want to. I just stayed in my cell till lights out, lookin at the photos on the wall, then I went to sleep.

I woke up cryin durin the night.

I'd had the dream again.

I didn't want to go back to car maintenance, I wanted to talk to Victoria again. But she wasn't there. So I went.

But I didn't enjoy it. I kept dropping things an driftin off. Some of the other lads said things an I had a go back but Mick the mechanics teacher stepped in. Told us to calm down otherwise we'd all end up on the seg for fightin.

I tried havin soch that night but I didn't want it. I just sat there watchin the other lads play pool an PlayStation an watch the telly. Not many spoke to me. A couple said, why don't you have a shower, you smelly cunt? I just said fuck off an they laughed an went away.

I just sat an thought. About me dad. An me mum.

They split up when I was five, my mum an dad. I can't remember much about it, just the pair of them used to shout a lot. I can't remember my dad hittin my mum. He said he never did an I believe him. He said he wanted to though. An I believe him.

I got brought up by me mum. I can never remember her lookin happy. She was always shoutin at me an hittin me. Didn't matter what I did, whether I was good or bad, she was always layin into me. I used to try an be good, do things that might make her smile, make her happy, like tidyin up or somethin, but it never worked. I'd still get shouted at an hit. After a while I stopped tryin.

Sometimes though she would get upset an cry, give me a hug an say she was sorry. She was gonna be good to me from now on. An I used to smile an hug her back an tell her I loved her.

But she didn't. The next day it would be just the same. At first I cried, but then after a while I stopped doin that as well.

An Sean would sometimes stay. He usually lived with his dad. He was just over a year older than me an he used to really scare me. He seemed really grown up, like he knew everythin. He used to tell me all these things that he'd done, like breakin into places an fuckin girls. He used to nick mum's fags an smoke them. Mum didn't mind, she used to laugh. She got on really well with Sean. They used to sit down together an smoke on the settee. They'd sit all cosied up, she'd put her arm round him an cuddle him in.

When they did that, I used to look at them then run round jumpin on things an shoutin, fallin off things and tryin to make them laugh. But mum would shout at me, tell me to stop fucking about, an belt me one. Sean used to sit there an laugh. After a while I started goin out, leavin them to it. Sean was about eight then.

Then one day these two blokes arrived.

I was playin in the backyard at the time, with my toy cars. I don't know where Sean was.

Here he is, I heard my mother say, an she pointed at me.

One of the blokes took somethin, some foldin cash it looked like, out of his pocket an gave it to her. She smiled an took it. One of the men crossed the yard an knelt down beside me. He was going bald an had a little round fat tummy. He smiled. There was somethin about him I didn't like but I didn't know what. A look or a smell or something that wasn't quite right. I just looked at him.

Hello, he said, my name's Graham. What's yours?

I looked at him. I didn't want to tell him but mum said I had to, so I did.

That's nice, he said. Then he started talking to me about my toy cars. He said he had some lovely ones round at his place. Why didn't I come round an play with them?

I just looked at him.

Go on, my mum said. Go on, you'll have fun. I'll be here when you get back. She was smiling an laughin. She looked really happy.

Okay, I said, an I stood up an Graham held my hand an led me out. I didn't want to go, but if it made mum so happy I would do it.

Only for her, though.

I've been dropped a level. Fightin on the wing. We've all got levels in prison, y'see, from one to five. An which one you've got depends on how well you behave. I was up for a review that would take me to level five. TV in my cell, PlayStation, the lot. Instead I'm back to three now. An it's not my fault. I told the wing guvnor that.

It's that fuckin bitch Kayleigh's fault, that's who.

I phoned her earlier tonight. Saved up me phonecard credits an was the first in the queue. She answered an straightaway I could tell there was somethin up. I started talkin, askin after Tod, tellin her I missed her an that, an she said,

Look, I was gonna write to you but since you've phoned I'll tell you. Cos I think it's best to be honest.

I didn't say anything.

I'm seeing somebody. His name's Adrian an he's moved in.

I went fuckin ballistic. I screamed an pleaded, I begged an shouted. I called her everythin I could think of an she hung up.

I put the phone down. Anderson an Glover was standin there.

Dropped you, has she? one of them said. Getting it off somebody else, ehe? I bet she doesn't want you near her, you fuckin stink. Yeah, do they not have showers where you come from, you smelly cunt?

I lost it. An I forgot everythin. How to block them, keep the out, show them you're goin one way then go another. Hit back. Hurt them. Everythin.

The next thing I remember is a couple of screws grabbin ahold of me an me cryin an goin limp. Then I was taken to see the guvnor an when I calmed down a bit I told him what had happened.

He nodded an said that since they provoked me, he wasn't goin to send me to the seg. But since I'd been fightin he had to drop me a level. He said he was sorry, though, he thought I was doin well.

Then he suggested it might help if I took a shower.

I said I wouldn't.

He sighed.

I said I wanted to see Victoria.

He said she'd gone home.

No more soch. I went back to me cell an sat there.

I tried not to cry. I tried not to think. I tried not to dream.

D'you like playin games, son? Graham asked.

I said I did. He smiled.

Good. Cos I've got some good ones to play.

An we played. Him an the other bloke chased me all over the house. We played catch. Hide an seek. We played all the games that my mother never played with me. An I had a great time. I loved it.

Whoo, Graham said eventually. I'm hot, are you?

I said I was.

I'll go an run you a bath then. You can cool off.

An he did. An I sat there in for ages, thinking, This is all right, this. What a good time I was havin. Then the door opened an Graham an the other bloke, Dave, came in wearin towels.

Budge up, said Graham. I'm gonna get in an do your back.

An that was the first time it happened.

Afterwards I was shakin. I wanted to cry. I wanted my mum. Graham musta saw this an he gave me a cuddle.

Listen, he said. You're a special little boy. What we did was special. A special kind of love.

An he went on, telling me I was special, an that he loved me. But that I hadn't to tell anyone else. I had to pretend that nothing was happenin. It was a secret. An then he gave me a toy. A big red fire engine. I loved it. An he said he'd see me again soon.

I went home. Mum was waitin. She didn't say anythin, she just looked at me. An I looked at her. Then I couldn't look at her anymore. I went upstairs into me bedroom, shut the door an lay on the bed. I laid like that for ages just starin at the ceilin. I heard noises from downstairs. Sean had arrived. I heard him an mum laughin. Then I heard them on the stairs. Then they went into mum's room an shut the door.

I just lay there. Then I thought about me secret. About Graham an Dave. An I got me fire engine out an started to play.

They used to come for me regular after that. They'd take me to theirs an start playin games. Let's pretend, they said.

We'll pretend now, they used to say. We'll play a special pretend game with you because we love you.

An I used to do it. Because they loved me.

An the games got bigger an bigger. An they started to hurt more an more. But I kept playin them. Because they loved me an I wanted to make them happy. I used to play me own game too. Pretend with them. Pretend I enjoyed it.

But one day I couldn't. I just couldn't pretend anymore.

An the best thing that ever happened to me happened. Me dad came to visit. An I told him what had happened. An I cried. An I clung to him. An I wouldn't let go. An I begged him to take me home with him.

An he did. An then it was the best time of me life.

Oh shit. Oh shit. I'm really worried now.

There's a couple of kids come onto my wing from Hollesley Bay. They say they know Sean. They say they know what he's really in for. He told them. So they beat the shit out of him. An they say they know what I'm really in for.

Armed robbery, I tell them. I paralysed a bloke with a shotgun.

Nah, they say. What you're really in for.

An they've been telling everybody else on the wing too.

I went to see the guvnor. I told him I needed to see Victoria right now.

He tried but said sorry, she was away on a course for a few days.

I didn't cry in front of him. I just asked to be taken back to me cell.

An I cried there instead.

Everythin was goin great living at me dad's, until I was fifteen. Until Sean showed up.

Me did didn't want him around.

I said he was family. An dad was always sayin family was important. Family was about love.

I've got no fuckin love for him, me dad would say.

I said all this, but really, Sean scared me. If I didn't see him, I thought he would . . . I don't know. Do something.

He wasn't livin with mum by this time. He was livin with some old boiler about fifteen years older than him. There was rumours goin round that she was on the game. There was rumours goin round that he'd put her there.

The good thing he did was takin me to meet this bloke who ran a garage. This bloke said he would take me on as an apprentice mechanic. I was really chuffed with Sean for that. It was a proper brotherly thing to do. Dad couldn't say anything about that.

Sean an me started hangin out a bit then. The pub, the snooker hall, just havin a laugh. He wasn't bad really. Liked a ruck, though. He used to start fights an that just for the fuck of it.

I didn't join in. I would just stand an watch.

Then I met Kayleigh an she got pregnant.

It made me feel good doin that, like a real man. I felt proud. I had a girlfriend who loved me, me dad an Marie telling me they loved me, an a job. A real job. I was fuckin sorted.

An then one night, Sean said he had an idea.

Marie sent me a letter. Me dad's gettin worse.

They've said at the hospital there's nothing more they can do with him. He said he wanted to go home to be with his family.

I got a letter from Kayleigh an all. Sayin she was sorry

an that, but her mind was made up. She also said that my mum had contacted her. I was nearly sick when I read that bit. Cos Kayleigh was alone with Tod me mum had been helping her. She said she seemed lovely. She didn't know what I had against her.

I'd never told her, you see. I'd hoped I'd never had to.

I phoned her up. Told her she must never allow my mum to get too close to Tod. She asked why not. An I couldn't tell her. She said if I couldn't tell her then that wasn't a good enough reason. She said I was a moody awkward bastard an me mother didn't deserve me.

Then she hung up.

I tried phonin dad but it just rang an rang. Maybe they unplugged the phone. Maybe he was tryin to get some sleep.

I've stopped doin the mechanics course.

Everyone else keeps lookin at me. Starin. I don't like it. It feels like somethin's waitin to happen.

I try an stay banged up as much as possible. I won't even talk to Victoria.

I just wanna be by myself. I want everyone else to go away.

I think about that red fire engine. I don't know why.

I'm down on the seg now. They moved me there after the fire.

The fire. I don't think I've ever been so fuckin scared in all my life. An I've been scared a lot.

I know who did it. Them two from Hollesley Bay. An if it wasn't then they got someone to do it. Bastards.

What happened was at soch one night someone came up to me cell door. I was banged up. I told them I didn't want soch. I heard something by the door an I looked up. An there was this paper that had been set on fire an slid under the door.

I just stared at it. I couldn't move. Then I heard some laughin in the hall.

Burn in Hell you stinkin rapist cunt!

Then I heard feet runnin away.

I ran to the paper an started stampin on it. But it had spread to a blanket that was in a heap at the bottom of the bed. An that really blazed up.

I screamed Fire! Fire! an I pressed the alarm bell.

It seemed like it took hours for the screws to arrive but it must have just been seconds. They got the fire extinguisher on it an took me down to healthcare. They said I was okay, not even too much smoke damage cos it hadn't had time to take hold. Then they took me to the seg for one night. For my own protection, they said.

The next morning Victoria came to see me. I was really pleased to see her. She looked all concerned for me, asked me what had happened.

She sighed. Look, she said, I think you've got to face up to things. I think you've got to confront your problems an ask for help.

No one can help me, I said. I don't need no help. I was startin to shake.

We can help you. I can help you. If you let me.

I shook my head.

Look, I know what you're in for. An I know what was done to you. But Graham Barnes and David Roper are locked up now. They can't touch you. Your dad saw to that. She sighed. An your dad. I'm sorry. Please let me help.

I was shakin. I tried to sit still, to stop.

You can't, I said. My throat was smoke-dry.

Why don't we take things one step at a time, she said, leanin forward. We'll work towards one thing an when we've accomplished that we'll move on to the next thing. Now, the shower situation-

I stood up. I couldn't hold myself in any longer.

I can't take a shower, can I? Eh? It's easy for you to say, but I can't do it.

Look—

No! You look!

I pulled my sweatshirt off.

Look! I shouted. Look! This is why I can't take no fuckin shower!

She looked. An I saw the horror on her face.

Remember earlier when I said I carried around my history with me?

Victoria knows now what I mean by that.

I've got this great idea, says Sean. It'll be a real laugh.

He had that look. The one he gets before he's about to have a fight or do something mad. It scared me. But I didn't want him to know that.

Yeah? I said.

Why don't we do over a petrol station? C'mon.

I don't—

Look, it's piss easy. He had this bag with him. He pulled out two black balaclavas. We stick these on, we go up to the counter an we tell them to give us the money.

Why will they do that? I asked.

He went back in the bag again. Because of this.

He pulled out a sawn off.

Fuckin' ell . . .

Yeah. C'mon. We'll have a laugh.

Sean kept talking. He kept talking for over an hour, telling me it would be a laugh, we'd get a real rush, we'd come out of it with some cash and with the masks on we'd never get caught.

I didn't wanna do it at first but Sean kept talking an talking until yeah, it would be a laugh. I looked at the gun sittin there. Pure power. Pure control. Easy power. Yeah, I thought, it'd be fun. So I told him I would. An he smiled. I didn't tell him I was doin it cos I was scared of what he'd do if I said no.

We waited til it was dark an drove to the service station. We parked out of sight, pulled the masks on an off we went.

There was no customers, just this fat Asian woman behind the counter. Sean was straight in before she had time to scream.

Open the till an hand over the fuckin money now! Now!

He stuck the business end of the sawn off in her face. She looked like she was gonna piss herself. She opened the till an I went round with the bag open.

Put it in there! I shouted.

She did as she was told. Don't hurt me, don't hurt me, she said in a whisper.

I got a tingle when she did that. Havin someone scared an doin what you tells them gives you a real thrill. I really liked it.

C'mon! C'mon! I shouted.

She piled the notes in faster.

I started to get a hard on. I started to feel hot an get pins an needles in me stomach. Me head started to spin.

I blinked. I looked at the woman but her face was goin blurry. It wasn't the same woman who was there when I came in. But I knew her. It was mum.

I got really angry then.

What the fuck are you doin here? I shouted. I grabbed ahold of mum an pushed her against the counter. She tried to fight back but I just slapped her down.

Fight me, would you?

Me cock was gettin harder. Me head was spinnin faster. I was feelin hotter. I had to do something. I pulled the front of her dress, tearin it, rippin it to shreds, buttons flyin an everythin. I pulled the front of her tights, pushed her back over the counter. I started to undo my jeans.

No, please, please no . . .

Shut up! Fuckin shut up! I slapped her again.

Then I was in er, up er, snarlin at er, lookin straight in er eyes, straight into me mother's eyes.

I hate you! I fuckin hate you!

Me mother's eyes were cryin.

Why couldn't you love me, eh? Why couldn't you fuckin love me? Properly, like other mothers, eh?

Why did you give me to them? Eh? D'you know what they did to me? D'you know what me body looks like under me clothes? The burns an the cuts, eh?

Me mother's eyes closed.

Open your eyes! Open your fuckin eyes! I slapped her. I hit her. I came.

I just stood there getting me breath back for about thirty seconds or a minute with me eyes closed. I opened them.

An me mother had gone. An there was just this scared, fat Asian woman. Cryin.

Oh fuck, I said. O fuck, I'm sorry . . .

I went to touch her. She flinched away.

Out the way!

It was Sean. He was laughin an hootin. He pushed me out the way an got in front of the Asian woman.

My turn now!

I didn't join in. I just stood an watched.

C'mon, he said, when he'd finished. Hurry up! We've got what we came for!

He grabbed the bag and did his jeans up. He slapped me on the shoulder. Stop fuckin dreamin! C'mon!

I followed him out. I couldn't look back at the woman.

In the car I couldn't believe what we'd done. What I'd done.

Oh fuck . . . Oh fuck . . . I kept sayin.

Sean laughed. You're a mad fucker, you. When you get goin.

We drove away.

They caught us two days later. We'd forgotten to wear gloves. Sean's prints are on file.

Me dad was devastated. That was when he started complainin of pains in his chest. We had a long talk. I cried. He cried. I told him all about it. I told him I was sorry.

He hugged me. He told me I was still his son an that whatever happened he would always be there for me.

That's what he said. He would always be there for me.

Me brief gave me a bit of advice. Tell them you're in for armed robbery, he said. If they ask you why you got such a long sentence tell them you shot someone an paralysed them or put them in a coma or somethin.

But don't let them know you're a rapist. Or your life won't be worth livin.

That's what he said. My life won't be worth livin.

Me dad died. They wouldn't let me go to the funeral. Said I'd caused too much trouble. Dropped too many levels. I'm on basic now. You can't go further down than that.

I phoned Marie. Said how sorry I saw. She was cryin. She told me not to phone again. Said it was worry about me that had started the cancer goin in me dad's body. Said she'd lost the man she loved. She put the phone down on me.

Me dad was wrong. He won't always be there for me. He let me down. Kayleigh won't speak to me. She's changed her phone number. All me letters get sent back. Victoria still comes to see me. Still talks to me. But it's not the same. She looks at me differently now.

I let them down. All of them. An not they've let me down.

The rest of the wing know what I'm in here for now. They just leave me by myself. An I've started havin showers now. I don't care. I don't know if they're lookin at me or not cose I don't look at them anymore. Anyway, I'll be gettin moved soon. I don't know where. I don't care.

But I still get letters. Mum's started writing to me. At first I ignored them, but she kept on doin it so in the end I gave in a started readin them. She still sees Kayleigh. She says Kayleigh says she wouldn't know what to do without her.

An she tells me about Tod. What a lovely boy he's gettin. How he's startin to be like his dad.

An she told me that Graham an Dave will be out soon. An they wanna contact me.

But I know this. Cos they already have. They've told me they wanna keep in touch. They've told me they miss me. They love me. They've told me they wanna see me when I get out, they've a job for me.

I know what it is. I'm not stupid. They want me to find boys to go visit them. Ones who like to play. Ones who like to pretend. I could join in if I liked. I would be on their side this time.

I wrote back an told them to fuck off. But they replied. They told me that they'd heard Tod was growin into a beautiful lad. An that his grandma was lookin after him really well. They asked me to think again about their offer.

I cried. An I cried. An eventually I couldn't cry anymore.

I thought about their offer. An I thought about mum. Whatever else she is she's still me mum. She's still family. An as me dad used to say, family is important. Family is about love.

An I thought about. Perhaps they weren't so bad really, I tell meself. Perhaps what they didn't wasn't so bad.

At least they said they loved me.

Or pretended they did.

The dream's back again. It's there just about all the time. But it's different now. Now there's no drive, no countryside, no dad. There's just me as a little boy, sittin all alone in a quarry, huggin me knees to me chest an cryin. An cryin an cryin an cryin.

An then I wake up.

An I'm still cryin.

# Geoffrey Says

Aliya Whiteley

Aliya Whiteley was born in Ilfracombe, Devon, in 1974, and currently lives in Germany. Her stories have appeared in *Shred of Evidence, SHOTS, Pulp.net, Word Riot,* and *The Guardian.* Her first novel, *Mean Mode Median,* was published in 2004 by bluechrome.

**I was only a baby** when she first told me about Geoffrey.

The story goes that, two weeks after my father left, I dropped my pacifier on to the kitchen floor. When I reached down for it and attempted to put it back between my lips, Mother slapped my hand away and delivered to me these words, the words that would become the soundtrack of my morality.

"Geoffrey says only bad boys put dirty things in their mouths."

I cried the first time she ticked me off that way in her sharp style, one finger pointing directly into my right eye. I was too young to understand the words; only the emotion would have penetrated my baby brain. Only the disapproval from the woman who I wanted to smile more than anything else in the world.

It took a few years before I realised it wasn't her disapproval I was dealing with, but Geoffrey's. And it took another year after that before I realised who Geoffrey is.

Geoffrey is the emerald green penguin who lives in my head.

Mother may have created him, but she never understood him. It was inevitable that my desire to please her would be subverted into the desire to make Geoffrey clap his sparkling flippers together with glee. My penguin friend was the better part of me and, whenever he spoke, firstly through Mother and later directly to me, I stopped whatever I was doing and listened.

I became known during my school years as the quiet child, the daydreamer. In fact I was being told the answers to mathematical puzzles or instructed on how to get free chocolate out of the vending machine. Geoffrey said many things, all of them interesting. I kept my head down and bore the brunt of my unpopularity with the other children, achieving good academic results and biding my time. My internal penguin told me my wonderful future would come.

And then, just as I was giving up on the hope of achieving happiness, something amazing occurred. Mother and Geoffrey disagreed.

There were two weeks to go to my exams, and I was invited to a party. It was my first invitation I had ever received.

"Geoffrey says wise boys stay in and study," Mother told me when she emerged from the kitchen to find me shrugging into my orange cagoule, a bottle of sweet sherry clutched in one clammy hand. Usually I would have accepted this with equanimity, believing she was party to Geoffrey's wisdom in this matter having known him for longer than myself, but at that moment my green mentor decided to intervene.

I saw him clearly in my head; he was wearing a baseball cap back to front and had slung a badge from one of those curvy little Beetle cars around his neck. There was a certain nonchalance in the way he rearranged his groin with one flipper.

"Geoffrey says go to the party."

I heard him distinctly. If there was anything odd about a penguin referring to himself in the third person and contradicting my mother in the same breath, it didn't occur to me and I needed no further command. I walked out of the house without a glance at Mother and when I returned at three o'clock in the morning, exultant with sherry and goose-pimpled from leaving my cagoul in a public litter bin, she had already retired for the night. She never mentioned the incident, or Geoffrey, again.

From then on I belonged, body and soul, to that penguin.

Geoffrey says get your head shaved.

Geoffrey says screw the A Levels.

Geoffrey says apply for benefits and spend the money on beer, pot and porn mags.

Geoffrey had promised me happiness, and he was delivering. It was only Mother who was attempting to hold me back now; Mother, with her tutting and crying and poking finger. When I smoked pot in the house she played her *Tom Jones Sings Gospel* tape at top volume. When I went out to the pub on the corner, skulking past the ever-present glares of the disapproving neighbours, she retrieved my porn stash from the bottom of the wardrobe and set fire to it in the back garden. When I retreated to my bed with a monster hangover she opened the curtains and insisted on hoovering. The house just wasn't big enough for the both of us.

Geoffrey, as always, provided the solution. He appeared to me, dressed in an open necked shirt in a silky material and with a selection of what is commonly known as bling hanging around his neck.

"Geoffrey says buy more porn."

That may not sound like much of a solution, but it was all in the delivery. I knew something huge was coming up.

There were many stages to the plan, and it took two months to get everything organised to Geoffrey's satisfaction. When the big day finally arrived, I had mentally rehearsed our timetable so often that I hardly had to think at all.

Step One: The Hook. Twenty-six copies of *Razzle, Asian Babes* and *Big Jugs* amongst others lay at the bottom of my wardrobe after being specially prepared as per my instructions. They were ripe for discovery.

Step Two: The Timing. Weather reports became crucial. Finally the atmospheric conditions were correct; grey, yet dry. Cold, yet frost-free. Perfect.

Step Three: The Alibi. I made sure to observe my usual routine. I stayed in bed until after twelve. I moaned and groaned and made noises about being bored in the house.

Those noises grew in volume until 3:08 that afternoon, at which point I left under the pretence of going to the corner pub whilst making sure that I had attracted the attention of the neighbours. The fat man with a bushy black moustache who has lived opposite for as long as I can remember was particularly observant. He eyeballed me as I left, and for once it did not irritate, fitting in exactly with the plan.

Step Four: The Stay-Away. I waited in that pub for hours. I made small talk with the homeless bloke who collects the glasses and ate crisps in a carefree fashion whilst my penguin soothed my mind with his reassurances and provided a running commentary as to exactly what should be happening back at the house.

Step Five: The Collection. Geoffrey says Mother is rooting around in the bottom of my wardrobe, wearing her rubber gloves so that she will not be defiled by my filthy habits. Now she's tutting under her breath as she flicks through the pages of my magazines. Now she's gathering them up—there are so many this time she can't see her feet as she descends the stairs. She misses one of the stairs; her foot flails; she makes contact once more; she takes a breath of relief; she makes it to the bottom of the stairs, her arms still piled high with magazines. Geoffrey says it was never going to be that easy.

Step Six: The Garden. Geoffrey says Mother is dropping the magazines on to the burnt patch of grass at the bottom of the back garden. She is bending low, a can of lighter fluid in one hand and a lit match in the other. She is putting the match to the magazines—they whoosh into blue life, having been coated liberally in hairspray and deodorant. They produce fierce and jumping flames that take her by surprise. She drops the can of lighter fluid as the fire leaps on to her rubber gloves, which have been given the same treatment as the magazines. Mother claps her hands together in an attempt to extinguish the fire in the second before the lighter fluid explodes.

Step Seven: The Crisp. Mother burns. The last sound she hears is that of her rubber gloves clapping together; she has applauded herself to death, becoming the first victim of murder by porn.

Step Eight: Discovery. Geoffrey says the nosy neighbour sees the flames and calls the fire brigade. The fire engine, siren shouting, will have to pass by the corner pub. And that means its time to go home and find the charred remains and opt for the cheapest coffin available and move into the bigger bedroom.

Eight steps to happiness. Who would have thought it could be so simple?

I gave the fire engine a half hour head start and then sauntered home. Sure enough, they were running around in the back garden, and the fat neighbour tried to stop me from going through, but I pushed past him and looked at the scene of the tragedy.

The fire was out. I squinted against the greasy smoke and saw one blackened rubber glove lying at the bottom of the garden. It poked out from under an unfamiliar pile which coalesced into the remains of Mother. The more I stared at it, the more I could see of her—the stick thin legs, the patch of hair which remained untouched and immaculate in its permanent wave, the wedding ring sitting on the hand which had come free of the glove. The index finger of the same hand, extended outwards, rigid in death, pointing, pointing directly at me.

It seemed to me that something monumental was being shown to me in the stiff accusation she threw from beyond her own mortality. Even when a fireman covered her over with a blanket, that statement remained, protruding and demanding. But demanding what? I knew there was a point to it. That finger always made a point. Mentally I reached for my penguin friend, and found him, sitting on a child's swing, contemplating his six toes.

Geoffrey said nothing.

I pressed him for an answer, for any kind of help. Eventually, after much internal pleading on my part, he gave a faint, puzzled kind of caw. I didn't even know penguins could caw.

We didn't speak the same language any more.

That was the lowest point of my life. Every day Geoffrey faded from his emerald green into a more traditional black and white. Every day he seemed to grow more distant from me. He got smaller, and stopped wearing clothes or chewing gum. He wouldn't even answer to his name. Eventually, on the day before the reading of the will, he simply waddled away and dived into an icy pool that I had never seen before in my imagination. He was gone. I did not imagine he would return.

It was a desolate and heartbroken young man who attended the solicitor's office the next day. I was barely listening as the reading of the will took place. It was only when the phrase, 'thirty days to vacate the property' filtered through my understanding that I began to feel uneasy.

"Hold on," I interrupted. "Say that again."

"You have thirty days as from today in which to remove yourself and all possessions, including those bequeathed to you by your mother, from the property unless a mutually agreeable solution can be arranged with the new owner."

'The new owner?" I said. This was a situation I had not envisaged. I wished fervently to feel Geoffrey's reassuring flipper on my mind.

"He's waiting for you in the lounge area. Now, if you'll allow me to conclude the reading . . . ?"

The dining table and chairs. The settee. The single bed. The watercolour of Clacton she painted in 1958. I had nothing and a man I eventually recognised only by virtue of his bushy black moustache had everything. He was cracking his knuckles, his ill fitting trousers cutting his round belly into two segments as he heaved himself to his feet upon my entrance.

"I'm so sorry," he said, before I had a chance to speak. "I always said she should tell you. But she said it would only upset you . . . that at first you were still missing your dad and then later, you were too unruly to accept another man in the house. But I never imagined she had put me in the will. Honestly. Never."

The man I only knew as a nosy neighbour stuck out his hand and I took it. "It's grand to finally meet you properly," he said. "I know so much about you, and to think, you know nothing about me, even though I was friends with your mum even before you were born."

"Were you . . . .?" I asked, not knowing where the question could go. He mistook my tone for an enquiry. "Are you . . . ?"

"Geoffrey," he supplied helpfully. "My name's Geoffrey."

Funnily enough, we get on like a house on fire. He lets

me live in the house, and comes over now and again for a chat. He says he feels close to me; that he spent so many years watching over me and that there is a special bond between us. He's helping me to find a job.

Still, I can't help wishing that one day he'll turn into a gigantic emerald penguin and incite me to smoke pot and get laid. If only life could be that simple once more.

# God's Dice

David White

David White is an eighth-grade English teacher and the Derringer Award–winning author of the Jackson Donne stories. His short fiction has been published in *Thrilling Detective, HandheldCrime, Shred of Evidence, Hardluck Stories,* and *Shots UK.* He currently resides in New Jersey and is at work on his first novel.

**The room spun.**

The bed, the nightstand, and the TV, all swirled in front of my eyes. I shut them hard. My side ached, and I could feel the blood flow between my fingers.

*Don't pass out,* I thought, *she's going to need you.*

Then I felt her hand cradle my head, heard a voice from somewhere out in the distance. "It might be a good time to start believing in something."

* * *

My favorite time to jog is ten A.M., right after the early morning thaw, before the day gets too hot.

St. Paul's, a towering brick church, is just down the street from my office, near the New Brunswick train station. I jog past it on my normal route, and each time I do—its two long steeples pointing toward the clouds, its stained glass sending cracked, colored reflections of the sun slicing through shadows on the street—I get a chill. I haven't been inside since Jeanne's funeral.

The only welcoming thing about the place was the old priest who seemed to be out sweeping the steps whenever I went by. He'd smile and say hello, and though I was usually out of breath, I'd try to do the same. Not thinking much of it, I'd turn right onto George Street and head back toward my building.

I was out on my route for the first time in weeks, one of the first nice afternoons in March. With most of the students away on spring break, the streets of New Brunswick were near empty. Finding my rhythm on Somerset Street, I saw St. Paul's in the distance, towering as usual. I squinted, surprised I didn't see the friendly priest sweeping or chatting with pedestrians.

I had pushed past the familiar chill, past the church, when I realized something else wasn't right. A black BMW was parked awkwardly, its front right tire over the curb across from the stairway. Someone was in a hurry. And that someone was probably from out of town. The locals couldn't afford Beamers and neither could the Rutgers students. The professors never parked this far from campus. And it wasn't the kind of car a priest drove.

*He always* swept from ten to eleven.

I jogged up the steps. A broom lay on its side on the landing, as if dropped. I pulled the large oak door open, the handle slipping in my sweaty palms, and stepped into the darkened church. I stood for a moment to let my eyes adjust, but tensed when I heard a loud crash, like tin rattling on the ground.

Then: "Please, I don't know where she's gone."

"Don't give me that. You know where she is. She told you. She wouldn't just leave the church. You can't lie to me. Isn't that a sin?"

Tracking the voices, I saw the old priest being backed against a closed door by a thick man who looked like he was about to tear through his suit. The door was tucked into an odd corner I wouldn't have noticed otherwise.

"You can either tell us where she is now or help us find her later. We'll take you along as a guide. If we don't find her then—"

The priest visibly paled. "All I know is she took today's donations. Said something about where she always used to go."

The big guy smiled. His face was cracked like old leather, and his nose and jaw curved like they'd been broken before. He wore a gray suit over a white shirt and black tie. His biceps pressed tight against the seams.

"'Where she always used to go.' I think we know where that is. Right, Charlie?"

It was then I noticed another man, standing off in the shadows, near the confessional, watching at a perfect angle. Charlie seemed to be an audience, only watching the situation, but not wanting to get too close to it. He looked like a negative of the big guy, wearing a black suit, white shirt, gray tie. Thin and balding, his face was piggish. His nose was round, his eyes small and beady. He didn't seem to notice me.

"Guess we won't have to take you along, but let me leave a message with you in case she comes back."

The big guy held the priest by the lapel with his left arm and cocked his right arm back—

"Hey, guys, how's it going?" I called, only a few feet from the big guy.

"Who the hell are you?" Charlie asked, his head twisting in surprise.

"Good Samaritan. Let the priest go."

I was closing in on the big guy, who didn't have enough room in the passageway to maneuver. I slid a bit to my left, to see if Charlie was coming up behind me. He wasn't. He called from his spot. "Come on Buddy. We both know where she is."

Buddy looked at the priest and dropped him on the ground. He didn't say a word. Just ambled back into the church.

"Buddy and Charlie, huh?" I asked, following him. I pointed at Charlie. "I guess he's in charge."

Buddy turned to me and growled, but didn't advance. Seconds later, they were both out the door.

I went to the priest who was trying to get up, huffing and puffing on his knees. His head was shaved, ebony skin dripping with sweat. He was thin, in the usual off-duty priest garb: black jacket, black pants, black shirt, and white collar.

"Father, are you all right?" I asked.

I took his wrist and pulled him to his feet. He brushed himself off. "I'm fine. Just a bruised ego."

I helped him into one of the pews.

"Who were those men?"

"It's nothing. Nothing. Thank you for your help." He finally took a look at me. "What happened to you, son?"

He had noticed my long hair and shaggy beard. Business had been bad. My name had been all over the papers and none of it was good news. My bank balance was drying up. To make the rent, my food budget had to take a hit. Shaving cream and haircuts were out of the question.

I said, "I'm going for a new look."

He took that in for a moment, not speaking. Finally, "You haven't been around since the funeral, Jackson. You might not even remember my name. Father Michael."

He stuck out his hand, and we shook.

"You remember me?" I asked. I never got the priest's name before, had even avoided eye contact. Then after Jeanne's funeral, I did my best to put him out of my mind.

He smiled. "Jeanne was a good friend of the parish. You and she used to come to Mass every Sunday"

I looked away.

"I've seen you in the papers. It looks like you've come across some rough times. The best time to return to God."

"Who were those men?" I asked again.

He looked back toward the doorway, putting his arm over the back of the pew, twisting his body. Above the doorway was a stained glass window, the image of Jesus pressing his palm against a kneeling man. Behind them an apostle seemed to be turning his back, his arm in the air as if waving more to join them. The kneeling man looked to be at peace, as if Jesus was forgiving him.

"I've always viewed that window as a sort of recruiting poster for the church. I feel like I'm the apostle, calling for others to join in the worship of Jesus. It's my favorite part of serving here. I've recruited someone else to stay here as well. A woman, Julia Carver has agreed to become a part of our parish. She is willing to become a nun, give herself to God. But she's run off. Disappeared, with some money from the church.

"I want to tell you more, but she's confessed to me. I can't break that trust." He pressed his thumb and index finger against the bridge of his nose. "But I know where she's gone to. And if you ride with me, we can find her."

He pulled his wallet. "And," he continued before I could say a word, "I'll advance you enough to get a shave and haircut."

More than three hours later, Route 30 was full of brake lights. I only hoped the black BMW was only a little ahead of us, stuck in the same traffic mess. I spun the radio dial, found nothing, and popped Coldplay's *A Rush of Blood to the Head.*

Showered and dressed in jeans, polo shirt, leather jacket, and holstered Glock, I had picked up Father Michael in front of St. Paul's. He was in jeans and a Yankees sweatshirt now. We cruised down the parkway and then hit the exit for Route 30, heading for Atlantic City. The road was lined with traffic lights that seemed to stick on red, small chain restaurants, Holiday Inns and a ton of strip motels that charge fourteen bucks a night. Perfect for all the losers who need a place to stay before they drop the rest of their quarters on a bus ride home the next morning.

"Who were those guys at the church, Father?"

Michael looked at me and shook his head. "She confessed." Then he smiled. "I do think it's a good idea if we check out Harrah's. I hear it's a good place to play craps."

We finally hit a few greens, and I was able to get to Harrah's in about ten minutes. From his lips to God's ears, I thought.

The casino isn't on the main strip. It's on the Marina, near two other new casinos, the Trump Marina and the Borgata. While it was only late afternoon, the sun still shining, we could see lights flickering and colors glittering in neon. Signs read: HIGH PAYOUTS! WIN A MUSTANG BEFORE TAX TIME! Even I was starting to believe I'd walk out a millionaire.

I parked in the parking deck, on the 3rd floor, and we took the elevator to the casino level.

"I haven't been here in a few years," Father Michael said, as the doors swung open. I could hear the canned '60s pop music, the ringing bells, the people talking and screaming, and couldn't even see the casino yet. "Too bad we can't stay around to play a few slots."

"You like this place?" I asked, squinting against the neon.

He smiled at me. "I used to like to come down once a month or so and spin the wheels. Sometimes I got lucky. Sometimes I didn't."

We kept walking toward the glitter and gaudiness.

"Father, I don't know what I'm looking for. I don't know who this girl Julia is, or why I'm here. I'm trusting you. Where are we headed?"

"You have faith in me?" he asked, as we walked around a corner.

The casino was a vast canyon of tables and video machines, all glittering in bright flashing lights. It was designed like a maze, so you could never tell whether it was day or night, and could never find your way out. Bells, whistles, and music assaulted the ears, and the place, while not mobbed, was crowded, especially at the tables. There were no clocks, and I couldn't see the entire room. The flashing lights were disorienting and I had already lost my sense of direction. Not to mention my sense of smell from all the cigarette smoke. The slots were many, grouped together pushing you away from the corners of the room toward the middle, toward the tables.

"Faith and trust are two different things," I said.

"Are they? I'm not so sure," Father Michael replied quickly.

"Why are Buddy and Charlie after Julia?" I scanned the crowd looking for Buddy and Charlie. I didn't see them.

"She ran off. She stole money from the parish and she ran off."

Father Michael wasn't really answering my question, but I let it go. "How do you know she's here?"

Father Michael picked up his pace and moved away from me. He headed toward the craps tables. A throng of people three deep milled around the tables, some hoots and cheers each time the dice rolled.

As he approached, people made way, as if they knew he was a man of the cloth despite the Yankees sweatshirt, allowing him to get close to the table. Father Michael popped a few dollars down on the table and placed a bet. I watched the crowd. It was four-thirty, according to my watch, and the crowd at the tables was mostly young men, frat boys and businessmen putting everything on one roll. Living on the edge. I scanned the crowd. Nothing jumped out at me. Most of the women were older and hanging out near the slots. I didn't see Charlie or Buddy either.

The dice must not have been in the priest's favor, because he turned away from the table empty handed and came my way.

"Is she here, Father?"

He glanced around, over my shoulder, behind him. "I don't see her."

"This place is huge. She could be anywhere."

"She'll be here at the craps table."

"When? How can you be so sure?"

He met my eyes. "She's a craps player."

I looked away.

"What happened to you, Jackson? You used to come to Mass with Jeanne."

"What happened? Jeanne died. That's what happened. God hasn't exactly been gracious to me." I could feel my anger rising. Then, either because I was sick of him already or because of the stress that had been on my shoulders for the past few months, I said, "If there even is a God."

Father Michael didn't move, the words barely fazing him. "Everyone has a crisis of faith."

Behind us the bells and whistles of a slot went off, the electronic sounds of "We're in the Money" blaring as a woman screamed with joy.

"I don't believe in God, Father. Sorry, but over the past

year I've seen people die. Hell, I've even killed a man, and it seems like it's all for nothing. You expect me to still believe there's a God?"

My muscles had bunched around my neck. I felt tight, coiled. I wanted to kick my way out.

I watched Father Michael, waiting for his counter argument. I expected some sort of rhetoric, something from my years of Catholic school, but he didn't say anything like that. He nodded and said "I don't expect anything from you."

"What do you mean?"

"I don't expect you to believe in God. You've shown in the past that you have believed in God. Now your life has taken a turn. Does that mean you should stop believing? Do Red Sox fans stop believing in their team just because they've had another losing series? It's all about faith. It's not about expectations. Mine. Or yours."

"Red Sox fans haven't seen what I've seen." I wanted to add "duh," but decided against it. "Haven't done what I've done."

"It's not all about you. Yes, bad things happen. Despite what Einstein's said, God does play dice with the universe. Just like a craps table, sometimes the good comes out, sometimes the bad. Random outcomes shouldn't stunt our belief or strengthen it. That's not what belief is about."

Two burly figures caught my eye. They pushed their way through the crowd on the other side of the casino. Charlie and Buddy, dressed the same as before. They were eying the crowd, searching the tables. I stepped in front of Father Michael, my back to them, hoping they wouldn't notice us.

"Is Julia here yet?" I asked.

"You need to be patient. She'll be here. Don't change the subject."

I thumbed at Charlie and Buddy over my shoulder, confident enough they wouldn't notice us. "I don't think they're going to be patient. If you see Julia, you need to get to her before they do. It's going to be tough to sneak out of here."

Father Michael looked over my shoulder. "She's here."

"You're kidding."

He smiled. "No. I told you to have faith. She's crossing the floor this way from the elevators."

I turned and looked.

"The one with the blue sweater?" I asked

"Yes."

There was a woman wearing a navy sweater, and jeans. She was walking quickly. Thin, with dirty blond hair, small frowning lips, and a face covered with too much makeup, she was going through her purse as she walked.

"Okay. Do you remember where the car is?"

He nodded.

I pulled my keys from my pocket and pushed them into his hand. "Go start it. I'll get her. We'll meet you in the lot."

"But—"

"Have a little faith, Father."

For once, I'd gotten to him. The man in him looked like he wanted to hit me. But the priest turned and headed away.

I caught up with Julia putting some chips down on the craps table. I moved up behind her as Charlie and Buddy's backs were turned. I wanted to get moving before they spotted us.

"Julia?" I said, stepping behind her, as if shielding her.

She turned quickly, surprised. "Who are you?"

"Father Michael sent me."

"Father Michael—?"

"I'm a private investigator. There are men after you. They are here now. We have to go."

"Charlie is here?"

"Yeah, and his friend." I took her by her arm.

"Let me cash these chips," she said, pulling back.

"No. There's no time." I didn't care if I sounded like the Terminator. We had to move.

I took her arm again and pulled her from the table. She followed, but we'd already caused enough commotion for Charlie to turn, squinting in our direction. He motioned to Buddy, and they both headed towards us.

Julia and I broke into a run, as I pushed past two guys in cowboy hats playing the one-armed bandits. We turned the corner, the elevators in sight.

Julia got to the elevators first and hit the button, but neither of the cars was on our floor. I had stopped running, turning to face Buddy and Charlie.

Buddy was the quicker of the two, built like a fullback, and moving like one too. If I stood back to handle him, I'd be flattened. Instead, I ran at him. When I hit him, I kept my legs moving, and wrapped him up with my arms, twisted and threw him to the ground. I jumped up, turned toward Charlie.

He smiled, bouncing on his feet like a boxer. I decided to play defense and let him come at me. Charlie swung, and I wasn't able to spin out of the way in time. He hit me in the left side. I gasped, but was able to spin off that and connect with a right hook. Charlie staggered back, and I heard the elevator doors ping open. Something with a glint clattered to the ground as Charlie fell. I ran toward the elevator.

I got inside behind Julia, hit floor three, and the doors shut, just as both thugs were trying to get up.

"What do those men want with you?" I asked, holding my side where Charlie had punched me. It throbbed, and I couldn't catch my breath.

Julia looked. "Oh my God."

Finally, I looked down at my side. My jacket and left hand were covered in blood. The pain didn't feel like a punch usually did. My side burned and stung. And as I replayed it in my head, I could tell it was a small penknife that had clattered to the ground next to Charlie.

"That bastard stabbed me." I said, gritting my teeth, and forcing my vision back into focus.

The elevator doors opened and Father Michael had the car waiting right at the casino's front entrance. Julia got in the front; I pretty much fell into the backseat. I pulled my knees up so I could fit in the small space of the two-door.

We got back on to Route 30, moving at a normal pace. I told Father Michael to try and appear inconspicuous.

"We have to get him to a hospital, Father," Julia said.

"No," I said. "It's not that bad. Besides, Charlie knows he stabbed me. Hospitals are the first place they'd check."

I lied. I didn't know how bad it was. I just knew it hurt like hell.

"Where to, then?" Michael asked.

"I just need a place to stop the bleeding. To rest." I told Father Michael to try for a fourteen-dollar room. I wasn't sure I was making any sense, but no one argued with me. I gingerly pulled my jacket off, and the left side of my polo shirt was soaked with blood. I pressed hard against my side.

"Oh my—" Julia started again, but a cell phone went off. It wasn't mine.

Julia dug through her bag, and pull out a small phone. She answered it, but an instant after saying hello she hung up quickly.

"It was them," she said. "They must have been the ones who called me before. I didn't check the display, I didn't answer. I figured it was you."

"Who are they? How do they have your number?" I asked.

Julia looked at Father Michael. "You didn't tell him."

"You told me in confession."

My vision blurred and my side ached. I took a few deep breaths, trying to get my body under control. I felt cold.

"Somebody better tell me," I said.

Julia turned to me. "They're loan sharks. Well, Charlie—Charlie Hafner—is. Buddy's just hired help."

*Some help. He went down easy.*

Julia looked at Father Michael, who was getting ready for to make a U-turn. "I like to gamble. I played craps. I used to come down here all the time. When I wasn't here it was sports—football, basketball. Charlie took my bets."

"You lost?"

"Everything. I couldn't pay."

"So you ran to Father Michael?"

"I'm going to give myself to God."

"What do you mean?"

"My life's always been a mess. I've been coming down

here since I've been eighteen, avoiding the security guards, just playing the slots. The first two times I came out ahead. After that I was hooked, couldn't help myself. Bet on sports, craps, roulette, everything. I borrowed money from more friends than I could keep track of. Never paid them back. They abandoned me, and I don't blame them. I even thought of committing suicide. Just ending it all."

"Why didn't you?"

"I heard God. God talked to me, and told me that if I gave myself to Him, everything would be okay. I'd always been religious, and I'd always prayed. But finally he answered back. I decided to become a nun. Father Michael said he'd give me a place to stay until I could take my vows. Until I was ready to give myself to God. Completely."

God is the last refuge of a desperate woman, I thought. "But you ran," I said aloud.

"Charlie called my new apartment. He found me, I don't know how, knew that I was staying under Father Michael's watch. Charlie told me if I didn't get the money by Friday he'd kill me and the Father.

"I had no choice. I told him that I was going to get his money. I thought I could win it back. But I didn't have any of my own money. I'm—I'm so sorry Father."

We were pulling into a parking lot of a one-story motel. It looked like a ranch. No other cars were in the lot.

"It's okay, Julia," Father Michael said.

"I wanted to give the money back. I was going to win it all back, plus. I could even things out. I didn't want you to even notice—You wouldn't even miss me—"

"I knew you had good intentions, Julia. But those men came looking for you."

Father Michael parked the car, hitting the brakes too hard, making me wince. Pain shot up my side.

"Check us in, Father," I said. "Pay cash. Don't give them our names. Don't give anything. I don't want Charlie or Buddy finding us."

I watched him shuffle into the office.

Trying to subdue the pain, I concentrated on my breathing. In through the nose, out through the mouth. It was just like jogging, finding a rhythm and something to focus on. Let the seconds pass and so will the pain.

Julia turned back to me. "How do you feel?"

"Lousy."

My hand felt soaked with blood. Hopefully, the motel room would have towels. But from the looks of the chipped paint, the cracked windows, and the splintered walls, towels weren't a guarantee.

"Why don't you pray?" Julia asked.

"I gave it up. Going to be a nun, huh?"

"God's always been there for me."

"Even when you lost it all?"

She paused, closed her eyes. "Especially when I lost it all."

"That doesn't make any sense."

"It's not something anyone can break down. I just knew there was a reason for what had happened to me. God was trying to tell me something. It sounds stupid, but—"

"God rolled the dice, and they didn't land your way."

"What?"

"Just something Father Michael said."

She pushed a strand of hair behind her ear. "I think I got pretty lucky, actually. I've always wanted to serve in some way. But when the gambling was going right, when I couldn't lose, I lost sight of that. Then I lost everything *except* God. I think it was meant to be. But I need to pay them back. I need to win the money back, though. They'll never leave us alone," she said.

"What do you mean?"

"Money's important to Charlie, but he gets more pleasure out of killing, holding that kind of power over life in his hands. He won't threaten you or break your legs. He'll just kill you. He gets off on it."

"That's not good business, killing your clients."

"You don't see that side of him until you miss a payment. He told me a story once. Another woman, she didn't pay. She was into college football and she was down thousands. They gave her a deadline. She didn't pay. So Buddy cut her brake lines. When the cops found her dead in a ditch, she had a briefcase. She was on her way to pay them. They didn't care. We need to get the money back."

Father Michael came back to the car and directed us to Room 12, farthest from the highway.

"I think the owner is deaf. He just took the money and gave me a key. No questions."

"These places aren't exactly reputable," I said.

Julia opened the door, went inside. I got out of the car, needing to wrap an arm around Father Michael for support. We hobbled into to the room.

"See if there are towels," I said. "I gotta stop this bleeding."

The room was bare. One night table, a stained brown carpet, a double bed, which I collapsed on to. It smelled like mothballs and paint. I didn't even want to know what the bathroom looked like.

Julia came back with a towel, as I pulled my shirt over my head. The wound didn't look too bad, It wasn't a long cut, but more a puncture wound. I just hoped the knife didn't hit anything important. I pressed the towel to my side, wondering how much blood I had lost. I pulled my belt from my jeans, and tied it around the towel and my stomach, so I wouldn't have to apply pressure myself.

And then the room pitched. Everything spun. And went black.

I could hear Father Michael. "It might be a good time to start believing in something."

Consciousness came back in the form of pain. It was a jolt of electricity through my entire body, settling in my side. I opened my eyes, and took a lot of air in through my mouth.

The room spun for a second, with my stomach, and then settled. The lights were off, the curtains drawn. Everything was dim. I was lying on the bed, on my back. Sweat dripped along my face.

My hearing was the last thing to function correctly. White noise fading in and out until there was only Father Michael and Julia whispering. I had to concentrate on what they were saying. They were praying.

I must have grunted. Julia looked up and rushed to my side. "Father, he's awake!"

"Yeah," I said through grit teeth. "I'm up."

I pushed on the bed, and tried to sit up. The room spun again, but righted itself.

"Don't move too much, Jackson." Julia was at my side.

"I'm fine," I said.

I heard Father Michael laugh. "You just passed out. Sure, you're just fine."

"I think the bleeding's stopped," Julia said to me. "We had to change the towel while you were out. It was soaked through. But this new one is okay."

I looked at my side. She was right. The towel was dry.

"We need to get you to a hospital," the priest said.

I shook my head. "Not yet."

"How can you say that? You might be dying."

"I'm fine."

Julia stood up. "You've been saying that. You're going to keep saying that. Do you even believe it?"

I looked her in the eye, trying not to blink. I didn't believe it, but I had to make her think I did until we could sort this out. "There are two dangerous, obvious places right now. A hospital either here or in New Brunswick or the church in New Brunswick will make it too easy for them to find us."

"So," she said, "what are we going to do?"

"Make them come to us on my terms."

"What are you talking about?" Father Michael asked.

Now they were both standing and all I could do was sit. My legs felt weak, and I was afraid if I stood too quickly I'd be down and out again.

"Father, I want you to take Julia away from here."

"But—" Julia cried.

"This is the only way. You aren't going to be able to pay them back Julia, and they're not going to stop coming until they either get their money or until they kill you. So we're going to have them show up here. And all that'll be waiting is me, my stab wound, and a bunch of cops."

"I can win the money back. I'll just pay them. You both shouldn't have come. I don't want the police involved." Julia rubbed her hands together hard. I thought she was holding her breath.

Father Michael took her hands in his. Looked her in the eye.

I pushed on the bed, trying to stand. No dice.

Father Michael took the keys and said, "I'll start the car."

As he went out the door, Julia stared me down. "I don't want to leave you."

"They will kill you," I said, "just like they killed that woman you told me about. She already had the money, too," I said.

I finally pushed hard on the bed and stood. I fought hard with my equilibrium, but I didn't go down.

"Julia," I said. "Call them. Tell them where we are. Then get out of here."

She looked at the cell phone in her hand. Dialed, waited for an answer. Then, in a wavering voice, she told them where we were. And that we'd meet them at seven.

She left the hotel room without looking at me. I went and found my pistol in the bathroom.

The sun had set. Standing in the parking lot behind an oversized SUV, I could smell the salt water from the bay and the ocean. It was still too early in spring for the air to stay warm into the evening, but the ocean smell, the fact that I could walk to the bay from the lot was enough to remind me of summer. I had my jacket on, but I felt warmer just thinking of it.

Father Michael and Julia were long gone. Before they pulled out, I told Father Michael I'd call when I got back. He agreed, and pulled on to the highway.

From my corner of the dusty lot, I could see the casinos' glitter reaching the sky. The rest of the city was mostly rundown. People were homeless or living in houses that should have failed safety inspection years ago. In New Brunswick, the city countered this problem by knocking the houses down, kicking the poor to the streets and building new houses, all in the name of economic improvement. The press made it look like New Brunswick cared. The casinos didn't even pretend to care about the city, or about the people, only money. In a way, they were loan sharks as bad as Charlie Hafner and Buddy.

My gun felt heavy in my hand, and my side ached as I checked my watch. They would be here any minute. I crouched behind a small bush, trying to remain focused. Trying not to pass out again.

The BMW cruised into the lot, its brakes squealing as it came to a stop outside our door. Two doors opened and shut, and I heard footsteps on the dust and gravel.

"If she's going to try and talk us out of this . . ." Charlie said.

"She doesn't have the money. I'm telling you. She wasn't even at the craps table long enough," Buddy said.

"I'm going to fucking kill her."

*Here we go again,* I thought. This wasn't going to end well, no matter who came out ahead.

I caught myself starting a prayer. A desperate man turns to God as well.

As I forced myself out of the crouch, I saw Buddy knocking on the door. Walking toward them, I clicked off the safety of my Glock. By the time I was behind the two of them, Charlie had pushed the unlocked door open himself.

I pressed my gun to the back of Charlie's head. He froze while Buddy continued in to the room.

"Don't fucking move another muscle. Either of you."

Buddy twirled around, ready to pounce, not figuring me to have a gun. He took a step toward us, but must have seen something in Charlie's face. He froze.

I pressed the gun hard against Charlie's skull, forcing him into the middle of the room, behind Buddy.

Charlie said, "Where's the bitch? I will kill you. Then I will find her and kill her. I have people everywhere. You can't hide."

"Shut up," I said.

For a moment, I wished I had asked Father Michael to pray for me. I had known what was going to happen, lied to make them both leave. Now I wanted someone praying for me, hoping for it all to be okay.

"We're going to take a walk. Behind the motel, out to the bay," I said.

"Buddy, kill this son of a bitch," Charlie said.

Buddy took a step toward me, reaching into his jacket. I turned his way, shot him in the chest. Blood spilled everywhere as he fell to the ground.

"Jesus Christ!" Charlie screamed. "Buddy!"

My gun was back on Charlie. "I'll fucking kill you, too."

He actually looked surprised.

"You ever going to leave her alone?"

He tried his hardest to say "Yes." To lie. But he couldn't. His pride was too strong. "I'll kill the both of you," he said again.

Before today, I had only killed one person, to save a woman I thought I could have loved. It was still the most difficult thing I've ever done. Today it was a lot easier to pull the trigger.

I sat in St. Paul's the next Sunday morning. My face was clean shaven, and my hair cut and cropped neatly. It had been nearly two months since I'd shaved, and now I felt like a different man.

Father Michael said Mass. If he saw me sitting in the back, he didn't show it. The church was nearly filled, mostly by older people. I decided not to take communion.

It had been three days since I waited in that motel room with two dead men. I scrubbed away the blood, taking whatever I could find out of the pockets of the dead, and wrapping the bodies in bed sheets. The rest of the time I spent trying to stay conscious.

In the darkness after midnight, I dragged both bodies from the room and dropped them into the bay. By the time I was done, I was soaked with sweat, and my wound had started to bleed again. I went back to the room and wiped it down once more, locked Room 12, and threw the keys into the bushes.

Using Charlie's keys, I drove the BMW to the Atlantic City International Airport and parked it in long term. With luck, it wouldn't be found for weeks. It may not even have been in Charlie's name.

I took a cab to New Brunswick. It cost a fortune, but I didn't care, just wanting to get the hell out of Atlantic City.

Finally, I passed out in the emergency room of Robert Wood Johnson Hospital. When I came to, I had been stitched up and given blood. It wasn't going to be serious, but they had a lot of questions on how I'd been stabbed. I told them I didn't know; I had been in a drunken blackout. I was surprised I even got to the emergency room.

They didn't buy it, but they didn't ask any more questions. Didn't even ask to do a blood alcohol test. If push came to shove, Artie would back me up. He'd say I walked out of the Olde Towne Tavern piss drunk at closing time.

I was released the next day.

When Mass ended, I hung around while the crowd cleared. Father Michael followed them out, shaking hands and saying hellos. The church was silent, the high ceilings and empty pews, the stained glass, the altar, the crucifix, I felt like they were all watching me. They were wondering why I was here.

Father Michael reentered the church and caught my eye. I nodded toward the confessional and he returned the nod. I stepped in. The priest entered a moment later, though I could hardly tell it was him behind the mesh that separated us. I didn't want to see his face. After what I had to tell him, he might not want to see mine.

"Bless me Father, for I have sinned."

"How long has it been since your last confession?"

"I don't remember."

"Have confidence in God."

I laid it out for him. Everything that had weighed on my conscience since Jeanne's death. Everything. Including Wednesday night. We were in there for a good twenty minutes.

He gave me my penance. I had a lot of praying to do. "Through the ministry of the Church, may God grant you pardon and peace, and . . ." Father Michael's voice trailed off.

I waited a second. Then said, "Father?"

"And," he said, his voice small. "And I absolve you from your sins in the name of the Father, Son, and Holy Spirit."

"Amen."

"Go in peace, and may God bless you."

So I had confessed, and still felt the weight of three dead men.

I turned to leave the confessional when I heard Father Michael clear his throat. I couldn't see his expression through the mesh. In a small voice, he said, "Please don't return. If you want to worship, find another church."

I had nothing to say to that. I left the confessional, stepping into the church. Father Michael didn't follow me.

On my way out, I noticed the stained glass window again. The light from outside stabbed through it, etching a cracked, inverted image across the floor. It looked to me like the turned apostle wasn't recruiting, but throwing his hands up in anger, not willing to give the same penance that Jesus was. I wondered how Father Michael would view the image.

I pulled the door open and stepped out into the harsh sun.

# The Consolation Blonde

Val McDermid

Val McDermid, a former journalist, is the author of sixteen mysteries, including three series starring Kate Brannigan, Lindsay Gordon, and the team of Tony Hill and Carol Jordan. *A Place of Execution* (1999) won the Macavity, Anthony, Dilys, and *Los Angeles Times* awards for best novel. Lately, her books have become not only genre favorites but international bestsellers as well. Her most recent work is *The Torment of Others,* published in 2004.

**Awards are meaningless, right? They're** always political, they're forgotten two days later and they always go to the wrong book, right? Well, that's what we all say when the prize goes somewhere else. Of course, it's a different story when it's our turn to stand at the podium and thank our agents, our partners and our pets. Then, naturally enough, it's an honour and a thrill.

That's what I was hoping I'd be doing that October night in New York. I had been nominated for Best Novel in the Speculative Fiction category of the U.S. Book Awards, the national literary prizes that carry not only prestige but also a $50,000 cheque for the winners. *Termagant Fire,* the concluding novel in my *King's Infidel* trilogy, had broken all records for a fantasy novel. More weeks in the *New York Times* bestseller list than King, Grisham and Cornwell put together. And the reviews had been breathtaking, referring to *Termagant Fire* as the first novel since Tolkien to make fantasy respectable. Fans and booksellers alike had voted it their book of the year. Serious literary critics had examined the parallels between my fantasy universe and America in the defining epoch of the sixties. Now all I was waiting for was the imprimatur of the judges in the nation's foremost literary prize.

Not that I was taking it for granted. I know how fickle judges can be, how much they hate being told what to think by the rest of the world. I understood only too well that the *succès d'estime* the book had enjoyed could be the very factor that would snatch my moment of glory from my grasp. I had already given myself a stiff talking-to in my hotel bathroom mirror, reminding myself of the dangers of hubris. I needed to keep my feet on the ground, and maybe failing to win the golden prize would be the best thing that could happen to me. At least it would be one less thing to have to live up to with the next book.

But on the night, I took it as a good sign that my publisher's table at the awards dinner was right down at the front of the room, smack bang up against the podium. They never like the winners being seated too far from the stage just in case the applause doesn't last long enough for them to make it up there ahead of the silence.

My award was third from last in the litany of winners. That meant a long time sitting still and looking interested. But I could only cling on to the fragile conviction that it was all going to be worth it in the end. Eventually, the knowing Virginia drawl of the MC, a middle-ranking news anchorman, got us there. I arranged my face in a suitably bland expression, which I was glad of seconds later when the name he announced was not mine. There followed a short, stunned silence, then, with more eyes on me than on her, the victor weaved her way to the front of the room to a shadow of the applause previous winners had garnered.

I have no idea what graceful acceptance speech she came out with. I couldn't tell you who won the remaining two categories. All my energy was channeled into not showing the rage and pain churning inside me. No matter how much I told myself I had prepared for this, the reality was horrible.

At the end of the apparently interminable ceremony, I got to my feet like an automaton. My team formed a sort of flying wedge around me; editor ahead of me, publicist to one side, publisher to the other. "Let's get you out of here. We don't need pity," my publisher growled, head down, broad shoulders a challenge to anyone who wanted to offer condolences.

By the time we made it to the bar, we'd acquired a small support crew, ones I had indicated were acceptable by a nod or a word. There was Robert, my first mentor and oldest buddy in the business; Shula, an English SF writer who had become a close friend; Shula's girlfriend Caroline;

and Cassie, the manager of the city's premier SF and fantasy bookstore. That's what you need at a time like this, people around who won't ever hold it against you that you vented your spleen in an unseemly way, at the moment when your dream turned to ashes. Fuck nobility. I wanted to break something.

But I didn't have the appetite for serious drinking, especially when my vanquisher arrived in the same bar with her celebration in tow. I finished my Jack Daniels and pushed off from the enveloping sofa. "I'm not much in the mood," I said. "I think I'll just head back to my hotel."

"You're at the InterCon, right?" Cassie asked.

"Yeah."

"I'll walk with you, I'm going that way."

"Don't you want to join the winning team?" I asked, jerking my head towards the barks of laughter by the bar.

Cassie put her hand on my arm. "You wrote the best book, John. That's victory enough for me."

I made my excuses and we walked into a ridiculously balmy New York evening. I wanted snow and ice to match my mood, and said as much to Cassie.

Her laugh was low. "The pathetic fallacy," she said. "You writers just never got over that, did you? Well, John, if you're going to cling to that notion, you better change your mood to match the weather."

I snorted. "Easier said than done."

"Not really," said Cassie. "Look, we're almost at the InterCon. Let's have a drink."

"Okay."

"On one condition. We don't talk about the award, we don't talk about the asshole who won it, we don't talk about how wonderful your book is and how it should have been recognised tonight."

I grinned. "Cassie, I'm a writer. If I can't talk about me, what the hell else does that leave?"

She shrugged and steered me into the lobby. "Gardening? Gourmet food? Favourite sexual positions? Music?"

We settled in a corner of the bar, me with Jack on the rocks, she with a Cosmopolitan. We ended up talking about movies, past and present, finding to our surprise that in spite of our affiliation to the SF and fantasy world, what we both actually loved most was film noir. Listening to Cassie talk, watching her push her blond hair back from her eyes, enjoying the sly smiles that crept out when she said something witty or sardonic, I forgot the slings and arrows and enjoyed myself.

When they announced last call at midnight, I didn't want it to end. It seemed natural enough to invite her up to my room to continue the conversation. Sure, at the back of my mind was the possibility that it might end with those long legs wrapped around mine, but that really wasn't the most important thing. What mattered was that Cassie had taken my mind off what ailed me. She had already provided consolation enough, and I wanted it to go on. I didn't want to be left alone with my rancour and self-pity or any of the other uglinesses that were fighting for space inside me.

She sprawled on the bed. It was that or an armchair which offered little prospect of comfort. I mixed drinks, finding it hard not to imagine sliding those tight black trousers over her hips or running my hands under that black silk tee, or pushing the long shimmering overblouse off her shoulders so I could cover them with kisses.

I took the drinks over and she sat up, crossing her legs in a full lotus and straightening her spine. "I thought you were really dignified tonight," she said.

"Didn't we have a deal? That tonight was off limits?" I lay on my side, carefully not touching her at any point.

"That was in the bar. You did well, sticking to it. Think you earned a reward?"

"What kind of reward?'

"I give a mean backrub," she said, looking at me over the rim of her glass. "And you look tense."

"A backrub would be . . . very acceptable," I said.

Cassie unfolded her legs and stood up. "Okay. I'll go into the bathroom and give you some privacy to get undressed. Oh, and John—strip right down to the skin. I can't do your lower back properly if I have to fuck about with waistbands and stuff."

I couldn't quite believe how fast things were moving. We hadn't been in the room ten minutes, and here was Cassie instructing me to strip for her. Okay, it wasn't quite like that sounds, but it was equally a perfectly legitimate description of events. The sort of thing you could say to the guys and they would make a set of assumptions from. If, of course, you were the sort of sad asshole who felt the need to validate himself like that.

I took my clothes off, draping them over the armchair without actually folding them, then lay face down on the bed. I wished I'd spent more of the spring working out than I had writing. But I knew my shoulders were still respectable, my legs strong and hard, even if I was carrying a few more pounds around the waist than I would have liked.

I heard the bathroom door open and Cassie say, "You ready, John?"

I was very, very ready. Somehow, it wasn't entirely a surprise that it wasn't just the skin of her hands that I felt against mine.

How did I know it had to be her? I dreamed her hands. Nothing slushy or sentimental; just her honest hands with their strong square fingers, the palms slightly callused from the daily shunting of books from carton to shelf, the play of muscle and skin over blood and bone. I dreamed her hands and woke with tears on my face. That was the day I called Cassie and said I had to see her again.

"I don't think so." Her voice was cautious, and not, I believed, simply because she was standing behind the counter in the bookstore.

"Why not? I thought you enjoyed it," I said. "Did you think it was just a one-night stand?'

"Why would I imagine it could be more? You're a married man, you live in Denver, you're good-looking and successful. Why on earth would I set myself up for a let-down by expecting a repeat performance? John, I am so not in the business of being the Other Woman. A one-night stand is just fine, but I don't do affairs."

"I'm not married." It was the first thing I could think of to say. That it was the truth was simply a bonus.

"What do you mean, you're not married? It says so on your book jackets. You mention her in interviews." Now there was an edge of anger, a "don't fuck with me" note in her voice.

"I've never been married. I lied about it."

A long pause. “Why would you lie about being married?” she demanded.

“Cassie, you’re in the store, right? Look around you. Scope out the women in there. Now, I hate to hurt people’s feelings. Do you see why I might lie about my marital status?”

I could hear the gurgle of laughter swelling and bursting down the telephone line. “John, you are a bastard, you know that? A charming bastard, but a bastard nevertheless. You mean that? About never having been married?”

“There is no moral impediment to you and me fucking each other’s brains out as often as we choose to. Unless, of course, there’s someone lurking at home waiting for you?” I tried to keep my voice light. I’d been torturing myself with that idea ever since our night together. She’d woken me with soft kisses just after five, saying she had to go. By the time we’d said our farewells, it had been nearer six and she’d finally scrambled away from me, saying she had to get home and change before she went in to open the store. It had made sense, but so too did the possibility of her sneaking back into the cold side of a double bed somewhere down in Chelsea or SoHo.

Now, she calmed my twittering heart. “There’s nobody. Hasn’t been for over a year now. I’m free as you, by the sounds of it.”

“I can be in New York at the weekend,” I said. “Can I stay?”

“Sure,” Cassie said, her voice somehow promising much more than a simple word.

* * *

That was the start of something unique in my experience. With Cassie, I found a sense of completeness I'd never known before. I'd always scoffed at terms like "soulmate," but Cassie forced me to eat the words baked in a humble pie. We matched. It was as simple as that. She compensated for my lacks, she allowed me space to demonstrate my strengths. She made me feel like the finest lover who had ever laid hands on her. She was also the first woman I'd ever had a relationship with who miraculously never complained that the writing got in the way. With Cassie, everything was possible and life seemed remarkably straightforward.

She gave me all the space I needed, never minding that my fantasy world sometimes seemed more real to me than what was for dinner. And I did the same for her, I thought. I didn't dog her steps at the store, turning up for every event like an autograph hunter. I only came along to see writers I would have gone to see anyway; old friends, new kids on the block who were doing interesting work, visiting foreign names. I encouraged her to keep up her girls' nights out, barely registering when she rolled home in the small hours smelling of smoke and tasting of Triple Sec.

She didn't mind that I refused to attempt her other love, rock climbing; forty-year-old knees can't learn that sort of new trick. But equally, I never expected her to give it up for me, and even though she usually scheduled her overnight climbing trips for when I was out of town on book business, that was her choice rather than my demand. Bless her, she never tried taking advantage of our relationship to nail down better discount deals with my publishers, and I respected her even more for that.

Commuting between Denver and New York lasted all of two months. Then in the same week, I sold my house and my agent sold the *King's Infidel* trilogy to Oliver Stone's company for enough money for me actually to be able to buy a Manhattan apartment that was big enough for both of us and our several thousand books. I loved, and felt loved in return. It was as if I was leading a charmed life.

I should have known better. I am, after all, an adherent of the genre of fiction where pride always, always, always comes before a very nasty fall.

We'd been living together in the kind of bliss that makes one's friends gag and one's enemies weep for almost a year when the accident happened. I know that Freudians claim there is never any such thing as accident, but it's hard to see how anyone's subconscious could have felt the world would end up a better or more moral place because of this particular mishap.

My agent was in the middle of a very tricky negotiation with my publisher over my next deal. They were horse-trading and haggling hard over the money on the table, and my agent was naturally copying me in on the e-mails. One morning, I logged on to find that day's update had a file attachment with it. "Hi, John," the e-mail read.

**You might be interested to see that they're getting so nitty-gritty about this deal that they're actually discussing your last year's touring and miscellaneous expenses. Of course, I wasn't supposed to see this attachment, but we all know what an idiot Tom is when it comes to electronics. Great editor,**

**cyber-idiot. Anyway, I thought you might find it amusing to see how much they reckon they spent on you. See how it tallies with your recollections . . .**

I wasn't much drawn to the idea, but since the attachment was there, I thought I might as well take a look. It never hurts to get a little righteous indignation going about how much hotels end up billing for a one-night stay. It's the supplementaries that are the killers. Fifteen dollars for a bottle of water was the best I came across on last year's tour. Needless to say, I stuck a glass under the tap. Even when it's someone else's dime, I hate to encourage the robber barons who masquerade as hoteliers.

I was drifting down through the list when I ran into something out of the basic rhythm of hotels, taxis, air fares, author escorts. *Consolation Blonde, $500,* I read.

I knew what the words meant, but I didn't understand their linkage. Especially not on my expense list. If I'd spent it, you'd think I'd know what it was.

Then I saw the date.

My stomach did a back flip. Some dates you never forget. Like the U.S. Book Awards dinner.

I didn't want to believe it, but I had to be certain. I called Shula's girlfriend Caroline, herself an editor of mystery fiction in one of the big London houses. Once we'd got the small talk out of the way, I cut to the chase. "Caroline, have you ever heard the term 'consolation blonde' in publishing circles?"

"Where did you hear that, John?" she asked, answering the question inadvertently.

"I overheard it in one of those chi-chi midtown bars where

literary publishers hang out. I was waiting to meet my agent, and I heard one guy say to the other, 'He was okay after the consolation blonde.' I wasn't sure what it meant but I thought it sounded like a great title for a short story."

Caroline gave that well-bred middle-class English-woman's giggle. "I suppose you could be right. What can I say here, John? This really is one of publishing's tackier areas. Basically, it's what you lay on for an author who's having a bad time. Maybe they didn't win an award they thought was in the bag, maybe their book has bombed, maybe they're having a really bad tour. So you lay on a girl, a nice girl. A fan, a groupie, a publicity girlie, bookseller, whatever. Somebody on the fringes, not a hooker as such. Tell them how nice it would be for poor old what's-his-name to have a good time. So the sad boy gets the consolation blonde and the consolation blonde gets a nice boost to her bank account plus the bonus of being able to boast about shagging a name. Even if it's a name that nobody else in the pub has ever heard before."

I felt I'd lost the power of speech. I mumbled something and managed to end the call without screaming my anguish at Caroline. In the background, I could hear Bob Dylan singing "Idiot Wind." Cassie had set the CD playing on repeat before she'd left for work and now the words mocked me for the idiot I was.

Cassie was my Consolation Blonde.

I wondered how many other disappointed men had been lifted up by the power of her fingers and made to feel strong again? I wondered whether she'd have stuck around for more than that one-night stand if I'd been a poor man. I wondered how many times she'd slid into bed with me after a night out, not with the girls, but wearing the mantle of the Consolation Blonde. I wondered whether pity was still the primary emotion that moved her when she moaned and arched her spine for me.

I wanted to break something. And this time, I wasn't going to be diverted.

I've made a lot of money for my publisher over the years. So when I show up to see my editor, Tom, without an appointment, he makes space and time for me.

That day, I could tell inside a minute that he wished for once he'd made an exception. He looked like he wasn't sure whether he should just cut out the middle man and throw himself out of the twenty-third-floor window. "I don't know what you're talking about," he yelped in response to my single phrase.

"Bullshit," I yelled. "You hired Cassie to be my consolation blonde. There's no point in denying it, I've seen the paperwork."

"You're mistaken, John," Tom said desperately, his alarmed chipmunk eyes widening in dilemma.

"No. Cassie was my consolation blonde for the U.S. Book Awards. You didn't know I was going to lose, so you must have set her up in advance, as a stand-by. Which means you must have used her before."

"I swear, John, I swear to God, I don't know. . . ." Whatever Tom was going to say got cut off by me grabbing his stupid preppie tie and yanking him out of his chair.

"Tell me the truth," I growled, dragging him towards the window. "It's not like it can be worse than I've imagined. How many of my friends has she fucked? How many five-hundred-buck one-night stands have you pimped for my girlfriend since we got together? How many times have you and your buddies laughed behind my back because the woman I love is playing consolation blonde to somebody else? Tell me, Tom. Tell me the truth before I throw you out of this fucking window. Because I don't have any more to lose."

"It's not like that," he gibbered. I smelled piss and felt a warm dampness against my knee. His humiliation was sweet, though it was a poor second to what he'd done to me.

"Stop lying," I screamed. He flinched as my spittle spattered his face. I shook him like a terrier with a rat.

"Okay, okay," he sobbed. "Yes, Cassie was a consolation blonde. Yes, I hired her last year for you at the awards banquet. But I swear, that was the last time. She wrote me a letter, said after she met you she couldn't do this again. John, the letter's in my files. She returned her fee for being with you. You have to believe me. She fell in love with you that first night and she never did it again."

The worst of it was, I could tell he wasn't lying. But still, I hauled him over to the filing cabinets and made him produce his evidence. The letter was everything he'd promised. It was dated the day after our first encounter, two whole days before I called her to ask if I could see her again.

***Dear Tom, Thanks for transferring the $500 payment to my bank account. However, I'm enclosing a refund check for $500. It's not appropriate for me to accept money this time. I won't be available to do close author escort work in future. Meeting John Treadgold has changed***

***things for me. I can't thank you enough for introducing us. Good luck. Cassie White.***

I stood there, reading her words, every one cutting me like the wounds I'd carved into her body the night before.

I guess they don't have awards ceremonies in prison. Which is probably just as well, given what a bad loser I turned out to be.

# The Shoeshine Man's Regrets

Laura Lippman

Laura Lippman attended Northwestern University's Medill School of Journalism, then, in 1981, after sending résumés to virtually every newspaper in New England, landed her first job in Waco, Texas, at *the Tribune-Herald.* After a decade of reporting at various newspapers in both Texas and Maryland, she turned to mystery writing in 1993. Her novels *Baltimore Blues* and *Charm City* were published in 1997, and since then she's written a book a year while working full-time at the *Baltimore Sun.* Along the way she's also won the Anthony, Edgar, Shamus, Agatha, and Nero Awards She lives in Baltimore, in a place with a view of the almost-demolished Memorial Stadium. Her latest novel is *To the Power of Three.*

**"Bruno Magli?"**

"Uh-uh. Bally."

"How can you be so sure?"

"Some kids get flashcards of farm animals when they're little. I think my mom showed me pictures of footwear cut from magazines. After all, she couldn't have her only daughter bringing home someone who wore white patent loafers, even in the official season between Memorial Day and Labor Day. Speaking of which—there's a full Towson."

"Wow—white shoes *and* white belt and white tie, and ten miles south of his natural habitat, the Baltimore County courthouse. I thought the full Towson was on the endangered clothing list."

"Bad taste never dies. It just keeps evolving."

Tess Monaghan and Whitney Talbot were standing outside the Brass Elephant on a soft June evening, studying the people ahead of them in the valet parking line. A laundry truck had blocked the driveway to the restaurant's lot disrupting the usually smooth operation, so the restaurant's patrons were milling about, many agitated. There was muttered talk of symphony tickets and the Oriole game and the Herzog retrospective at the Charles Theater.

But Tess and Whitney, mellowed by martinis, eggplant appetizers, and the perfect weather, had no particular place to go and no great urgency about getting there. They had started cataloging the clothes and accessories of those around them only because Tess had confided to Whitney that she was trying to sharpen her powers of observation. It was a reasonable exercise in self-improvement for a private detective—and a great sport for someone as congenitally catty as Whitney.

The two friends were inventorying another man's loafers—Florsheim, Tess thought, but Whitney said good old-fashioned Weejuns—when they noticed a glop of white on one toe. And then, as if by magic, a shoeshine man materialized at the elbow of the Weejun wearer's elbow.

"You got something there, mister. Want me to give you a quick shine?"

Tess, still caught up in her game of cataloging, saw that the shoeshine man was old, but then, all shoeshine men seemed old these days. She often wondered where the next generation of shoeshine men would came from, if they were also on the verge of extinction, like the Towson types who sported white belts with white shoes. This man was thin, with a slight stoop to his shoulders and a tremble in his limbs, his salt-and-pepper hair cropped close. He must be on his way home from the train station or the Belvedere Hotel, Tess concluded, heading toward a bus stop on one of the major east-west streets farther south, near the city's center.

"What the—?" Mr. Weejun was short and compact, with a yellow polo shirt tucked into lime-green trousers. A golfer, Tess decided, noticing his florid face and sunburned bald spot. She was not happy to see him waiting for a car, given how many dinks he had tossed back in the Brass Elephant's Tusk Lounge. He was one of the people who kept braying about his Oriole tickets.

Now he extended his left foot, pointing his toe in a way that reminded Tess of the dancing hippos in *Fantasia,* and stared at the white smear on his shoe in anger and dismay.

"You *bastard,*" he said to the shoeshine man. "How did you get that shit on my shoe?"

"I didn't do anything, sir. I was just passing by, and I saw that your shoe was dirty. Maybe you tracked in something in the restaurant."

"It's some sort of scam, isn't it?" The man appealed to the restless crowd, which was glad for any distraction at this point. "Anyone see how this guy got this crap on my shoe?"

"He didn't," Whitney said, her voice cutting the air with her usual conviction. "It was on your shoe when you came out of the restaurant."

It wasn't what Mr. Weejun wanted to hear, so he ignored her.

"Yeah, you can clean my shoe," he told the old man. "Just don't expect a tip."

The shoeshine man sat down his box and went to work quickly. "Mayonnaise," he said, sponging the mass from the shoe with a cloth. "Or salad dressing. Something like that."

"I guess you'd know," Weejun said. "Since you put it there."

"No, sir. I wouldn't do a thing like that."

The shoeshine man was putting the finishing touches on the man's second shoe when the valet pulled up in a Humvee. Taxi-cab yellow, Tess observed, still playing the game. Save the Bay license plates and a sticker that announced the man as a member of an exclusive downtown health club.

"Five dollars," the shoeshine man said, and Weejun pulled out a five with great ostentation—then handed it to the valet. "No rewards for scammers," he said with great satisfaction. But when he glanced around, apparently expecting some sort of affirmation for his boorishness, all he saw were shocked and disapproving faces.

With the curious logic of the disgraced, Weejun upped the ante, kicking the man's shoeshine kit so its contents spilled across the sidewalk. He then hopped into his Humvee, gunning the motor, although the effect of a quick getaway was somewhat spoiled by the fact that his emergency brake was on. The Humvee bucked, then shot forward with a squeal.

As the shoeshine man's hands reached for the spilled contents of his box, Tess saw him pick up a discarded soda can and throw it at the fender of the Humvee. It bounced off with a hollow, harmless sound, but the car stopped with a great squealing of brakes and Weejun emerged, spoiling for a fight. He threw himself on the shoeshine man.

But the older man was no patsy. He grabbed his empty box, landing it in his attacker's stomach with a solid, satisfying smack. Tess waited for someone, anyone, to do something, but no one moved. Reluctantly she waded in, tossing her cell phone to Whitney. Longtime friends who had once synched their movements in a women's four on the rowing team at Washington College, the two could still think in synch when necessary. Whitney called 911 while Tess grabbed Weejun by the collar and uttered a piercing scream as close to his ear as possible. "Stop it, asshole. The cops are coming."

The man nodded, seemed to compose himself—then charged the shoeshine man again. Tess tried to hold him back by the belt, and he turned back, swinging out wildly, hitting her in the chin. Sad to say, this physical contact galvanized the crowd in a way that his attack on an elderly black man had not. By the time the blue-and-whites rolled up, the valet parkers were holding Weejun and Whitney was examining the fast-developing bruise on Tess's jaw with great satisfaction.

"You are so going to file charges against this asshole," she said.

"Well, I'm going to file charges against him, then," Weejun brayed, unrepentant. "He started the whole thing."

The patrol cop was in his mid-thirties, a seasoned officer who had broken up his share of fights, although probably not in this neighborhood. "If anyone's adamant about filing a report, it can be done, but it will involve about four hours down at the district."

That dimmed everyone's enthusiasm, even Whitney's.

"Good," the cop said. "I'll just take the bare details and let everyone go."

The laundry truck moved, the valet parking attendants regained their usual efficiency, and the crowd moved on, more anxious about their destinations than this bit of street theater. The shoeshine man started to walk away, but the cop motioned for him to stay, taking names and calling them in, along with DOBs. "Just routine," he told Tess, but his expression soon changed in a way that indicated the matter was anything but routine. He walked away from them, out of earshot, clicking the two-way on his shoulder on and off.

"You can go," he said to Whitney and Tess upon returning. "But I gotta take him in. There's a warrant."

"Him?" Whitney asked hopefully, jerking her chin at Weejun.

"No, him." The cop looked genuinely regretful. "Could be a mix-up, could be someone else using his name and DOB, but I still have to take him downtown."

"What's the warrant for?" Tess asked.

"Murder, if you really want to know."

Weejun looked at once gleeful and frightened, as if he were wondering just whom he had taken on in this fight. It would make quite a brag around the country club, Tess thought. He'd probably be telling his buddies he had taken on a homicidal maniac and won.

Yet the shoeshine man was utterly composed. He did not protest his innocence or insist that it was all a mistake, things that even a guilty man might have said under the circumstances. He simply sighed, cast his eyes toward the sky, as if asking a quick favor from his deity of choice, then said: "I'd like to gather up my things, if I could."

"It's the damnedest thing, Tess. He couldn't confess fast enough. Didn't want a lawyer, didn't ask any questions, just sat dawn and began talking as fast as he could."

Homicide Detective Martin Tull, Tess's only real friend in the Baltimore Police Department, had caught the shoeshine man's case simply by answering the phone when the patrol cop called him about the warrant. He should be thrilled—it was an easy stat, about as easy as they come. No matter how old the case, it counted toward the current year's total of solved homicides.

"It's a little too easy," Tull said, sitting with Tess on a bench near one of their favorite coffeehouses, watching the water taxis zip back and forth across the Inner Harbor.

"Everyone gets lucky, even you," Tess said. "It's all too

incredible that the warrant was lost all these years. What I don't get is how it was found."

"Department got some grant for computer work. Isn't that great? There's not enough money to make sure DNA samples are stored safely, but some think tank gave us money so college students can spend all summer keystroking data. The guy moved about two weeks after the murder, before he was named in the warrant. Moved all of five miles, from West Baltimore to the county, but he wasn't the kind of guy who left a forwarding address. Or the cop on the case was a bonehead. At any rate, he's gone forty years wanted for murder, and if he hadn't been in that fight night before last, he might've gone another forty."

"Did he even know there was a warrant on him?"

"Oh, yeah. He knew exactly why he was there. Story came out of him as if he had been rehearsing it for years. Kept saying, 'Yep, I did it, no doubt about it. You do what you have to do, Officer.' So we charged him, the judge put a hundred grand bail on him, a bail bondsman put up ten thousand, and he went home."

"I guess someone who's lived at the same address for thirty-nine years isn't considered a flight risk."

"Flight risk? I think if I had left this guy in the room with all our opened files, he would have confessed to every homicide in Baltimore. I have never seen someone so eager to confess to a crime. I almost think he wants to go to jail."

"Maybe he's convinced that a city jury won't lock him up, or that he can get a plea. How did the victim die?"

"Blunt force trauma in a burglary. There's no physical evidence, and the warrant was sworn out on the basis of an eyewitness who's been dead for ten years."

"So you probably couldn't get a conviction at all if it went to trial."

"Nope. That's what makes it so odd. Even if she were alive, she'd be almost ninety by now, pretty easy to break down on the stand."

"What's the file say?"

"Neighbor lady said she saw William Harrison leave the premises, acting strangely. She knew the guy because he did odd jobs in the neighborhood, even worked for her on occasion, but there was no reason for him to be at the victim's house so late at night."

"Good luck recovering the evidence from Evidence Control."

"Would you believe they still had the weapon? The guy's head was bashed in with an iron. But that's all I got. If the guy hadn't confessed, if he had stonewalled me or gotten with a lawyer, I wouldn't have anything. Only witness died almost fifteen years ago."

"So what do you want me to tell you? I never met this man before we became impromptu tag-team wrestlers. He seemed pretty meek to me, but who knows what he was like forty years ago? Maybe he's just a guy with a conscience, who's been waiting all these years to see if someone's going to catch up with him."

Tull shook his head. "One thing. He didn't know what the murder weapon was. Said he forgot."

"Well, forty years. It's possible."

"Maybe." Tull, who had already finished his coffee, reached for Tess's absentmindedly, grimacing when he realized it was a latte. Caffeine was his fuel, his vice of choice, and he didn't like it diluted in any way.

“Take the easy stat, Martin. Guy’s named in a warrant, and he said he did it. He does have a temper, I saw that much. Last night it was a soda can. Forty years ago, it very well could have been an iron.”

“I’ve got a conscience, too, you know.” Tull looked offended.

Tess realized that it wasn’t something she knew that had prompted Tull to call her up, but something he wanted her to do. Yet Tull would not ask her directly, because then he would be in her debt. He was a man, after all. But if she volunteered to do what he seemed to want, he would honor *her* next favor, and Tess was frequently in need of favors.

“I’ll talk to him. See if he’ll open up to his tag-team partner.”

Tull didn’t even so much as nod to acknowledge the offer. It was as if Tess’s acquiescence were a belch, or something else that wouldn’t be commented on in polite company.

The shoe shine man—William Harrison, Tess reminded herself, she had a name for him now—lived in a neat bungalow just over the line in what was known as the Woodlawn section of Baltimore County. Forty years ago, Mr. Harrison would have been one of its first black residents, and he would have been denied entrance to the amusement park only a few blocks from his house. Now the neighborhood was more black than white, but still middle-class.

A tiny woman answered the door to Mr. Harrison’s bungalow, her eyes bright and curious.

“Mrs. Harrison?”

*"Miss."* There was a note of reprimand for Tess's assumption.

"My name is Tess Monaghan. I met your brother two nights ago in the, um, fracas."

"Oh, he felt so bad about that. He said it was shameful, how the only person who wanted to help him was a girl. He found it *appalling.*"

She drew out the syllables of the last word, as if it gave her some special pleasure.

"It was so unfair what happened to him. And then this mix-up with the warrant . . ."

The bright catlike eyes narrowed a bit, "What do you mean by mix-up?"

"Mr. Harrison just doesn't seem to me to be the kind of man who could kill someone."

"Well, he says he was." Spoken matter-of-factly, as if the topic were the weather or something else of little consequence. "I knew nothing about it, of course. The warrant or the murder."

"Of course," Tess agreed. This woman did not look like someone who had been burdened with a loved one's secret for four decades. Where her brother was stooped and grave, she had the regal posture of a short woman intent on using every inch given her. But there was something blithe, almost gleeful, beneath her dignity. Did she not like her brother?

"It was silly of William"—she stretched the name out, giving it a grand, growling pronunciation, Will-yum—"to tell his story and sign the statement, without even talking to a lawyer. I told him to wait, to see what they said, but he wouldn't."

"But if you knew nothing about it . . ."

"Nothing about it until two nights ago," Miss Harrison clarified. That was the word that popped into Tess's head, clarified, and she wondered at it. Clarifications were what people made when things weren't quite right.

"And were you shocked?"

"Oh, he had a temper when he was young. Anything was possible."

"Is your brother at home?"

"He's at work. We still have to eat, you know." Now she sounded almost angry. "He didn't think of that, did he, when he decided to be so noble. I told him this house may be paid off, but we still have to eat and buy gas for my car. Did you know they cut your Social Security off when you go to prison?"

Tess did not. She had relatives who were far from pure, but they had managed to avoid doing time. So far.

"Well," Miss Harrison said, "they do. But Will-yum didn't think of that, did he? Men are funny that way. They're so determined to be *gallant*"—again, the word was spoken with great pleasure, with the tone of a child trying to be grand—"that they don't think things through. He may feel better, but what about me?"

"Do you have no income, then?"

"I worked as a laundress. You don't get a pension for being a laundress. My brother, however, was a custodian for Social Security, right here in Woodlawn."

"I thought he shined shoes."

"Yes, *now*." Miss Harrison was growing annoyed with Tess. "But not always. William was enterprising, even as a young man. He worked as a custodian at Social Security, which is why he has Social Security. But he took on odd jobs, shined shoes. He hates to be idle. He won't like prison, no matter what he thinks."

"He did odd jobs for the man he killed, right?"

"Some. Not many. Really, hardly any at all. They barely knew each other."

Miss Harrison seemed to think this mitigated the crime somehow, that the superficiality of the relationship excused her brother's deed.

"Police always thought it was a burglary?" Tess hoped her tone would invite a confidence, or at least another clarification.

"Yes," she said. "Yes. That, too. Things were taken. Everyone knew that."

"So you were familiar with the case, but not your brother's connection to it?"

"Well, I knew the man. Maurice Dickman. We lived in the neighborhood, after all. And people talked, of course. It was a big deal, murder, forty years ago. Not the *happenstance* that it's become. But he was a showy man. He thought awfully well of himself, because he had money and a business. Perhaps he shouldn't have made such a spectacle of himself, and then no one would have tried to steal from him. You know what the Bible says, about the rich man and the camel and the eye of the needle? It's true, you know. Not always, but often enough."

"Why did your brother burglarize his home? Was that something else he did to supplement his paycheck? Is that something he still does?"

"My brother," Miss Harrison said, drawing herself up so she gained yet another inch, "is not a thief."

"But—"

"I don't like talking to you," she said abruptly. "I thought you were on our side, but I see now I was foolish. I know what happened. You called the police. You talked about pressing charges. If it weren't for you, none of this would have happened. You're a terrible person. Forty years, and trouble never came for us, and then you undid everything. You have brought us nothing but grief, which we can ill afford."

She stamped her feet, an impressive gesture, small though they were. Stamped her feet and went back inside the house, taking a moment to latch the screen behind her, as if Tess's manners were so suspect that she might try to follow where she clearly wasn't wanted.

The shoeshine man did work at Penn Station, after all, stationed in front of the old-fashioned wooden seats that always made Tess cringe a bit. There was something about one man perched above another that didn't sit quite right with her, especially when the other man was bent over the enthroned one's shoes.

Then again, pedicures probably looked pretty demeaning, too, depending on one's perspective.

"I'm really sorry, Mr. Harrison, about the mess I've gotten you into." She had refused to sit in his chair, choosing to lean against the wall instead.

"Got myself into, truth be told. If I hadn't thrown that soda can, none of this would have happened. I could have gone another forty years without anyone bothering me."

"But you could go to prison."

"Looks that way." He was almost cheerful about it.

"You should get a lawyer, get that confession thrown out. Without it, they've got nothing."

"They've got a closed case, that's what they've got. A closed case. And maybe I'll get probation."

"It's not a bad bet, but the stakes are awfully high. Even with a five-year sentence, you might die in prison."

"Might not," he said.

"Still, your sister seems pretty upset."

"Oh, Mattie's always getting upset about something. Our mother thought she was doing right by her, teaching her those Queen of Sheba manners, but all she did was make her perpetually disappointed. Now, if Mattie had been born just a decade later, she might have had a different life. But she wasn't, and I wasn't, and that's that."

"She did seem . . . refined," Tess said, thinking of the woman's impeccable appearance and the way she loved to stress big words.

"She was raised to be a lady. Unfortunately, she didn't have a lady's job. No shame in washing clothes, but no honor in it either, not for someone like Mattie. She should have stayed in school, become a teacher. But Mattie thought it would be easy to marry a man on the rise. She just didn't figure that a man on the rise would want a woman on the rise, too, that the manners and the looks wouldn't be enough. A man on the rise doesn't want a woman to get out of his bed and then wash his sheets, not unless she's already his wife. Mattie should never have dropped out of school. It was a shame, what she gave up."

"Being a teacher, you mean."

"Yeah," he said, his tone vague and faraway. "Yeah. She could have gone back, even after she dropped out, but she just stomped her feet and threw back that pretty head of hers. Threw back her pretty head and cried."

"Threw back her pretty head and cried—why does that sound familiar?"

"I couldn't tell you."

"Threw back her pretty head . . . I know that, but I can't place it."

"Couldn't help you." He began whistling a tune, "Begin the Beguine."

"Mr. Harrison—you didn't kill that man, did you?"

"Well, now, I say I did, and why would anyone want to argue with me? And I was seen coming from his house that night, sure as anything. That neighbor, Edna Buford, she didn't miss a trick on that block."

"What did you hit him with?"

"An iron," he said triumphantly. "An iron!"

"You didn't know that two days ago."

"I was nervous."

"You were anything but, from what I hear."

"I'm an old man. I don't always remember what I should."

"So it was an iron?"

"Definitely, one of those old-fashioned ones, cast iron. The kind you had to heat."

"The kind," Tess said, "that a man's laundress might use."

"Mebbe. Does it really matter? Does any of this really matter? If it did, would they have taken forty years to find me? I'll tell you this much—if Maurice Dickman had been a white man, I bet I wouldn't have been walking around all this time. He wasn't a nice man, Mr. Dickman, but the police didn't know that, for all they knew, he was a good citizen. A man was killed, and nobody cared. Except Edna Buford, peeking through her curtains. They should have found me long ago. Know something else?"

"What?" Tess leaned forward, assuming a confession was about to be made.

"I *did* put the mayonnaise on that man's shoe. It had been a light day here, and I wanted to pick up a few extra dollars on my way home. I'm usually better about picking my marks, though. I won't make that mistake again."

A lawyer of Tess's acquaintance, Tyner Gray, asked that the court throw out the charges against William Harrison on the grounds that his confession was coerced. A plea bargain was offered instead—five years probation. "I told you so," Mr. Harrison chortled to Tess, gloating a little at his prescience.

"Lifted up her lovely head and cried," Tess said.

"What?"

"That's the line I thought you were quoting. You said 'threw,' but the line was lifted. I had to feed it through Google a few different ways to nail it, but I did. 'Miss Otis Regrets.' It's about a woman who kills her lover, and is then hanged on the gallows."

"Computers are interesting," Mr. Harrison said.

"What did you really want? Were you still trying to protect your sister, as you've protected her all these years? Or were you just trying to get away from her for a while?"

"I have no idea what you're talking about. Mattie did no wrong in our mother's eyes. My mother loved that girl, and I loved for my mother to be happy."

So Martin Tull got his start and a more-or-less clean conscience. Miss Harrison got her protective older brother back, along with his Social Security checks.

And Tess got an offer of free shoeshines for life, whenever she was passing through Penn Station. She politely declined Mr. Harrison's gesture. After all, he had already spent forty years at the feet of a woman who didn't know how to show gratitude.

# For Benefit of Mr. Means

Christine Matthews

Christine Matthews is a veteran short story writer with more than sixty to her credit. Her mysteries have appeared in dozens of anthologies, and the best of them were anthologized in the short story collection *Gentle Insanities and Other States of Mind.* With Robert J. Randisi, she also co-authors the Gil and Claire Hunt cozy mystery series, which includes the books *Murder Is the Deal of the Day, The Masks of Auntie Laveau,* and *Same Time, Same Murder.*

*Devotees of cinema history will know well the cause célèbre of 1921 when the popular film star, Roscoe "Fatty" Arbuckle, was accused of raping and causing the death of the young actress Virginia Rappé. He had done no such thing and was found not guilty, but the case had ruined his career and he was blacklisted by Hollywood. He later directed films, but turned to drink and died at the age of only forty-six from heart failure—Buster Keaton said it was of a broken heart. In the following story we see the real Roscoe.*

**YOU ARE CORDIALLY INVITED**
**TO JOIN LILY ARMSTRONG-SMITH**
**IN CELEBRATING HER TWENTY-FIFTH BIRTHDAY**
**ON THE FOURTH OF SEPTEMBER**
**ONE THOUSAND NINE HUNDRED and**
**TWENTY-SEVEN**
**EIGHT O'CLOCK IN THE EVENING**
**AT HER BENTON COVE ESTATE**
**NEWPORT, RHODE ISLAND**

**gifts required**

"If I told ya once, I musta told ya fifty times—you'll be swell."

Irma bit her red fingernail. "But I don't know all the words. Not like Peggy does."

"If ya get into trouble, just give us a nod and we'll cover ya."

Cal turned toward Johnny Long and nodded a signal. Johnny reached up to straighten his bow tie and then played the first six notes solo before the rest of the band joined in.

Cal shoved Irma toward the microphone. "Just remember—smile!"

It was the caliber of people in the mansion that got the butterflies flapping in her stomach, not being up there on stage. She'd been singing most of her eighteen years . . . that was the easy part. And what God had cheated her out of in talent, He'd made up for by loading up the charm.

She sang the first three lines of the song and then hesitated for a moment. Raising her eyebrows and then her small hand, she waved as Harold Lloyd entered the room. Now, why had she done that? Like she knew the man, jeepers! But the guy was a real gentleman and bowed slightly, even waved back before continuing through the crowd. "The man I love . . ." Piece of cake, she thought. If I can just keep from going gaga every time one of them hot shots looks at me, I'll be fine.

"There's three of them. All perfectly matched. I heard Lillian had those chandeliers made in France. Mustn't be outdone by the Astors!"

The woman's companion looked up at the pale lavender ceiling, then inspected the crystal lights evenly spaced across the expanse of the great room.

"You can bet your Aunt Sally they cost more than Lillian's dearly departed father plus his father made in their entire lifetimes—even throwing in that haberdashery her brother runs up in Providence," he said.

"And just how would you know that, if I may ask?" she asked.

"I was her accountant years ago."

"Do I detect a tiny smidge of bitterness in your tone?"

He laughed.

A man with a grudge. The evening was going to be fun! "And now?" She leaned in closer. "You work for her in some other capacity?"

"No, she has an entire office—hand picked—just to

handle her affairs." More bitterness. "Men highly qualified to run at the drop of her imported hat."

Now it was her turn to laugh. After composing herself, Zelda Fitzgerald pressed on. "Twice divorced! That's our Lily. I bet that would require more than one lawyer indeed."

He gulped down his martini. "She's become quite an expert at the fine art of matrimony but when it comes to divorce, Madam Curie couldn't keep up!"

"Will you look at that carpet! Really look at it!" the newcomer said loudly as he interrupted the two guests. "Hand stitched. Custom made! Exquisite. Simply exquisite."

Before Zelda could get rid of the obnoxious intruder, her accountant friend walked away.

"Well?" Dorothy exhaled the word, slowly. Smoke from her second cigarette of the evening hung above her head in a halo. "Where is our birthday girl? Is she decent yet?"

"If she were, she wouldn't be giving herself another birthday party."

"Now, Bill—be nice."

He looked at her with disdain.

"You have to feel sorry for poor Lily. Three birthdays in one year. And twenty-five? How on earth did she come up with that laughable number? A bit eccentric or pathetic, I haven't quite figured it out yet," she said.

"Keep at it, old girl, I'm sure you'll come up with something."

This time it is was she who scowled.

"Why, you're W. C. Fields, aren't you?" A round, balding man stood in front of the group seated on a long divan covered in velvet the color of burnished pewter. "I've enjoyed you on Broadway . . . oh, and of course, the films. Yes, I've spent many enjoyable hours laughing at you and Chaplin . . ."

"*He,* sir, is not an actor. I'll thank you to never mention him in my presence."

The man looked puzzled.

Fields continued, "Chaplin is a goddamn ballet dancer, nothing more." Picking up the book that lay in his lap, he resumed his reading as if he were the only person in the room.

"Don't mind him," the woman said. "He's just a cantankerous old man."

The stranger shifted his weight, unsure how to proceed until his ego kicked in. "Allow me to introduce myself. My name is Means. Gaston Bullock Means." He waited a moment for some sort of reaction. When she didn't say anything he elaborated. "I'm the author of *The President's Daughter.*"

"Oh." She withdrew her hand. "Of course I've heard of you. Who hasn't?"

Fields huffed. "You, sir, are a hack—a gossip monger who happened to luck into a scandal. Now Mrs. Parker here is a writer."

Fields had enough of the boorish crowd and stood up. Without a nod backwards, he walked across the room to the bar.

"Gin. And keep pouring, my good man, until I pass out," he said to the bartender.

"Sure thing, Mr. Fields."

The band was getting ready to wrap up "Someone to Watch Over Me," as two couples danced slowly.

"Have you seen Miss Armstrong-Smith?" he asked the bartender.

"Gee, Mr. Fields, can't say as I have."

With a glass in each hand, the actor made his way to a large seating group in the middle of the room. The sweet young thing singing with the band caught his eye. He raised a glass and blew her a kiss.

She tried concentrating on the words, but he was W. C. Fields—in the flesh! She stopped to return his kiss and Cal leaned over.

His tuxedo didn't fit as well as it could have but the call to play for the party had come at the last minute, it being a Saturday and all. His regular suit was at the cleaners so he borrowed his brother's tux and scrambled to replace Peggy with Irma. Irma Levine, what a mixed-up dame! But so far—so good. And Mrs. Armstrong-Smith paid well, had a lot of parties at the Cove and he wanted to get in solid with her. Now, baton in hand, he tapped on the music stand propped in front of him and asked Irma, "Need some help?"

"What? Oh, sorry, no, I'm fine."

As she sang, she never lost eye contact with Fields. "I hope that he, turns out to be . . . someone to watch over . . ." Ramon Novarro walked into the room and she lost it again.

In contrast to the glamorous, inviting atmosphere downstairs, the air on the second floor was charged, like a storm ripping through a Kansas town.

"Where are Mrs. Smith's pearls?" the maid asked, panicky. "If we don't find them, there'll be hell to pay, I can guarantee you that! She's out for blood tonight."

"Alice!" Lily's voice boomed down the long hallway. "Hurry! Alice!"

* * *

"So, tell me my good man," Gaston Means said, "what is the source of your supply and will I die of alcohol poisoning later this evening?"

The bartender studied the pompous little man for a moment and then decided to take his comment as a joke. "Don't worry, sir, it will be a most pleasant death. Mrs. Armstrong-Smith only serves the best."

"Then I'll have a brandy." The man patted the bar, happy with his decision. "Yes, brandy."

After carefully pouring, the bartender slid the crystal glass toward the man. "There you go sir. Napoleon, the best we have. Enjoy."

He swirled the amber liquid around in the snifter. After a moment spent inhaling, he finally sipped. "Ahh, yes, excellent."

Truth be told, Mr. Means couldn't tell bad brandy from good. As he stood there, surveying the room, he watched the parade of celebrities pass by and felt confident he belonged. A gentleman came and stood beside him, recognizing the voice, he turned. "Mr. Crosby." Means held out his hand. "I'm a great fan of your trio, The Rhythm Boys. Allow me to introduce myself."

Bing Crosby started to shake hands until he heard the name Gaston Means, then quickly withdrew his hand. "Sorry, I don't associate with swindlers or spies."

"I beg your pardon?"

"You and your kind make me physically ill."

"But . . ."

"I've read all about you, Mr. Means. How you sold information on Allied shipping to the German embassy, were fired from the FBI, got yourself involved with that Ohio

Gang scandal. Then without missing a beat, rolled around in the dirt with that Nan Britton woman."

"She hired me to investigate her husband . . ."

"*The President's Daughter!* You expect the American public to believe that a president of the United States fathered an illegitimate child?"

"He was a senator at the time . . ."

Crosby wasn't interested in anything Means had to say. "You, sir are a coward, benefiting from people's delusions . . ."

"But I assure you Miss Britton's claims are true!"

"Why don't you try doing something useful with your life?" After taking a minute to stare at Means with disgust, Crosby walked off.

It wasn't embarrassment that swirled around in Means's brain, no, it was disbelief. Hadn't H. L. Mencken written favorably about *The President's Daughter?* Right there in the *Baltimore Sun?* Who the hell was this Bing character anyway? What did some lousy crooner know about politics? Literature? Means shrugged and headed for the buffet table,

"Gee, Cal, when are we gonna get a break?" Irma asked. "My feet are killing me in these shoes." She pointed down to her new red satin pumps that had been custom-dyed to match the roses stitched across the black velvet of her chemise. While the band played, Irma fingered a spit curl which curlicued across her left cheek. "Come on, Cal, I need to sit down a minute," she whispered. "Be a pal, will ya?"

The last note of "Lady be Good," ended when Cal brought his baton down. "Ladies and gentlemen, thank you for your enthusiasm. We're going to take a short break but don't worry, we'll be back to play more of your favorites in fifteen minutes."

A few people applauded but most seemed not to notice.

"There, are ya happy?" he asked Irma.

"Yeah, thanks." It wasn't her feet that were hurting—it was her heart. She had to go meet Ramon Novarro. What a dream boat! As she hopped off this bandstand, her long string of pearls bounced in time with the matching earrings that hung almost to her shoulders.

Judy McKeon hated her employer. If she could have gotten away with slitting the throat of that obnoxious cow, she would gladly have done so. But then she'd not only be out a big fat pay check each week, but have to clean up the mess as well.

"Juuudith! Come here this instant!"

Ordinarily, Judy would have run to help Lily (Mrs. Armstrong-Smith insisted she call her Lily). But this particular evening she wasn't feeling very helpful. As she rushed past the bedroom door she kept her eyes down and her mind set on escape. The party had started, the guests were sucking up the free hootch and one of the maids could surely tend to their demanding mistress.

"Gaston Bullock Means," he said as he shook the man's hand in almost a violent manner. He was sick and tired of being looked down on. "Author of *The President's Daughter.* You must have heard about the book. It's almost certain to become a bestseller."

The poor fellow had been in the middle of a conversation with the beautiful woman next to him when this imbecile interrupted him. His anger forced the truth to erupt from inside like a volcano. "I sir would never soil my hands let alone my intellect with such garbage. Besides, I thought that piece of trash was written by a woman."

"Well yes, Nan Britton and I did collaborate."

"Maybe you should mention that next time you introduce yourself. By saying you're the author gives the impression you had an original idea—did all the difficult work of writing yourself. Maybe next time . . ."

Means walked away.

A large man sat in the corner, alone. Means headed toward the loner to introduce himself. This time he would leave out the part about writing a book. All he wanted to do now was get drunk. The booze was free, the food exceptional. If he just kept his mouth shut he could have a good time.

After twenty minutes, Cal went looking for Irma. Aside from the ballroom and library, the first floor of the mansion was quiet. Walking through the French doors, he scanned the pergola which had been strung with red and gold lacquered Chinese lantern. A few couples stood admiring the view of Narragansett Bay. The air was cool and clean, the grass slightly damp. Even though an additional bar had been set up outside, the evening was too chilly to have many takers.

The bartender waved across the expansive lawn to the Bandleader.

"You seen Irma anywheres?" Cal shouted.

The man pointed toward the water.

Cal walked across the lawn, wondering why on earth Irma would be out in the cold. He could hear water slapping against the rocks and as he wandered away from the artificial light of the lanterns, his pace slowed a bit while his eyes adjusted to the darkness beyond.

Finally, he was able to make out two figures. One, short—female, and one considerably larger—male. He stood there, conflicted. Not wanting to intrude, not wanting to walk any further in the dampness and dark. But even more anxious than ever to find his girl singer.

He started to shout out to the pair but was interrupted by the low bellowing from a nearby lighthouse. He waited, then shouted, “Irma!”

The female turned toward him. “Just a sec, Cal. I’m kinda busy here.”

“No, Irma. You’re on my time now, break’s over!”

“Okay, okay!”

He turned and headed back to the house.

The crowd seemed to have grown considerably in the short time he had been outside. His men sat waiting impatiently for their instructions.

“Come on, Cal,” the trumpet player complained. “Are we playin’ or ain’t we?”

“Quit your gripin’. You’re gettin’ paid, aren’t ya? Whether you play or just sit back on your rented tails, you’re gettin’ paid.”

Looking away, in the direction of the drums, Cal stood waiting for Irma, silently daring the musician to say another word.

The drummer, oblivious to the situation, stared out across the crowd.

“Fascinating Rhythm,” Cal finally said. “And ah-one, ah-two.” Bringing his baton down, he continued, “ah-three.”

The band had only gotten a minute or so into the number when Irma appeared. Frantically, she scrambled across the small stage. Cal was too angry to notice the long tear in her dress.

"I'm sorry," she whispered.

Cal ignored her.

"Gee, give me a break, will ya?" she asked. "It was only a few minutes. So I got a little carried away. Come on, Cal, I said I was sorry. I promise it won't happen again."

Before he could respond, a woman pushed her way through the crowd. The bandleader couldn't make out what she was shouting until she got closer.

"Mrs. Armstrong-Smith is missing!"

The musicians froze, conversations hung unfinished in the air.

"What do you mean by 'missing?' " W. C. Fields asked.

"I'm sure she's around here someplace," an older woman said. "You know how fond Lily is of surprises."

"She was upstairs in her bedroom just a moment ago."

"And who might you be?" Gaston Means asked.

The hysterical woman looked around, unsure who had asked the question and even more unsure if that person was speaking to her.

"Young woman," he started again, "calm down. And please, tell us just who in Sam Hill you think you are, coming in here shrieking like a banshee, ruining our—"

"Judith McKeon. I'm Mrs. Armstrong-Smith's personal secretary, sir, that's who the hell I am! And would you be so kind as to tell me why you're standing here wasting my time instead of helping me look for Mrs. Armstrong-Smith? She's vanished—maybe been kidnapped—or worse. We have to find her!"

Means approached the woman. "Surely your employer couldn't have just disappeared."

"But I saw her less than ten minutes ago. Well . . . I didn't see her . . . with my eyes. She was in her room, dressing and wanted her . . ." That's when Judith's eyes settled on the sapphire clasp of Irma's pearls. Wide-eyed she pointed and screamed. "Those pearls! You stole them! They belong to Mrs. Armstrong-Smith!"

Irma was mortified. Clutching her throat she shook her head violently. "I didn't steal nothin'. These are mine!"

"What did she say?" someone asked.

"What's happening?" a lanky man sporting a pin striped suit wanted to know.

"Should we call the police?" one of the maids who had been serving hors d'oeuvres asked, after swallowing the small toast point and last bit of caviar she had swiped.

"No!" The large man standing near the French doors shouted. "No police!"

Everyone's attention turned. As he walked into the room, a unified gasp rose from the crowd.

"I can certainly understand your concern, Mr. Arbuckle," Judith began, "but I don't think . . ."

"Fatty Arbuckle?" Gaston Means asked. "*The* Fatty Arbuckle? The man who killed that Rappé woman?"

"He was acquitted," Judith snapped.

"And if your memory is good enough to dredge up that poor woman's name after six years, then I'm sure you remember I was exonerated twice."

"Hey! He told me his name was William Goodrich," Irma explained to Cal. "He said he was a director."

Cal whistled through his teeth. "Yeah, honey, and I bet he told ya he could get ya in the moving pictures." As he spoke, Cal noticed the rip in Irma's dress. "Was he the one who did that?"

"Well . . . yes . . . but not like you . . ."

Cal walked to the microphone. "Miss McKeon, I suggest ya detain Mr. Arbuckle. He attacked my singer, here."

"What?"

"I did no such thing," the large man said. Sweat broke out across his forehead; his round face was slowly turning a deep crimson. "I would never do that!"

"He's right." Irma was now talking into the microphone. "Mr. Arbuckle and I was just talking. He was a perfect gentleman. And then we spotted the. . . ." Irma stopped abruptly. Her eyes slammed shut and she stood there, head down, staring at the floor.

"Spotted what? What did you see?" Cal asked.

"Sorry, Mr. Arbuckle. Sometimes I can be a real dope."

Fatty had hoped for enough time to take care of his "situation." But when she had started to run for the house he had to stop her, grabbing for her arm. She was younger and quicker and all he had managed to do was rip her sleeve. The thing that had upset her the most about this incident was the damage to her dress. When he promised to not only replace it but throw in another with matching shoes and evening bag, she agreed to give him half an hour to take care of things.

"I think I know where Lily is," he slowly told the crowd.

"Well, for God's sake tell me," Judith demanded. "I've spent days putting this party together and now, maybe, some of the evening can be salvaged."

"If one of the men will go with me," Fatty suggested, "we can escort Lily . . ."

"Anything. Do whatever you want. As long as she's not been kidnapped."

"No, I can assure you she hasn't," Fatty told her.

"Fine, then." Judith McKeon pivoted around on the heels of her practical shoes, annoyed, and marched out of the room. "Just like that old cow," she muttered to herself. "Selfish, ungrateful . . ."

"Mr. Means?" Fatty said. "If you would be so kind as to come with me."

"And just what are the rest of us supposed to do?" Bing asked.

"Eat, drink and be merry. Isn't that why we're here?" Fatty asked.

"I suppose it is," the crooner answered. Then, turning to Cal, he said, "Play something light. How about a Charleston?"

"Sure thing, Mr. Crosby."

As the music started up again, Means and Arbuckle headed through the ornate doors. When they had crossed the patio and stepped into the plush grass, Means asked his companion, "Why me?"

"Because we are two of a kind, I suppose."

"How can you say that? Before tonight, we've never met." "Not face to face, you're right about that. However, I am very well acquainted with your reputation, Mr. Means. We both have scandalous backgrounds. And it's that fear of being disgraced again that puts us on our best behavior."

Means stopped dead. "So, if each of us in on his best behavior, then it stands to reason we are the most honorable of all the men—or women—here."

"Exactly. Now, follow me. I want to show you something."

The men continued walking in the direction of the jagged shoreline. The only light guiding their way came from the full moon.

"There." Arbuckle pointed. "See her?"

Means studied the area he was being shown. After a moment he was able to differentiate between rock, sand, water and a human form. He gasped. "Is that? No . . ." He leaned as far as he dared. "It can't be."

"I spotted her while talking to that girl with the band. Of course she went all hysterical. She even started to run back into the party. Well, I wasn't even sure it was Lily down there . . ."

"And you couldn't afford another scandal, now, could you, Mr. Goodrich?"

"Come on," Fatty said, removing a cigarette from a silver case. "We both know I can't use my real name if I want to work in the movies. The Hays office saw to that."

"Cleaning up Hollywood. There's a good one for you," Means said. "The town's crawling with hookers and drugs, bootleg hootch—"

"Men like William Randolph Hearst who flaunts his mistress, men who think nothing of the lives they ruin. No, nothing matters to them except money," Fatty said with contempt. "You certainly are aware of the kind of diseased vermin making huge profits in the film industry, Mr. Means. So you can certainly understand why I tried delaying Irma's exit."

Means nodded. "Well, I guess we should get down there and see if that is in fact our hostess before worrying about what decisions need to be made."

"How do we do that without causing a riot?" Arbuckle

asked. "You're the investigator. The ex-FBI man. What do we do?"

"We're not alone in our need for propriety, Arbuckle. Why, just from the misfortune that has befallen the two of us, every single person in that house knows how easily their careers can tumble down around them and their families. We have to go back in there and stoke that fear."

It was as if they had all forgotten about Lily completely. When the two men entered the grand ballroom, not one guest turned to ask them what had become of her. The music was loud, the glasses were full and the majority of voices were competing for attention. Gaston Means walked the length of the room alone without attracting one glance.

When he had come to what looked to be the library, he was met by a butler.

"May I help you, sir?"

"Please get Miss McKeon for me."

"Certainly, sir." The elderly man bowed and slowly, as if each step caused pain, walked out of the room.

She must have been just down the hall, because Judith McKeon returned within a moment.

"Well? Where is she?"

"I assume Lily . . . Mrs. Armstrong-Smith has a gardener on the premises? A caretaker?" Means asked.

"Yes, William. He lives in the cottage up the road."

"Call him. I need his help."

"May I ask . . ."

"You may not. Call him and tell him to meet me by that dead evergreen near the cliffwalk. Tell him to bring a lantern and a rake."

"Fine."

"Oh, and Miss McKeon," he said, looking up at the tall woman, "I'll need you to stay close by."

She glared down at him as if he were an imbecile. "I live here, Mr. Means. Where else would I go?"

"That's her, all right," William said as he watched Means drape Lily's body with a tablecloth. "I kept telling Mrs. Armstrong-Smith that she should put a fence up along here. But she'd just laugh. Told me it would detract from the 'wildness' of this place. Can you believe that?" he asked, eyeing Arbuckle as he approached. "Wildness? After all the money she poured into this property? After the landscapers and architects, builders, fancy artists? There ain't nothin' wild left out here except maybe that water down there."

"Thank you, William," Means said when Arbuckle was standing next to him. "Please, don't say anything to alarm the staff. We'll have Miss McKeon send for the doctor who will in turn, no doubt, send for the police."

"Whatever you say, Mr. Means. But I want it on the record that I warned her many times. She was very headstrong; she didn't listen to many people."

Means nodded, watching Fatty bend over to lift the cloth from Lily's face. "I'll make sure the authorities are made aware of your concerns."

"That's all I'm asking, Mr. Means." William removed his cap from his jacket pocket and pulled it down over his thinning hair. "That's all I'm asking." Satisfied that he was blameless, William quickly walked back to his cottage.

Fatty stood up. "She fell, then? But I don't understand why . . ."

Means waited until William was out of sight. "That's what I thought at first. And that's exactly what I want William to believe. At least for the time being. But if you'll look closely at her neck you can see the bruises."

Fatty slowly lowered his hefty frame again. Means held the lantern closer to the body. "Well, I'll be. You can see the imprints of hands, right there, plain as day."

"The person who did this had to be very strong."

Fatty wheezed as he stood up. "How do you know that?"

"Well, not only did they strangle Lily but they dragged her body all the way out here. How do you suppose they did that? Without being seen?"

"What makes you so sure she didn't come out here on her own? Maybe she just wanted some fresh air."

"Not likely. She'd be getting ready for her party. You know how much she looked forward to these productions of hers. Besides, did you happen to notice she only has on one shoe? And her stockings are worn away only on the heels."

"So? Maybe she didn't have new stockings for the party. And her other shoe probably came off when she was thrown into the water."

"No, if I'm not mistaken, that's it over there."

The two men walked toward the object Means pointed out.

Holding the lantern close to the ground, it was easy to see a black velvet pump half buried in the soft earth.

"Whoever killed Lily had to be strong enough to drag her out here."

"I don't like the way you're looking at me, Means." Fatty was angry. "I thought we were in this together."

"Relax, I didn't mean that to sound like an accusation. I'm just thinking out loud."

"So what do we do now? We have to go back in there."

Means looked toward the mansion. "And we have to convince everyone to trust us enough so they don't leave until we can figure out who killed Lily."

"Why does everyone have to stay for us to do that?" Fatty asked.

Means brushed off his jacket. "Because, Arbuckle, what we both fear the most will happen quicker than you ever imagined. If you thought you had troubles before, wait until you see what they do to you now. Both of us have been put through the grinder, had our reputations ruined. But somehow, we managed to make lives for ourselves again."

"Yeah, things are a helluva lot better than they were a few years ago."

"And I have the new book," Means said. "But this, getting our names connected to a murder? This would bury us alive! There'd be no coming back . . . ever."

Fatty didn't understand what Means had planned; all he knew was he was scared. "Okay," he said, "just tell me what to do." He reached in his pocket and pulled out a large handkerchief to blot the sweat.

"What time is it?" Means asked.

"I don't know." Fatty shrugged.

"But you have a pocket watch. There," Means pointed to the chain hanging from Arbuckle's gray flannel vest.

Arbuckle looked down, embarrassed. "That's just for show. I had to hock the watch years ago."

Means didn't care about his companion's sad financial state. "Well, I imagine we've only been out here for twenty minutes—half an hour at the most. From the sound of things inside, I don't think we've even been missed."

* * *

When Irma saw Arbuckle enter the brightly lit room, she immediately thought of Lon Chaney. The way he'd contorted his face—his whole body—when he played the Hunchback of Notre Dame had given her the willies for days. His eyes bugging out that way. Poor Fatty, she thought. He looked so ill-at-ease that she felt deeply sorry for him. The lights made his skin look waxy. She stopped singing without realizing she had done so. And when she stopped, the band stopped. And when the musicians broke off so abruptly, everyone in the room froze.

It was Zelda Fitzgerald who came to life first. "So," she giggled, apparently drunk, "where is our little Lily? Our precious little flower? Our lovely, lost Lily?" Her laughter embarrassed practically everyone in the room.

Gaston Means walked onto the dance floor. "Gather around," he said. "I have an announcement."

"Oh, a game! We're going to play a game!" Zelda clapped her hands together.

"Hush," someone shouted.

"You wouldn't talk to me like that if Scott were here." She took another gulp of her drink and then retreated into a pout.

"But he's not, so kindly hush up," the same person told her.

Satisfied he had their attention, Means began. "First off, is Miss McKeon here?"

"I certainly am," she said as she walked over to stand beside him.

"Good. What I am about to tell you is very upsetting but I want you all to remain calm and quiet until I've finished."

Judith straightened her back and folded her arms across her chest. "Just tell us, Mr. Means, we're not children."

"Our hostess is . . ."

"Dead! I knew it!" Irma said.

The crowd ignored the singer and continued staring at Means as if she hadn't spoken.

"She's right, I'm afraid. Lily must have fallen. We found her body down in the water."

"How terrible," Judith said.

Disbelief ricocheted around the room, hitting each guest in their gut, then their heart. Shock, then commotion. "Dreadful!" "Unbelievable." "How very awful." "Poor Lily."

Fatty looked at Means, confused.

Means motioned for him to remain quiet. Then turning to Judith, he asked, "Do you have a guest list?"

"In my office. I'll go get it."

Several people asked the butler for their coats. Means hurried over to the servant and told him to stay where he was. "Listen. Please. No one can leave here yet."

"The party's over, as they say, old chum," Bing said, slapping the man on the back.

"The police have to be called," Means said. His words quieted the room.

"Then we should clear out so they can do their work. Write up their reports. Whatever it is they do." Dorothy Parker walked to the bar and sat her empty glass on a coaster.

Judith returned with the list and handed it to Means. He held it over his head. "I have the names of every person in this room and I'm going to check to see if we're all here."

An elderly woman wearing a diamond choker timidly asked, "But what does that matter? Lily had an accident and . . ."

"It wasn't an accident!" Arbuckle shouted from his side of the huge room.

"Is this true?" Judith asked.

"Well, possibly. Maybe. I believe her death was caused by someone other than . . . herself."

Fatty came closer. "He means she was murdered."

"I have to get out of here," W. C. Fields said. "I can't be associated with any of you. Look what happened to ole Fatty there. No, no, this would definitely ruin me. Excuse me, but I must be on my way."

"Sorry, Mr. Fields. That is precisely why you should not leave. We must all stay here and be accounted for. There is strength in numbers. If we all remain calm and vouch for each other, we're safe."

"Then tell me, my good man," Fields asked, looking down at Means with disgust, "why did you tell us Lily succumbed to an accident when in fact she was murdered?"

"I'll tell you why," Fatty said, "because he was a hot shot with the FBI, then a private investigator after he got involved in one too many scandals. Now he's looking to solve a murder—make the headlines and a new name for himself. Think all will be forgiven, Mr. Means? Think you can write a brand new book about the murder of Lillian Armstrong-Smith?"

Means was the confused one now. "No, why would you ask me that? I thought we had an agreement? An understanding of sorts."

"I did too until you lied to me out there, when you showed me Lily's shoe."

"What do you mean?"

"Oh, I know you think I'm just a big, fat, dumb clown. Everyone does. But I'm real good at what I do. I spent years practising falls, tumbling, figuring out where arms and legs land when you chase someone. Hell, I did nothing else for hours at a time with the Keystone Cops. I'm a professional, Mr. Means, and damn good at what I do—did.

"The shoe you showed me was dug deep into the ground. If someone dragged Lily, as you assumed they did, her shoe would have slid off and fallen away—not pushed down into the soil. For the shoe to end up where and how we found it, would have meant one of three things: someone pushed her forward, she walked to that place willingly, or she was running away from her attacker. However, it was you who found the shoe, in the dark. Odd, considering I had been out on the grounds in the yard—on that very spot—earlier and missed it. Imagine! In the light of the full moon, I missed a silver object the size of a shoe, sparkling there—like a spotlight. Therefore, I can only assume you planted it yourself, Mr. Means."

Means fell down into a plush club chair forcing it against the wall. "All right, I admit I put the shoe there, but only after I'd stumbled over it earlier."

"Why would you do such a thing?" Judith asked, stunned.

Embarrassed to look the woman in the eye, he spoke slowly. "I needed to be believed."

"You mean admired," Fatty said. "You thought this was just the opportunity you needed to regain some credibility."

"Is that true?" Bing asked.

"Yes," Means said, still too cowardly to look up. "I worked for the FBI. I had respect, a position close to the president of the United States. The most powerful man in the world."

"And you brought disgrace down upon yourself," Bing

ranted. "You brought disgrace to your office and your country. There is no one to blame for your misfortunes except you, sir."

"I know. Don't you think I know all that?"

"So," Judith said, "let me see if I understand this. You took Mrs. Armstrong-Smith's death as an opportunity to benefit yourself?"

Dorothy Parker sniffed. "Typical man, you'll always land on somebody's feet."

Judith McKeon shook her head. "Poor Mrs. Armstrong-Smith."

"Oh come now, you hated her . . ." Arbuckle's fat hand swiftly clamped over his mouth.

Means's head jerked upward to look at the secretary. "You did?" And then shifting his eyes to Arbuckle he asked, "How would you know something like that? Have you met Miss McKeon before this evening?"

"Well, yes, and . . ." He looked to the woman contritely.

"It's okay, Roscoe, I'm not ashamed of our friendship."

"Friendship? This is all so cozy I can't stand it," Parker quipped.

"Miss McKeon wrote me several letters while I was going through my ah, trouble."

"Fan letters?" Means asked.

"It started out that way," Judith told them. "I was infatuated with . . ."

"A star. It happens all the time," Crosby said. "But the papers, magazines, they were full of stories. All the gory details. Weren't you afraid you were corresponding with a murderer?"

Judith looked at Fatty adoringly. "Oh, no. I could tell

Roscoe would never hurt anyone. He's a gentle, kind, sensitive soul."

"And you could tell all of this from . . . what?" Bing asked. "What ever led you to believe you knew this man so intimately . . . unless . . ."

"No! Don't even think it! Nothing happened between the two of us."

Means studied the guest list he had gotten from Judith. "I notice here that your name is not among those invited, Mr. Arbuckle,"

"And if you look closer, Mr. Means, neither is yours," Judith pointed out.

"I don't understand."

"*I* invited you—both of you. It was easy just to slip in a few extra guests, being responsible for the invitations and all. Mrs. Armstrong-Smith never saw what went out in the mail or what I didn't want her to know came back."

Dorothy Parker finished her martini, held the empty glass up to attract a waitress. "So why the invites?" she asked.

W. C. Fields laughed. "Life is certainly a stage and how we all do strut. Our little lady here set us up. We were all here for her entertainment. Isn't that so, my dear?"

"No. I just wanted to see Roscoe. I knew he'd never consent to meet me otherwise. So I spoke through Mrs. Armstrong-Smith. But it wasn't as if she would have appreciated a man like you," she said to Arbuckle. "Truth is, she always thought you were a killer."

"So knowing what her reaction would be at the very sight of me, you wanted to shock her? Upset her?" Arbuckle's face fell into a soft frown.

"It's terrible," Judith admitted, "I know it's unforgivable but, Lord help me, as much as I wanted to be with you, I wanted to see her uncomfortable more. I wanted to see her frightened."

Cal walked over, Irma trailing behind. "Miss McKeon, should I tell the boys they can pack up and go home? Or do we have to wait around for the police?"

Judith was glad for the interruption. "What do you suggest we do, Mr. Means?"

"Why in Sam Hill are you asking that imbecile?" W. C. Fields wanted to know.

"Because he's the closest thing we have right now to any kind of law."

"Law by association? That's rich." Parker laughed.

"Tell your band to hang around," Means addressed Cal, ignoring Dorothy.

"Sure thing." Cal turned to leave and Judith spotted the necklace around Irma's neck.

"Hold on a minute, you." She grabbed Irma by the arm. "Just where did you get those pearls?"

Means stood up and advanced on the woman, hoping to frighten her into an answer.

"Cal gave them to me. Honest! I ain't no thief, I'm a good girl!"

The bandleader started for the French doors. Means chased after him.

A group of drinkers sitting in lawn chairs laughed as Means shouted for help. It was Novarro who ended up tackling the man.

"Get offa me!" Cal shouted to the actor. Then to Means, "I found them. Honest, Mr. Means. Over there. I swear!

Just go ask that guy." He pointed to the bartender stationed under a green awning.

"Bring him over here," Means told Novarro.

Grabbing the man by the collar of his tuxedo jacket, the actor dragged Cal across the lawn.

The bartender smiled, oblivious to the commotion. His attention had been focused on one of the attractive waitresses. "What'll it be, gentlemen?" he asked when he saw them.

"The gentleman here," Means said pointing to Cal, "claims he found a strand of pearls out here and that you can vouch for his story."

"Name's Howard Pearson, sir, and no, I'm sorry but I never saw any such thing. I'm afraid he's lying to you."

Cal's shoulders went limp. Novarro released his hold but stood close. "Come on, Howard, tell them how I found those damn pearls right over there." Cal pointed to a spot near the cliffwalk. "Ya saw me. I showed ya them. Ya acted like you didn't know where they came from, that ya'd never seen them before."

Howard rubbed his chin, the stubble looked like dirt stuck to his face. "Sorry, Cal."

Before anyone could stop him, Cal lunged across the bar and grabbed the bartender. "I thought we were friends here, Howard. Ya told me if I covered up for you, I could have the pearls for Irma. Ya told me . . ."

"Get him off me," Howard grunted.

Hearing the commotion, Judith McKeon came running, leaving the rest of the party inside, watching the scene as if it were a moving picture. "Howard," she said jerking to a stop. "I didn't know you were here."

"Isn't he one of the bartenders you hired?" Means asked.

"I called the agency and they sent over some people. I've used Howard in the past. There's never been any trouble before. We have a good working relationship."

Howard pushed himself away from the men. "Working relationship? Judith, we both know it was a hell of lot more than that."

Before she could speak, Means addressed the man. "Tell us how you would define your relationship with Miss McKeon."

"I have connections, know what I mean? I'm very popular with the upper crust, especially in these difficult times. Understand what I'm saying here? I can get alcohol—illegal hooch. High quality and lots of it. I've helped her out on more than one occasion."

"That's true," Judith said. "Mrs. Armstrong-Smith is very demanding and when she wants something I either accommodate her or I'm not only out of a job, but as she has threatened many times, never going to find work in this country."

"It's a big world out there, Miss McKeon," Means said, "and I'm sure an intelligent woman such as yourself . . ."

"You don't understand how influential Mrs. Armstrong-Smith is . . . I mean was. And excuse me, Mr. Means, but you of all people should understand how difficult it is to start over with a questionable reputation. It follows you everywhere. I've watched it happen over and over again."

Means nodded. "You're right; I do understand." Turning to Howard he asked, "So you've done some favors for Miss McKeon from time to time, and worked as a bartender at a few parties. That's all there is to it, then?"

"Yes," Judith answered. "That's all."

"And when did you last see the pearls?" he asked her.

"Days ago. In fact, Mrs. Armstrong-Smith was still looking for them earlier this evening."

"Cal, do you want to stick to your story or are we calling the police now? I think we can drum up a burglary charge if not murder."

"Okay, no police. I swiped them—so what? I didn't know they were hers. I didn't know who they belonged to."

"Explain," Novarro said, anxious to hear the man's story.

"I got here earlier this afternoon to check things out—set up. I saw the pearls on the floor in the hall. I picked them up, put them in my pocket, and gave them to Irma. Thought maybe I'd get lucky after we were done tonight."

"And if Irma got caught wearing them, she'd be the one in trouble, right?"

"To be honest, I never thought that far ahead. I had other things on my mind."

Arbuckle joined the group in the middle of Cal's story.

"Let's go back inside," Judith suggested. "It's getting cold out here."

Means stood fixed in thought. "You never saw Mrs. Armstrong-Smith leave the house?" he asked Judith.

"No, I told you, the last I heard she was getting dressed in her room."

"What side of the house is your room on?"

"The opposite side."

"Why? Wouldn't she want you close by?"

"Yeah, you were always telling me what a tyrant she was," Fatty said.

"Precisely, that's why I insisted I be in the other wing. I needed some privacy. I do have a personal life."

"I'll say," Howard laughed.

Everyone turned.

"Shut up, Howard!" Judith snapped.

"Shut up! Go away! Be quiet! I'm sick of your orders, Judy. You can't treat me like that anymore."

Means saw his opportunity and sympathetically asked the man, "Like what Howard? Does she treat you badly? Women can be so . . ."

"She's a bitch! She lies to me; she treats me like a dog."

"But you love her anyway, right?" Means asked.

"Yes, but she loves someone else."

Means turned to Arbuckle. "Did Miss McKeon ever confess her love for you in any of her letters?"

"Well . . ."

"Come on, man, no one can hold you responsible for what another person writes."

"Occasionally she would say something along those lines."

"And you told me you loved me, too," Judith said. "Tell them. Tell everyone now how much you love me and how we're going to be together. Forever! That's what you said . . . forever!"

"And just how did you expect that to happen, girlie, when you was with me?" Howard shouted. "All the time telling me how that bitch boss of yours was the only thing keepin' us from being together and now I find out you was writing this fat man, planning to be with him. But I was the one who got rid of . . ."

"Continue, Mr. Pearson," Means insisted. "You were the one who got rid of who?"

"No one."

"Call the police," Means told Judith.

She didn't move. It took a moment but when she spoke, she erupted. "You, Howard? You killed Mrs. Armstrong-Smith?"

"For you, Judy. For us."

Howard jumped over the bar and started for the cliffwalk. Arbuckle and Novarro were on his heels. The smaller man tripped him and Arbuckle pinned him to the ground.

Judith ran inside for the phone.

"Gaston Bullock Means," he told the reporter. "M . . . e . . . a . . . n . . . s."

"I've heard that name before. Wait a minute. Don't tell me." The pretty young thing was anxious to get all her facts straight.

"I used to work with the president; I was with the FBI." He beamed.

"And now you've solved a murder!" she said.

"I guess I was just born to be of service to my fellow man."

"Well jeepers, Mr. Means, I can't thank you enough for talking to me. None of the other people at Mrs. Armstrong-Smith's party will give me the time of day."

"Don't mention it, my dear. Don't mention it."

# East Side, West Side

Max Allan Collins and Matthew V. Clemens

Max Allan Collins, an MWA Edgar nominee in both fiction and nonfiction categories, has earned fourteen PWA Shamus nominations for his historical thrillers, winning twice. His graphic novel *Road to Perdition* is the basis of the Tom Hanks film; prose sequels, *Road to Purgatory* and *Road to Paradise,* have followed. His many comic book credits include *Dick Tracy, Ms. Tree, Batman,* and *CSI: Crime Scene Investigation,* based on the hit TV series for which he has also written a best-selling series of novels. An independent filmmaker in his native Iowa, his latest indie feature, *Shades of Noir* (2004), is an anthology of short films. He and his writer wife Barbara frequently collaborate, sometimes under the name Barbara Allan.

Matthew V. Clemens has, along with Max Allan Collins, co-authored numerous short stories that appear in anthologies like

*Murder Most Confederate,* the *Hot Blood* series, the *Flesh & Blood* series, and *Buffy the Vampire Slayer.* Clemens is also the co-plotter and researcher for Collins on a series of books based on the television series *CSI: Crime Scene Investigation, CSI: Miami,* and *Dark Angel.* Collins and Clemens have also written comic books, graphic novels, a computer game, and jigsaw puzzles all based on the successful *CSI* franchise.

**The tuxedo fit well, but** Mickey Ashford still felt like he'd strapped himself into a straitjacket. A slender man, rather like a taller, unmustached William Powell, Ashford would have preferred something more casual. Dinner at Twenty-One meant dressing to the nines, but at least he'd have the soft muted sounds of a jazz combo in the background and could savor a martini while he suffocated inside this penguin suit. Though two and a half years had passed since the repeal of the Volstead Act, Mickey still felt the urge to genuflect every time a martini glass touched his lips.

Across the table, her own drink still untouched, MaryAnne Wallace, his fiancée of seven months—blond, twenty-nine, her slender yet buxom figure sheathed in a glittery white evening gown—managed to maintain an almost schoolgirl giddiness that made Mickey grin.

"I can't believe that this time tomorrow night," she said, sotto voce, "we'll finally be married," as if speaking the words too loudly might jinx their wedding. Half of his native Chicago, and half of her native Iowa, and many of their mutual East Coast show business friends, were even now converging on Manhattan by train, bus, auto, and even air, for fancy doings in a Waldorf-Astoria ballroom.

"And the day after that," MaryAnne was saying, "we'll be honeymooning aboard the *Queen Mary,* on our way to England."

The quiet conversations of the other well-dressed diners fluttered around them like cooing birds, but Mickey heard MaryAnne just fine. "What was that about 'finally' married?"

Her rouged lips paused in a brief kiss before they split into a wide smile. "I've wanted to be Mrs. Michael Ashford since the moment we met."

Mickey beamed at her. No matter how long they were together, no matter how many times he gazed at her, her beauty stole his breath away. Nor was he the only man to react in such a manner. Having seen perhaps one too many Ruby Keeler talkies, MaryAnne had left her parents' farm five years ago to find fame and fortune on the Great White Way, and though she hadn't yet landed a starring role, several producers had noticed her heart-shaped face, deep jade eyes, elegant nose, and full, ruby-rouged lips—not to mention her trim, well-rounded figure—and she'd already made a name for herself in secondary ingenue roles.

"You wanted to marry me how long?" he asked.

"Since the moment we met."

He stuck out his fine Irish chin and flashed what he'd been told were piercing blue eyes, hoping she'd ignore his thrice broken nose. "Is it my dashing good looks?"

Her smile revealed straight white teeth, worthy of a tooth powder advert. MaryAnne shook her head, dark blond hair shimmering; she wore it longer than was fashionable, almost brushing her bare shoulders.

"It must have been my piano playing." Mickey had

worked his way through college playing with jazz combos, and had even made a few recordings with the Staccato Seven. The night they'd met, in a Rush Street joint, he'd been sitting in, for old times' sake.

"Well, you are a wonderful piano player, but . . . no. I make it a point to stay away from show business romances."

"So that worked against me, if anything."

"That's right."

"It *was* my dashing good looks, then."

"No, silly . . ." She arched an eyebrow. "Don't you know it's your money I'm after?"

"You didn't know I had money when we first met," Mickey said, and took a drag from his cigarette and pretended to pout a little, even as the giggle erupted across the table.

Patting his hand as it hovered over the edge of the ashtray, she said, "You really are quite a good detective, aren't you, dear?"

Mickey Ashford was indeed a "good" detective; more to the point, he was a successful businessman. The Ashford Detective Agency had grown from a one-man operation nine years ago into a fifty-operative affair headquartered in Chicago's Rookery. Pinkerton and Margraves—his major competitors—had even been sniffing around, about wanting to buy Mickey out. So far he'd resisted their advances, but the amounts of money they discussed had definitely gotten his attention. He wondered if thirty-eight was too young to retire.

Knocking back the rest of his drink, Mickey glanced at the Rob Roy at MaryAnne's elbow. "Care for another, darling?"

"Before dinner?" she asked, mock shocked. "Are you trying to get me tight, Mr. Ashford? Can't you wait one more night?"

"Now look who's playing detective."

She smiled again, this time keeping her teeth to herself, a self-satisfied, wicked cat-that-ate-the-canary smirk.

"I can't believe that after you've known me this long," he said as he discreetly signaled the waiter to bring another round, "you have so little trust."

"That's precisely why I don't trust you. I've known you long enough to learn how you think."

The waiter brought their drinks, and MaryAnne managed to ignore both of hers as Mickey gulped most of his martini, the old glass not yet removed from the table. Before the waiter could exit, Mickey signaled for one more martini.

"You better watch that," MaryAnne said, "or you won't be any good to me later."

With some effort, he lifted an eyebrow. "Later?"

"In your room, of course."

"You're coming to my room?"

"If you're a good boy and don't drink yourself silly, I just might."

It was his turn to smirk. "Any other reason?"

"To make sure you're not trying to sow any wild oats before you march down the aisle. I've seen you turning your private eye on my maid of honor."

"Some maid of honor." Mickey affected a pained expression. "At least she won't be trying to get away with wearing a white dress."

She laughed, once. "Oh, so we're going to hit below the belt now, are we?"

"With any luck."

The teasing was a game they'd been playing for some time now. But the intimacy to which they both referred was recent. When they met, they'd both been around the block and back again; neither had been anxious to repeat past mistakes. They had decided not to fall into bed with each other, even though they both longed to do just that. Instead they took it slow, got to know each other, becoming friends before lovers—and they had stuck to their vow.

At least they had until that night a month ago in Mickey's Chicago apartment . . .

After dinner and a movie at the Biograph, the pair had retired to his flat for a nightcap before he escorted MaryAnne home. Mickey's place occupied half of the top floor of a six-story building at the corner of Addison and North Broadway, with a spectacular view of Lake Michigan and scads of art moderne furnishings and knickknacks that Mickey never seemed to remember exactly how he had acquired. Behind the sofa, one tall silver lamp kept the room from being enveloped in darkness.

Two drinks into their nightcap, the couple found themselves on the couch in a clinch. His lips pressed hard against hers, his hands roaming over her evening gown, her arms wrapping around his neck, her fingers gliding through his thick hair, as they rubbed against each other, their need growing.

Pulling away, her voice husky in the moment, she said, "We should slow down . . ."

His answer was to pull her closer and kiss her neck, his lips sliding down to her exposed shoulder.

Again she eased away from him, this time putting her

hands against his shoulders, holding him off as she spoke. "Mickey, Mickey, we've got to stop."

He pulled back from her, brushed his hair back with a hand. "Do you really want to?"

MaryAnne's head drooped. "No, of course not . . . but we promised ourselves."

"That was before we knew how we really felt—before we decided to get married."

"I know," she said, her voice tiny now.

"Are you planning to have second thoughts about us?"

"No—certainly not!"

"Then why"—he nuzzled the nape of her neck—"why should we have any second thoughts now . . ."

Mickey kissed her mouth, gently, then, as she yielded, more urgently. She returned the kiss and didn't fight when he eased the spaghetti straps of her gown over her ivory shoulders.

"My God," he whispered as he exposed her creamy breasts, nipples pink and perked, "you are so lovely."

MaryAnne pulled his face to her, but he needed no coaxing as he buried his face in her breasts, sucking first one hard nipple, then the other. She moaned and pulled gently at his hair as his tongue worked against the tiny bud.

Clothes went flying as they gave in to each other. Though she was nude in a matter of seconds, Mickey had more hoops to jump through to join her, and she tried to assist him.

"My Lord, you've got more layers than an onion," she said, a wicked smile playing at the corner of her mouth.

"Just pull the damn socks off, will you?"

One at a time, laughing as she jerked on the toes of his black silk stockings, she got him free and they collapsed onto the couch in each other's arms.

She smiled at him, held his face in her hands. "Maybe you're right—it is time."

"If we've come this far," he said, "it had better be."

Mickey eased her onto her back and slid to the floor as he kissed her breasts, stomach, thighs, MaryAnne moaning with pleasure as he filled her. The couple moved slowly at first, adjusting to each other as their passion swept them away. Mickey groaned as MaryAnne's nails dug into his back; soon she let out a long, low gasp of pleasure as they each reached their climax—

Mickey, lost in his reverie in the midst of the busy nitery, snapped out of it when MaryAnne reached across the table and took his hand.

"Are you all right? You looked like you left me there for a moment."

He grinned sheepishly. "Sorry, dear. I assure you, I was with you . . . just remembering that night in Chicago."

She arched an eyebrow. "Which night would that be?"

Frowning at her fondly, he said, "I think you know what night."

"Aah, the night I seduced you."

"The night you seduced me?" he asked, surprise in his voice. "Don't you mean the night you finally succumbed to my charm?"

The waiter interrupted their repartee by bringing dinner. As they began to eat, MaryAnne looked into Mickey's eyes and said, "It's a good thing they brought you food, dear. I think you must be a little tipsy."

"Me tipsy? I never get tipsy—roaring drunk, possibly. Never tipsy."

"Roaring drunk, then—which you'd have to be, if you think the likes of you could seduce me. Your memory, were it not pickled at this very moment, would be of me seducing you."

"Of course you're right, my dear. Can you possibly forgive me?" He held up his martini glass in toast to her.

"Now you're patronizing me."

"Oh, am I?"

She waggled her fork at him, a scolding schoolmarm, if an enticing one. "Finish your dinner, Mickey Ashford. I'm going to take you back to the hotel and show you exactly what happened in Chicago."

His eyes met hers, saw the intent, and he raised his hand for the waiter. "Check, please."

Twenty minutes later, they found themselves on a couch even nicer than the one in Mickey's apartment. The Waldorf-Astoria prided itself on its appointments, and management probably wouldn't have approved of what the sofa in room 1725 was being used for at this particular moment.

MaryAnne was astride him, full breasts swaying, as she rode him harder and faster, her beautiful face drunk not with alcohol but abandon. With each passing second their passion grew until they exploded together, and this time he cried out, in wonderful agony, then together they slumped in a heap on the sofa,

"Okay, okay," he managed between long gasps, "you seduced me. You were right. I was wrong."

"And don't you forget it," she said, tousling his hair, then bending in to kiss his cheek.

"Still . . . and I hate to be a, uh stickler . . ."

"Do you, now?"

"But this was not precisely the way things went the first time."

"Are you saying I . . . we . . . need to try again?"

An eyebrow raised.

She slapped playfully at his chest. "Michael Ashford, you are incorrigible. Shouldn't we leave something for our honeymoon?"

"Is there something else?"

Pulling away, dodging the question, she said, "I have to go make sure Mae has checked into her room, and besides, it's supposed to be bad luck for you to see me before the wedding."

"Too late," he said, tapping her on her dimpled backside as she bent to pick up her clothes.

"If you'll look at the clock instead of me, you'd see it's still not quite midnight. Not the day of our wedding, at all."

"Have it your way. Call the desk, and then I'll walk you to your room."

Ten minutes later they were both dressed and MaryAnne was hanging up the telephone, her expression confused.

Mickey asked, "What's the matter?"

"It's Mae," MaryAnne said referring to her maid of honor, singer/actress Mae West. "She's checked in, but she's not answering her telephone."

Shrugging, Mickey asked, "So? You know Mae. Christ, she could be sleeping or bombed, or out on the town for all we know."

MaryAnne's forehead tightened. "It's not like her to not

let me know. She's well aware we'd want to know she arrived safely. I thought she'd at least leave a note."

"You want me to do something, don't you?"

MaryAnne brightened. "Would you?"

He shook his head, laughed a little. "Okay, I'll go to her room and knock on the door. You call the desk back and see if they have any messages for us. Now, what's her room number?"

She told him, and Mickey slipped his shoes on and headed down the hall to the elevators. The hotel was quiet at this hour, and Mickey had the lift to himself as he rode up to the twenty-sixth floor where Mae's suite was located. Wandering down the hall, he couldn't tell if he smelled a hint of Mae's perfume or if that was just wishful thinking on his part.

He wouldn't have traded MaryAnne for Mae West, of course, nor would he betray his sweetheart, his bride-to-be . . . but he was human, and the petite yet voluptuous singer was one of the most sexually charged women he'd ever met. She radiated sex—and trouble. After all, she'd been the girlfriend of top gangster Owney Madden, at least till New York's answer to Capone recently got sent up.

Stopping in front of her door, Mickey tilted his head and listened. He noticed no light under the door, and he knocked three times before giving up. The singer didn't seem to be in her room, and Mickey had no idea where to look for her. The clock had edged past midnight when he returned to his room.

MaryAnne practically jerked the door out of his hand, the key he had just twisted in the lock slipping through his fingers.

"Any sign of her?"

He shook his head.

"I'm getting worried, Mickey. She should have been here by now."

"I take it there were no messages?"

"No."

"I'll walk you back to your room, then I'll go down and talk to the desk clerk myself."

"I should stay here. At least until you get back."

"I thought it was bad luck for me to see you on our wedding day."

She gave him a wan smile. "It already is our wedding day."

After pulling on his suit coat and tie and giving his hair a quick whip with his comb, Mickey led MaryAnne to her room across the hall.

"Maybe I should go down with you."

He took her in his arms and felt her tremble against him. "You really are worried, aren't you?"

MaryAnne nodded. "I'm afraid something's wrong. You've done security for her before."

That brought a smile to his face. Though he'd asked MaryAnne to marry him seven months ago, they had actually met when Mickey had been hired by Owney Madden to keep an eye on his girlfriend, appearing in Chicago at Colosimo's; MaryAnne had been in Mae's chorus, having met the star working on the film *Belle of the Nineties*—she'd been working as a bit player on that shoot, and she and Miss West had become good pals.

Madden, who owned the famed Cotton Club, had been worried that his enemies might hurt Mae to get at him. He was about to go up the river for a spell, and he hadn't trusted his own men to protect her, so in came Mickey.

"Stay in your room. I'll talk to the desk clerk and be right back."

MaryAnne shook her head, but handed over the key and Mickey unlocked her door.

"You promise to come right, back?"

He nodded. "Ten minutes, tops."

She said, "Okay," but he never heard. He'd already shut the door.

The lobby, as Mickey had expected, was vacant. He strode through the palatial hallways, passed the paintings on the wall in their ornate frames, and heard his heels clacking like gunfire as he crossed the mosaic in the lobby floor. Ceiling fans whirred like airplane propellers, doing a decent job of cooling. He wished he'd worn the rubber-soled shoes that he wore while working—literal gum shoes. Though he saw no one behind the desk, his echoing footfalls must have roused someone because a tall, thin man appeared there before Mickey could touch the bell.

"May I help you, sir?" the desk clerk asked, although his voice was so condescending the question sounded like an insult. His hair was slicked back, parted in the middle. He wore a natty black suit, white shirt, and maroon tie with a maroon kerchief showing just enough out of the breast pocket. Mickey could tell the fellow was an officious ass, and he doubted this would be much help.

"Yes. My name is Michael Ashford. I'm trying to locate one of your guests."

The clerk's nod was both bland and blank.

Mickey said, "Mae West—the actress? She's in twenty-six nineteen."

"Yes, sir. The house phone is just around the corner to your left."

"She's not answering the telephone or her door."

"Perhaps, sir, she would prefer not to be disturbed."

"A possibility, I grant you," Mickey said, trying to control his growing frustration. "But not likely since she is scheduled to be the maid of honor in a wedding tomorrow. Mine. I think Miss West might want to speak with the bride-to-be before the event, however, so I doubt she's barricaded herself in her room."

Somehow the desk clerk's expression managed to turn even mote vacant. Mickey pulled out his wallet and eased out a five.

The desk clerk said nothing.

A second five joined the first, and yet the man said nothing.

When the third Abe Lincoln joined his pals, a small smile nudged at the corner of the desk clerk's slack mouth.

"Perhaps," the clerk said, watching the bills creep out of the wallet and then across the marble counter, "I might have glimpsed the guest in question leaving the hotel shortly after nine thirty."

"Perhaps isn't worth paying for, buddy." Mickey said, the bills still tucked under his palm.

"Ah—I did indeed glimpse the guest in question."

Mickey raised his hand, and the bills disappeared. So much of sleuthing was the judicious application of bribery.

The detective asked, "Which entrance?"

The clerk said nothing, but his eyes flicked toward the Park Avenue side.

Out on the sidewalk, beyond the reach of the fans, the heat remained oppressive, even in the middle of the night. A doorman in red livery, his collar button unbuttoned, stopped fanning himself with his cap, put it back on, and stepped forward. He was around sixty, potbellied, and sweating rivulets. "Get you a cab, sir?"

"Not just yet. Were you on duty when Mae West left the hotel?"

The man nodded. "You a cop?"

"Private."

The doorman nodded again, took off his hat, and resumed fanning himself, turning away. Mickey's admission of non-official capacity meant the doorman didn't have to bother with him.

Back to bribery. Mickey held up a five spot. "You know which cab she got in?"

The doorman's hand snatched it out of the air like a frog's tongue clipping a fly. "Yeah, that'd be Bernie. Second cab in line over there—he just got back."

"Thanks, buddy," Mickey said.

"Thank you, sir . . . but we're gonna have to have a little something for the first guy. He's been sittin' here for over an hour waitin' for a fare. If you take the other one . . . well, you get the picture."

Nodding, Mickey wondered if the whole damn town was on the pad; he longed for Chicago, where a cop gave you change on your five spot. He had taken two steps toward the cab when MaryAnne swept up and entwined her hand in his elbow. She looked lovely in that sleeveless white dress with the red polka dots and the little red waistcoat that accompanied it at night.

"What are you doing here?" he asked.

She gave him the movie-star smile. "I tipped the desk clerk five dollars to tell me where you'd gone."

Mickey rolled his eyes.

She batted hers. “Was that too much?”

“No, but that bastard may he able to afford the cabin next to us on the *Queen Mary* by now. I may have a line on Mae, and I need to follow it.”

She shrugged. “Fine—let’s go.”

“Let’s go?” His hands went to his hips. “You think you’re going with me?”

Her hands went to hers. “You think you’re leaving here without me?”

He turned away from her. “I’ll telephone as soon as I know something.”

“You won’t have to,” she said, latching on to his elbow again. “I’ll he right there next to you.”

“MaryAnne—”

“Mickey, did you ever imagine you were marrying a stay-at-home girl?”

He was still searching for a comeback when she said, “Good. Now tell me where we’re going.”

“To talk to Bernie,” he said numbly.

“Who’s Bernie?”

“Drives that cab over there.” He pointed toward one of the two Checker cabs at the curb.

Mickey held the door while MaryAnne climbed in the back and slid across the seat. He got in next to her.

“Where to?” Bernie asked. He was in his forties, blond, very pale, sweat pouring down his face, half a cigarette dangling from narrow lips.

Mickey asked, “You know who Mae West is?”

“Yeah.” Bernie grunted. “I also know who Donald Duck is, and also Gary Cooper.”

"Well, did you drive any of 'em, earlier?"

"I'm not sure."

Mickey pitched two bucks over the seat.

"Well, the duck and the cowboy I ain't seen tonight. But the dame with the shape, yeah, I took her downtown."

"Can you take us to the same place?"

The driver tripped the meter. "A man with money can go anywheres he wants to in this country."

Very little traffic moved through the city, and it wasn't very long before the taxi pulled up to the corner of Twenty-first and Lexington.

"Gramercy Park Hotel," Bernie said, nodding toward it. "Left her off there couple of hours ago."

As they pulled around the corner to the front of the hotel, Mickey saw a black car parked across the street, two big guys in rumpled suits sitting in it trying to look inconspicuous. He caught them eyeballing the cab as it rolled by.

"Around the corner," Mickey said. "Out of sight of that car."

The cabby didn't gun it. He just kept the same easy speed as they cruised past the black sedan, the front door of the hotel, then turned the corner.

Mickey passed the guy another two bucks as he and MaryAnne exited the cab. New York wasn't a city; it was a damn casino, and the people were walking slot machines. The couple crossed both streets so they were on the same side as the black sedan, coming up behind it arm in arm, just two lovers out for a late-night stroll.

"This hotel is where Bogart got married back in '26," Mickey explained as they neared the car.

"Oh, really," MaryAnne said, her voice high, light. In a hoarse whisper she added, "What the hell are you doing?"

"Making it up as I go," he whispered back. "That's how detectives do it."

Then they stepped off the curb, as if about to pass behind the sedan. Mickey tugged lightly on MaryAnne's elbow, indicating for her to stay put while he moved to the driver's side window. The driver slouched, his hat pulled down over his eyes, and Mickey couldn't tell anything about the guy except he had at least one cauliflower ear and had to be pretty big—even slouching the guy stuck up over the back of the seat. The passenger seemed only fractionally less imposing as he, too, tried to shrink farther into the seat.

Pulling a cigarette from his silver case, palming his cylindrical lighter, Mickey said, "Plenty hot tonight, huh, pal?"

"Buzz off, buster. I ain't in no mood to talk."

Mickey leaned closer, the cigarette now in his mouth. "C'mon, pal, I just need a light. You've got a light, haven't you?"

"Ya ain't very bright, are ya? I told ya to buzz off."

Mickey, moving quickly, jammed the round bottom of the lighter into the back of the guy's neck.

Feeling the cold metal and taking it for a gun barrel, the driver tensed but didn't move.

His partner did move, though, and fast. He threw open the passenger door and came barreling out. An icicle of fear cut through Mickey's gut as he looked over the car roof to see that MaryAnne had moved directly into the man's path. The guy had jerked a revolver out of his jacket and now had it leveled at MaryAnne.

To Mickey's surprise, MaryAnne pulled her skirt up over her thighs, revealing her long, glorious legs. The guy's eyes moved down to check MaryAnne's gams. As the clown gaped at her, she took a step forward to knee the guy in the nuts, but he stepped back, his gun still leveled at her, his eyes snapping up to meet hers.

She shook her head slowly, letting her skirt lower. "Well, it worked for Claudette Colbert . . ."

The driver used the diversion to slam the car door into Mickey, driving him backward and knocking the lighter out of his hand as the wheelman came piling out of the car and into the detective.

The passenger grinned at MaryAnne, who look one quick step and smashed her spiked heel down on the man's toes. As he yelped in pain, she finally delivered her knee to his groin, dropping him to the sidewalk in a moaning heap.

Grabbing the guy's gun, MaryAnne stepped around the car to find the driver sitting on top of her fiancé, about to drive a ham-size fist into Mickey's face. Pressing the revolver into the man's back, she said, "Please don't hit him—I'm marrying him later today, and I want to keep him adorable."

As the driver's head spun around, MaryAnne stepped back and let him see this was no fake, no cigarette lighter, but a real pistol. The man rose, his eyes on MaryAnne's gun. Mickey scrambled to his feet and tapped the driver on the shoulder. When the man turned to face him, Mickey hit him with a solid right cross, knocking the guy cold.

They went around to the other side of the car, where the passenger finally seemed to be catching his breath. When he saw MaryAnne coming toward him with the pistol, he cringed and held up his hands palms out. "Keep her away from me, mister. She's nuts."

"That's right," MaryAnne replied pleasantly. "Nutty as a Baby Ruth bar—and don't you forget it."

Mickey squatted next to the man. "Who are you boys?"

The guy shook his head and MaryAnne took a half step forward.

"Okay, okay! We work for Paramount."

Mickey frowned. "The movie studio?"

The guy nodded slowly. "Security."

"For Mae West?"

Confusion spread like a rash over the man's pockmarked puss. "Mae West? No. We're supposed to make sure no one bothers Mr. Raft."

Mickey and MaryAnne traded a look.

Motioning toward the street, Mickey said, "You better help your buddy back into the car."

As he started to rise, the guy asked, "What about my gat?"

MaryAnne shook her head. "You don't appreciate my legs, you don't deserve a . . . a gat."

A fiver got the room number from the bellboy and, with MaryAnne in tow, Mickey rode the elevator up to the seventh floor, using the time to add up all the money they'd spent on this little errand already. The total did not make him happy. They went down the hall, and he found the correct room about halfway down. Still thinking abut the money, he pounded on the door. He succeeded in getting two other occupants of the floor to open their doors, but the door he'd knocked on remained closed, and behind it he could hear no sound. Either Raft slept sounder than the dead or he wasn't in there.

“Maybe they’re . . . uh . . . busy,” MaryAnne offered.

Mickey shook his head. “If they’re that quiet, they’re not doing it right,” he said, giving her a wicked little smile.

“Well, if they’re not in there and the goons are still outside,” she said, her pretty features screwing up in confusion, “just where the hell are they?”

He considered that for a moment, before snapping his fingers and taking off back toward the elevator, MaryAnne now hustling along in his wake.

“Where are we going?” she panted as she finally caught up with him just as he pushed the button to call the lift back.

“The roof,” Mickey said, as if that explained everything.

Before she could ask him anything else, the door opened and the little white-haired elevator operator smiled at them. “What floor?” he asked.

“The roof,” Mickey said again as they entered, and the little man closed the big door.

“The roof it is. You two going up for a nice romantic dance?”

“That and a cocktail or two.”

“Ah, youth . . .”

Suddenly, MaryAnne understood why Mickey was taking them upstairs. The elevator opened into a glass-enclosed room that resembled—and felt like—a hothouse where all the plants had been replaced by men and women. The gents all wore tuxedos, though most of them looked like they would have preferred something much cooler. The ladies more closely resembled the colors one expected to find in a garden, long dresses like blossoms of red, blue, green, white, and assorted pastels. At one end of the, glass room, an orchestra played a Duke Ellington piece, not badly. Looking over the crowd, Mickey tried to spot Raft and Mae West; if they were up here, they were swallowed in the throng that probably numbered nearly two hundred despite the heat of the night.

"Let's split up," MaryAnne suggested. "We'll have better luck that way."

Before he could argue, she pointed toward the bandstand and took off in the opposite direction. He moved to his left, the lights of the Chrysler Building twenty blocks to the north plainly visible through the glass ceiling of the room, a spectacular view—but Mickey wondered how they kept snow from destroying the ceiling in the winter. The thought of winter did little to stave off the heat, however, so he kept moving, eyes on the crowd as he searched for two stars not in the heavens.

As he edged closer to the orchestra, he realized that this was Ronnie Staccato's big band, an expansion of the combo he'd appeared with in Chicago. As Staccato segued into another Ellington piece, the crowd barely had time to applaud before they were dancing again. Mickey was almost to the bandstand when he caught Ronnie's eye. Short, thin, his blond hair combed straight back, Staccato was the blue-eyed singer of the orchestra as well as its leader, and the one that drove the women wild.

The bandleader winked at Mickey and signaled toward the stage. Mickey tried to shake his head, but it was already too late. Staccato's baton slowed the tempo of the band, and he stepped forward to the microphone.

"Ladies and gentlemen, you're in for a rare treat. We have a special guest in the audience tonight, all the way from Chicago, our former keyboard man—who traded in the ivories for a magnifying glass and roscoe—Mis-ter . . . Mickey Ashford."

The crowd applauded automatically, and as Staccato held his hand out toward Mickey, there was nothing to do but climb the bandstand and take a bow. He did, falling in next to the blond bandleader, the spotlights at the back of the room blinding him, making it impossible for Mickey to see Raft, Mae West, MaryAnne, or for that matter the Statue of Liberty, had it been beyond the first few feet in front of the stage.

He waved, took a step toward the stairs, then Staccato leaned into the mike again. "Folks, wouldn't you like to hear Mickey noodle a tune?"

The applause grew even louder, and Mickey realized that he had no alternative. He hoped that while he was playing, MaryAnne was searching for her missing maid of honor. Acknowledging the applause, Mickey moved to the piano and sat down.

"Cole Porter?" Staccato asked.

Thinking about his current investigation, Mickey nodded. "Make it 'Anything Goes.' "

Staccato counted it off, and then they were going, the two men doing a duel on the vocal while the band followed along. When the vocal chorus ended, Mickey did a nice long easy ride, giving these Manhattanites a taste of some jazz, Chicago style.

Lost in the music for a while, Mickey just played and played; then when he'd given it back to the band for their more straightforward dance-band rendering, he gazed out at the crowd. Seated there, Mickey could see the audience only slightly better than before; and he didn't see Raft or Mae West. As the song wound down, he finally spotted MaryAnne, and she pointed toward the elevator doors. He could just see them closing in the distance and thought he caught a glimpse of a silver dress, but that was all.

As the song ended, he rose, but the applause of the audience kept him on the bandstand for "Night and Day," before he finally got off the stage and he and MaryAnne were able to snag the elevator to hot foot it back to Raft's room.

"Guess you haven't lost your touch," MaryAnne said.

"As you'll see tomorrow night . . ."

He knocked on the hotel room door and waited until it cracked open.

"Ashford!" The small, Valentino-handsome dancer was in a wine-colored silk robe, his dark, slicked-back hair immaculate; his expression was uncharacteristically alarmed, for so cool a customer. "What the hell are you doing here? I thought you were still playing with the band upstairs."

"So, you did see me."

"How did you get my room number?"

"You can buy anything from the desk clerks in this town. The fun part was getting past those studio goons."

"How did you even know I was here?"

"I'm a detective, remember?"

Mickey had met Raft while the latter was working for Owney Madden. The actor and the gangster were best friends; in fact, anybody who knew them both could tell that Raft's underworld personality on screen was a dead copy of Madden's style.

Anger flared in Raft's eyes. "What do you want at this hour?"

"I need to talk to Mae."

"Mae who?"

"George, not all dicks are thick. . . . With Owney your best friend and all, makes you look kind of bad, doesn't it?"

After a short tense silence, Raft said, "Mae and Owney, they broke up."

"Yeah, he went to prison. That tends to slow romance. Boy-girl kind, anyway."

Raft's mouth flickered in his version of a grimace. A hand dipped into the pocket of the robe and emerged with a small automatic in it. "Look, Ashford, I'm not gonna be shaken down by the likes of you."

Despite the weapon, Mickey did not back up. "This isn't a shakedown, George—I just wanna talk to Mae a minute."

"She ain't here, I tell ya."

"Fine. I'm going down to the lobby. If it comes to you, in a trance or something, how to get ahold of Mae . . . have her call me on the house phone in five minutes."

And approximately five minutes later, in the lobby, the detective answered the phone and the unmistakable voice came on the line: "Mickey, why don't you come up and see me?"

"I tried, sweetheart, but that dance partner of yours wouldn't let me in."

"You makin' a comeback? Tinklin' the ivories again, like that?"

"Not hardly."

"You're not working for Owney, are you, sweetheart?"

"No! Is that what Raft thinks? Here—"

Mickey handed the phone to MaryAnne. The two women seemed to talk forever. Long enough for Mickey to find a paper cup of coffee and go outside to enjoy the sunrise. Finally, MaryAnne joined him on the sidewalk.

"You look tired."

He nodded. "Feel tired."

"Too tired to get married?"

"Nope. Ready, to do it right now."

"It'll wait for the Waldorf. I'll make an honest man out of you yet." She hugged his arm. "This is the beginning of more than just a mere marriage, you know."

"Yeah?"

"We've solved our first mystery together."

"Darling, George Raft shacking up with Mae West is no mystery. It may be a crime, but—"

Then he was hailing a cab, and soon they were both getting in the back, to bicker over where they should have breakfast, and whether it should be food or something else—that sweet, loving bickering that is music to the ears.

# The Promotion

Larry D. Sweazy

Larry D. Sweazy's short stories have appeared in the *Texas Rangers* (Berkley Publishing Group) anthology—for which he won the 2005 Spur award for best short fiction—*Hardboiled, Kracked Mirror Mysteries,* and other small press magazines. His poetry has appeared in *The Red River Review, The Raintown Review, The Tipton Poetry Journal,* and other literary reviews. Larry is also a freelance indexer with over 375 back-of-the-book indexes to his credit. He lives in Indiana with his wife, Rose, and his dog, Brodi, a Rhodesian ridgeback.

**There was the usual stir** at night as Darly carefully slid out of bed. Her steps were light, intentional, and Samuel "Red" Wolfe knew the path his wife of twenty-two years would take. She would ease along the bed and down the hall under the control of a nightmare that would not, could not, go away, to their son's empty room. He would find her at first light, balled up on the floor next to the bed, a shirt or a blanket wrapped tight in her fist.

Red tossed and turned after his wife left their bed, but sleep came more easily for him, even in the days following Jason's death. Holding onto Darly and what remained of their life took all of the energy he had left. And now they were moving back to Lubbock from San Antonio, leaving the house Jason grew up in. Darly had protested at first, but in the end, even she could not deny Red the opportunity to become the Texas Rangers' Assistant Commander of Company C.

"Life goes on," she had said, and then did not speak a word to anyone for a week.

Red awoke a few hours later in bed alone. The house was a maze of cardboard boxes, with the exception of Jason's room. Darly was lying on the bed this time, staring at the ceiling. The room remained just as it was the day Jason died. A shrine to a ten-year-old boy who dreamed of playing football for Texas Tech and becoming a Texas Ranger just like his father had. The walls were red-and-white-striped, a poster of the Masked Rider wearing black riding clothes, mask, bolero hat, and red cape, mounted on a black quarter horse, leading the football team on to the field, hung over the bed. The school fight song, the paper yellowed, hung sideways on a peg just above a row of Pop Warner football trophies on the dresser. Jason had the makings of a great quarterback. Everybody said he was the next gift to Tech from the Wolfe family.

"Hey, baby," Red said. "I have to meet with the moving company and tie up some loose ends at the office. Can you do a few things for me?"

Darly, Darlene to her parents and the church, did not acknowledge Red. There was no sign of the former college cheerleader he once knew and worshiped; she was nothing but a withering yellow rose, her blond hair dull and unkempt, and her blue eyes lifeless as a stagnant pond.

"We can't leave him, Red. I won't."

He had tried arguing, even pleading, to get past her grief, but time was running out. "I'll call Betty. She might be your sister, but she's getting darned tired of helping out. She's done her fair share, Darly."

Darly exhaled, looked over at him and said, "He's alone, Red. All alone. I'm his mother, what am I supposed to do?"

After leaving the movers, Red drove to the headquarters of Company D in San Antonio. In the fields beyond the highway, Indian paintbrush, prairie phlox, with a few bluebonnets and scarlet pimpernels mixed in, were in full bloom. South Texas was unusually colorful and fragrant this year, but Red had barely noticed it was spring.

He had the window down, the radio turned down low. A muffled Guy Clark song droned on about too much to drink and lost love. Two files sat underneath his Stetson. The contract from the movers, and the other, tattered and worn, held all of his notes from the Hardy case.

It was the one case that haunted him, a case Red Wolfe had sworn to solve before he left San Antonio.

Jason was a little over four years old and Red had been at Company D for about a year when he caught the case. Life was good then. Everything was bright and hopeful. Now, it looked like he had failed; even though he was almost certain he knew who the killer was, there was just not enough evidence to bring the case to trial.

Red dug into the glove box and pulled out a pack of Marlboros. He lit a cigarette, chastising himself, but resigned to the fact that his health no longer mattered like it used to. After a couple of long drags, he played the Hardy case over and over in his head, like he'd done a million times before.

*The first thing Red saw was a pool of dried blood in the road, an unusual oil spot that shimmered in the reflection of the setting sun.*

*July in Government Canyon was as beautiful as it was miserable. The temperature had peaked at over one hundred degrees for the last seventeen days, but the Edwards Aquifer, the lone source of San Antonio's drinking water, kept the area lush. Oak-juniper-mesquite woodlands peppered the hill country, and it was not unusual to see a feral hog, or hear a bobcat scream at night.*

*Spanish moss dripped from oak trees just beyond the road that led to the back entrance of the park boundaries that encased most of the canyon, casting a mosaic of shadows on the blood. Red was heartened, excited that the blood might be the first break in the disappearance of Peggy Hardy, a sixteen-year-old high school long-distance track star, who had vanished three days before.*

*Winslow Trout, the sheriff of Bexar County, sauntered up to Red. A group of deputies were scouring the roadside and the woods beyond.*

*"You sure this isn't a wild-goose chase, Win? Could be nothing more than roadkill," Red said.*

*The sheriff chuckled. "Some things never change. You're*

*the biggest damn skeptic in Texas. I figured the same thing when I got the call. Probably a goddamned porcupine. But those skid marks over there, and the fact that this was Peggy Hardy's daily-training route, gave me reason to check it out. Trail's getting cold the way it is, so here we are. Where's Skylar? I thought you two were joined at the hip."*

*Winslow Trout chuckled again; his spare-tire belly shook inside his uniform like a bowl of chocolate pudding. He was a little over fifty years old, and the years of sitting behind a desk and in a police cruiser was taking its toll on the sheriff. Red never doubted Trout's ability, though; he was as smart as a fox and could still run down a bull, or a twenty-year-old punk, if he had to.*

*"Skylar'll be here, don't worry. He wouldn't want to miss seeing your smiling face."*

*"Good, I got a couple of new jokes for him."*

*"Who called?"*

*"Anonymous. Said we ought to come out and check it out. Skid marks and blood. That's it. Whoever they were they called from a pay phone downtown."*

*"Figures."*

*"My sister's kid goes to the same school as the Hardy girl," Trout said. "This thing's got everybody shook to the bone. Things like this don't happen around here."*

*"I know," Red answered, staring at a deputy who was studying something on the ground intently. "From what I can see, Peggy Hardy had everything going for her. It won't be long before the press gets wind we're out here. They've been camped out at her house like a bunch of damn vultures, holing up the parents inside like prisoners. I sure do feel sorry for them."*

*The deputy stood up and shouted, "I found a running shoe."*

* * *

Eight years had passed since they found Peggy Hardy stuffed in a culvert in Government Canyon, her body broken and battered by the impact of a vehicle. The worst part of it was she had been raped. Forensics pointed to the occurrence of rape before Peggy died. Speculation was she had escaped and her attacker had run her down. But speculation was as far as they got in the investigation. There were no footprints at the crime scene other than the attending officers', which confounded Red to this day. How could the killer not have left any tracks? Two suspects had been cleared. A teenage boy Peggy Hardy had broken off a relationship with a week before was cleared because he was out of town at the time of the disappearance, and Peggy's father was cleared almost immediately.

The only other suspect they could never clear was Junior Barton, a backyard mechanic who lived just up the road from where they found body. Barton had admitted to talking to Peggy that day. But Red was sure, even after eight years, that Junior wasn't telling him everything he needed to know about his relationship with Peggy Hardy.

After he made his stop at the office, Red's last unofficial act of duty in San Antonio was to give Junior one last visit.

He flipped the cigarette out the window and pushed down on the accelerator. It took him ten minutes to arrive at the cement block building that housed Company D. Traffic buzzed up and down the highway, but all Red could hear was the memory of Peggy Hardy's mother pleading with him to find the killer.

Two months after they buried Peggy, Martha Hardy took a handful of sleeping pills, intent on seeing her daughter sooner rather than later, in the afterlife. She failed, at least immediately. Martha Hardy lay in a coma for eight months and eight days before she finally died. Red had worried that Darly would do the same thing after Jason's death. He was sure he would come home and find her sprawled on the sofa, an empty pill bottle on the floor. The fear had passed after a few years, but recently, he'd seen that same faraway look in Darly's eyes, just like he'd seen in Martha Hardy's.

Ray Hardy, Martha's husband and Peggy's father, was left behind in more pain than any man ought to be able to survive. But Ray hung in there, hoping, praying that someday Peggy's killer would be brought to justice.

"Hey, Red, Skylar's been lookin' for ya," Bess Tildeman, the dispatcher, said. Someone had failed to inform Bess that beehive hair went out in the sixties. Normally, just the sound of her voice made Red smile, but not today. "I think he wants to take us all to Luby's for lunch."

"I won't be here. Tell Skylar I'll be in my office for about ten minutes," Red said.

"You're gonna miss Luby's? Shoot, today is meatloaf day."

The door buzzed open and Red walked past Bess without answering. He could hear her moaning about the meatloaf being just like her momma's until the door slammed shut.

His office was in the same state as his house; nothing but a pile of cardboard boxes ready for transport. Everything was packed away, his desk clear. He needed to call Winslow Trout and make sure Junior Barton was still at home.

Red had asked Win to stake out the Barton place two days earlier just to make sure he wouldn't miss his last chance to catch Junior by surprise. Win felt strongly that Junior was involved in Peggy's death too. But no matter how hard he tried, Red could not make the link to nail Junior down. Junior's story never changed, no matter the threats, or how intensely he was interrogated. Junior said he saw her on her normal run, waved, gave her some water, then went into town and grabbed a beer. The bad thing was that Winslow Trout saw him pull into the bar.

A sealed manila envelope sat squarely on his desk. He knew immediately what the envelope contained.

"You might want to wait to open that until you're on your own," Jane Sewell said as she poked her head in the door.

Red looked up, always glad to see Jane. Today she had a long face and a look in her eye that made him think she'd just done something she didn't want to. Jane was a forensic artist who came to the post in 2000 with the creation of UCIT, the Unsolved Crimes Investigation Unit. Red and Skylar were the lead team, and it was that position that had garnered him the promotion to Lubbock.

"You didn't have to do this," he said.

"You asked." Jane walked in the office and faced Red across the desk.

Jane Sewell was ten years younger than Red, a leggy A&M grad who had talent seeping from her unpainted fingernails. There were times when he fell a burst of energy between them, and had been tempted on more than occasion to find out if the attraction was mutual. But he could never force himself to cross the line. He loved Darly too much to hurt her like that, and had enough respect for

Jane not to reach out to her from the depths of his own loneliness.

"It was the least I could do," Jane said. "I can't imagine what it's going to be like around here without you."

"I won't be far."

"Lubbock's a world away."

"True," Red said, gently turning the envelope in his hands.

"Bess is scared to death you're going to miss your party. . . ."

"Meatloaf is one thing. But I already have lunch plans. I'll be at the party. Tell her not to worry her fool head off."

Jane smiled. "All right."

"See you there?"

"I wouldn't miss it." Jane turned to leave, but stopped midway to the door. She started to say something, drew back, shook her head, and said, "You need to wait, Red. Don't open it until you're in Lubbock."

"All right." When she was gone from his sight, Red exhaled, restrained his temptation, and put the envelope aside. He picked up the phone and called Winslow Trout. It was a quick conversation. Junior Barton was at home putting a new engine in his truck.

"I was about to put up a missing sign for you," Skylar Beaumont said as he walked into the office. "We need to go over some things before you leave."

"I'm going to be gone for a while. Going out to Wayland to have lunch with Winslow Trout."

Red knew Skylar was a little anxious about taking over the UCIT team, but it sure felt like he was in a hurry to show him the door and make the office his own. It might have been Red's own discomfort, not telling Skylar what he was up to, but the last thing he needed was Skylar tagging along. His visit with Junior wasn't going to be a by-the-book visit.

"Come on, Red, we need to go over schedules and transfers. I still don't have a handle on all this paperwork crap. And passing up Luby's for lunch with Winslow Trout doesn't seem like a fair deal."

"Bess'll help you through the paperwork. Besides, I won't be gone long, Win and I go back a long way you know that. He really helped me with the lay of the land when I was first starting out here. What the hell did I know about the hill country? I would've been lost without his help."

"You're right," Skylar said. "I guess I'm more nervous than I thought. But any time you sit down with Winslow Trout it turns into an all-day affair."

"Not today. Really, trust me, I'll be back in plenty of time."

"If you say so."

"I do."

Skylar backed away, hands in the air. "I'll see you later then."

Red nodded.

"Tell Winslow a joke for me," Skylar said.

"You know I'm not any good at telling jokes."

"It wouldn't be same and you know it."

"All right, what's the joke?"

"You know what the fish said when it hit a cement wall?"

"Nope," Red answered.

"Dam."

* * *

Red could drive to Wayland blindfolded. In the days after Peggy Hardy's body was found, he'd made the trip a hundred times. The last couple of years had kept him away, though if he had a chance, he'd stop by and see Ray. Those visits were few and far between, especially after Jason's death. The silence of the Hardy house reminded him too much of his own home. And no matter how hard he tried every time he was there, he could not keep his eyes off the locked door that led into Peggy's room. He wondered if Ray ever went in there. The last time he had stopped by to see Ray was a week ago. He had been putting off the trip, putting off telling Ray he was leaving for Lubbock. Ray had said something that affirmed his belief that Junior Barton was hiding something. He'd looked at Red and said, "Junior worked on Martha's car a lot. He always was a little sly. Every time she needed a tune-up she went out to see Junior."

It was common knowledge that Junior and Peggy knew each other, in an acquaintance kind of way, but this was the first time Ray had given Red any hint that there might've been something going on between Junior and Martha.

"I never could keep that woman fenced in," Ray had said.

Wayland was an old stagecoach town, a heritage that was forgotten as much as it was frowned upon. Mostly, it was a last stop for tourists heading into Government Canyon. A mix of trailer parks, barking dogs, a bait shop, a Stop-n-Go, and a row of broken-down buildings that suggested a moment of prosperity had existed and then evaporated all too quick.

Junior Barton lived in an old house that butted up against Rivell Creek about a mile and a half up the road from where Peggy Hardy's body was found.

Red pulled into Junior's driveway without hesitation.

He could see Junior bent over the front of an old Chevy truck. Two tick-hounds stood up warily and let out a few low-level barks. Red waited for Junior to turn around before he opened the door.

Junior was in his mid-thirties, skinny as a rail, a true nuts-and-bolts genius who had fallen on hard times since the Hardy case had put him in a bad light. Red wasn't sure how Junior made his living these days, nor did he care.

"You better get the hell off my land, Wolfe, unless you got a warrant."

Red stopped at the bumper, arms crossed, his glare shielded by his sunglasses.

"Just a social visit, Junior. Call off the dogs."

"I ought to let them tear you to shreds."

"I'd hate to have to shoot a good dog, Junior."

Junior ran his hands through his scraggly hair and threw a wrench to the ground. "Tiny, Blackie, shut the hell up."

The dogs quit barking, but continued to growl as they skulked to the other side of the porch.

"A social visit? I guess that means I don't need my lawyer, now does it, Wolfe?"

"Can't see why an innocent man would need a lawyer after so many years, Junior. But you're right, you won't be needing a lawyer today."

"That a threat?"

"No threats, Junior. I just have one question for you, and then I'll be on my way."

Junior smiled. “You still think I’m stupid, don’t you, Wolfe?” And then the smile faded. “Where’s your partner? I thought Rangers always worked in pairs.”

“Not today. I told you, this is a social visit.”

“Yeah, and I’m the friggin’ Easter Bunny,” Junior said. “Don’t expect no iced tea.”

“Just an answer, Junior, and I’ll be on my way.”

“I already answered every question I’ve been asked.”

“New question.”

Junior muttered something under his breath, and then leaned hack against the truck. “You’re not going to leave, are you?”

“You’re going to answer me one way or another, Junior. Just depends on how hard you want to make it.”

Junior studied Red for a moment, looked up and down the empty road, and then said, “All right, ask. But I’m tellin’ you, I already told you everything I know.”

Red uncrossed his arms. “You saw Peggy Hardy every day, waved at her. Even gave her a glass of water a couple of times.”

“Yeah, nothing new there.”

“Let me finish.”

Junior nodded.

“Ray Hardy told me you worked on a Martha’s car a couple of times in the months before Peggy disappeared.”

“I worked on a lot of cars back then, what of it?”

“Ray kind of insinuated that you worked on Martha’s car a little more often than everybody knew about the last time I talked to him.”

“Can’t rightly say. But Ray Hardy would say just about anything to see me burn.”

Red walked toward Junior. "Let me put it this way, Junior. Were you and Martha Hardy having an affair?"

"That's the stupidest question anybody's ever asked me, Wolfe. I knew Martha Hardy ever since she was in high school. I liked her, but not like that, she was too messed up. She came out here a lot, dropped off her car, and disappeared for a while. I can tell you who she was having an affair with, though. . . ."

Farley's Diner sat at the crossroads of Highway 45 and 51. North would take you straight to the Alamo, south to Mexico, east to Tyler, and west to Lubbock. All Red wanted to do was head north, sweep Darly into his arms, and head for Lubbock. But he knew he couldn't. He had to finish what he'd started.

Right now, he sure wished Skylar was with him.

Winslow Trout's county cruiser was sitting in Farley's parking lot. Two other cars sat at the back of the building.

Red walked in to the smell of chicken-fried steak and the sound of Win laughing, probably at one of his own jokes.

"'Bout time you showed up, I was gonna send the posse out to look for you," Win said.

Seems like a lot of people are looking for me today, Red thought. He was feeling a little nervous, a little uncertain, and that was not a feeling he was used to dealing with.

A waitress in her early forties with too much makeup on backed away from the booth Win was sitting in.

"Can I get you anything, sweetie?" she said to Red.

"A Dr. Pepper'd be just fine."

"Anything else?"

"That'll do."

"Bring him some of those cheese fries, Wanda. I'm god-damned addicted to those things," Win said.

"I'm not hungry."

"Well, bring 'em out anyway, I'll eat 'em."

Wanda headed for the kitchen, shouting, "Another order of fries for the sheriff, Ernie, and put some extra sauce on them. Win likes it hot."

"I sure do, baby," he said with a belly laugh.

Red slid into an orange vinyl booth and lit a cigarette.

"That's going to kill you one of these days, Red."

"Yeah, like those cheese fries are the foundation of the food pyramid." "Damn, Red, when did you get a sense of humor?"

"Skylar's rubbing off on me."

Win sopped up the last bit of cheese on the plate in front of him with a limp fry and inhaled it. "How is Skylar?"

"Nervous. He sent a joke for you."

"Good, I haven't had much to laugh at today."

Red stared at Win for minute, studying his face, thinking of all of the time they had spent together. He stubbed out the cigarette and dropped his right hand to his side.

"What do you get when you cross a Texas Ranger with a mechanic?"

Win stopped chewing. "This don't sound like a joke Skylar would tell. I don't know, what do you get?"

"Sooner or later," Red said, "you get the truth."

"How come I'm not laughing?"

"Because I already been out to Junior Barton's place. I always knew he was holding back, but I figured he was guilty. That's what you wanted isn't it, Win?"

"I don't know what the hell you're talking about, Red."

"I made a mistake a long time ago. I was looking at the biggest clue there was in the investigation and I didn't know it."

Win shifted in his seat. His face was drawn tight, flushed, and his eyes were darting around the room avoiding contact with Red at all costs.

"Now, if you're thinking about doing anything stupid, you ought to know my finger's on the trigger, and I'll blow your balls off before you can say boy howdy."

"Before you start accusin' a man of something, Red, you better know . . ."

Wanda walked to the table with a white china plate full of cheese fries. "Here you go, boys," she said.

Win slid his foot out from underneath the table and tripped the waitress. As she fell, distracting Red, Win jumped up, grabbed Wanda around the neck, and put his gun to her head.

The plate of fries shattered on the table and Wanda screamed at the top of her lungs. Red reacted out of instinct. He threw his left hand up to deflect the shards of china while he kept a tight grip on his weapon. He raised the Colt revolver, automatically training on the center of Win's forehead.

"Looks like we got us a Mexican standoff, Red. Now lay down your gun, and nothing will happen to sweet Wanda here."

"I never figured you for a man who went after young girls, Win. Junior told me about you and Martha. Ray thought Junior and Martha were running around, but Junior cleared that up for me. It wasn't until he told me about you strong-arming him that I began to wonder whether or not you might have killed Peggy. So, I looked at my notes, at your reports, and damn if there wasn't a few things just a hair out of whack the day we found Peggy. You had about two hours unaccounted for. But why would we question you? Hell, I never even looked at it until today. My guess is it was you that called us out to the canyon, figuring you could throw the trail onto Junior. Your boot prints were everywhere around Peggy's body, but that made sense, didn't it? I never could understand how the killer got away without leaving prints. Now I do. Junior's alibi was tight other than nobody being around when Peggy ran by. But it was enough, wasn't it, Win? Enough not to send an innocent man to prison and to keep the scent off you. As long as Junior kept his mouth shut about you and Martha, you were never a suspect. And you had that covered, didn't you, affirming Junior's alibi?"

Tears were streaming down Wanda's face.

"I had to do something, Red. The little brat found out about me and her momma. She was gonna tell her daddy."

"And you raped and killed her to keep her quiet? Come on, Win."

Red saw Ernie out of the corner of his eye slowly making his way out of the kitchen with a butcher knife in his hand.

"Things got out of hand," Win said. "I figured she liked it hot, like her momma."

Ernie was about three feet behind the sheriff when a customer walked in the door.

Win jumped at the bell and caught sight of Ernie. He swung Wanda around and shot Ernie in the stomach.

The customer, a weary traveling salesman, ran back out the door.

Red lunged at Win, knocking Wanda into the booth, and rolled onto the floor. He got one shot off as he gained his balance.

Winslow Trout staggered backward as a bloody hole appeared just below his heart. "Damn, Red, that was the worst joke I ever heard," Win said, and then fell to the floor with a resounding thud.

Two hours later, Red was walking out of Ray Hardy's house. He wasn't surprised when he saw Skylar pull into the drive.

"How's Ray?"

"He'll be all right," Red said. "He didn't take it too well when he found out that Martha and Win were having a fling, but he knew she was stepping out with somebody. He just kept saying how all this was his fault. If he would have left when he found out, Peggy would still be alive. I know how he feels. If I wouldn't have let Jason walk home from school that day, he would've never been hit by a car. We can't change the past, I guess, but we'll keep playing it over and over in our heads wishing we could."

Skylar put a hand on Red's shoulder. "It's been a lot of years and that's still a hard one to swallow. It sounds like Ernie and Wanda are going to be all right." he said, waiting a beat before saying anything else. "I don't figure you're going to be up to your party, but I talked to Betty a while ago, and she said Darly would be there."

A slight smile crossed Red's face. "I'll be there."

"All right, then."

Red exhaled. “Funny, but I’m going to miss Win.”

Skylar nodded. “Me too,” he said, and then drove away.

Red took one last look at the Hardy house, and saw Ray cross the living room and head toward Peggy’s room. Red looked away, went to his vehicle, sat down, lit a cigarette, and picked up the envelope that Jane Sewell had given him.

He pulled out a picture of Jason, fully rendered in acrylics. Jane had aged him to the present. All he had asked her to do was give him a head shot, an idea of what his son would look like today if he were still alive. Like always, Jane had gone above and beyond the call of duty and talent.

Jason was dressed in a Texas Tech football uniform, holding the football up in a victorious touchdown stance, smiling to a faceless crowd.

# Me and Mitch

Bill Pronzini and Barry N. Malzberg

Bill Pronzini has written more than fifty mystery, science fiction, horror, and western novels, including the Nameless Detective series. A former newspaper reporter, Pronzini began his writing career with the 1971 publication of *The Stalker.* He has also written more than three hundred short stories and articles, and several of his books have been adapted for film. As has been said in these anthologies before, his Nameless books form a vital and important chronicle of one of crime fiction's most credible and human private detectives ever written. His most recent novel is *Nightcrawlers.*

Barry N. Malzberg has had a successful if sometimes controversial career in the field of science fiction where, in the course of winning kudos and awards, he has written novels and short stories that challenged the field to take itself seriously. His novels

*Guernica Night* and *Herovit's World* demonstrate his wide range of styles and technique and are considered lasting contributions to the literature of science fiction. In addition to his writing career, Malzberg has also been an editor, agent, and critic.

**Well, all this happened a** long time ago. Almost fifty years. Dodgers were still in Brooklyn where they belonged and Ebbets Field was still the best place in the country to watch a ball game, never mind what the Cubs fans say about Wrigley. Draft beer was two bits a schooner, you could eat a big meal for a buck at Longchamps, the Rockettes were still kicking at Radio City Music Hall, and if you took a date to Coney Island you still had a chance to get lucky under the boardwalk.

Better world back then. Some people say so, anyway. Me, I don't think so. World was just as crazy in those days, what with the polio scare and Korea and everybody worried that the Russians would drop the bomb. People were just as crazy, too—hurting each other, hurting themselves.

Me and Mitch and a bunch of other regulars used to hang out at Mooney's Saloon, an old workingman's tavern in the shadow of Ebbets. Two generations of Mooneys had kept it operating for better than sixty years, even during the Prohibition; old man Mooney said nobody but God Almighty could tell him not to serve cold beer to a thirsty man, and he paid graft to pretty much run wide open for the duration. Place had a brass rail, spittoons, sawdust on the floor, big crock of pickled eggs on the bar. And framed, signed photos of sports greats on the walls. Fighters like Dempsey and Louis and Marciano, but mainly Bums. Durocher, Jackie Robinson, Pee Wee Reese, the Duke, the

Preacher, dozens more. Not Ralph Branca, though, not after he served up that fat home run curve to Bobby Thompson in '51. Night that happened, Mitch tore Branca's photo off the wall and stomped it into the floor and nobody tried to stop him.

We were both from the neighborhood, me and Mitch. Both young punks, both worked construction, both liked to shoot pool and sip suds and play the pinball machines. Bar buddies, not real friends. Didn't see much of each other outside of Mooney's, except once in a while we'd take in a game at Ebbets or roll a few lines for brews at Studemeyer's Bowlarama. Different guys away from the tavern, you know what I mean? Different as night and day.

Thing about Mitch, he was a little guy wanted to be a big guy. Wore his hair in a slicked-back ducktail like Elvis, wore T-shirts with a pack of Camels rolled up in one sleeve. Talked tough and swaggered when he had a load on. Nobody paid much attention to him; even Swede Johannsen, who seemed to be a genuine tough guy, pretty much ignored Mitch when he started mouthing off. So did I. He was all bark and no bite. That's what everybody thought, anyhow.

Back then, I went by Lenny. Actually my name's Leonard, which is what I preferred to be called when I was away from Mooney's. Now that the L.A. Dodgers are a joke and about bankrupt thanks to the sellout to that bastard Murdoch, now that the world's gone crazy again, I prefer L. J. Don't ask me why. It's just what I prefer, that's all, even though Gloria, my late wife, was of the opinion that it's kind of sad when a guy my age changes his name for no good reason. Yeah, I know this has nothing much to do with what happened; it's just background information of the kind that Branch Rickey wanted on Jackie Robinson before he signed him to that first contract. Or, hell, maybe it does have something to do with it. I don't know.

Delaying the story is what I'm doing, I guess, the way I was delaying real life back there in Mooney's nearly fifty years ago. The way you do when you're young and single and don't have a mortgage and money troubles and all the rest of it. You know what I mean?

I'd've gone on delaying my life and me and Mitch would've gone on being bar buddies for who knows how long, even after O'Malley yanked the Dodgers out of Brooklyn and hauled them all the way out to La La Land, if it hadn't been for Stella Kleinfelt. Swede Johannsen, too, but mainly Stella. After what happened with them, nothing was ever the same again. Not for any of us.

This Stella was Patsy Dorfman's cousin, from over in Jersey. She'd got a job in the city and moved in with Patsy until she could find a place of her own, and they'd just started coming into Mooney's. She was sure something to look at, Stella was. Big woman—not fat, just big all over, close to six feet tall with blond hair and Monroe-type boobs in a push-up bra. All the guys had a letch for her, but the ones that drooled the most were Mitch and Swede Johannsen.

The Swede was big, too. And he liked to hear himself talk, the same as Mitch. Always yacking about his life, his tryout with the Senators in '48 and how they offered him a Class D contract which he was too proud to take, and his deal with Rheingold for an exclusive distributorship and the crew he had doing all the work while he raked in the lion's share, and what a big stud he was. We pretty much figured most of it was bullshit, but who could tell with a guy like that? He looked tough and acted tough and claimed he carried a gun because one of his delivery slaves had threatened him and he wasn't taking any chances. So nobody called him a liar. Nobody messed with him, either.

He was there that night, carrying a bigger load than usual on account of some deal he was bragging on. Me and Mitch were playing pinball. Mitch had a load on, too, and when Stella and Patsy walked in he stopped and stared and licked his chops. She looked oh so fine in a tight red dress, those headlights bulging half out of the top.

"Man," he said in that cocky way of his. "Man oh man oh man."

"Forget it, Mitch," I said.

"Forget what?"

"You'll never get next to her. None of us will."

"You wanna bet? I seen the way she looks at me sometimes."

"That's all in your head. She's not interested in anybody, she comes in for the same reason we do—to have a good time."

"I got a good time I can give her."

"Yeah, sure. Lookit—Swede's already moving in on her."

"Hell with that big jerk." He pasted a Camel to his lower lip, left it there unlit. But he didn't do anything else. Just stood there holding his bottle of Rheingold and sucking on his unlit Camel and staring at Stella.

The Swede was moving in on her, all right. He'd done it before, just as fast, and every time she'd held him off at arm's length like she did every other guy in Mooney's. Only this night he didn't back off. He started whispering to her, real earnest, like he was telling her all the secrets of the universe. All she did was laugh and pay more attention to Patsy than she did to him. Then he started pawing her a little, slobbering on her neck. She didn't like that. She told him to cut it out. He was the one who laughed then, loud, like a donkey braying.

Mitch started to get steamed, watching. His hand got tight around the neck of the Rheingold bottle like maybe he was imagining it was the Swede's neck. "The big slob," he said. "If he don't leave her alone . . ."

"What do you care? It's none of your business."

"She deserves to be treated better than that. I ought to go over there and tell him off."

"You don't want to do that. Stay out of it." That was Brooklyn wisdom then and probably now. You stayed out of trouble whenever you could, especially bar fights. Things had to jump all over you first, and even then you fought only to save your own ass, not some other guy's.

The Swede whispered something else to Stella. This time she glared at him. So he laughed loud and swigged his brew and then nibbled her ear again. Whatever it was he said that time, she turned bright red, jerked around on her stool, and belted him across the face.

She was a big woman and she put a lot of muscle into that roundhouse slap. It knocked Swede right off his stool, spilled beer all over the front of his pants. The regulars couldn't help but bust out laughing. The laughter as much as the slap yanked the Swede's chain. He sat there for about five seconds, fuming, and then he hauled off and whacked her as hard as she'd whacked him.

Well, that was too much for Mitch. The rest of us just stood around gawking, while Stella started bawling and rubbing her cheek, but Mitch took off running across the sawdust to the bar. He stopped in front of the Swede and leaned up in his face and said, "What's the idea hitting a woman, you big son of a bitch?"

It got real quiet in there. If there'd been a ballgame on that night, you'd've been able to hear the crack of a bat over at Ebbets.

The Swede loomed over him by a good eight inches, but Mitch had more guts than we'd given him credit for. He stood his ground. "You, you son of a bitch."

"Say that again and I'll bust your head for you."

Mitch had just enough of a load on, and just enough of a letch for Stella, to say it again. And sure enough, the Swede busted his head. I mean that's just what he did. He hit Mitch three times in the face, right, left right, so fast that his hands were a blur. Mitch went down and sailed backward through the sawdust until he smacked up against the pool table. His head was all bloody and his eyes were glazed over. He didn't move. Down for the count.

I started over to help him, but the Swede got there first. He was half crazy by then and he picked Mitch up and started beating on him some more. Must've punched him half a dozen times before me and some of the other regulars pulled him off.

Mitch was in a bad way. The bartender, Herman, called for medical help but he didn't call the law. In Brooklyn back then you didn't have anything to do with the law if you could avoid it. Swede left before the ambulance guys got there, muttering and grumbling and glaring; nobody tried to stop him.

Well, Mitch ended up in the hospital with a broken nose, busted cheekbone, three teeth knocked out, and assorted cuts and abrasions. Some of us went to see him. He claimed Stella came to see him, too, told him how sorry she was and what a brave thing he'd done for her and held his hand for him, but we didn't believe it. He had a lot of fantasies, Mitch did, where women were concerned.

He could've pressed assault charges against the Swede, but he didn't. I asked him why and he said, "I'll fix that bastard my own way one of these days. I'll fix him good."

"You don't mean you're gonna go gunning for him?"

"You'll find out, Lenny. When the time comes."

The Swede quit coming into Mooney's. So did Stella and Patsy. And Mitch didn't show when he got out of the hospital. I was still hanging out there some evenings, because I wasn't ready to move on yet and didn't have anywhere else to go. That's where I was about a week later, when we heard what'd happened on the TV news.

The Swede had been found in an alley next to Patsy Dorfman's apartment house, shot to death with his own gun.

I guess it was natural enough that Mitch would be suspected of being the shooter, after the fight in Mooney's. Everybody sure figured he was guilty when he all of a sudden disappeared, two days after Swede was found. Cops came around to the tavern to talk to us regulars, and one of them let it slip that they'd grilled Mitch and when they went around to his place to grill him again, he was gone bag and baggage.

Well, you'd think the law would've made an effort to find him. But I doubt that they did. No cops ever came around to Mooney's again, or talked to any of us individually that

I know about, and I figure that after a week or so they back-burnered the whole thing. Fact was, Swede Johannsen wasn't an important or even a respectable citizen. Turned out his Rheingold distributorship was just a lot of hooey—he'd been nothing more than a deliveryman himself—and he had a shady past to boot. Convicted once of assault and once of possession of an illegal firearm. Plus he had no flock of friends or family demanding justice. Neither did Mitch, for that matter. These were just casual guys in casual times, if you catch my drift.

None of the bar regulars cared much, either. The Swede had been nobody's pal and Mitch had been only what you call an on-premises friend to me and most of the others. I hoped he'd stay lost—I wished him well, but I didn't miss him even a little. As I'd said to him once, "Mitch, I don't think I've ever seen you without half a bag on." We'd laughed at that, but looking back I can see it wasn't funny. A hell of a comment on the way we lived in those days, you know? Lenny the Loser hanging out with Mitch the Loser and Swede the Loser and all the other Losers in the shadow of Ebbets Field.

Stella, though—Stella was a different story.

The day Mitch disappeared, I went over to see her at Patsy Dorfman's and she wasn't there. Patsy said she'd decided all of a sudden to quit her job and go back to Jersey. Maybe Patsy believed that and maybe she was covering up, I don't know. All I know is that I contacted Stella's folks and some of her friends over in Jersey, and if any of them knew where she was they wouldn't tell me.

Once the news that Stella had also disappeared got circulated in Mooney's, there was all sorts of speculation.

One theory was that she was dead, that Mitch had killed her, too, for some crazy reason, and chucked her body in the East River. The other theory was that the two of them had been secret lovers and had run off together, which made a lot more sense. That was pretty much the way I saw it. Remember what Mitch had said about her coming to see him in the hospital and holding his hand? It hadn't been a fantasy after all.

The talk went on for a while and then, with nothing to feed it, it died out. Before long nobody even mentioned Mitch or Stella or the Swede anymore. Life moves on. O'Malley was cooking his plan to split Flatbush with the Dodgers, teasing the mayor, Robert Wagner, with the possibility that he'd stay and poor Wagner, a hard-of-hearing bum, didn't realize that the fix was already made. Then O'Malley pulled Horace Stoneham on board and made his announcement that the Giants were heading west, too. That was all anybody in Mooney's talked about or cared about from then until I finally quit hanging out there and got on with my life.

Is that all to the story? No. Hell, no. You been patient, sitting there listening to me talk and wondering if I'd ever get to the point, and don't think I don't appreciate it. So I'll buy you another drink before closing time and tell you the rest of it. It's time I told it, straight out. Maybe it will do me some good to get it told. But I doubt it. Nothing about what happened back there in Brooklyn ever did me any good. Mitch didn't shoot the Swede in that alley next to Patsy Dorfman's building. I guess you could say I shot him, but the real truth is, he shot himself.

No, it wasn't suicide. What happened was this: That night,

late, I was half in the bag when I left Mooney's, feeling lonesome and wanting company, so I went over to see Stella. She wasn't there, but the Swede was. Waiting for her outside, even drunker than I was and in one of his mean moods. He started throwing his weight around, bragging on how he planned to put that little bastard Mitch back into the hospital for a lot longer stay next time he saw him. It rubbed me the wrong way, and I called him on it. He said, nasty, "You in love with Mitch, maybe? Maybe I oughta put you in the hospital too, both of you in the same bed."

I didn't bite on that, but then he started in on Stella. What a sweet piece she was, how he couldn't wait to get next to her, what he would do to her when he did. That was what put me over the line, that and all the Rheingold I'd thrown down my neck. I jumped him and while we were wrestling in that alley, he yanked his gun out and tried to brain me with it. I got hold of his wrist, and the next thing I knew the gun went off and the Swede grunted and quit fighting and then quit moving. Bullet went straight through his heart. Alive one second, dead the next.

Well, I got away fast without being seen, and nobody ever knew I was there. I never told anyone until tonight. Maybe I'd've told Mitch if he hadn't disappeared, but probably not. I don't think he ever suspected me. Or that Stella did, either.

What happened to the two of them? I never found out. Only thing I know for sure is that they ran off together. Stella and Mitch, an unlikely couple, but the world is full of unlikely couples. I like to believe that wherever they went they've been happy. Had and are still having a beautiful life together.

I guess you've figured out by now why I feel that way. Sure, that's right. I was in love with Stella myself. I'd've been good to her, too, maybe just as good as Mitch if I'd had the chance. But I didn't. I never had any luck at all.

Sometimes—lately, a lot of the time—I think what my life might've been like if Stella hadn't fallen in love with Mitch, if the Swede hadn't blown himself up and in a way blown me up along with him. If I'd stayed in Brooklyn, instead of moving out here to Southern California—running out on my roots the same as the Dodgers did in '57. I'm pretty sure it would've been better than the life I've had. More real. More honest.

But here I am, an old man now, a widower alone after thirty years of a loveless, childless marriage, hanging out in taverns the way I did back then, swilling beer and bitching about the Dodgers and how they're being destroyed by their greedy owner. I've come full circle, you might say. Me and the Bums, both.

# The Necromancer's Apprentice

Lillian Stewart Carl

Lillian Stewart Carl finds herself inventing her own genre, mystery/fantasy/romance with historical underpinnings. She enjoys exploring the way the past lingers on into the present. Her twelfth novel, *The Secret Portrait,* takes the story of Bonnie Prince Charlie into a contemporary setting; the sequel, *The Murder Hole,* tackles the legend of the Loch Ness monster. She has also published over twenty short stories in a variety of magazines and anthologies. Lillian has lived for many years in North Texas, in a book-lined cloister cleverly disguised as a tract house. She is a member of SFWA, Sisters in Crime, Novelists Inc, and the Authors Guild. Her Web site can be found at www.lillianstewartcarl.com.

**Robert Dudley, master of the** Queen's horses, was a fine figure of a man, as long of limb and imperious of eye as one of his equine charges. And like one of his charges, his wrath was likely to leave an innocent passerby with a shattered skull.

Dudley reached the end of the gallery, turned, and stamped back again, the rich fabrics of his clothing rustling an accompaniment to the thump of his boots. Erasmus Pilbeam shrank into the window recess. But he was no longer an innocent passerby, not now that Lord Robert had summoned him.

“You beetle-headed varlet!” His Lordship exclaimed. “What do you mean he cannot be recalled?”

Soft answers turn, away wrath, Pilbeam reminded himself. “Dr. Dee is perhaps in Louvain, perhaps in Prague, researching the wisdom, of the ancients. The difficulty lies not only in discovering his whereabouts hut also in convincing him to return, to England.”

“He is my old tutor, he would return at my request.” Again Lord Robert marched away down the gallery, the floor creaking protest at each step. “The greatness and suddenness of this misfortune so perplexes me that I shall take no rest until the truth is known.”

“The inquest declared your lady wife’s death an accident, my lord at the exact hour she was found deceased in Oxfordshire, you were waiting upon the Queen at Windsor. You could have had no hand—”

“Fact has never deterred malicious gossip. Why, I have now been accused of bribing the jurors. God’s teeth! I cannot let this evil slander rest upon my head. The Queen has sent me from the court on the strength of it!” Robert dashed his fist against the padded back of a chair, raising a small cloud of dust, tenuous as a ghost.

A young queen, like Elizabeth could not be too careful what familiar demonstrations she made. And yet, this last year and a hall, Lord Robert had come so much into her favor, it was said that Her Majesty visited him in his chamber clay and night . . . No, Pilbeam assured himself, that rumor was noised about only by those who were in the employ of Spain. And he did not for one moment believe that the Queen herself had ordered the disposal of Amy Robsart, no matter how many wagging tongues said that she had clone so. Still, Lord Robert could hardly be surprised that the malicious world now gossiped about Amy's death, when he had so neglected her life.

"I must find, proof that my wife's death was either chance or evil design on the part of my enemies. The Queen's enemies."

Or, Pilbeam told himself, Amy's death might have been caused by someone who fancied himself the Queen's friend.

Lord Robert stalked back up the gallery and scrutinized Pilbeam's black robes and close-fitting cap. "You have studied with Dr. Dee. You are keeping his books safe whilst he pursues his researches in heretical lands."

"Yes, my lord."

"How well have you learned your lessons, I wonder?"

The look in Lord Robert's eye, compounded of shrewd calculation and ruthless pride, made Pilbeam's heart sink. "He has taught me how to heal illness, how to read the stars. The rudiments of the alchemical sciences."

"Did he also teach you how to call, and converse with spirits?"

"He—ah—mentioned to me that such conversation, is possible." "Tell me more."

"Formerly, it was held that apparitions must be spirits from purgatory, but now that we know purgatory to be only papist myth, it must he that apparitions are demonic, angelic, or illusory. The devil may deceive man into thinking he sees ghosts or . . ." Pilbeam gulped. The bile in his throat tasted of the burning flesh of witches.

"An illusion or deception will not serve me at all. Be she demon or angel, it is Amy herself who is my best witness."

"My—my—my lord . . ."

Robert's voice softened, velvet, covering his iron fist. "I shall place my special trust in you, Dr. Pilbeam. You will employ all the devices and means you can possibly use for learning the truth. Do you understand me?"

*Only too well.* Pilbeam groped for an out. "My lord, whilst the laws regarding the practice of magic are a bit uncertain just now, still Dr. Dee himself, as pious a cleric as he may be, has been suspected of fraternizing with evil spirits. My lord Robert, if you intend such a, er, perilous course of action as, well, necromancy . . . ah, may I recommend either Edward Cosyn or John Prestall, who are well known in the city of London."

"Ill-nurtured cozeners, the both of them! Their loyalty is suspect, their motives impure. No. If I cannot have Dr. Dee, I will have his apprentice."

For a moment Pilbeam considered a sudden change in profession. His beard was still brown, his step firm—he could apprentice himself to a cobbler or a baker and make an honest living without dabbling in the affairs of noblemen, who were more capricious than any spirit. He made one more attempt to save himself. "I am honored, my lord. But I doubt that it is within my powers to raise your . . . er, speak with your wife's shade."

"Then consult Dr. Dee's books, you malmsey-nosed knave, and follow your instructions."

"But, but . . . there is the possibility, my lord, that, her death was neither chance nor villainy, but caused by disease."

"Nonsense. I was her husband. If she had been ill, I'd have known."

Not when you were not there to be informed, Pilbeam answered silently. Aloud he said, "Perhaps, then, she was ill in her senses, driven to, to . . ."

"To self-murder? Think, varlet! A fall down the stairs could no more be relied upon by a suicide than by a murderer. She was found at the foot of the staircase, her neck broken but her headdress still secure upon her head. That is hardly a scene of violence."

Pilbeam found it furtively comforting that Lord Robert wanted to protect his wife's reputation from hints of suicide . . . Well, her reputation was his as well. The sacrifice of a humble practitioner of the magical sciences—now, that would matter nothing to him. Pilbeam imagined His Lordship's face amongst those watching the mounting flames, a face contemptuous of his failure.

"Have no fear, Dr. Pilbeam, I shall reward you well for services rendered." Lord Robert spun about and walked away. "Amy was buried at St. Mary's, Oxford. Give her my respects."

Pilbeam opened his mouth, shut it, swallowed, and managed a weak "Yes, my lord," which bounced unheeded from Robert's departing back.

The spire of St. Mary's, Oxford, rose into the nighttime murk like an admonitory finger pointing to heaven. Pilbeam had no quarrel with that admonition. He hoped its author would find no quarrel with his present endeavor.

He withdrew into the dark, fetid alley and willed his stomach to stop grumbling. He'd followed Dr. Dee's instructions explicitly, preparing himself with abstinence, continence, and prayer made all the more fervid for the peril in which he found himself. And surely the journey on the muddy November roads had sufficiently mortified his flesh. He was ready to summon spirits, be they demons or angels.

The black lump beside him was no demon. Martin Molesworth, his apprentice, held the lantern and the bag of implements. Pilbeam heard no stomach rumblings from the lad, but he could enforce Dr. Dee's directions only so far as his own admonitory fist could reach. "Come along," he whispered. "Step lively."

Man and boy scurried across the street and gained the porch of the church. The door squealed open and thudded shut behind them. "Light," ordered Pilbeam.

Martin slid aside the shutter concealing the candle and lifted the lantern. Its hot-metal tang dispelled the usual odors of a sanctified site—incense, mildew, and decaying mortality. Pilbeam pushed Martin toward the chancel. Their steps echoed, drawing uneasy shiftings and mutterings from amongst the roof beams. Bats or swallows, Pilbeam hoped.

Amy Robsart had been buried with such pomp, circumstance, and controversy that only a few well-placed questions had established her exact resting place. Now Pilbeam contemplated the flagstones laid close together behind the altar of the church, and extended his hand for his bag.

Martin was gazing upward, to where the columns met overhead in a thicket of stone tracery, his mouth hanging open. "You mewling knotty-pated scullion!" Pilbeam hissed, and snatched the bag from his limp hands. "Pay attention!"

"Yes, master." Martin held the lantern whilst Pilbeam arranged the charms, the herbs, and the candles he dare not light. With a bit of charcoal, he drew a circle with four divisions and four crosses. Then, his tongue clamped securely between his teeth, he opened the book he'd dared bring from Dr. Dee's collection and began to sketch the incantatory words and signs.

If he interpreted Dee's writings correctly—the man set no examples in penmanship—Pilbeam did not need to raise Amy's physical remains. A full necromantic apparition was summoned for consultation about the future, whereas what he wished was to consult about the past. Surely, this would not be as difficult a task. *"Laudetur Deus Trinus et units,"* he muttered, *"nunc et in sempiterna seculorum secula . . ."*

Martin shifted, and a drop of hot wax fell onto Pilbeam's wrist. "Beslubbering gudgeon!"

"Sorry, master."

Squinting in the dim light, Pilbeam wiped away one of his drawings with the hem of his robe and tried again. There. For a moment he gazed, appreciatively at his handiwork, then took a deep breath. His stomach gurgled.

Pilbeam dragged the lad into the center of the circle and jerked his arm upward so the lantern would illuminate the page of his book. He raised his magical rod and began to speak the words of the ritual. "I conjure thee by the authority of God Almighty, by the virtue of heaven and the stars, by the virtue of the angels, by that of the elements *Domine, Deus meus, in te speravi. Damahil, Pancia, Mitraton . . .*"

He was surprised and gratified to see a sparkling mist begin to stream upward from between the flat stones just outside the circle. Encouraged, he spoke the words even faster.

". . . to receive such virtue herein that we may obtain by thee the perfect issue of all our desires, without evil, without deception, by God, the creator of the sun and the angels. *Lamineck. Caldulech. Abracadabra.*"

The mist wavered. A woman's voice sighed, desolate.

"Amy Robsart, Lady Robert Dudley, I conjure thee."

Martin's eyes bulged and the lantern swung in his hand, making the shadows of column and choir stall surge sickeningly back and forth. "Master . . ."

"Shut your mouth, hedgepig!" Pilbeam ordered. "Amy Robsart, I conjure thee. I beseech thee for God his sake, *et per viscera misericordiae Altissimi,* that thou wouldst declare unto us *misericordiae Dei sint super nos.*"

"Amen," said Martin helpfully. His voice leaped upward an octave.

The mist swirled and solidified into the figure of a woman. Even in the dim light of the lantern Pilbeam could see every detail of the revenant's dress, the puffed sleeves, the stiffened stomacher, the embroidered slippers. The angled wings of her headdress framed a thin, pale face, its dark eyes too big, its mouth too small, as though Amy Robsart had spent her short life observing many things but fearing to speak of them. A fragile voice issued from those ashen lips. "Ah, woe. Woe."

Pilbeam's heart was pounding, livery nerve strained toward the doors of the church and through the walls to the street outside. "Tell me what happened during your last hours on earth, Lady Robert."

"My last hours?" She dissolved and solidified again, wringing her frail hands. "I fell. I was walking down the stairs and I fell."

"Why did you fall, my lady?"

"I was weak. I must have stumbled."

"Did someone push you?" Martin asked, and received the end of Pilbeam's rod in his ribs.

Amy's voice wavered like a set of ill-tempered bagpipes. "I walked doubled over in pain. The stairs are narrow. I fell."

"Pain? You were ill?"

"A spear through my heart and my head so heavy I could barely hold it erect."

A light flashed in the window, accompanied by a clash of weaponry. The night watch. Had someone seen the glow from the solitary lantern? Perhaps the watchmen were simply making their rounds and contemplating the virtues of bread and ale. Perhaps they were searching for miscreants.

With one convulsive jerk of his scrawny limbs, Martin scooped the herbs, the charms, the candles, even the mite of charcoal, back into the bag. He seized the book and cast it after the other items. Pilbeam had never seen him move with such speed and economy of action. "Stop," he whispered urgently. "Give me the book. I have to . . ."

Martin was already wiping away the charcoaled marks. Pilbeam brought his rod down on the lad's arm, but it was too late. The circle was broken. A sickly-sweet breath of putrefaction made the candle gutter. The woman-shape, the ghost, the revenant, ripped itself into pennons of color and shadow. With an anguished moan those tatters of humanity streamed across the chancel and disappeared down the nave of the church.

Pulling on the convenient handle of Martin's ear, Pilbeam dragged the lad across the chancel. His hoarse whisper repeated a profane litany: "Earth-vexing dewberry, spongy rump-fed skainsmate, misbegotten tickle-brained whey-faced whoreson, you prevented me from laying the ghost back in its grave!"

"Sorry, master, ow, ow . . ."

The necromancer and his apprentice fled through the door of the sacristy and into the black alleys of Oxford.

Cumnor Place belonged not to Lord Robert Dudley, but to one of his cronies. If Pilbeam ever wished to render his own wife out of sight and therefore out of mind, an isolated country house such as Cumnor, with its air of respectable disintegration, would serve very well. Save that his own wife's wrath ran a close second to Lord Robert's.

What a shame that Amy Robsart's meek spirit had proved to be of only middling assistance to Lord Robert's—and therefore Pilbeam's—quest. No, no hired bravo had broken Amy's neck and arranged her body at the foot of the stairs. Nor had she hurled herself clown those same stairs in a paroxysm of despair. Her death might indeed have been an accident.

But how could he prove such a subtle accident? And worse, how could he report such ambiguous findings to Lord Robert? Of only one thing was Pilbeam certain he was not going to inform His Lordship that his wife's ghost had been freed from its corporeal wrappings and carelessly not put back again.

Shooting a malevolent glare at Martin, Pilbeam led the way into the courtyard of the house. Rain streaked the stones and timber of the facade. Windows turned a blind eye to the chill gray afternoon. The odors of smoke and offal hung in the air.

A door opened, revealing a plump, pigeonlike woman wearing the simple garb of a servant. She greeted the visitors with "What do you want?"

"Good afternoon, mistress. I am Dr. Erasmus Pilbeam, acting for Lord Robert Dudley." He offered her a bow that was polite but not deferential.

The woman's suspicion eased into resignation. "Then come through and warm yourselves by the fire. I am Mrs. Odingsells, the housekeeper."

"Thank you."

Within moments Pilbeam found himself seated in the kitchen, slurping hot cabbage soup and strong ale. Martin crouched in the rushes at his feet, gnawing on a crust of bread. On the opposite side of the fireplace a young woman mended a lady's shift, her narrow face shadowed by her cap.

Mrs. Odingsells answered Pilbeam's question. "Yes, Lady Robert was in perfect health, if pale and worn, up until several days before she died. Then she turned sickly and peevish. Why, even Lettice there, her maid, could do nothing for her. Or with her, come to that."

Pilbeam looked over at the young woman and met a glance sharp as the needle she wielded.

The housekeeper went on. “The day she died, Her Ladyship sent the servants away to Abingdon Fair. I refused to go. It was a Sunday, no day for a gentlewoman to be out and about, sunshine or no.”

“She sent everyone away?” Pilbeam repeated. “If she were ill, surely she would have needed an attendant.”

“Ill? Ill used, I should say . . .” Remembering discretion, Mrs. Odingsells contented herself with “If she sent the servants away, it was because she tired of their constantly offering food she would not eat and employments she had no wish to pursue. Why, I myself heard her praying to God to deliver her from desperation, not long before I heard her fall.”

“She was desperate from illness? Or because her husband’s . . . duties were elsewhere?”

“Desperate from her childlessness, perhaps, which would follow naturally upon Lord Robert’s absence.”

So then, Amy’s spear through the heart was a symbolic one, the pain of a woman spurned. “Her Ladyship was of a strange mind the clay she died, it seems. Do you think she died by chance? Or by villainy, her own or someone else’s?”

Again Pilbeam caught the icy stab of Lettice’s eyes. “She was a virtuous God-fearing gentlewoman, and alone when she fell,” Mrs. Odingsells returned indignantly, as though that were answer enough.

It was not enough, however. If not for the testimony of Amy herself, Pilbeam would be thinking once again of self-murder. But then, as His Lordship himself had said, a fall down the stairs could no more be relied upon by a suicide than by a murderer.

The housekeeper bent over the pot of fragrant soup.

Pilbeam asked, "Could I see the exact staircase? Perhaps Lettice can show me, as your attention is upon your work."

"Lettice," Mrs. Odingsells said with a jerk of her head. "See to it." Silently, the maid put down her mending and started toward the door. Pilbeam swallowed the last of his soup and followed her. He did not realize Martin was following him until he stopped beside the fatal staircase and the lad walked into his rump. Pilbeam brushed him aside. "She was found here?"

"Yes, master, so she was." Now Lettice's eyes were roaming up and clown and sideways, avoiding his. "See how narrow the stair is, winding and worn at the turn. In the darkness—"

"Darkness? Did she not die on a fair September afternoon?"

"Yes, yes, but the house is in shadow. And Her Ladyship was of a strange mind that day, you said yourself, master."

Behind Pilbeam, Martin muttered beneath his breath, "The lady was possessed, if you ask me."

"No one is asking you, clotpole," Pilbeam told him.

Lettice spun around. "Possessed? Why would you say such a thing? How . . . What is that?"

"What?" Pilbeam followed the direction of her eyes. The direction of her entire body, which strained upward stiff as a hound at point.

The ghost of Amy Robsart descended the steps, skirts rustling, dark eyes downcast, doubled in pain. Her frail hands were clasped to her breast. Her voice said, "Ah, woe. Woe." And suddenly, she collapsed, sliding down the last two steps to lie crumpled on the floor at Pilbeam's feet, her headdress not at all disarranged.

With great presence of mind, Pilbeam reached right and

left, seizing Martin's ear as he turned to flee and Lettice's arm as she swooned.

"Blimey," said Martin with feeling.

Lettice was trembling, her breath coming in gasps. "I did not know what they intended, as God is my witness, I did not know . . ."

The revenant dissolved and was gone. Pilbeam released Martin and turned his attention to Lettice. Her eyes were now dull as lead. "What have you done, girl?"

"They gave me two angels. Two gold coins."

"Who?"

"Two men. I do not know their names. They stopped me in the village, they gave me a parcel and bade me bring it here."

"A parcel for Her Ladyship?"

"Not for anyone. They told me to hide it in the house was all."

Pilbeam's heart started to sink. Then, as the full import of Lettice's words blossomed in his mind, it reversed course and bounded upward in a leap of relief. "Show me this parcel, you fool-born giglet. Make haste!"

Lettice walked, her steps heavy, several paces down the hallway. There she knelt and shoved at a bit of paneling so worm-gnawed it looked like lace. It opened like a cupboard door. From the dark hole behind it she withdrew a parcel wrapped in paper and tied with twine.

Pilbeam snatched it up and carried it to the nearest windowsill "Watch her," he ordered Martin.

Martin said, "Do not move, you ruttish flax-wench."

Lettice remained on her knees, bowed beneath the magnitude of her defeat, and made no attempt to flee.

Pilbeam eased the twine from the parcel and unwrapped

the paper. It was fine parchment overwritten with spells and signs. Beneath the paper a length of silk enshrouded something long and hard. Martin leaned so close that he almost got Pilbeam's elbow in his eye. Pilbeam shoved him aside.

Inside the silk lay a wax doll, dressed in a fine gown with puffed sleeves and starched stomacher, a small headdress upon its tiny head. But this was no child's toy. A long needle passed through its breast and exited from its back—Pilbeam's fingertips darted away from the sharp point. The doll's neck was encircled by a crimson thread, wound so tightly that it had almost cut off the head. A scrap of paper tucked into the doll's bodice read: Amy.

Pilbeam could hear the revenant's voice: *A spear through my heart and my head so heavy I could barely hold it erect.* So the spear thrust through her chest had been both literal and symbolic. And Amy's neck had been so weakened it needed only the slightest jolt to break it, such as a misstep on a staircase. A misstep easily made by the most healthy of persons, let alone a woman rendered infirm by forces both physical and emotional.

It was much too late to say the incantations that would negate the death spell. Swiftly, Pilbeam rewrapped the parcel. "Run to the kitchen and fetch Mrs. Odingsells," he ordered Martin, and Martin ran.

Lettice's bleak eyes spilled tears clown her sunken cheeks. "How can I redeem myself?"

"By identifying the two men who gave you this cursed object."

"I do not know their names, master. I heard one call the other by the name of Ned is all."

"Ned? If these men have knowledge of the magical sciences, I should know . . ." She did not need to know his own occupation. "Describe them to me."

"One was tall and strong, his black hair and beard wild as a bear's. The other was small, with a nose like an ax blade. He was the one named Ned."

*Well, then!* Pilbeam did know them. They were not his colleagues, but his competitors, Edward Cosyn, called Ned, and John Prestall. As Lord Robert had said, they were ill-nurtured cozeners, their loyalty suspect and their motives impure.

Perhaps His Lordship had himself bought the services of Prestall and Cosyn. If so, would he have admitted that he knew who they were? No. If he had brought about his wife's death, he would have hidden his motives behind sorrow and grief rather than openly revealing his self-interest and self-regard.

God be praised, thought Pilbeam, he had an answer for Lord Robert. He had found someone for His Lordship to blame.

At the sound of a footstep in the hall Pilbeam and Lettice looked around. But the step was not that of the apprentice or the housekeeper. Amy Robsart walked down the hallway, head drooping, shoulders bowed, wringing her hands.

Lettice squeaked in terror and shrank against Pilbeam's chest.

With a sigh of cold, dank air, the ghost passed through them and went on its way down the hallway, leaving behind the soft thump of footsteps and the fragile voice wailing, "Ah, woe. Woe."

* * *

Pilbeam adjusted his robes and his cap. Beside him Martin tugged at his collar. Pilbeam jabbed the lad with his elbow and hissed, "Stand up straight, you lumpish ratsbane."

"Quiet, you fly-bitten foot-licker," Lord Robert ordered.

Heralds threw open the doors. Her Majesty the Queen strode into the chamber, a vision in brocade, lace, and jewels. But her garments seemed like so many rags beside the glorious sunrise glow of her fair skin and her russet hair.

Lord Robert went gracefully down upon one knee, his upturned face tilled with the adoration of a papist for a saint. Pilbeam dropped like a sack of grain jerking Martin down as he went. The lad almost fumbled the pillow he carried, but his quick grab prevented the witching-doll from falling off the pillow and onto the floor.

The Queen's amber eyes crinkled at the corners, but her scarlet lips did not smile. "Robin, you roguish folly-fallen lewdster," she said to Lord Robert, her voice melodious but not lacking an edge. "Why have you pleaded to wait upon us this morning?"

"My agent, Dr. Pilbeam, who is apprenticed to your favorite, Dr. Dee, has discovered the truth behind my wife's unfortunate death."

Robert did not say "untimely death," Pilbeam noted. Then Her Majesty turned her eyes upon him, and his thoughts melted like a wax candle in their heat.

"Dr. Pilbeam," she said. "Explain."

He spoke to the broad planks of the floor, repeating the lines he had rehearsed before His Lordship: Cumnor Place, the maidservant overcome by her guilt the death spell quickened by the doll, and behind it all the clumsy but devious hands of Prestall and Cosyn. No revenant figured in the tale, and certainly no magic circle in St. Mary's, Oxford.

On cue, Martin extended the pillow. Lord Robert offered it to the Queen. With a crook of her forefinger, she summoned a lady-in-waiting, who carried both pillow and doll away. "Burn it," Elizabeth directed. And to her other attendants, "Leave us." With a double thud the doors shut.

Her Majesty flicked her pomander, bathing the men and the boy with the odor of violets and roses, as though she were a bishop dispensing the holy water of absolution. "You may stand."

Lord Robert rose as elegantly as he had knelt. With an undignified stagger, Pilbeam followed. Martin lurched into his side and Pilbeam batted him away.

"Where are those evildoers now?" asked the Queen.

"The maidservant is in Oxford gaol, Your Majesty," Robert replied, "and the malicious cozeners in the Tower."

"And yet it seems as though this maid was merely foolish, not wicked, ill used by men who tempted her with gold. You must surely have asked yourself, Robin, who in turn tempted these men."

"Someone who wished to destroy your trust in me, Your Majesty. To drive me from your presence. My enemy, and yours as well."

"Do you think so? What do you think, Dr. Pilbeam?"

What he truly thought, Pilbeam dared not say. That perhaps Amy's death was caused by someone who intended to play the Queen's friend. Someone who wished Amy Robsart's death to deliver Lord Robert Dudley to Elizabeth's marriage bed, so that there she might engender heirs.

Whilst some found Robert's bloodline tainted, his father and grandfather both executed as traitors, still the Queen could do much worse in choosing her consort. One could say of Robert what was said of the Queen herself upon her accession: that he was of no mingled or Spanish blood but was born English here in England. Even it he was proud as a Spaniard . . .

Pilbeam looked into the Queen's eyes, jewels faceted with a canny intelligence. Spain, he thought. The deadly enemy of Elizabeth and Protestant England. The Spanish were infamous for their subtle plots.

"B-b-begging your pardon, Your Majesty," he stammered, "but I think His Lordship is correct in one regard. His wife was murdered by your enemies. But they did not intend to drive him from your presence, not at all."

Robert's glance at Pilbeam was not encouraging. Martin took a step back. But Pilbeam barely noticed, spellbound as he was by the Queen. "Ambassador Feria, who was lately recalled to Spain. Did he not frequently comment to his master, King Philip, on your, ah, attachment to Lord Robert?"

Elizabeth nodded, one corner of her mouth tightening. She did not insult Pilbeam by pretending there had been no gossip about her attachment, just as she would not pretend she had no spies in the ambassador's household. "He had the impudence to write six months ago that Lady Robert had a malady in one of her breasts and that I was only waiting for her to die to marry."

His Lordship winced but had the wisdom to keep his own counsel.

"Yes, Your Majesty," said Pilbeam. "But how did Feria not only know of Lady Robert's illness but of its exact nature, long before the disease began to manifest itself? Her own housekeeper says she began to suffer only a few days before she died. Did Feria himself set two cozeners known for their, er, mutable loyalties to inflict such a condition upon her?"

"Feria was recently withdrawn and replaced by Bishop de Quadra," murmured the Queen. "Perhaps he overstepped himself with his plot. Or perhaps he retired to Spain in triumph at its—no, not at its conclusion. For it has yet to be concluded."

Lord Robert could contain himself no longer. "But, Your Majesty, this hasty-witted pillock speaks nonsense. Why should Philip of Spain . . ."

"Wish for me to marry you? He intended no compliment to you, I am sure of that." Elizabeth smiled, a smile more fierce than humorous, and for just a moment Pilbeam was reminded of her father, King Henry. Robert's handsome face lit with the answer to the puzzle. "If Your Majesty marries an Englishman, she could not ally herself with a foreign power such as France against Spain."

True enough, thought Pilbeam. But more important, if Elizabeth married Robert, then she would give weight to the rumors of murder, and might even be considered his accomplice in that crime. She had reigned for only two years; her rule was far from secure. Marrying Lord Robert might give the discontented among her subjects more ammunition for their misbegotten cause and further Philip's plots.

Whilst Robert chose to ignore those facts, Pilbeam would

wager everything he owned that Her Majesty did not. His Lordship's ambition might have outpaced his love for his wife. His love for Elizabeth had certainly done so. No, Robert Dudley had not killed his wife. Not intentionally.

The Queen stroked his cheek, the coronation ring upon her finger glinting against his beard. "The problem, sweet Robin, is that I am already married to a husband, namely, the Kingdom of England."

Robert had no choice but to acknowledge that. He bowed.

"Have the maidservant released," Elizabeth commanded. "Allow the cozeners to go free. Let the matter rest, and in time it will die for lack of nourishment. And then Philip and his roadies will not only be deprived of their conclusion, they will always wonder how much we knew of their plotting, and how we knew it."

"Yes, Your Majesty," said Lord Robert. "May I then return to court?"

"In the course of time." She dropped her hand from his cheek.

He would never have his conclusion, either, thought Pilbeam. Elizabeth would like everyone to be in love with her, but she would never be in love with anyone enough to marry him. For then she would have to bow her head to her husband's will, and that she would never do.

Pilbeam backed away. For once he did not collide with Martin, who, he saw with a glance from the corner of his eye, was several paces away and sidling crabwise toward the door.

Again the Queen turned the full force of her eyes upon Pilbeam, stopping him in his steps. "Dr. Pilbeam, we hear that the ghost of Lady Robert Dudley has been seen walking in Cumnor Place."

"Ah, ah . . ." Pilbeam felt rather than saw Martin's shudder of terror. But they would never have discovered the truth without the revenant. No, he would not condemn Martin, not when his carelessness had proved a blessing in disguise.

Lord Robert's gaze burned the side of his face, a warning that matters of necromancy were much better left hidden. "Her ghost?" he demanded. "Walking in Cumnor Place?"

Pilbeam said, "Er—ah—many tales tell of ghosts rising from their graves, Your Majesty, compelled by matters left unconcluded at death. Perhaps Lady Robert is seeking justice, perhaps bewailing her fate In the course of time, some compassionate clergyman will see her at last to rest." Not I, he added firmly to himself.

Elizabeth's smile glinted with wry humor. "Is that how it is?"

She would not insult Pilbeam by pretending that she had no spies in Oxfordshire as well and that very little failed to reach her ears and eyes. And yet the matter of the revenant, too, she would let die for lack of nourishment. She was fair not only in appearance but also in her expectations. He made her a bow that was more of a genuflection.

She made an airy wave of her hand. "You may go now, all of you. And Dr. Pilbeam, Lord Robert will be giving you the purse that dangles at his belt, in repayment of his debt to you."

"Yes, Your Majesty." His Lordship backed reluctantly away.

What an interesting study in alchemy, thought Pilbeam, that with the Queen the base metal of His Lordship's manner was transmuted to gold. "Your Majesty. My lord." Pilbeam reversed himself across the floor and out the door, which Martin contrived to open behind his back. Lord Robert followed close upon their heels, his boots stepping as lightly and briskly as the hooves of a thoroughbred. A few moments later Pilbeam stood in the street, an inspiringly heavy purse in his hand, allowing himself a sigh of relief—ah, the free air was sweet, all was well that ended well . . . Martin stepped into a puddle, splashing the rank brew of rainwater and sewage onto the hem of Pilbeam's robe.

Pilbeam availed himself yet again of Martin's convenient handle. "You rank pottle-deep measle! You rude-growing toad!" he exclaimed, and guided the lad down the street toward the warmth and peace of home.

# The Banshee

Joyce Carol Oates

Joyce Carol Oates is one of the United States' most prolific and versatile contemporary writers. With a career that spans more than thirty years, she is the author of more than one hundred books, including novels, short-story collections, poetry volumes, plays, literary criticism, and essays. Her writing has earned her much praise and many awards, including the National Book Award for her novel *them* (1969), the Rosenthal Award from the American Academy Institute of Arts and Letters, a Guggenheim Fellowship, the O. Henry Prize for Continued Achievement in the Short Story, the Elmer Holmes Bobst Lifetime Achievement Award in Fiction, the Rea Award for the Short Story, and in 1978, membership in the American Academy Institute. She also has been nominated twice for the Nobel Prize in Literature. Her most recent novel is *Missing Mom.*

**On Hedge Island, in Nantucket** Sound, a twenty-minute ferry ride from Yarmouth Harbor, Massachusetts. On the promontory above the wide raked beach, the Hedge Island Yacht and Bailing Club. On another matching spit of land to the east, the Hendricks' "cottage"—stately weathered-gray Victorian clapboard, three stories, numerous tall narrow windows, a tower and a widow's walk, steep shingleboard roofs and a wraparound veranda, with a floor so shiny-gray it appeared lacquered. On the veranda, wicker furniture with bright chintz cushions. On the choppy waters of the Sound, sailboats looking like white paper cutouts.

Cries of gulls. Mixed with the wind. And that flap-flapping sound overhead! Each time she glanced up fearful she would see giant birds flapping their wings as they swooped down upon her, but it turned out to be just the flag whipping in the wind at the top of the gunmetal pole.

The flag was Daddy's flag. But this summer Daddy was gone. She wandered among the guests seeking Mummy. In her new coral-pink tank top and wraparound denim skirt with the big patch pocket in the shape of a kitten from Gap Kids. So many strangers! Mummy had so many friends. On the flagstone terrace, and around the swimming pool, and on the grassy lawn where the bar had been set up, even on the tennis-courts. Bloody Marys and long-stemmed glasses of white wine, mushrooms stuffed with crab meat, Russian caviar smeared on dark bread like jelly, smoked salmon and thin-sliced cucumbers on Swedish crackers. Music booming so loud, almost you couldn't hear it. Women like Mummy in sleek swimsuit tops, silk slacks with pencil-thin legs. Bronze-skinned men in white trousers, sports shirts open to mid-chest. Men like Gerard, Mummy's new friend with a wide white smile that glistened. Oh here's a pretty girl! Here's the princess! Face like a flower! The strangers marveled, but were soon bored with her. The Irish girl had brought Baby to Mummy who'd showed Baby to her friends, for a while Baby had stirred interest, but babies are even more boring than six-year-olds and soon the Irish girl was sent back up to the house for it was time for Baby's diaper change, Baby's bottle, and Baby's nap.

Oh, there was Mummy: that waterfall-of straw-colored hair spilling on bronze-tanned bare shoulders. Laughter like glass breaking.

Mum-*my?* Plucking at Mummy's hand. Which Mummy did not like, not at such times. Mummy with Gerard in his dark glasses and windblown hair bleached from the sun, Gerard in white-dazzling sailing clothes and Mummy was wearing her "funky" top that was just a black silk scarf tied about her narrow chest and her wraparound silk skirt the color of neon strawberries. Barelegged Mummy in high-heeled: sandals that made her teeter. Mummy's fingernails were neon-strawberry too and perfect like plastic. Mummy slap-slapped at her as you'd brush away a pesky fly meaning go away! go back to the house! isn't that Irish girl supposed to be watching you! even as Mummy was laughing at Gerard telling one of his comical stories.

When she'd been a little girl Mummy had curled up to nap with her sometimes. It had not been that long ago on Hedge Island in the summer. In the big old iron bed in Mummy's and Daddy's room with the goose-feather pillows. Cuddled together in mid-afternoon which was a special time. Whispering and laughing and suddenly sleepy on the bed facing the window so you could see (through, your eyelashes) the sky, and a little of the Sound. You could imagine sailing in the sky, in thin floating clouds. Now she was no longer little but six years old and soon to start first grade in the city and a new baby had come: She was given to know *There can be only one baby.* She had believed always that she was this baby but now Baby had come and so she could not be Baby. And yet when Mummy and Gerard went sailing they refused to take her with them, she was *too little.*

*Too little,* and it was dangerous. Gerard's route eastward between Monomoy Island and Nantucket Island and into the open Atlantic, doubling back then westward and circling all of Hedge Island to return in triumph to the Hendricks' dock.

She was running back to the house. Pushing through the legs. Oh she hated Mummy's friends even Gerard smiling at her pretending she was special!

She hated Daddy, for going away. For leaving Hedge Island. This is the safe place, Daddy used to say. Why'd Daddy say that if it wasn't true! And anyway it wasn't true, on Hedge Island there were summer squalls, there were hurricanes sometimes and howling winds and the dock had been torn, up by ice (over the winter) and had had to be repaired. Daddy lived in the city now, but it was a different city. She'd been looking for Daddy hiding among the guests at the party for it was that kind of party, neighbors dropped by, summer guests and visitors to Hedge Island, the Yacht and Sailing Club people, so maybe Daddy had slipped among them, he'd changed how he looked, last time she'd seen Daddy he'd had scratchy black whiskers and a vertical line between his eyebrows she'd rubbed at with her fingers wanting to erase. Oh Daddy.

Daddy was not Baby's daddy (that was strange, but Mummy said) but Daddy was still her daddy (yes, Mummy said that was so) and that was why he might be at the party except—how could, they find each other, in such a crowd?

If!—if she stood on the veranda!—on the wicker sofa on the veranda!—in her pretty new summer outfit from Gap Kids maybe Daddy would see her? But there were too many people on the veranda, too.

Inside the house the walls were blinding-white, there was a mirror over a chintz sofa that reflected more light that made your eyes hurt. She rubbed at her eyes. She was not crying! Panting like a little dog that has been kicked but she was not crying.

There was Baby in his downstairs crib. Upstairs in the nursery Baby had another crib. Both cribs were white.

Baby was a *little boy.* As she was a *little girl.* Mummy said oh she loved both! Mummy said she Had not wished to stop with just one, and that one a *little girl.*

Mummy said when you're a mother you become superstitious you think what if? what if something happens to—? Oh it's the worst thought, it's the unthinkable thought so you start obsessing about more than one kind of disaster insurance, maybe it's just primitive instinct but we are primitive aren't we?

The Irish girl was laughing with the dark-tanned boy wearing a Red Sox cap. He was the son of one of Mummy's friends, he lived a few houses down on the beach. He'd brought a "joint" for the Irish girl and himself to smoke, they were laughing together as Baby lay in his crib by the French doors opening onto the veranda and the breezy salt air. Baby's eyelids fluttered as her shadow passed over his face.

Ba-*by?*

She knew to lilt her voice, like Mummy's voice. Carefully she lifted Baby in her arms. Her little brother!—that is what he was. She was fascinated by Baby's eyes that were so small and blue and bright with moisture and always moving, trying to focus on her face. She liked to touch the smooth skin like a doll's rubber skin. And there was the small perfect mouth. Yet Baby had a temper: You could not believe the sounds that issued from that mouth. In the night, the Irish girl had to tend Baby if he woke, and would not sleep, and made his fierce choking noises. For sometimes Mummy was away. And sometimes Mummy was home, and with Gerard in the big bedroom and at such times she did not appreciate being wakened by the screams of a banshee.

What is a *banshee,* Mummy? she asked but Mummy seemed not to know, and was annoyed at her for asking. Gerard always knew what a word, meant saying a *banshee* is some kind of Southwest Indian like Apache. But the Irish girl who kept to herself mostly and rarely said anything to Mummy except yes ma'am, no ma'am, thank you ma'am, now said in a thrilled voice Oh ma'am, a *banshee* is a wild spirit sounding like the wind, it screams in the night in a household where someone is soon to die.

Mummy laughed. Like glass being broken. So you knew that Mummy was displeased. The Irish girl's pale-freckled face reddened, and she said Oh ma'am! I am sorry. Sometimes in the night this summer on Hedge Island which was a lonely summer she would slip from her bed in the room close-by the nursery and tiptoe barefoot; and breathless into the nursery to peer into Baby's crib that was so white, it seemed to float in the shadows like a little boat in the water. When there was a moon, especially. When the moon was shining like a milky eye. When the Irish girl was snoring in her sleep. Like a ghost she would come to stand beside Baby's crib she had overheard Mummy saying had been her crib once upon a time and it was so strange to think that a long time ago she had been Baby, but now Baby was someone not-her she could, look at as he slept. Baby slept so very hard, his small body quivered with the heat of his mysterious dreams. Oh, what was Baby dreaming? He was so small, he had not yet learned to speak. And so his baby-dreams were lost when he wakened.

It was so thrilling, she was holding Baby in her arms! And no one knew, and could scold.

She was holding Baby as the Irish girl held Baby snug in the crook of her left arm when she gave him his bottle. And her elbow lifted a little to support the nape of Baby's neck for they said that an infant's neck is not yet strong enough to support his head Baby was not-asleep and not-awake. This was a good time for Baby for he was not likely to cry just now. How warm Baby was! Hedge Island was always cooled by sea breezes but Baby's body was hot from such hard sleeping. She liked it that Baby was trying to smile at her. His little snail mouth wet with spittle. For Baby knew her, and trusted her.

She had no trouble carrying Baby. Baby didn't weigh

much more than her big ceramic antique doll, Grandma had given her. Past the doorway opening out onto the veranda and the noisy guests she carried Baby, and past the doorway leading to the pantry where the Irish girl and the boy in the Red Sox cap were standing very close together. Up the creaking stairs to the second floor. Along the corridor. Past doors opening upon sun-lit rooms. Past the nursery, and past the bedroom that had been Daddy's and Mummy's but was now Mummy's and Gerard's. And there was her own room, with her little bed snug in a corner, her bedspread was snowy white ducks and kittens on a blue background like the sea. Her curtains matched the bedspread. On a little rocking chair, the big ceramic Victorian doll in what's called a pinafore. She carried Baby to the window seat where they could rest. She showed Baby the people below. The tennis courts, and the grassy lawn, and the terrace. Amid so many strangers she could not see Mummy, and she could not see Daddy. It was difficult to know if Baby was seeing what she pointed out to him. Baby gurgled, and wheezed, and made his little cooing noises, and squirmed, and one of his pudgy baby-hands touched her cheek. As if in gentle rebuke. *We can't stop here, we are not high enough for them to see us.*

The tower! The widow's walk! She would, carry Baby there.

It came to her so fast: like switching on TV with the remote.

But on the stairs to the third floor, that were so much narrower than the other stairs, and where the carpeting was worn almost through, she had to stop more than once, to lean Baby against the railing. Suddenly Baby was heavier, and warmer. A sweetish-sour smell from Baby's diaper. She was panting again, and her left arm was aching. Clumsily she shifted Baby to the crook of her right arm. Baby did not feel comfortable there for she had never before held Baby in the crook of her right arm and she had not seen the Irish girl hold Baby that way, and she did not think she'd seen Mummy hold Baby that way.

But it was all right, Baby surprised, her by laughing!

Only once that summer had Mummy climbed with her to the tower, but Baby had not been with them. The higher we can climb the clearer our perspective, Mummy said. If we could fly to the moon and look back to earth we would "see" ourselves better. We would laugh at our so-called tragedies. From the window's walk you could see farther inland, sand dunes and sand fences and wild rose briars twined about the fences. You could see out into Nantucket Sound where the waves were always choppy and dark blue, leaden blue, greeny-blue depending upon the sky. The gulls look free, see the gulls! Mummy said, shading her eyes but gulls are creatures driven by hunger, every waking minute of their lives is a matter of hunger. If Mummy wanted her to feel sorry for the gulls, or to think that the gulls were silly, she could not know.

It was harder for her to remember, the summer before when Daddy had taken her up into the tower. She tried very hard to remember Daddy climbing the third-floor stairs with her and hand-in-hand with Daddy the almost unbearable excitement of stepping through the door onto the roof where there was a platform protected by a railing: This was the "widow's walk." She'd been frightened at first but Daddy held her hand saying it was absolutely safe.

Yes they were high-up and there was no roof here but they were not in any danger of falling. Many times she'd blinked her eyes startled at the bright blinding air that was so much windier up here than on the ground. The widow's walk was so exciting! Like flying in the eight-passenger plane to Hedge Island, from the Boston airport. Much more exciting than the ferry ride from Yarmouth Harbor that was so boring, you stayed inside your car and could hardly see the water.

She had to lean Baby against the wall, fumbling to open the door. She was panting hard now, her skin prickled with heat. It war hard to believe, Baby was so *heavy*. And Baby was beginning to fret as if impatient with her, wanting to get outside in the bright air and kicking his plump little legs in the way of a cat you've picked up to hug but the cat struggles and squirms trying to get away.

Baby, *no*.

Baby, see where we *are!*

Oh they were outside now, in the open air. Suddenly there was just the sky overhead. Blinding-bright windy air whipping her hair and clothes and making the flag, that was close-by and only a little higher than the roof of the house, flap like it was a live thing desperate to loosen itself from the gunmetal pole and fly off into the sky. Oh Baby, *see!*

By standing on her toes, and leaning over the railing, she could see some of the people on the ground below. But it was disappointing, she could not see them very well, and they could not see her. The railing was high as an adult's waist, and she was so much smaller. So she could not see anything very exciting except the sky, where a small propeller plane, was passing by droning its motor like a hornet, and she could not be seen. And Baby could not be seen. Nobody below was noticing!

She would have to crawl through the railing out onto the roof, and bring Baby with her. She could do this, she thought. Last summer a crew of dark-skinned men had torn out old shingleboards and nailed new shingleboards onto the roof. Five or six men with hammers walking about the roof hunched over, sometimes squatting on their haunches, slip-siding, crawling, then again walking straight-up on the different sections of the roof. For there were steeper sections than others and the section beyond the widow's walk was not one of the steep ones.

So she laid Baby down on the floor of the widow's walk, and pushed her head through the railing, and squeezed the rest of her through like a cat. Now she was outside the railing, on the roof!—one leg on either side of the peak, to balance herself. This was more daring than a cat, this was a monkey! She was able to turn herself around saying aloud "Don't look down!" for this was what Mummy said in the rattly little plane as it circled to land at the Hedge Island airport; with its single dirt runway fading out into a field of sand, dunes and wild rose briars. Don't look down! she told herself sternly Baby don't look! as she reached through the railing for Baby who was oblivious of her command lying on his back flailing his arms and legs like a silly beetle, beginning to go red in the face with that look of baby-vexation that made you want to laugh sometimes it was so comical, other times you wanted to shake Baby quick, to prevent the banshee wail. Baby, *no.*

Because Baby was kicking it was difficult to pull him through the railing. The rungs were far enough apart but

Baby was not cooperating. Oh, she was becoming impatient with Baby! For what if Daddy was here waiting to see them, Daddy was below at the edge of the noisy party, Daddy was about to glance up at the roof to see her and Baby—and there was no one visible, to be seen? And Daddy lost interest, and went away. And Mummy didn't see, either.

When Baby was new, and very little, she'd been jealous, maybe. The Irish girl had said Oh don't be jealous! You are the pretty one, you will always be the princess. And so she knew, what she was feeling was *jealous.* She'd been sulky, and sullen, and cried easily, and was mean to her doll, and hated Mummy. She'd cried for Mummy to take Baby back where she'd gotten him. (Why was that silly? Mummy was a shopper! Big packages tied with ribbon. Heavy glossy-paper bags with plastic handles. Sometimes Mummy returned what she'd bought in the stores, why couldn't she take Baby back too?) But Baby had not been taken back. Baby had stayed, and everyone adored Baby. And after a while she hadn't minded Baby so much being told he was her *little brother.* She has wanted a puppy but instead she had a *little brother.* Every time she peeked at him there were Baby's moist blue eyes fixed on her ace. Oh, she had to laugh at Baby! Except sometimes she became confused and her thoughts hurt her head: She was Baby, and Baby was her? Was that how it was meant to be? Or had Baby come to take her place?

She had tried to ask Daddy this. If Baby was her, and had taken her place, where was *she?*

Daddy laughed as if she'd meant to be funny. Daddy kissed and hugged her but his whiskers scratched her.

She was on the roof, and Baby was with her. When Daddy saw he would be impressed. My little monkey! Daddy would tease.

This section of the roof was not so steep, or so high. There was another, higher roof with a steeper pitch where the brick chimney pushed through. If she could get to that roof! By sliding along this roof as long as she straddled the peak she would not lose her balance and as long as she didn't look down. She was grunting, carrying Baby in this new way. Bump-bumping Baby along. Baby did not like the bump-bumping and began to fret. His head was rolling back because the crook of her arm wasn't right. She could see how it wasn't right, but she could not correct it. And the sun was so strong, and blinding. And the wind from inland, from the west, miles away at the far end of the island where there was an enormous garbage dump and a frenzy of gulls and other scavenger birds and the wind blew these smells to the inhabitants of East Beach as it was called. And there were gulls here, too. Swift-darting shadows on the roof. The panicky thought came to her *They will peck out our eyes.* She would have to protect her eyes from the gulls yet she could not drop Baby!

Now she could hear the strangers' voices below, more clearly. Laughter, and loud thumping music like a heartbeat.

The gulls circled near as if curious, only just screamed at her and Baby and spun away on the wind. And Baby blinked at them gaping and his little snail-mouth was wet with spittle preparing to scream back at them but they were gone.

Oh, her bottom! Beneath her denim skirt she was wearing pink cotton panties. The shingleboards were rough and scratchy. Her bottom was tender, and beginning to hurt.

Like a swift hard slap from Mummy. From Gerard, too. Only what she deserved they said. A spoiled little girl always sulking! Her arm was hurting, too. Where Baby flailed and kicked like a crazed cat, her arm was *so tired.*

Hush Baby! Hushaby Ba*by!*

By slow inches she was pushing her bottom along the peak of the roof. This wasn't so much fun as she had thought it would be. It was more like work, having to clean up something she'd spilled, or crawl beneath her bed to retrieve something she'd kicked there. No one had seen her yet. It was taking so long! Possibly she wasn't fully in sight yet, and had to go further. Her head felt strange. Like sharp-edged insects were inside buzzing to escape, *Don't look down* she told herself in Mummy's stern voice which was a voice to be obeyed but in the corners of her eyes she was beginning to see, she could not help herself. There was shouted laughter below, a blond blur that was (maybe) Mummy's hair, and so she looked, and gave a little scream of fear she was so high! She and Baby were so high above the ground! She was dizzy suddenly, and drymouthed paralyzed staring at the people below who had not yet seen her and Baby, Oh and Baby was kicking and fretting at such a bad time, so heavy in the crook of her arm, her heartbeat hard in her ribcage she could not seem to catch her breath as if she'd been running biting her lip to keep from crying, Oh how many more minutes before one of them glanced up to see her and Baby and all their eyes flew open?

# Sounds of Silence

Dennis Richard Murphy

Dennis Richard Murphy is a Canadian documentary writer, director, and producer with over two hundred films to his credit. He is producing a true crime series for The Discovery Network and Court-TV that will appear in seventy countries and thirty-three languages. Television is created by committee, which is why Murphy finds fulfillment with crime on his mind, a tale in his heart, and a blank page. He has been nominated for three major short story awards in two years and has won the top prize in *Storyteller Magazine* two years running. "Sound of Silence" first appeared in *EQMM* in December 2004.

**There he is, the son** of a bitch. Or her. Someone just walked past that window and the two of them are home. The Right Honorable Bergerons dine in tonight. A rare event. The wheels of government stand still.

My view over a fieldstone fence dividing two snow covered lawns, through dead shrub branches to the gap in the curtains is not perfect, but it's as good as it will get. The scope helps although the tiny figures inside look wavy behind the leaded glass. There's more lead in vintage glass. That's why old windows sparkle with a cleaning. I know about windows. The two security goons are in position; I can see one to my far left standing just inside the driveway gate; the other is on a seventeen-minute circuit around the property. They switch roles after every rotation. I know their habits. I see the irony of their presence—it provides tangible evidence the Bergerons are home. Bodyguards don't bother guarding where there are no bodies to guard, when the white-walled wheels of Bergeron have carried their masters off to politically apt receptions or throne speeches or vote gathering photo opportunities.

More ironic is that it's the wheels of Bergeron that brought me to this. Brought me to them. There's a straight dark line between an affluent young Bergeron speeding past my frozen thumb and me freezing my ass off in an upscale tree fort next door to his party provided manor house. That straight line is twenty-five years long.

Political Science. We were in the same class, PolySci 1E6. I couldn't afford to live on campus and home was too far away without a car, not that I could stand to live there anyway. I rented a cheap room with some other students a mile and a half down the highway from school. I'd hitchhike to class every day. It wasn't a big deal back then—there weren't perverts looking to kill people who couldn't afford cars. Early in the morning I'd get rides from wordless working men on their way to day shifts in the east end.

Later I'd get picked up by businessmen driving to downtown offices who chattered about quitting school in grade ten and making lots of money in spite of it. If I didn't have a class till midmorning I'd get rides from housewives headed for the city shopping centers who'd lecture me on the importance of a good education. I was a thankful yet captive audience, subservient to their thoughts.

The figure passing back and forth in front of the dining room window must be a servant or a maid. She passes too often and too regularly to be casually employed. In the distorted instant I see her, she might be wearing a uniform. I picture the Bergerons at opposite ends of a long mahogany table, with this maid dashing between them with a gravy boat or water jug. "More ice water for Mr. Bergeron, Emma." "Yes'm." "The Parmigiano for Mrs. Bergeron, Emma." "Yes sir." While they're dining I can afford to rest my trigger hand for a few minutes. I have a soft moleskin pocket in my Barbour jacket just for that purpose. Designed for autumn grouse hunters, it's surprisingly warm. My stomach's rumbling and I can feel the cold starting to cramp my right leg again. Off the scope I can barely see the gap in the curtains.

Gaps in the traffic rhythm were part of the daily hitching routine, calm periods that were only painful when the weather was cold or wet, which is most of the school year in this part of the world. After a month or two I could identify regulars on the route, including some fellow fledgling pupils of politics who came from a world where parents paid tuition and bought their bright children colorful cars. Bergeron was one of them. He had an orange MGB, the GT hardtop model that was my favorite then. I used to pray he'd notice me as other than a shivering shadow at the side of the road.

Someone—the server I imagine—just closed the gap in the curtain. I can only see dull gray shadows behind the white curtains through the scope now, and then only when they move. There'll be a server and a cook, but they'll leave after they've cleaned up. I can wait. I've waited before.

I'm sure Bergeron knew I was going to the same class as he was. Rose and I had sat beside him at the back of the lecture hall more than once. In his cozy car he'd stare straight ahead or look off to his left, pretending to see something more interesting than a poor student waiting in the roadside waste, his thumb sticking out and shoulders hunched forward to keep the cold away. I'm exaggerating. It wasn't that bad. Despite the waiting, I usually made it to school on time and if I missed Rose in class I'd see her after the lecture in the library, usually at the big table closest to the window on the ground floor. We smiled at each other the first time because we had the same textbook. Then we had coffee together twice. Three times really, counting the time she was already sitting with a crowd. She had frizzy black hair, pale skin with tiny freckles on her arms, and a nose too big for her face. She was pleasant to me and wore nice clothes. I liked her very much.

She was in the library the day Bergeron drowned me. My down ski jacket was limp and dripping, my books soaked and stained with filthy water and my jeans dark with wet. I thought the librarian was going to stop me but I walked toward Rose with such purpose that she didn't dare. I must have looked furious. I was. Even Rose looked frightened.

"God, Dave. What happened to you? You're soaking wet.

You'll catch your death of cold." I remember her exact words. I remember how she cared. I told her how Bergeron had pulled into the curb lane as he approached me, told her that I'd felt pretty good he was pulling over because a ride with him could become a regular thing for the winter. Then, at the last minute, he geared down and sped up and swung left into a pile of slush the size of a suitcase, covering me in ice and filthy water from head to toe. I was so damned angry I couldn't talk. I should have gone home but I wasn't thinking straight. I walked the highway to school. No one stopped for a drenched rat. By the time I got there the class was over and my teeth were chattering uncontrollably, so I went to the library to tell Rose and get warm.

If they're sheer curtains they're certainly thick ones. Maybe doubles. With a liner to keep the heat from seeping out those leaky leaded panes. The dull gray shadow passes back and forth, back and forth, soothing as a slow metronome, an adagio for dining. "Take the courgettes to Mr. Bergeron, Emma." "Yes'm." "Tell Cook they're overdone, Emma." "Yes sir." The Brits call them courgettes. We call them zucchini. My leg hurts.

Rose was comforting. She taught me the head pinching trick. Look from a distance at a person who's pissed you off, she said, and hold your thumb and forefinger about a half an inch apart in front of your eye so that their head fits in the gap between them. Then close the gap. Squish. It felt good when I tried it on some people in the library, people I didn't even know. Rose did it too, making a squishing noise with her tongue and saliva pushed through he teeth. Squish. Squish. We laughed so hard the librarian asked us to leave. We couldn't stop laughing.

After that I used it often when people didn't pick me up or pretended I wasn't there, especially Bergeron. Squish. I must have squished his head a hundred times that year.

My stomach won't stop growling. I ate a late lunch on purpose so I could wait this out. I have half a sandwich but it's against the other wall in my bag and stale by now. I have to get here early to avoid the police patrols, the bodyguards and the nosy neighbors. I park over on Rowbotham in the liquor store lot, where I change into my old man clothes. I take the walker out of the trunk and shuffle slowly into this part of town the pillars of our society call home. Concealing the rifle in the Barbour is easy and the streets are usually empty anyway. They use big SUVs just to go to the liquor store so the only people walking are the hired help—Filipino women pushing expensive prams. When the rich see strange men wandering their meticulously ministered boulevards they report them, unless they have a white van and a uniform like a pest control guy or a gas man. Or unless they're old. Service people and the elderly are invisible to the wealthy. I chose old because I need to be here late, and you can't leave a truck on the street around here after dark.

I knew Rose was taking polysci as a prerequisite for law. She told me. And I knew she planned to switch to law school after two years. Still, I wasn't prepared when she left. Just like that. As if we'd discussed it which we never did. As if we weren't best friends. As if she wasn't my girl. I'd never really said that to her but I kind of accepted it and I thought she did too. We had fun together and we didn't have fun with anyone else. Or see anyone else. As far as I knew. I didn't. That's special. Isn't it? Apparently not. She just left.

There they go now. Dull gray shadows. More of them. Dinner's done. Now to repair to the living room, or library or salon or whatever they call it. Yeah. There's the maid turning lights on in the room to the left of the dining room. The curtains are still wide open and I can see through the French doors. Steel clad, Extrusco I think, top of the line double glazed with the small pane rectangles beveled to match the original glass. I blow on my fingers and duck automatically when I see the circuit guard's silhouette pass below their full-length panes. The maid disappears in the direction of the dining room where the lights become brighter. They must be on a dimmer. I guess she's clearing up the dinner dishes. "Coffee and dessert in the library Emma." "Yes, sir." "Remember Mr. Bergeron's Sweet 'n Lo, Emma." "Yes'm."

I was upset with Rose's departure. Not really angry. I was hurt, I guess, because she seemed to feel nothing. Like we hadn't shared anything worth keeping. I knew where the law school was. It's a large campus of old limestone buildings with copper roofs gone green in the smoggy middle of the city. It's been there for years, or it looks like it. Around it is an ornate stone fence with inset curly black iron spindles that make it appear impenetrable, but there are gates on three sides where anyone can walk in and out. I did it myself, worried a bit that she'd see me and think I was weird or something. So I hung around across the road from the south gate where I could hide in the crowds waiting for the streetcar. I went there four or five times before I saw her.

There's Bergeron now. Bingo. In a smoking jacket. Christ. A smoking jacket. Do people still wear smoking jackets? Does Bergeron smoke? He's come in through the arch from the center hall in his shiny smoking jacket. Jesus. Now he's behind the bookcase. The dining room just went dark, so the cleanup's done. Yellow light spills out onto the snow from the kitchen windows at the back of the house. Shadows roll as dishes are done. The second guard has reached the front gates now and they're sharing a smoke before his partner leaves for his circuit.

The first time I tried to follow Rose I wasn't prepared. She walked out the south gate with a friend, both hugging their books against their chests like they were cradling babies, talking a mile a minute. She'd cut her hair short, which bothered me. It wasn't like she should have asked me or anything, but it was a pretty major change and she might have asked my opinion or told me she was thinking about it. Her girlfriend had short hair, too. Maybe they'd cut it together. Maybe they were roommates. Girls in the city with boyfriends back home. I boarded the streetcar first and sat at the back where I could hide behind a newspaper until they got off. It was almost rush hour and they had to stand up near the front. I could see Rose talking to her new friend, holding her books in one arm, using her free hand a lot the way I liked. Smiling and shaping and talking and making her friend laugh. Then they jumped off. I wasn't expecting it. I was blocked by people standing in the aisle and couldn't get to the doors in time. I looked out the window for a street name but could only see an orange and white beer store sign and a storefront with dirty windows and a sign saying they rented tools. I saw Rose waving good-bye to her friend so they weren't roommates. She looked right at me but I don't think she saw me.

There's a wide paved lane that runs past the rear of these big houses and the block behind, lined with stone garages and solid back gates. It's well lit at night and regularly patrolled by sleepy cops in overheated cruisers who have been told to be seen keeping the taxpayers safe, especially those who pay the high taxes. I usually arrive about two in the afternoon, long before the threat of nighttime crime. I hobble down the side street and steer the walker into the lane and no one pays any attention. Passing nannies ignore me. Dog walkers smile and nod hello and yank their yappy animals out of my way. The fieldstone wall that surrounds this place has a rear gate set into a recess off the lane. I can slip into the recess and not be seen from either end of the alley. I can wait there until I'm sure the coast is clear before I put my key into the thick silver lock and slip into the yard. I bought the lock. The people who live in this house spend the cold months somewhere warm. Maybe Florida. They have an alarm system in the house and a security patrol checks the windows and doors nightly, but they don't check the back gate or yard. Still, I hide the walker well in the shrubs inside the stone fence before I climb the wooden ladder to my fort. Some rich kids must have had fun up here. Years ago.

It took me a couple of trips on the street car, watching for beer stores and tool rentals, before I found Rose's stop. There was an elementary school on the north side of the road, behind a half-inch tempered plate glass public waiting booth with a cold metal bench inside. I waited in there until several streetcars passed and people in the school yard began looking at me strangely. I didn't want to be taken for one of those sick bastards who likes children too much so I left. I just liked Rose too much. The third time I went there I only waited a short time before she got off the car and walked down the block. She went in the main door of a four-story apartment building on the right without a glance behind. I waited a good ten minutes before I went in and saw that R. Goldberg lived in apartment 2A. It was at the front, on the left side of the building when you looked at it from the street. Across the road was a single-story auto body shop with a large green neon sign that rose above the roof level and said “The Dent-ist.” It wasn’t difficult to climb on an abandoned car at the back to the flat graveled roof and hide behind the sign. At dark Rose turned her lights on. She had a nice place—neat like I’d imagined, with a little cloth mat in the middle of the kitchen table and some dried flowers in a vase on it. Just like we’d have done. She had two big bookcases on the far wall. The windows looked like steel-framed single-glazed double-diamond glass, which would be cold in the winter. The blinds were made out of reeds or something and they wouldn’t keep out the cold. Before she lowered them I squished her head, but it didn’t feel right. Squishing heads was our joke. Rose’s and mine.

Bergeron has moved out from behind his bookcase now. He’s carrying a thick hardcover book with an orange-and-white dust cover and leafing through it as he walks toward a chair, a big overstuffed leather wing chair with shiny brass upholstery nails down the front of the arms and around the tall back. He puts his feet up on a matching footstool and crosses his ankles. He’s hearing something because he’s stuck his finger in the book to keep his place and he’s looking toward the dining room. He’s saying something back now and then he's sitting down. I'm taking my hand out of my moleskin pocket. I'm still hungry. I can almost read the book title through the scope.

I watched Rose from behind the sign three or four days a week from then on. Sometimes she'd study at the kitchen table and sometimes she'd have friends over and they'd laugh and share bottles of wine and forget to lower the blinds. I took to making my hand into a pistol, with my index finger extended and my thumb raised, and sighting down my finger to her friends' heads, then lowering my thumb and making a little "pew" sound as if I had a silencer barrel. It was better than squishing. Less of a joke. I never used it on Rose until the night Bergeron showed up with a bottle of wine and some flowers and kissed her again and again until she stood up to lower the blinds. Her front buttons were undone. I shot both of them with my hand and went home. Pew. Pew.

There she is now. She's wearing a caftan or whatever they call those long robes. A smoking jacket and a caftan. Jesus. She has a tray with tea things on it and some kind of dessert. A car with a light on top is pulling up in front of the driveway gate and the guard steps forward with his hand on his hip. Rose says something toward the hall and two figures leave the house and get into the cab. Cook and Emma. Rose sets the tray down on a table beside Bergeron's chair. He stops reading, looks at her and smiles, then takes his feet off the stool and pats it so she'll sit there.

I didn't flunk out because I was following Rose around or thinking about her all the time. I just wasn't about to become a lawyer or a politician and with Rose gone I had no idea what I was doing there. So it wasn't hard to stop. I worked a few jobs over the years but never found anything that involved me much until Windoscapes—you've probably heard of them. They're best known for making those huge industrial picture windows for libraries and museums and offices, but they have a residential line as well. They had an opening for a salesman which I certainly was not, but I took it for the money and the benefits. I did my homework. I usually do. Within a few months I knew everything about the business, about the competition, about all kinds of windows and doors: wooden frames, extruded aluminum, composites, vinyl clad and solid vinyl, and all types: sliders, casements, sashes, bows, double sashes, bays, self-cleaners, triple format hinges, e-glass, solar reflection . . . you name it. I was well known around the factory, and even at the conventions, for what I knew. Just ask Dave. Dave'll know that. Where's Dave? But I wasn't famous for great sales and I'd been told enough times that I'd better move some product or think about another career.

She's serving him dessert, for Christ's sake. Like some . . . some waitress. Like Emma. She's cutting little slices of something with creamy stuff on top of it and putting them on a little flowered plate. And he's smiling at her and touching her face, tracing her jaw line with his finger. His slicked back hair shines in the reading light when he leans forward to accept a little silver fork. I wiggle my shoulders and stretch my right leg again.

I finally engineered the sale that would guarantee me my job even if I never sold anything again. These things take time and I'd been hitting on this government purchasing guy for months, telling him all about Windoscapes and how we could provide anything he wanted and beat the price of anyone else, especially Extrusco. I promised him we'd beat them by 10 percent. Finally he invited me to a special meeting to make a pitch to provide glass for the new library which had finally been approved by the ministry, that architect's fantasy transparent pyramid project down on Stanford. Things happened so quickly that day they didn't make sense until later. I was pumped and ready. I had a guaranteed supply of 7.22-mm solar-controlled low-E anti-ray glass in anodized, thermally broken aluminum frames with a 60-minute fire rating that far exceeded local codes. I bought a new suit. I was there early. A secretary told me where sit and wait because the minister was very busy. Then the guy from Extrusco showed up. Before I could ask why, Rose came out of the office and walked by me without even looking. She looked different somehow. Before I could call out her name, a male voice yelled that we should come in, and the secretary made hurry-up flutters with her hand. The minister was very busy.

I didn't know Bergeron was the minister. I went first. I didn't do my best. I don't think he remembered me from school or maybe he did. I didn't remind him. All the time I was talking he looked at his hands and his pencil, and smiled at the Extrusco guy. He never once looked me in the eye. Like when he was driving. Extrusco got the job and I lost mine. The guys from the factory said they'd miss me.

That's when I bought the gun, scope and all. They lived out in the country then. I'm not much for politics or papers so I didn't know Bergeron and Rose had married or that

Bergeron had become a local politician and then a minister in the latest Cabinet shuffle. They owned the biggest and best gingerbread Victorian house in the medium-size town that was the center of their political world. They had a law office together on the Main Street called Bergeron and Goldberg. Partners in Law, it read. Partners in life as well. The office was too exposed for my purposes, and they never worked much past dark anyway, so I chose the house. It backed onto a lane like the one they have now, now that he's even more important. There was no need to lock the back gate in a small town where you knew everyone and everyone knew you. I could walk right in and squat in the shadow of an old glass greenhouse (eighth-inch clear untempered single diamond) and see them watching TV and walking around the house. They had no kids. Rose's nose was smaller. That's what was different. I shot him with the finger gun that first time but, like the squishing thing with Rose, it didn't make me feel any better. It wasn't satisfying. So I bought the rifle I have now and sat in their backyard, just out of the light pouring through their new Extrusco replacement vinyl-clad double casements. I could pan between them using the scope and I could put Bergeron's head in the cross-hairs and squeeze the trigger. There was a calibrated resistance on the finger, then a solid, satisfying "Click." I had no bullets. I wasn't crazy. It just felt a lot more satisfying to see each of them in a real cross-hair sight and pull a real trigger than to use a stupid finger gun. Or squish heads like a child. Squeeze. Click. Pan. Click.

He's standing up now at a table crowded with bottles. With little silver tongs he's moving ice cubes from a silver bowl into two cut-crystal glasses. Now he's holding up a bottle and asking her something, flashing his satin sleeve, arching his groomed eyebrows so his forehead looks like a washboard. She's raising her hand, thumb and forefinger extended, a small gap between them. Just a little alcohol. The circuit guard shuffles past, slipping on the icy path they've worn like nags on a longe line. Bergeron looks up. Maybe he's seeing the guard or realizing the curtains are open. She's beside him now, taking her drink. Kissing him on the cheek. He's smiling and kissing her back and they're clinking glasses. It's as if I can hear the sound. They sip.

"Oh dear," she says, drink spilled on her robe, glass set down, fingers to pursed lips, then both palms raised and formed into cartoon pistols aimed playfully at his happy face. "Too much scotch for me." The cross-hairs meet inside his mouth. The scope blurs as she walks in front. I look away, to the side, to see her coming toward me, toward the curtains, laughing over her shoulder. He's laughing, too. She's pointing down and dabbing at her wet robe, reminding him of something funny. Something they share. Something wet. Maybe me. I pan slowly with her as she reaches up to draw the curtains. Squish. Pew. Click.

Bang. Pan. Bang.

# Permissions

"The Year in Mystery and Crime Fiction: 2004," copyright © 2005 by Jon L. Breen • "A 2004 Yearbook of Crime and Mystery," copyright © 2005 by Edward D. Hoch • "The Mystery in Great Britain," copyright © 2005 by Maxim Jakubowski • "The Newest Four-Letter Word in Mystery," copyright © 2005 by Sarah Weinman • "The Adventure of the Missing Detective" by Gary Lovisi. Copyright © 2004 by Gary Lovisi. First published in *Sherlock Holmes, The Missing Years*. Reprinted by permission of the author. • "The Westphalian Ring" by Jeffery Deaver. Copyright © 2004 by Jeffery Deaver. First published in *Ellery Queen's Mystery Magazine*, September/October 2004. Reprinted by permission of the author. All rights reserved. • "The Hit" by Robert S. Levinson. Copyright © 2004 by Robert S. Levinson. First published in *Alfred Hitchcock's Mystery Magazine*, July/August 2004. Reprinted by permission of the author. • "The Last Case of Hilly Palmer" by Duane Swierczynski. Copyright © 2004 by Duane Swierczynski. First published in *Plots with Guns*. Reprinted by permission of the author. • "Everybody's Girl" by Robert Barnard. Copyright © 2004 by Robert Barnard. First published in *Mysterious Pleasures*. Reprinted by permission of the author. • "Imitate the Sun" by Luke Sholer. Copyright © 2004 by Luke Sholer. First published in *Ellery Queen's Mystery Magazine*, November 2004. Reprinted by permission of the author. • "Father Diodorus" by Charlie Stella. Copyright © 2004 by Charlie Stella. First published in *The Mississippi Review*. Reprinted by permission of the author. • "A Nightcap of Hemlock" by Francis M. Nevins. Copyright © 2004 by Francis M. Nevins. First published in *Ellery Queen's Mystery Magazine*, February 2004. Reprinted by permission of the author. • "The Best in Online Mystery Fiction in 2004," copyright © 2004 by Sarah Weinman • "Just Pretend" by Martyn Waites. Copyright © 2004 by Martyn Waites. First published in *Plots with Guns*, issue 30, Summer 2004. Reprinted by permission of the author. • "Geoffrey Says" by Aliya Whiteley. Copyright © 2004 by Aliya Whiteley. First published in *Shred of Evidence*, Vol. 2, issue 4, November 2004. Reprinted by permission of the author. • "God's Dice" by David White. Copyright © 2004 by David White. First published in *Thrilling Detective*, Spring 2004. Reprinted by permission of the author. • "The Consolation Blonde" by Val McDermid. Copyright © 2004 by Val McDermid. First published in *Mysterious Pleasures*. Reprinted by permission of the author. • "The Shoeshine Man's Regrets" by Laura Lippman. Copyright © 2004 by Laura Lippman. First published in *Murder and All That Jazz*. Reprinted by permission of the author. • "For Benefit of Mr. Means" by Christine Matthews. Copyright © 2004 by Christine Matthews. First published in *The Mammoth Book of Roaring Twenties Whodunits*. Reprinted by permission of the author. • "East Side, West Side" by Max Allan Collins and Matthew V. Clemens. Copyright © 2004 by Max Allan Collins and Matthew V. Clemens. First published in *Murder and All That Jazz*, edited by Robert J. Randisi. Reprinted by permission of the author. • "The Promotion" by Larry Sweazy. Copyright © 2004 by Larry Sweazy. First published in *Texas Rangers*. Reprinted by permission of the author. • "Me and Mitch" by Bill Pronzini and Barry N. Malzberg. Copyright © 2004 by Bill Pronzini and Barry N. Malzberg. First published in *Problems Solved*. Reprinted by permission of the authors. • "Necromancer's Apprentice" by Lillian Stewart Carl. Copyright © 2004 by Lillian Stewart Carl. First published in *Murder and Magic*. Reprinted by permission of the author. • "The Banshee" by Joyce Carol Oates. Copyright © 2004 by The Ontario Review, Inc. First published in *Ellery Queen's Mystery Magazine*, June 2004. Reprinted by permission of the author. • Sounds of Silence" by Dennis Richard Murphy. Copyright © 2004 by Dennis Richard Murphy. First published in *Ellery Queen's Mystery Magazine,* December 2004. Reprinted by permission of the author.